"YOU DRIVE ME OUT OF MY MIND, RAINE."

Jonah's voice was hoarse, full of torment. "When I touch you, I forget all my resolutions."

He captured her face between his hands, forcing her to look at him, then he lowered his hands to her belt, slowly untying it. As if hypnotized by his words, his touch, Raine could only stare into his eyes as the robe fell open, exposing her still-damp body to his gaze. He drank in her nudity while she stood there motionless, caught up in the fire that flamed in his eyes.

"I want you, Raine," he murmured, and his words, the throb of his voice were an aphrodisiac, stirring her to wildness. "I want you so much—and you want me, too. Remember how it was the night we made love? Let me love you the same way. . . ."

WELCOME TO...

HARLEQUIN SUPERROMANCES

A sensational series of modern love stories.

Written by masters of the genre, these long, sensual
and dramatic novels are truly in keeping with today's
changing life-styles. Full of intriguing conflicts
and the heartaches and delights of true love,
HARLEQUIN SUPERROMANCES are absorbing
stories— satisfying and sophisticated reading
that lovers of romance fiction have long been
waiting for.

HARLEQUIN SUPERROMANCES
Contemporary love stories for the woman of today!

Irma Walker
Sonata for My Love

Harlequin Books

TORONTO • NEW YORK • LONDON
AMSTERDAM • PARIS • SYDNEY • HAMBURG
STOCKHOLM • ATHENS • TOKYO • MILAN

For Mildred Fish—in gratitude and in friendship

Published February 1984

First printing December 1983

ISBN 0-373-70104-7

CHAPTER ONE

IT WAS LATE JUNE, a time of the year when a few days of perfect weather, sandwiched between the usual foggy summer mornings, sometimes favored San Francisco. So it shouldn't have surprised Raine as she walked briskly across Union Square that the morning sun should be so warm against her face. Instead it seemed wrong, an affront to her father's memory, that the city he'd loved so much should sparkle under a benign sun on this particular day. With her grief so raw and searing, with her father's funeral only two weeks behind her, how dare the sky be such a flawless blue, the sun so golden, the air so clear?

The people she passed should be frowning, their eyes reflecting her own sadness. Instead they strolled along, some of them actually smiling, obviously enjoying the rare fogless morning. Which was why it was with such a feeling of relief that she finally turned off the sunny street into the lobby of an office building where the lighting was dim and the air dank, a little musty.

The way I feel, she thought bleakly.

Briefly her father's image moved across her mind. He had been a quiet man who showed little outward emotion. Although his hair, the same silvery blond as her own, had thinned a little during the years, it had changed to white so gradually that she couldn't remember exactly when she'd realized he was getting old. Even to the end of his short terminal illness his eyes had retained their icy blueness, so remote that she knew some people had been uncomfortable around him. But those eyes had shown only kindness to her, and although he wasn't demonstrative, she had never doubted his love or her importance in his life.

Oh, dad, I miss you so. . . .

She took the elevator to the third floor, but when she reached the door that bore the name of her father's lawyer and old friend, she paused briefly to take a deep breath, steeling herself. Mr. Partridge had been at her father's funeral. Seeing him could only bring back painful memories. Well, no use postponing the inevitable. If she'd learned anything in her twenty-three years, it was to face up to bad news. Her father's estate must be settled—and settled soon. So much depended upon the state of his finances, not only for herself but for her brother.

Unconsciously she winced. It seemed so crass to worry about money with her father dead such a short time. And yet her life wasn't the only one that would be affected by what Mr. Partridge had to tell her that day. Her brother's future also depended on how much money was left, now that her father's debts had been settled.

When she opened the door the middle-aged

woman sitting at the reception desk looked up. Behind gold-rimmed glasses, her eyes took on a warmth as she recognized Raine. "It'll be a few minutes, Miss Hunicutt. Mr. Partridge is with a friend now—and Mr. Johnson has the appointment before yours, too."

She nodded toward a well-dressed man who was sitting on one of the reception room's leather chairs before she added, her voice a little too bright, "Congratulations on your graduation from Juilliard. Your father was so proud of you, especially when you won that last piano competition. He was so sure you'll win the one in Russia next year—what is it they call it?"

"The Tchaikovsky competition, Mrs. Clark," Raine said, a distressing lump in her throat. She saw the woman's expression soften, and to forestall any words of condolence she added quickly, "I'm a little early. I decided to walk over from my brother's apartment instead of taking the bus because it—it's such a nice day. Martin couldn't come with me. He's working double shifts at the hospital this week."

To her relief, Mrs. Clark asked her a question about her brother, who was an intern at a local hospital. She then went on to discuss, with the relish of a native San Franciscan, the unusually fine Bay Area weather. A few minutes later when Raine sank gratefully into a chair to wait, the desire to cry had passed.

She picked up a magazine at random, opened it and tried to read, but the page blurred in front of her and she finally gave up. In a few minutes she would find out the truth—and if it was as bad as she suspected it would mean the end of so many dreams. She swallowed hard and told herself sternly that it wouldn't be the end of the world if she couldn't compete in Russia the following year. It hadn't been certain even before her father's death. After all, there were so many expenses involved— the high fees a really good teaching coach would charge to supervise her preparations, her living expenses during those months, because the rigors of full-time training almost automatically precluded holding down a job, too. And then the travel costs and other expenses—no, it had never been something she could take for granted.

She had to be realistic. After all, she was still young. There would be other competitions. She could get a job, maybe in a bookstore, save her money. Eventually she would get to Russia or to another of the prestigious competitions that were so vital to the career of a concert pianist.

But it was different with her brother. This last year of Martin's internship was vitally important to him, his wife Gloria, and their small daughter. Martin shouldn't have married until he was established as a doctor, but it *had* happened, and now he needed money to support his family while he finished his internship.

It wasn't as if Gloria could go back to work, not with little Debra needing her full attention. When they'd learned the baby was asthmatic, Gloria had quit her job as a registered nurse. Somehow they had managed, with Raine's father's financial help, while Martin finished medical school.

And that's why so much depended upon the size of the estate. Strange, Raine had never worried much about money before. Why had she taken the checks that appeared every month in her mailbox so much for granted? Oh, she'd had to skimp and do without and make every penny count, and without the scholarships she'd won she couldn't have stayed at the Juilliard School of Music. But the allowance from her father had enabled her to get along without taking a job so she could have the precious time she needed for study and her daily hours of practice.

Of course during vacations she had worked for her father at his small antiquarian bookstore on Powell Street—not that this had been a sacrifice. She'd always loved old books and the thrill of finding something rare and wonderful in an auction odd lot or a carton of dusty books bought at an estate sale. But somehow it had never occurred to her to wonder how prosperous her father's business was. It wasn't until after the funeral, when she'd examined his records in the dusty little office behind his shop, that she'd realized how small his margin of profit was, and an awareness of the sacrifices he must have made to keep Martin and her in school so many years had come home to her.

A little belatedly, she thought now, filled with regret.

Well, she would soon find out the truth. Mr. Partridge had proved his friendship by offering to handle the sale of her father's book collection, the shop furnishings and the contents of his small apartment. After all outstanding debts had been settled, how much would be left? Enough to send her to the competition in Russia and also to provide for Gloria and the baby until Martin was a full-fledged doctor?

Suddenly Raine felt uneasy, as if someone were staring at her. She looked up into the appraising eyes of the middle-aged man Mrs. Clark had called Mr. Johnson. Although she returned her attention to the magazine that lay open in her lap, she knew he was still staring at her, just as she knew what had prompted his bold smile.

Because she had inherited her silver blond hair from her English father and her dark brown eyes and tawny skin from her Italian mother, Raine was used to being stared at by strangers, but that didn't mean she liked it. In fact, the last thing she wanted was the attention of men. To forestall it she used very little makeup, arranged her hair in a simple style, wore plain understated clothing, all protective coloring intended to thwart just this kind of unwanted attention.

There had been a time when she had gone even further to blend in with the crowd. Early in her freshman year at Juilliard she'd realized that her striking appearance was earning her the wrong kind of attention and keeping others, including some of her teachers, from taking her talent seriously. Just after she returned for her sophomore year she dyed her hair dark brown, but her own pride had eventually convinced her to let her hair grow back to its natural color. Since then she'd learned to live with speculative stares.

But it still rankled when someone ogled her as this man was doing now, his eyes moving over her long slender legs, her narrow waist and rounded hips and breasts with insulting thoroughness. After all, it wasn't as if she dressed or behaved in a manner to draw attention to herself.

She looked up with a feeling of relief when the door to Mr. Partridge's office opened. Then, when she heard a deep voice saying, ''You'll have to come out to Mendocino for dinner soon, Arnold,'' the blood drained from her head, leaving her weak and shaken.

She knew that voice. Oh, how well she knew it! It came straight out of her past, from a time in her life that she'd spent the past three years trying to forget.

The owner of the voice turned, his wide shoulders filling the doorway, and she wanted to get up and run away. But it was already too late. She sat rooted to her chair, her heart pounding in her throat, her hungry eyes devouring the man across the room.

He was a giant of a man, well over six feet four, but as she knew so well, there wasn't an ounce of superfluous weight on that strong muscular body. Dark hair, unruly and thick and the color of mahogany, fell over his forehead. His deep-set eyes were such a dark gray that when she'd first met him, three years earlier, she'd thought they were brown. His skin was dark, too, the inheritance, he'd told her, of some Scottish highlander ancestor, as were his high-planed cheekbones. Right now, as he responded to something Mr. Partridge said, the unexpected sweetness of his smile, at such odds with the ruggedness of his features, started a painful ache inside Raine's chest.

She'd been so sure that she was over her obsession with Jonah Duncan. So why was her heart beating out a chorus of pain inside her chest? Why was her breathing so erratic at the sight of a man she knew to be ruthless, uncaring and indifferent to the pain he inflicted upon others?

As she stared, unconsciously looking for signs of change, Jonah moved forward into the reception room. Yes, he did look a little older. There was a line between his eyebrows that hadn't been there three years ago, and wasn't there a shadow of some deep sadness in his eyes? Had someone else, another woman, done what she hadn't been able to do—make an impression upon that impregnable heart?

Her breath caught as Jonah Duncan's eyes rested upon her, paused a moment, then drifted away. The expression on his face didn't change, and she knew, the knowledge cutting her like a thin dagger of ice, that he didn't recognize her, that she hadn't mattered enough three years ago for him to remember her. And then he was gone, the minty odor of his after-shave lotion lingering in the air, the only evidence that she hadn't dreamed him up out of whole cloth.

Raine realized she was clenching the wooden sides of the chair with bloodless fingers. She tried to relax, but the memories that buffeted her were too strong. She could only sit there, helpless and unmoving, while the past, like a movie unreeling before her eyes, surged through her mind, blotting out the present. . . .

CHAPTER TWO

RAINE HAD JUST TURNED TWENTY and was in her second year at Juilliard when she'd first met Jonah Duncan.

Of course, long before that she'd known who he was. Like every music lover in the country, she was familiar with the work of the brilliant young concert pianist and composer who had become a household name even to people who ordinarily wouldn't have known a fugue from a fandango. Jonah was that rare combination—a performer who'd not only won the critics' praise but had the charisma to capture the imagination of the public, a fact that was fast making the piano the most popular musical instrument since Van Cliburn had won the Tchaikovsky competition.

Raine, like other Juilliard students, tried to attend as many of his New York concerts as she could, most of the time standing in the back of the auditorium because she couldn't afford a better ticket. But when she listened to his sensitive interpretations, the exquisite nuances of tone, the virility and vitality that set his performances apart from other pianists, the sacrifices she made to pay for her ticket didn't seem important.

Whenever she could afford them she bought his tapes, playing them over and over again, marveling at a talent that was so uniquely his. That he was something of a man of mystery, his private life unknown to his public, didn't matter. It was his music, not the man, that fired her imagination and earned her respect.

Which is why, when she learned that Jonah Duncan would be making a one-time appearance at a benefit concert for the scholarship fund of an upper New York State college, she knew she must go, even though she didn't own a car and the college, in the Catskills, was almost inaccessible any other way.

Ordinarily she wouldn't have accepted an invitation from Jimmy Whitfield. The spoiled son of a multimillionaire, he had a bad reputation among the hardworking students of Juilliard, who had him pegged as a dilettante who got by only because of his naturally fine baritone voice and his father's generous endowments to the schools he'd attended. Raine had already turned down several invitations from Jimmy, knowing that his interest in her was strictly sexual. But this time she weakened, reasoning that surely he wouldn't come on too strong on their first date. Even if he did try something, she told her roommates confidently, she could handle it.

Well, she'd been wrong—dead wrong. After the concert, during which Jimmy had emptied a pocket flask, he made an unscheduled side trip off the highway onto a country road. Ignoring her protests, he parked the car and then, supremely confident that she would willingly fall into his arms, tried to make love to her. When Raine's arguments, then her struggles hadn't convinced him how mistaken he was, she escaped from the car and hid in a nearby patch of woods until Jimmy finally got tired of searching for her and drove off.

Which was why she was walking along a dark back road on a cold November night, somewhere between the college where the concert had been held and New York City—a place she devoutly wished she'd never left.

Aware of how dangerous her position was, a woman alone on a country road at night, she stayed close to the shoulder, ready to hide at the sound of a car. It didn't help, knowing how stupid she'd been, putting herself into such a position. Well, there was nothing she could do about it now. She was in for a long walk to the nearest town, where, she hoped, she could catch a bus back to New York—provided she had enough money in her purse for the fare. Well, she'd worry about that detail when the time came. She was just lucky the situation hadn't been worse. Even now the thought of Jimmy's groping hands made her shudder. Thank goodness she'd gotten away from him before the incident had turned into something really ugly. . . .

Preoccupied with her thoughts, she was taken unaware when a car roared toward her out of the darkness, moving along at such a fast clip that she just had time to dart off the shoulder of the road before it swept past. In her haste her feet slid out from under her and she tumbled down into a ditch half-filled with rain water. She gasped with shock as icy water drenched her clothes and splashed up over her face and hair.

At first she was sure she was unhurt. But when she tried to get up, pain shot through her leg, and she realized she'd twisted her ankle, maybe even broken it. She lay there shaken from her fall, and in her anger she said a few words that would have earned her a mouthful of soap from her father a few years earlier.

"Is that any way for a lady to talk?" a deep and unmistakably amused voice said from the road above the ditch.

Raine's body chilled. She squinted up at the man, outlined against the moon, suddenly aware how vulnerable she was. Had she exchanged one danger for a far worse one?

"Don't be afraid," he said, almost as if he could read her thoughts. A flashlight clicked on, aimed not at Raine but upward, at the man's face. In the circle of light she saw a prominent, well-shaped nose, high-planed cheekbones and a mobile mouth that seemed too sensitive for such a craggy face.

Raine's breath caught sharply. She knew that face. Just a couple of hours ago she had sat in the hushed darkness of a theater, listening while this man's music had woven patterns in the air, filling her ears, her soul with the majesty and passion of a Bach concerto.

"My name is Jonah Duncan, and I'm perfectly respectable," he said. "I'm afraid I'm to blame for scaring you off the road. Are you hurt?"

"I—I think something's wrong with my ankle," she said, her voice thin. Although her heart still beat at an accelerated rate, it was for a reason other than fear now.

"Well, let's take a look at it. If you need a doctor, I'll see you get one. Dammit—I don't usually drive so fast, but I was in a rush tonight...."

A few moments later he was beside her. The flashlight flooded her face, lingered there a long moment, then moved down her body. He cursed under his breath as he saw that her legs were submerged in water. Setting the flashlight on the muddy bank, its beam pointing upward, he slipped out of his camel's hair coat and draped it around her shoulders.

Warm with body heat, the coat felt like arms, embracing her. Raine was aware of ambiguous feelings as the man lifted her out of the water as easily as if she were a child. She felt embarrassed at the trouble she was causing him, and yet, with his heart beating so strongly under her ear and his arms warm and comforting around her chilled body, she felt absurdly happy—after all, he was only doing what any civilized man would do, helping someone in trouble.

Even so, when they reached the car she discovered she didn't want him to put her down. Which, she thought, was a surprising kind of admission from someone who prided herself on her independence, who had carefully avoided the male species when she'd discovered how distracting they could be to a girl with a burning ambition to be a concert pianist.

Jonah's car, a black Mercedes, stood with the door open, spilling warm light out into the darkness of the night. Gently he lowered her to the passenger seat, then bent over her ankle. As he removed her boot, a strange sensation, as unexpected as it was strong, made it hard for Raine to breathe. His fingers, the blunt strong fingers of a pianist, touched her ankle and then moved along the arch of her foot. With a strong application of willpower, she ignored the weakness in the pit of her stomach and, at his request, wiggled her toes. She appraised the twinge of pain his touch provoked, finally judging it not to be too bad.

"It doesn't seem to be broken," he said. "But you'd better not try to walk on it until we can have it checked by a doctor."

"I'm sure that's not necessary. In fact, the pain is almost gone. It was being doused so unexpectedly by cold water that gave me such a shock, I guess."

"Well, better not take any chances. What were you doing walking out here alone this time of night, anyway? Do you live around here?"

"No, I live in New York. I'm a student at Juilliard—I was at your recital tonight, but unfortunately I came with the wrong person. He—well, he drove off the highway for a little fun and games. I couldn't handle it so I jumped out and hid. When I heard your car I thought it might be Jimmy coming back, so—''

"So you jumped into that ditch," he finished for her. "Look, it's a long way into the city, and you're soaking wet. I've borrowed a friend's lodge for the weekend—it's just up the road. Suppose I take you there so you can dry your clothes. After we've had some coffee, I'll see you home to—where exactly do you live?''

"I share an apartment with three roommates—it's near Lincoln Center," she said, thrilled with the prospect of spending a few hours with Jonah Duncan. *Wait until I tell the girls about this,* she thought. *They'll never believe it. Maybe I should get his autograph for proof.*

Jonah closed the passenger-seat door and moved around the car in front of the headlights. Raine gasped with dismay, realizing for the first time that the front of his tux and pleated shirt were splattered with mud.

"Your clothes will be ruined," she said contritely as he slid behind the wheel. "I'm really sorry—''

"Not to worry," he said carelessly. "Clothes can be replaced—broken bones are a little harder to deal with.''

He smiled at her then, but it was a long moment before she smiled back. If anyone had ever bothered to ask Raine what she thought of Jonah Duncan's appearance, she would have said that while he was attractive, he wasn't particularly handsome. Now, at close range, when she saw how his smile transformed his rugged face, she realized how wrong she'd been.

And why was he still smiling, still staring at her? She must look terrible, her clothes covered with mud and her hair straggling around her face.

"You're a very lovely young woman—and a damned good sport," he said softly.

For some reason, perhaps because the compliment was so unexpected, Raine felt a rush of tears to her eyes. Although she hadn't allowed herself to give into her fear, she'd been quite afraid walking alone down that country road so late at night. The realization that she was safe now, triggered by the concern she saw in Jonah Duncan's eyes, affected her in an unexpected way. She wanted to bury her face in his chest and bawl her eyes out. That she didn't, that she managed another smile, however wobbly, was because she had too much pride to show weakness in front of a stranger.

An expression she couldn't interpret crossed his face. He started to say something, and then, as if he'd changed his mind, he turned away. The dome light went off as he closed the car door, and during the next few minutes Raine found herself answering questions about her background, talking so naturally that it was only later that she realized how skillfully Jonah had put her at ease.

"—and then, just after my mother graduated from the Cincinnati Conservatory of Music, she developed a weakness in her fingers," she said. "It was the beginning of the arthritis that gradually became so bad. At the time the doctors thought it was stress, so they advised her to take a vacation. She met my father while visiting a relative in San Francisco. By the time my brother and I were born, she knew that her disability was permanent."

"I'm sorry," he said, as if he truly meant it. "Was she the one who encouraged you to be a pianist?"

"Oh, yes. Even before I was big enough to reach the pedals she taught me the scales and had me doing simple pieces. Later she arranged for me to take lessons from a good local teacher. Until she passed away—when I was twelve—she never lost her faith that I could take up where she left off."

She paused, thinking of the sacrifices her parents had made for her—the best teachers in San Francisco, the expensive grand piano they couldn't afford, the tuition for a school for the performing arts so she would have more time for practice.

Jonah nodded his understanding. "If the seed isn't sown early it doesn't take root," he told her. "And you need every advantage if you hope for a career as a concert pianist—or in any of the classical music fields. The competition is incredible these days. They seem to come out of the woodwork—the bright, talented, dedicated ones. Have you entered any competitions?"

"Yes—that's how I got my scholarship to Juilliard," she said, suddenly feeling shy. For a while she had almost forgotten who he was. Next to his accomplishments, her own successes seemed so minor.

"Don't knock it," he said, as if he'd read her mind. "If you won a scholarship to Juilliard you must be very talented. But it takes more than that—it takes guts, the kind that keeps you in there plugging away while the rest of the competition are resting on their laurels." There was a grimness in his voice that made her stare at him. "Do you have the right stuff for the long haul, young lady?"

"I think so—"

"*Think* so!" he said explosively. "You'd better be sure before you commit your life to music. If you can't ride roughshod over the competition, subjugate everything else, forget it now. Take up something else, because you can't have it both ways. If you take your eyes off the brass ring for one second, someone else will snag it out from under your nose. So make sure it's what you really want before you sacrifice your personal life for it."

Raine stared at his profile, at his strong nose, his equally strong chin, outlined by the faint light of the dashboard. Was that bitterness she heard in his voice? Why was he talking to her like this, as if he really cared whether or not she knew what she was up against? *Did* she really have—what had he called it—the right stuff? So far she had allowed nothing to distract her from her goal, but then she'd hardly begun to compete. Could she keep it up for as long as it took to become one of the rare people who earned their living on the concert circuit?

And if she never grabbed the brass ring, would

she someday regret that she'd devoted her life to something that was beyond her reach?

Raine was glad when Jonah changed the subject and asked her about her teachers at Juilliard, which had been his school, too, some twelve years earlier. For a while they discussed a teacher they both knew and then fell into a companionable silence. A few minutes later they pulled up in front of a rustic building constructed wholly from logs.

"Here it is—a little self-consciously quaint, but also very comfortable. Best of all, it's completely isolated from the madding crowd."

Raine felt a guilty pang at his wry tone. "I'm sorry I intruded upon your privacy," she said a little stiffly.

He threw back his head in a laugh so uninhibited that she found herself smiling. "Believe me, you're the kind of companion I don't mind. It's the groupies that bug me. That sort of attention, for all the wrong reasons, really turns me off. Of course, it's part of the game—but I'm glad you aren't one of them."

Guiltily Raine thought of the stack of tapes in her room, the only ones she ever spent her slim allowance on. Would Jonah consider her a groupie if he knew that every night she went to sleep with one of his concertos playing softly in her ears? That his picture, cut from a program, was pinned on her wall beside her dressing table?

Well, perhaps she was a groupie, but surely not in the way he meant. She, for one, had never tried to meet him, talk to him, get his autograph. No, it was the music he created that she was interested in. Busy with her own thoughts, she was startled when Jonah opened the door at her elbow and slid his arm under her knees, lifting her. She started to protest that she could walk, and then the words died on her lips. It felt so good, being in Jonah's arms, his breath warm against her face. The scent of after-shave lotion, minty and masculine, mingled with another, one that made her nostrils flare. Part of it was the good honest sweat the physical effort of a full-length concert demanded, but there was something else, too—the clean, musky scent of a healthy male.

She grimaced at the trend her thoughts were taking, and Jonah frowned, obviously mistaking it for a twinge of pain. "We'll have you warm and dry and comfortable in just a few minutes," he promised. He set her on her feet only long enough to unlock the door and switch on a light before he swept her up again and carried her into the cabin.

Raine looked around the living room with appreciative eyes. After the Spartan furnishings of her father's apartment and the clutter of the flat she shared with her roommates, this looked like a movie set to her. Several deep chairs and a comfortable-looking sofa, all covered with a cheery paisley print, complemented the rough texture of the long walls and the stone fireplace. A hooked rug in the same colors as the slipcovers and several cherry-wood tables and chests completed the furnishings.

Through an open door she glimpsed the gleaming appliances of a very modern kitchen. Whoever Jonah's friend was, he obviously had the best of both worlds, she thought.

She expected Jonah to set her down again, but he carried her across the room and lowered her onto the sofa. Contritely she looked down at the coat he'd put around her shoulders. Not only was it thoroughly wet inside, but the hem was stiff with mud where it had dragged on the ground. When she started to take it off to brush off the mud, Jonah stopped her.

"Wait until I get a fire going. Then I'll bring you something else to put on while your clothes dry," he said briskly.

Suddenly conscious of the cold, she huddled inside the coat while he made a fire. Only when it was burning briskly and radiating warmth did he allow her to remove the coat. He didn't examine it before flinging it carelessly over a nearby chair, but she couldn't help thinking that the cost of its replacement, if it came to that, would be enough to pay her living expenses for the next couple of months.

A few minutes later Jonah brought her a man's robe to put on. It was dark blue velour, fleecy and warm, and after he'd discreetly disappeared into a bedroom she slipped out of her clothes quickly, then pulled on the robe and belted it securely around her slender waist. She heard the sound of a shower running, and by the time Jonah reappeared, her jeans and jersey shirt, underwear and boots were arranged on the hearth in front of the fire.

Jonah had changed, too, into jeans and a thick Irish fisherman's sweater. As she eyed him surreptitiously, taking in his still-damp hair, she decided he looked very much at home in outdoorsy clothes, and then wondered why she would think such a thing about an obviously sophisticated man like Jonah Duncan.

"If you want to take a shower there's plenty of hot water. I'll toss your clothes in the washer and dryer. They should be ready for you by the time I fix us something to eat." He caught her surprise and explained, "My friend fancies a retreat in the wilderness but not enough to give up the amenities. There's a microwave oven in the kitchen—and even a waterbed in the master bedroom. All the basic necessities of roughing it."

After he'd picked up her discarded clothes and disappeared into the kitchen, Raine hobbled into the bathroom and found it, with its nile-green tiles and brass fixtures, as luxuriously appointed as the kitchen. She took a bath instead of a shower, soaking the cold out of her bones in a tub of hot steaming water before she washed the mud from her hair. She found a hair dryer in the cabinet under the sink, but when her hair was dry, she hesitated, tempted to leave it hanging free around her shoulders. In the end she coiled it into a tight knot at the nape of her neck as usual.

When Jonah returned to the living room, she was back in front of the fire, her leg propped up on a cushion. He dropped down on the edge of the sofa and bent over her leg; his fingers were gentle as he probed her ankle, then flexed her toes, watching her face for signs of pain.

She stared back, fascinated by this close-up look at him. Because of the picture pinned on her wall, she already knew every line of his face, his well-shaped nose and mouth, the unruly eyebrows that shadowed deep-set eyes. But she realized now that his eyes were not brown as she'd thought, but so dark a gray they looked black in the dancing light from the fireplace. Nor had she known that the creases beside his mouth were laugh lines, or that energy seemed to radiate from his body even when he was sitting still, or that when he spoke, asking her if it hurt when he moved her foot, his voice would set up shameful vibrations deep inside her, or that when he touched her, her bones would melt so disconcertingly, making her want her to touch him back. . . .

No, she hadn't known these things, but now that she did, she knew she must fight off this—this purely physical attraction before she humiliated herself by giving it away. So her voice was cool, her words stilted as she answered his question. "It doesn't hurt much now. I'm perfectly all right."

Jonah frowned at her. With an abruptness that startled her, he reached forward and took both her hands in his. "Look—don't be afraid of me. I don't seduce young women, especially ones in distress."

The flush started at Raine's throat and spread over her face. She was sure that under the velour robe the rest of her body was bright pink, too.

"I—I don't know what you mean," she stammered.

"You've been as skittish as a colt ever since you changed into that robe. You're obviously having second thoughts about coming to an isolated place like this with someone you don't know. And after your experience tonight, I don't blame you. But for what it's worth, you have my promise that as soon as your clothes are dry, I'm bundling you up and taking you back to the city—and for a very good reason. Since I don't happen to be a masochist—or a saint—that face of yours, and especially that smile, could get to be quite a problem to someone who's just promised to keep hands off."

"I'm not afraid of you," she said, which was the truth, since it was herself she was afraid of. "I know you're a gentleman."

Jonah threw back his head and laughed. Raine stared with fascination at the brown column of his throat, at the muscles that moved in his jawline. He sobered quickly, and as he returned her stare, his eyes darkened and some strong emotion moved across the face that she'd thought was a little impassive until that moment. He leaned forward as if he were about to kiss her, but then he drew back, his face strained.

"If you don't want me to forget my promise, you'd better stop staring at me like that. Because I'm not a gentleman. Anything but. I'm a street fighter who came up from the gutter and got where I am by bucking odds you couldn't possibly understand, not if I told you the story of my life for the next two hours. You might remember that when you get into the competition thing. You'll be pitted against the real roughies—a nice young woman like you just might not stand a chance.''

She started to tell him that she was a fighter, too, but then she held her tongue. Next to his background, her own life might seem easy. Yet it hadn't been, not when every minute since she was old enough to sit at the piano she had been aware that she must succeed, must fulfill her mother's unrealized dream and justify her parents' sacrifices. . . .

He left her then, saying he was ravenous and would make them something to eat. A few minutes later, feeling a little lonely, she hobbled into the kitchen to watch with amazement as he expertly put together an omelet.

"How on earth did you learn to cook like that?" she asked.

"The hard way. My mother cut out on my dad and me when I was four or five, so I've been cooking since I was big enough to hold a spatula. Beans from a can and franks, hamburgers and fried potatoes—those were my specialties. When I was fourteen I got a job as an all-around flunky at a truck stop in Jersey. The man who owned the diner let me sleep in a room in the rear. I watched the short-order cook until I was pretty sure I could handle it, and when he quit I took over his job. Upward mobility, you might say.'' Again there was wryness in his voice.

Deftly he flipped the omelet, buttered it

generously and slid it onto a warmed plate, then surrounded it with hot wedges of toast. He gave her a generous portion, and as she dug hungrily into the food he looked so complacent that she had to laugh.

As they ate she told him something about her own culinary efforts, of the way she'd tried so hard after her mother's death to cook the Italian food her father loved—and had failed more often than not. Though she offered to help do the dishes when they had finished their meal, Jonah sternly ordered her to stay off her foot. As he moved around the kitchen, she noted the grace of his body, so surprising in a man his size, and she reflected that if things had gone differently, he probably would have earned his living as a boxer.

When they were back in front of the fire, drinking coffee, she asked him curiously, "How did you happen to become interested in music, Mr. Duncan?"

"That's Jonah. My father was a classical music freak. He was a cab driver, but somehow he always came up with the money to pay for my music lessons. Not from the best teachers—he couldn't afford that. In fact, they were pretty pedestrian teachers, and later on I had to unlearn some bad habits. But it was enough to show me what I wanted to do with my life."

"Your father must be very proud of you."

"He's dead—I was thirteen when a diesel truck hit his cab and killed him. Since I had no other relatives, they put me into a foster home. I wanted to keep on with my music lessons, so I decided I'd better get a job. That's why I ran away to Jersey and went to work at the truck stop and spent my wages on lessons. Then, when I was sixteen, Bruno Wolfheim, a really top New York teacher, became interested in me, and after he'd worked the bad habits out of my system, he got me an audition for the School of Performing Arts. I spent the next two years there, which gave me a high-school diploma and some decent instruction. Then I won a four-year scholarship to Juilliard. One of my teachers found a music enthusiast patron for me, who paid my living expenses so I could concentrate on my studies. That's how I got a stab at the Tchaikovsky competition in Russia. Winning it gave me the boost I needed to be taken seriously by the important critics."

Raine was silent, aware of the parts he'd left out—the grueling work, the endless hours of practice, the constant financial struggle, the sacrifices to his personal life such dedication must necessarily have cost him.

"And what about you, young lady?" The quizzical look was back in his eyes. "Do you have the stamina for that kind of struggle?"

"I wish you wouldn't call me that," she said crossly, sure she read doubt in those too-observant eyes.

"But I don't know your name—no, don't tell me. I'll call you Carmen. If you were a soprano instead of a pianist you'd make a perfect Carmen. I think Bizet must have had someone just like you in mind—a slender girl with a cloud of dark hair, a Madonna face and eyes that flash fire when someone like me gets too personal.''

At her flush he laughed and added, ''And I hope you do have the right stuff. Only the tiniest minority make it to the top in the classical music field, you know. The rest end up teaching or turn to other professions. Most of the women get married, have kids—and wonder all their lives if they could have made it if they hadn't given it all up for love.''

''If ever I've heard a sexist remark, that's it,'' Raine snapped. Her awe of him had disappeared about the time she'd seen him in a white butcher's apron, grating cheese.

''Sexist? It wasn't meant that way—although there *is* a tendency to take a man pianist more seriously than a woman with similar talent. I suppose the reasoning is that a woman will eventually drop out to raise a family.''

''Well, I don't intend to get married—not for a long time,'' she said. ''I have no time for distractions, which is why—'' she stopped, biting her lower lip.

''Which is why you try to make sure that you aren't subject to temptation,'' he said, his eyes amused.

''I don't know what you mean,'' she said quickly.

''It doesn't work, you know,'' he told her. ''There's nothing you can do to hide that figure or that flawless complexion or those remarkable eyes. Even without lipstick, your mouth—''

This time he was the one who stopped. The pulse in his throat leaped and she was suddenly aware that his legs, stretched out beside hers, were so close she could feel his body heat through her robe.

He reached out and touched the coil of hair at the nape of her neck. "Why don't you let your hair do what comes naturally, which is to curl around your face? That washerwoman's knot doesn't make you look older, you know. In fact, you look like a schoolgirl playing a part. I'd like to see it down, hanging loose...."

Raine couldn't seem to look away. She was aware of the flames crackling in the fireplace, of the pungent odor of burning pine, the stirring of her own quickened breath. The warmth of his hand against her neck seemed to burn her skin, setting her whole body on fire. Suddenly she wanted to put her hand against the pulse that beat so strongly in his throat, wanted him to kiss her, wanted him to make love to her....

When she realized what she was thinking, she jerked away from his hand and started to get up. But her ankle, still weak from the twisting it had taken, gave out on her and she was pitching forward—into Jonah's arms. As his hands caught her, as his arms closed around her, she felt as if she were drowning, as if water had closed over her head, cutting off her breath.

His lips touched hers. It was such a gentle kiss at first that it disarmed her and kept her from pulling away. Then, as the pressure of his mouth deep-

ened, her lips parted, admitting his supple tongue.
He gave a smothered groan, and his kiss became
more demanding. Without conscious volition she
melted against him, her senses reeling, her limbs
weak with a languor so new to her that she had no
defenses against it. As he probed the softness of
her mouth with his tongue, strange sensations
assaulted her. His hands moved down her back,
and her arms, again as if she had no will of her
own, lifted and fastened around his neck.

With a groan he pushed aside the neckline of the
robe and buried his face in the moist hollow between her breasts. She felt a rush of warmth that
seemed to invade every part of her body, and an
ache swept through her loins, a hunger that swept
away her inhibitions, her common sense. As if he
were a wave and she a ship without a rudder, she
was helpless, caught in the trap of her own un-
tutored passions.

Even when his lips wandered further, capturing
her breasts, enveloping them in the warm moistness of his mouth, she didn't resist. As his hands,
so gentle and yet so strong, took other liberties, as
they caressed her, exploring the mysteries of her
body, raising the hunger to a peak, a warning
stirred sluggishly, but it had no chance against the
drives of her newly awakened body. She was
trapped by a need so powerful and overwhelming
that nothing, not even her strong sense of self-
preservation, could stop the spiraling excitement,
the aching, the wanting.

He slipped the robe off her shoulders and then

gently pushed her back on the couch. As his body blotted out the amber light of the fire, as she realized he was removing his own clothes, tossing them carelessly aside, she felt a smothering panic. Then he was beside her on the sofa, and she knew the delight of being caressed by a man's hands, of feeling a man's hard virile body pressing against hers, fitting into hers, molding their two bodies into one.

Again he kissed her, and as new sensations washed over her she knew she couldn't deny him. She had no defense against this sweet explosion of her senses. His mouth moved down her throat, his face nuzzled the curve of her shoulder and she arched her back, giving him access to her throbbing breasts. Gently he teased them with his lips, then with a smothered moan he was exploring the rest of her body with his hands, his lips, his warm, pliant tongue.

Filled with wonder at the delight his touch evoked, she let her own hands drift over his shoulders and down over the crisp hair that curled on his chest, wanting to know him as he knew her, wanting to pleasure him as he pleasured her.

And then he was lifting her, his hands cupped under her hips, and she felt the full power of his body as he penetrated her, making her one with him. Briefly a fierce pain shot through her, but it was lost in the midst of such a rush of pleasure that she hardly noticed it.

She was spiraling upward, caught in a searing, pulsating flood that raised her higher and higher.

The world had condensed to this moment, to this narrow place, to Jonah's hard demanding body, to her softer yielding one. As the wave, exquisitely sweet, carried her even higher and rose to a peak of pure ecstasy, she knew that this moment, this man, would be etched on her heart forever. No matter what the future brought her, she would always judge other men by Jonah Duncan, by this small slice of time that had changed her from a girl to a woman.

CHAPTER THREE

IT WAS ONLY AFTERWARD, when her turbulent breathing and her wildly leaping pulse had slowed, that reason returned and Raine felt a rush of regret. Jonah raised himself on his elbow and looked down at her, his eyes so sober that she wondered if he was disappointed because she was so inexperienced and hadn't known the things to do to satisfy a man. But no, his kiss on her forehead was tender, and his hand, when he pushed the hair away from her face, was very gentle.

"I'm sorry, Carmen. I had no idea this was your first time. If I'd known, I would have stopped with a kiss."

Hurt flooded through Raine. Rather than let him see how his words had wounded her, she reached for the velour robe and pulled it on, avoiding his eyes. "Not to worry," she said, borrowing his own phrase. "I wasn't an unwilling participant. If it hadn't been you, eventually it would've been someone else. I've been too busy for men until now. Maybe I'd better reevaluate my priorities in the future."

His next move took her by surprise. He reached for her and took her face between his hands, forcing her to look at him. "There is no way you're going to experiment with other men," he said softly. "If I've hurt your feelings, I'm sorry. That wasn't a criticism. But if I'd known you were inexperienced, I would have handled it differently. I would have wooed you, dined you, taken it by easy stages. Because you're very special, Carmen. You're like a—a fresh breeze. No acts, no games. Just a completely honest girl who happens to be one of the most beautiful women I've ever known. Okay, I lost control and took advantage of your vulnerability. But it would have come to that eventually, anyway, because I'm only human. Do you have any idea how hard it is for me, right at this moment, to keep from making love to you again?"

She looked at him for a long time; half a dozen thoughts went through her mind. Caution—yes, that was part of it. She wasn't sure if she could handle the intensity of her own feelings for this man. If he made love to her again...something primitive, feminine and wise told her that if she experienced the ecstasy of Jonah's lovemaking again she would be completely under his spell. And yet he hadn't committed himself to anything more than this one night. What if she were just a refreshing diversion, a convenient one-night stand, a way of releasing the tensions that follow a concert?

Raine took a long steadying breath. She opened her mouth for a light remark, one calculated to turn off the high voltage between them. Which was why she was so surprised when she heard her own voice, husky and without its usual crispness, saying, "But I *want* you to make love to me again, Jonah."

The pupils of Jonah's eyes dilated; a moment later she was enfolded in his arms and he was kissing her, searing kisses that rekindled the flame she'd so recently discovered within herself. He picked her up, carried her into the dark bedroom and lowered her onto the waterbed. With its softness surrounding them he led her leisurely through the stages of passion, and she knew that she had just passed a landmark in her life, that no matter how their relationship turned out, any other men who might follow would always be second best. . . .

WHEN RAINE AWOKE the next morning she was aware of a feeling of happiness even before she realized where she was or remembered the sweet hours she'd spent in Jonah's arms during the night. It was the cheerful sound of Jonah's whistling and the odor of sausages frying and coffee perking that brought it all back to her.

For a long time she lay there, her eyes closed, reluctant to leave the world of dreams even for the reality of being with Jonah. Her body felt different, incredibly sensitive and yet deeply relaxed. Gently she touched her breasts, remembering how stirred she'd been as Jonah's lips had teased those tiny sensitive peaks into hardness. She ran an experimental hand over her body, the body that had been one with Jonah's such a short while ago.

Was it this way with other women after love—this deeply sensual aftermath, this heightened awareness of their own bodies? If not—oh, how sorry she was for them that they didn't have Jonah for a lover! At the moment nothing else seemed important. Not her music or the future, nothing except this exciting and wonderful thing that had happened between Jonah and her.

Suddenly eager to see him, she threw back the covers. After she'd pulled on the borrowed robe, she went into the bathroom to shower. She was drying herself with a luxuriously thick towel when she caught sight of her own image in the full-length mirror behind the bathroom door. She stopped to give her reflection a bemused appraisal. Instead of the wan pale look of a woman who'd been awake half the night, her skin glowed and her eyes burned with an inward fire. In fact, she felt more alert than she'd ever felt before in her life.

How long has this been going on, she thought wickedly. She'd had no idea what she'd been missing, but oh, how glad she was that she'd waited for Jonah to initiate her to love!

When she came out of the bathroom, still wearing the robe, Jonah was standing in the kitchen doorway watching her. He was wearing the white butcher's apron again and he was holding a spatula in his hand. His smile was so smug that she gave an involuntary giggle.

"You should do that more often, you know," he told her. "You're something of a sobersides, aren't you? Well, we'll change all that. If you want to be my girl you'll have to smile more often. You can even giggle on occasion, as long as you don't overdo it, even though it does make me feel like an old man.''

She widened her eyes mischievously at him. "But you *are* an old man.''

"Here now—none of that talk with me. You'll have to treat me with more respect. The fact is, I'm thirty-four, in the prime of my life.'' His eyes grew serious suddenly. "How old are you, Carmen?''

"I'm twenty,'' she said, laughing.

A strange expression crossed his face, but before she could question it he was smiling again. "And you must be starved. Luckily, knowing you're still a growing girl, I fixed plenty.''

He led the way into the kitchen. She stared at the plates piled high with golden waffles and richly brown sausages. "You fixed enough for five growing girls,'' she observed wryly.

He gave her a mock leer. "It's only fair to feed you well since I kept you up half the night. I don't want you going home weak and pale.''

She met his eyes and something passed between them, the electricity that seemed so close to the surface when they were near each other. She discovered her mouth was dry, there was a distressing weakness in her knees, and she knew he felt the same when he drew her gently toward him and gave her a long lingering kiss. He whispered a soft question against her hair, and when she nodded he swept her up in his arms and carried her back into the darkened bedroom.

As he lowered her to the bed she had a fierce desire to feel his warm body against hers. She unhooked his belt buckle, and as if he knew it was important to her to undress him, he stood there smiling down at her as she took off his belt, then fumbled with his jeans.

"Right now, with that pucker between your eyebrows, you look like a little girl trying to figure out the answer to a puzzle. The shoes come off first—or it gets a little complicated."

She laughed. "Well, I don't really know the technique for undressing a man. This *is* my first time, after all."

"I know, I know. Here, let me help you." A few seconds later he was standing nude before her. Although it was shadowy in the tree-shaded bedroom, his strong well-muscled body, unmistakably virile and masculine, made her tremble. Tentatively she touched his chest, then his taut stomach, her hands moving over his body in slow sensual circles.

When her hands drifted lower he gave a muffled groan, and then he was beside her on the bed, his head blotting out the light from the window, his hands and lips creating small rivulets of flame along her body, arousing it to wildness. Wanting to return the pleasure he was giving her, she let her instincts take over as she returned his caresses, following his lead, touching him as he touched her.

"Sweet, sweet Carmen," he murmured, his breathing so strident that his words had a strangled sound.

It was much later when they returned to breakfast. By this time, the sausages were cold and the butter had congealed on the waffles. Extravagantly Jonah tossed them out and fixed more, and a few minutes later, as he watched Raine hungrily packing the food away, he shook his head.

"Just a growing girl," he muttered, and then ducked when she tossed a crumpled paper napkin at him.

"This is more food than I usually eat in a day," she said. "But for some reason I'm famished this morning—and I think you missed your calling. You should have been a chef."

"And you should have been a courtesan, the rage of Paris at the turn of the century—or a hetaera in the golden days of Greece."

"Well, I doubt I could qualify for either of those things. Most of my wardrobe is jeans and sweatshirts," she said ruefully. "Even if I wore the apartment dress, I would still look like a college student."

"What the devil's an 'apartment dress'?"

"It's a Halston original that one of my roommates found in a secondhand-clothing store. She couldn't afford it, even on sale, so we all went together and bought it. Luckily we're about the same size, so when one of us has a really special date we take a vote, and if it's important enough, that person gets to wear it for the evening—and the rest of us wait up until she gets home to make sure there are no rips or tears."

Jonah's stare was quizzical. "It must be quite a

responsibility for your dates—making sure nothing happens to the community gown.''

''Well, to tell the truth, I haven't worn it yet. Nothing's come up that seemed that important.''

''Until now. Will you wear it for me?''

Her heart seemed to stop, and she had to take a deep breath before she said softly, ''Yes—if that's what you want, Jonah. I—I'd do anything for you.''

A muscle tightened in his jawline, and he shook his head. ''Carmen, Carmen—you're so damned vulnerable. Don't you know how dangerous it is, wearing your heart on your sleeve?''

''I don't know any other way to be,'' she told him. ''After all, this is all so new to me.''

A glint of amusement showed in his eyes. ''You know the important thing—how to set a man on fire.'' He kissed her, careless of his coffee cup, which his sleeve knocked to the floor.

As she helped him mop up the spilled coffee, Raine was glad for the diversion, because she was afraid that he would guess how his kiss, meant only to tease, had inflamed her again.

''Is it always like this?'' she said when they were back in their chairs again with fresh cups of coffee. ''Will I always feel this way after—after making love?''

''How *do* you feel, Carmen?'' he asked, smiling at her.

''Wonderful. So alive and—and wonderful,'' she said.

''Uh-huh. You'll have to decide that for yourself after the next time," he told her, his tone teasing.

"Then there will be a next time?" she said.

He was silent, watching her. "I want there to be," he said finally. "But I wonder if I'm being fair to you. Maybe I'm too old, too...burned out. I've made so many mistakes, so many compromises. You deserve someone younger, less battered by life."

"But I don't want someone younger. I want you," Raine said softly. "Last night was the most wonderful night of my life."

"I wish you weren't so young—or even so lovely," he said. "This isn't one of those younger women-older men things, but no one is going to believe it." At her puzzled look he laughed, but not as if he were really amused. "Well, at least you aren't a blonde. That would really stir up the gossip, wouldn't it?"

She felt the shock all through her body. Not a blonde? But of course she really was a blonde. And what did his remark mean? That so many people thought of blondes as being sex objects, as she had good reason to know? Or did he have some personal prejudice against blondes?

Questions trembled on her lips but she didn't ask them aloud. She knew so little about him and their relationship was so new. Did she dare put any strain upon it? She wanted so badly to be everything he wanted in a woman. If it meant remaining a brunette, even though she'd decided to let her hair grow back to its natural color, so be it. A brunette she would be....

But her mood had changed, she discovered, as she dressed in her own freshly laundered clothes and then waited while Jonah banked the fire, turned out the lights and locked the door. Somehow, putting on her own jeans and wool jacket had brought it home to her that the interlude was finished, that it was time to face reality again. It didn't help that Jonah suddenly seemed a stranger.

He turned, his eyes swept over her face, and then she was in his arms, his lips nuzzling her throat. "It isn't over yet," he said against her warm flesh. "You don't think I'd let you get away from me, do you?" And suddenly the magic was back and she was laughing as he held her close against his chest.

They drove back to the city leisurely, stopping on the way for lunch. As they sat lingering over their coffee, she found it so easy to open up to Jonah, to tell him something about her dreams and hopes, things she'd never admitted to anyone else.

Later, during so many sleepless nights, she would go over and over the things she'd said, looking for clues, for some answer to the question of what had gone wrong. Had it been her ambition, which she'd been so frank about? Had she revealed her callowness, boring him? Or had it been that all along he had simply been using her?

But at the time she didn't notice how little he said about himself. Oh, he talked about music and told her amusing anecdotes about a conductor she admired. He hummed a few bars of a concerto he was working on and described the problems with the logistics of coordinating a long concert tour. But he didn't mention his personal life, an omission that didn't seem important then because they had so many other things to talk about. Every time Raine met his gaze the possessiveness in his eyes thrilled her. It seemed incredible that just one short day ago she hadn't even met Jonah and now she felt as if she'd loved him all her life.

When he dropped her off in front of her apartment building he held her hand for a long time, ignoring the honking horns of traffic he was holding up while she hurriedly told him her phone and apartment numbers.

"I'll call you this evening," he promised. "There are so many things we should talk about. I don't want to rush you, Carmen, so I'm not going to make love to you again, not until you're very sure. So be prepared for a conventional courtship—that is, if I can keep my hands off you."

"And if you can't?" she said, so confidently, so ignorantly.

He gave her a twisted smile. "Then this will be the fastest courtship in history."

Raine's head was still reeling from his thorough and very leisurely goodbye kiss when she went upstairs to face the worried questions of her roommates. Something inherently private in her nature prevented her from sharing the adventure, so she said only that she'd had a bad experience with her date and had ended up spending the night alone in a Catskills motel.

Later she would be glad she hadn't confided in

them. At least she never had to face the humiliation of her friends' knowing what a fool she'd been. Because Jonah didn't call that night, didn't call the next day, and when, afraid that something had happened to him, Raine tried to reach him by phone, his number wasn't listed.

Two days later a bouquet of white roses and an exquisite—and very expensive—sapphire bracelet were delivered to the apartment, addressed simply to "Carmen." Perhaps Raine already knew in her heart what the note inside would say, because she ignored the curious stares of her roommates and took the gifts and the note, still unread, into her bedroom and closed the door.

The handwriting on the note was angular, so sprawling that it covered most of the page. Jonah had written:

I hope your ankle has healed and there won't be any unfortunate repercussions of last night. You'll understand, I'm sure, when I tell you that while it was all very pleasant, it must be a one-time thing. There are too many obstacles between us to continue with our relationship. I hope this gift will be enough compensation.

For a long time Raine sat on the bed, staring at the note, before she shifted her eyes to the flowers. White roses... for purity?

Under the force of the pain, the shame, her whole face convulsed. Rising, she took the roses from the box and one by one tore them apart. When there was nothing left but broken stems and crushed petals, she ripped the note to shreds, too. Her face stiff and frozen, her hands and feet so cold they could have been encased in ice, she gathered up the torn petals, the scraps of paper and ribbon, the sapphire bracelet and carried them downstairs to dump them in the trash cans behind the building. It wasn't until later that she realized the rose's thorns had pricked her fingers so badly that practicing was painful for a few days. Somehow it seemed fitting that Jonah's gift should leave her with physical as well as emotional pain as a remembrance of their brief affair.

And even that hadn't been the end of it. A week later in the music section of the *Times* she had seen a picture of Jonah, standing beside a beautiful elegantly dressed woman and a small dark-haired boy. The caption beneath made it clear that this was Jonah's wife and son, who had just returned from a vacation in Mexico.

Somehow Raine had weathered the pain, the knowledge that Jonah had not only seduced a vulnerable girl but betrayed his wife, as well. But it had changed her, hardened her. Since then she had completely cut men out of her life, not allowing anyone to get past her defenses. What had originally been a means for avoiding distractions for the sake of her career had become permanent, an insurance against ever again enduring such pain.

Now, three years later, as she sat staring at the

office door through which Jonah had just passed, words from the past came back to her. *What a fool I was,* she thought.

If ever she'd had any secret hope that somehow it had all been a mistake and there was a good explanation for what Jonah had done to her, that hope was dead now. The knowledge that their night together had made so little impression upon Jonah that he hadn't even remembered her shouldn't hurt so after all this time, but it did... terribly.

Well, she wasn't going to put up with it. Unconsciously Raine squared her slim shoulders. It was time she purged not only Jonah but the old hurt and bitterness from her memory once and for all. Yes, that's just what she would do. From this moment on, Jonah Duncan no longer existed for her—just as she obviously hadn't existed for him for a long time.

CHAPTER FOUR

RAINE HAD OFTEN THOUGHT that Arnold Partridge's office was a perfect setting for the old lawyer with his formal manner, his rustling voice and his kind eyes. It radiated order and tradition and a rather fussy cleanliness, like the man who rose to greet her. Since she had known Mr. Partridge all her life, she had long ago discovered his secret—his outward appearance of austerity hid a deep compassion for others. And that is how she knew, even before he spoke, that the news he had for her was bad.

Wanting to get the disappointment over with, she got right down to business. "Okay, Mr. Partridge, let's have it, please. I already know the news isn't good."

Mr. Partridge cleared his throat, looking unhappy. "Well, there *were* a lot of debts. Your father had borrowed quite a bit of money, and of course he did rather neglect his business there at the last when he was so ill, you know."

"No, I didn't know," Raine said, a lump in her throat. "It seems dad—and my brother—were in some kind of conspiracy to keep me from finding out how sick he was. I should have guessed when he told me he couldn't come to New York for my graduation because he had some business to attend to." She looked at Mr. Partridge with bleak eyes. "I was so busy feeling sorry for myself that it never occurred to me that nothing except illness would keep him away."

"Oh, my dear Raine, it wasn't your fault. It was Earl's own choice. Once your father made up his mind about something, he could be as stubborn as—" he paused, looking uncomfortable.

"As me," Raine said, and found that she could smile after all.

"As you. In many ways you're like your mother, and yet—yes, you do have many of your father's qualities, too. Which will do you more good in the long run than a solvent estate would."

"Are there still a lot of debts?" she asked, her heart sinking.

"No, no—nothing like that. All the bank loans have been paid, although it took every cent I got from the sale of the business, I'm afraid. There were a few things that weren't part of the inventory, such as his signed limited editions of Faulkner and the Lawrence first editions, which he bought for speculation. Even though the market is so sluggish right now, they brought in enough to cover the rest of the bills."

He paused to shuffle the papers on his desk before he added, "Of course, there's still your father's private collection of leather bounds. You did ask that they not be put up for sale, but—well, you could raise a nice sum from them. I'm afraid he sold the most valuable ones during the past few years, but there's still a few left, the ones he treasured the most.''

"No," Raine said firmly. "Whatever's left of dad's private collection I'd like to keep. I'm sure my brother feels the same way.''

He nodded, his eyes showing understanding. "Yes, yes. . . in so many ways, that collection personifies what your father stood for. A lifetime dedicated to conserving quality and aesthetic beauty is reflected in those books. I'd like to think that someday they'll be passed along to Earl's grandchildren. 'The world of books is the most remarkable creation of Man,' as—now who was it who said that?" He peered at her over his rimless glasses, his eyes expectant.

"Clarence Day?''

"Of course. How could I forget? Well, my memory isn't so faulty that I don't remember that it was Voltaire who said that 'Rare books make rich men wise and wise men rich.' ''

Raine hid a smile. Where literary quotes were concerned, Mr. Partridge had a memory like an elephant, and this was a game they had played ever since she was old enough to read. "I believe that was Sir William Rees-Mogg, Mr. Partridge," she said gently.

"Yes, yes, of course." He gave his dry cough again. "And you haven't changed all that much from the little girl who used to sneak away from her piano to lose herself in a book. I can still see you—that long ponytail hanging down your back, the part crooked more often than not, with such a serious expression that it made a person want to make you smile. Well, your mother would feel justified for keeping you at your piano all those hours." He paused, then went on. "Your father was so proud of you, you know. You aren't going to allow this financial setback to prevent you from trying for the Tchaikovsky competition, are you?"

"No...but I'll have to find some way to support myself while I train." She didn't think it necessary to point out that to be ready for the competition in Moscow, the toughest in the world, she needed hours of daily practice and a top-rated teacher to monitor her work.

"But surely that won't be necessary—oh, how thoughtless of me! I haven't explained about the insurance, have I?"

"Insurance?"

"Your father made you the beneficiary of his insurance. Not a fortune, but it should be enough to support you while you prepare for the competition."

"But—but what about my brother? Surely dad intended it for both of us."

Mr. Partridge shook his head. "You're the sole beneficiary. Earl's will left the business and his collection to both of you. I'm sure he never dreamed the business would be left insolvent because of his medical bills and other things."

"Other things," she said dully. "Such as my allowance for the past four years."

"And your brother's expenses," he reminded

her. "Don't forget that he supported your brother for almost seven years—and paid very high tuition for him at Stanford, too." He hesitated, then added, "Martin will be earning an allowance as an intern, won't he? And his wife—isn't she an R.N.? Surely she could work for a while."

"Their daughter, Debra, still needs constant care, which is why Gloria hasn't been able to work. The doctors are hopeful that the source of Debra's allergies will be pinpointed eventually, but Martin will need financial help for another year, probably longer. And that means the insurance money should go to them." She forced back her disappointment and smiled at him. "There's no reason why I can't take a job in a bookstore. That's something I'm qualified for."

Mr. Partridge's eyes were thoughtful as he studied her, but she had the feeling his mind was elsewhere. When he spoke, he had changed the subject so abruptly that it was a moment before his words sank in.

"I need your advice, Raine. I've been offered a first edition of Raymond Chandler's *The Big Sleep* for five hundred dollars. Usually I don't buy from anyone except dealers I know and trust, but this man approached me and—well, it's a book I need to fill in my Chandler collection. He left it here for my inspection. How about looking it over and giving me your opinion?"

Mr. Partridge's sphere of interest as a bibliophile was collecting classic mysteries and other related books. Over the years her father had earned many commissions from the old lawyer by searching out rare first editions in this field.

"I'd be glad to take a look at it, but you do realize that I'm not an expert, don't you?" she cautioned.

"Earl often told me that he'd taught you just about all he knew about the business. Since I value his judgment I'm sure you're just being modest."

Although Raine knew his praise was undeserved, it was true that her father had taught her a lot about the antiquarian book business. After her mother's death she had wanted desperately to be with him as much as possible. She had asked questions about his collection, about the books he bought and sold, and eventually, as so many lonely men do, he had let her share the passion that was both his hobby and his profession.

What had started out as a bid for her father's attention had soon become an engrossing interest, and now Raine cherished old books so much that she would have been a collector had she been able to afford it. Next to her father, who had been highly respected in his field, she was only an amateur. Still, in comparison to most dealers, she could probably qualify enough to give an educated opinion to her old friend.

So she waited silently while Mr. Partridge unlocked a desk drawer to take out a hardcover book. Handling it carefully she examined the book page by page. It was ten minutes before she looked up at him, her face troubled.

"There are definitely signs of tampering." She

pointed out a ragged edge on the frontispiece, a long crack in the spine, differences in the texture and color of the paper. "This seems to be a composite of two, possibly three books. Cleverly done, but not worth anything to a collector. As an oddity—perhaps a few dollars. I'm really sorry. If it were genuine, it would be worth—oh, something in the neighborhood of two thousand dollars, perhaps a few hundred dollars more."

Mr. Partridge didn't seem very disappointed. In fact he was smiling as he put the book away in the drawer again. "I thought the price was much too low for the genuine article," he said. "You seem up on market values, too."

"Just what I read in trade magazines and Mandeville's *Used Books Price Guide*—and of course I've taken advantage of living in New York to attend the World Antiquarian Book Fair as often as possible. I even did some buying for dad last year," Raine said, trying not to show her puzzlement. Mr. Partridge knew more about his own sphere of interest than most dealers did. Surely he must have noticed the alterations in the spine of the book, the slight differences in the paper. It was clearly a fake, and she had heard her father talk about his friend's shrewdness, his talent for sniffing out real value. Was he trying to divert her from her disappointment, or was there something else he was reluctant to tell her?

"What is it, Mr. Partridge?" she said. "Is there something more I should know?"

Mr. Partridge's eyes developed a twinkle.

"You're still the same blunt person you were as a child, aren't you? Well, you're right. An idea came to me that . . . well, you might say I've been testing you."

"If it's more bad news—"

"Oh, no. In fact, it could be very good news. You say you need a job, and I think I might be able to help you. And because of unusual circumstances, it might solve some of your problems."

"A job . . . what do you mean by 'unusual circumstances'?"

"It's a short-term proposition. One of my clients is looking for someone to catalog a very large collection of books he inherited several years ago. From what he tells me, it's quite an eclectic collection. His father-in-law, Granton Arlington, was the last of the old timber barons and a rather eccentric man. Perhaps you've heard of him?"

"Isn't he the man who endowed a collection of old maps and bound galleys for the de Young Museum?"

"Among other things. Anyway, my client wants the books cataloged with an eye toward giving anything really rare and valuable to the de Young Museum and getting rid of the rest of the books through sale or donation. He'll also be keeping some of the books himself. What he needs now is a complete assessment by someone who is qualified to catalog the collection and give a general estimate of its value on a book by book basis—he needs this for tax purposes. Since he knows I'm something of a bibliophile, he turned over the power of attorney to me so I can issue the contract on his behalf. You just passed the test with flying colors. The job is yours if you want it. It should take you about three months."

He went on to discuss the fee, which was so generous that Raine's breathing almost stopped. If she lived frugally it would be enough to pay her expenses while she trained for the Tchaikovsky competition and even cover her travel expenses to Russia....

"Would you like to tackle it, Raine?" Mr. Partridge asked, and since she'd lost her voice, she nodded so vigorously that he gave one of his rare laughs.

A few minutes later Mrs. Clark's typewriter was tapping busily in the outer office, preparing a contract for signing, while Mr. Partridge and Raine discussed his collection of mystery and detective books, which ranged from the works of Wilkie Collins and Edgar Allan Poe to Raymond Chandler and Dashiell Hammett. It was only when Raine was leaning over his desk to sign the contract that a shocked gasp escaped her lips. For a long moment she stared down at the name written on the contract, her mouth dry, before she raised stricken eyes to Mr. Partridge's face.

"Is something wrong?" he asked.

"Your client is Jonah Duncan!"

"Why, yes, didn't I tell you—but of course I didn't. Yes, it's Jonah Duncan. Unfortunately you won't get the chance to listen to his practice sessions, my dear. That's one of the terms of the contract.''

"I don't understand—"

"Jonah has retired from the concert arena. His wife's death—a terrible, terrible tragedy—left him prostrate with grief. Now he won't touch the piano, and anybody who works for him is forbidden to mention music in his presence. Which means you'll have to manage your practice sessions off the estate somewhere. Since you'll have ample free time, I don't think this will be a problem. I'm sure you can make some arrangements in Mendocino town—"

"I've changed my mind, Mr. Partridge," Raine broke in. "It's very kind of you to consider me but I can't work for—I can't take the job."

"But it's perfect for your needs. And you're certainly qualified. After the books have been cataloged, Jonah intends to bring in an expert from New York to put a final value on them. Your responsibility ends with the cataloging."

"I can't explain. It's a personal matter," Raine said, trying to hide her bitter disappointment. "I do thank you and—you won't volunteer any information to Martin about my being the beneficiary of dad's insurance, will you?"

"Of course not. But I do wish—well, I'm sure you have your own reasons for turning down the job. However, I'll hold it open for another couple of days before I look around for someone else.

Jonah will be out of town for a few days so there's no real hurry. Perhaps you might change your mind."

Raine left it like that, although she knew there was no possibility that she would change her mind. The thought of seeing Jonah again, of stirring up the old hurt and shame, was intolerable. No, even though the contract had seemed a godsend, she couldn't possibly endure being near Jonah for even a few minutes, much less three months.

She would turn elsewhere for a solution to her financial problems—find a job as a bookstore clerk or maybe play at a supper club or in a ballet school. In fact, she would do anything, she thought, rather than work for a man who had won her heart, then broken it so badly that for the past three years she hadn't been able to look at another man.

MARTIN'S THREE-ROOM APARTMENT was located on the top floor of an old building at the edge of the Mission district. After Gloria had let her in, Raine looked around, her eyes taking in the small touches that showed her sister-in-law's efforts to turn the crowded apartment into a home. Although it was cluttered with the paraphernalia of three people living in a space that was only adequate for one, it was tidy and very clean.

Raine had suspected that Martin and Gloria were having a hard time financially as soon as she'd returned to San Francisco for the funeral, but it was only now, with the insulation of her own grief wearing thin, that she took a really close look at her sister-in-law and realized how much Gloria had changed in her three years of marriage. Although still pretty, with her heart-shaped face and her dark hair, she had lost weight, and the jeans she wore had a baggy look. Her eyes, too, were different. What had happened to the stars that had shone there on her wedding day?

"Is Martin home yet?" Raine said, realizing her sister-in-law was waiting for her to speak.

"He's due any minute now." Although Gloria's voice was calm, her eyes gave away her anxiety. "For his sake I hope it isn't bad news. It's been one thing after another ever since we found out about—about the baby."

Raine's heart twisted. There was so much pain behind those understated words. How could she possibly equate her own problems with something as important as the health of a child?

"No problems," she said, making up her mind. "In fact, it's very good news. There's going to be enough money to let Martin finish his internship."

For a moment Gloria's face sagged, as if she had been braced for a blow that hadn't come. Her eyes closed—in thankfulness, Raine knew. There was a sound behind her, and then Martin, his face drawn and apprehensive, was coming through the door. He stared at his wife, then at Raine.

"Is—how did it go?" he asked huskily.

Martin was a tall rangy man four years Raine's senior. Like her, he had inherited his mother's dark eyes and his father's fair hair. Although his

personality was more outgoing than their father's
had been, the two men were much alike in their
total dedication to their wives and children.

"It went fine," she told him. "The bills are all
paid and there's enough left over to turn you into a
full-fledged M.D., big brother."

Martin gave a whoop. He snatched his wife up
and twirled her around. When he set her down, he
gave Raine a shamefaced smile. "Hey, that out-
burst seems pretty insensitive so soon after—it's
just that we've really been sweating it out. And
dad would understand...."

"He would, indeed. He wanted the best of
everything for both of us," Raine said.

"When you win that Tchaikovsky competition,
you can dedicate it to dad," he said. "Where will
you be training, anyway? Your old piano's still in
storage, so there's no reason why you can't rent a
place here in San Francisco. There are some fine
teachers in this area—"

"No hurry about that," she said quickly. "The
next competition isn't until next year. In fact, I've
been playing with the idea of getting myself a job
for a while."

"Wait a minute. Why would you do that? Dad's
insurance should be enough to support you while
you train."

"His insurance? You know about—" She broke
off.

"Sure I know about it. Dad talked it over with
me when he made his will. Since my tuition and expenses have always been so much higher than

yours, he thought it only fair that he sign that policy over to you. He couldn't increase its amount because of his age, so he—hey, wait a minute! What are you trying to pull? Is it dad's *insurance* that you've been talking about? If so, you can just forget it. That money was intended for you. I know what the Tchaikovsky competition means to you—"

"Believe me, there's no hurry. I'm young and—"

"How many times have I heard you and dad talking about the importance of getting an early start in the concert business? By the time the next competition comes around, a hundred younger competitors will be waiting in line—and they have the advantage. So just forget it. Even though you're willing to make the grand sacrifice, I'm not about to let you."

Raine stared at him, speechless for the moment. From the corner of her eye she caught the disappointment that flooded her sister-in-law's face. Although Gloria covered it up quickly with a stiff smile, Raine knew the depth of her despair. After all, hadn't she herself just gone through the same thing when she'd realized she couldn't possibly take the book cataloging job? But the difference was that for her it had been a very personal and selfish disappointment. . . .

She forced her lips to curve into a smile. "Well, as usual, you're suffering from foot-in-mouth disease, big brother. The fact is that I am quite well taken care of without that insurance money.

Mr. Partridge has arranged for me to do the cataloging of a book collection for Jonah Duncan.''

"The concert pianist?'' Martin said.

"The very one. It pays a very nice fee, enough for my needs for a long time. And even if it didn't I'd jump at the chance to be in the same house with a man of Jonah Duncan's stature. Who knows? If I play my cards right I just might coax him into being my mentor—and for a fledgling concert pianist that would be worth as much as winning a dozen competitions.''

CHAPTER FIVE

THAT EVENING AFTER MARTIN, who was on double-shift status, had returned to the hospital, Raine volunteered to put Debra to bed. After she'd tucked the sleepy two-year-old into her crib, she looked around the tiny room, a converted walk-in closet, noting the attempts Gloria had made with wallpaper and paint to turn it into a proper nursery. How small and unimportant her own problems seemed next to the life and death struggles that sometimes went on in this room when Debra had one of her asthmatic attacks. And how weak of her to even consider rejecting the solution to all their financial problems simply because she knew how painful seeing Jonah again would be.

After Gloria went to bed, Raine called Mr. Partridge, knowing it was his habit to stay up late, to tell him she'd changed her mind about the cataloging job. Always tactful, he didn't ask her any questions and she didn't volunteer the reasons for her original refusal or her about-face. Nor did she share her apprehensions about her decision. After all, what could she say? That the thought of the next few months filled her with dread? That she knew how painful it would be pretending to be a stranger when she was forced to talk to Jonah again? Since she couldn't be honest, she simply said that she'd thought it over and now she believed she could do the job.

The next morning she went into Mr. Partridge's office to sign the contract. After she'd affixed her signature to the bottom of the brief document, the lawyer told Raine that Jonah Duncan's sister-in-law, who also lived at Arlington House, would be expecting her sometime during the next couple of days.

"Her name is Crystal Arlington. She oversees the domestic help at Arlington House, supervises the care of Jonah's boy, and also acts as Jonah's secretary. After Jonah retired from the concert stage he purchased a promising local winery. In the past two years it's already received several prestigious awards, and I understand it will soon be distributing nationally."

Raine waited, hiding her impatience, as he went on to tell her that the winery's zinfandel was particularly outstanding.

"How old is Mr. Duncan's sister-in-law?" Raine asked when he stopped for breath.

"In her mid-twenties, I believe. She was several years younger than her sister. Always rather dominated by her, to tell the truth. Elaine was—well, for one thing, she was a strikingly beautiful woman and quite aware of it. Very strong willed. Crystal was completely loyal to her and content to live in her shadow. She has the same kind of devotion to Jonah and the boy. A rather nice little thing. I'm sure you two will get along.''

Raine listened silently as he went on to explain that, for convenience, she would be staying at Arlington House, which Mr. Partridge described as an interesting old place a few miles north of Mendocino town. Later, as she packed, Raine reflected that she was going into the whole situation blind, that it might have been better if she could have talked to Jonah's sister-in-law directly to find out what would be required in the way of clothing.

For one thing, would she be expected to appear at any kind of social function? Surely not. After all, she would be there strictly as an employee—and the harder she worked, the sooner she would be finished and could be gone. She wasn't really worried that Jonah would recognize her. He had looked directly at her in Mr. Partridge's office without one flicker of recognition. If he remembered her at all, it was as a brunette, a Juilliard student. Why would he connect the naive girl he'd seduced, a dark-haired girl he'd called Carmen, with a blond book cataloger? No, he wouldn't recognize her. But just to make sure, she would take pains to stay out of his way, and when the job was finished she would turn her back on Mendocino and never look back, never think of Jonah Duncan again.

That night she had the old dream, the one that had come with such regularity during the months after Jonah had betrayed her trust. She dreamed he was making love to her, that she was returning his kisses, his caresses, her body burning with a fire that only his touch could quench. And then suddenly he was pulling away, his mocking laughter ringing in her ears. As she held out her arms to him he began to retreat, to grow smaller and smaller until he finally faded away, and when she awoke she found that her pillow was wet with tears that she'd shed in her sleep.

Later, as she loaded her suitcases and makeup case into her father's car, she resolved to put the dream out of her mind, to enjoy the ride ahead. She had always loved driving along the coast. Why not consider this a holiday and try to forget for a while the problems that undoubtedly lay ahead?

At first it seemed she would succeed in putting worrisome thoughts out of her mind. The car, a vintage Mustang her father had kept in pristine condition, purred contentedly as if it too were glad to be out of the city on a sparkling clear morning, crossing the lovely span of the Golden Gate Bridge, passing through the wooded hills of Marin County.

At Petaluma, a small town whose business district still retained an aura of the thirties, she turned off Highway 101, drove along a street lined with old Victorians, and was soon passing through rolling hills of ranchland and dairy farms. The road was crooked and narrow and there was little traffic. Several times she slowed the car to stare at a particularly lovely view, reflecting that it was hard to believe she was in California. In fact, it could have been any of a dozen hill countries of the

Midwest or East—until she came to a farmhouse bordered with tall palms and orange trees in one of the valleys, minute pockets of semitropical climate that permitted the growing of citrus this far north in California.

It occurred to her now how little she knew of Sonoma and Mendocino counties, even though she'd spent her childhood in San Francisco. Her father had been so occupied with his business and she with her music that there had been few excursions away from the city. As she passed a small crossroads general store she made herself a promise. Since she couldn't possibly work every minute of the day, she would do a little sight-seeing while she was in Mendocino County, and she would take advantage of being so close to the beach, too, and get in some swimming.

She reached the coast a few minutes later, and for the next two hours the coastal highway opened up one seascape vista after another, each more wildly beautiful than the last. There was little traffic, and she couldn't help thinking that the same magnificent views in the East—or even in southern California—would be packed with tourists and sightseers even this early on a weekday morning.

At Jenner, a small port town at the mouth of the Russian River, Raine stopped for a lunch of abalone. It was expensive but so delicious that she couldn't begrudge the price. Because she felt in a festive mood she asked for a glass of white wine. She was told that their house wine, a French colombard, came from a local winery. As she sipped the wine with its delicate hint of apples, she wondered if it possibly could have come from Jonah's winery.

But the thought, conjuring up images of Jonah, was a mistake. As she finished her lunch and paid her bill, she discovered her mood had changed, and although the views grew even more spectacular once she'd passed the fashionable Sea Ranch area and was approaching Point Arena, the trip had become more of a chore than an outing, and she was sorry that she had chosen the coastal highway with its endless twists and turns rather than the less scenic but much quicker Route 101.

By late afternoon she was too tired to go on. She stopped in the small town of Little River and rented a room in an old inn that featured Victorian furniture and superb food. She slept late, then had a leisurely breakfast at the inn before she drove on toward the town of Mendocino. Since the map Mr. Partridge had drawn for her was so clear, she didn't bother to stop for directions, a decision she regretted half an hour later when she was creeping along the highway north of Mendocino trying to find the sign he'd told her to watch for.

On both sides of the highway were rolling hills, still green from the late May rains. She had seen flocks of sheep dotting the sometimes very steep slopes and had passed an occasional car or truck, but there were very few houses. Just as she stopped on the shoulder of the road to examine the map Mr. Partridge had given her, she spotted a small sign a few feet ahead, half-hidden in a cluster of tall dill plants. Her skin prickled as she read the words neatly painted on the sign—Private Road. Keep Out.

A few minutes later she passed between two rows of tall gaunt eucalyptus trees. As she reached the last of the trees, the house ahead burst upon her sight so suddenly that instinctively she put on the brakes, stopping dead in the middle of the road. Mr. Partridge had said it was an interesting old house, but his words hadn't prepared her for the sprawling Victorian before her—a riot of cupolas, porches, balconies, fish-scale shingles, recessed bays and clapboard sidings, topped by a rounded corner turret with a witches'-hat tower. Although predominantly in the Queen Anne style, it was a Victorian brew of periods—medieval, baroque and colonial revival. It also tugged at her memory. Surely, she had seen pictures of this house somewhere. In a newspaper article? A book of Victorian houses?

A bubble of laughter rose in her throat and escaped. The thought of Jonah, with his New York street toughness, choosing this particular house to live in was unbelievable. Had she taken the wrong road after all? Before she could decide whether to go on, the front door opened and a small slender woman came out. Although it was impossible to make out her features because of the distance that separated them, Raine was sure from the confident way the woman moved that she wasn't a servant or someone in a subordinate position at Arlington House.

The woman shaded her eyes with her hand and stared at the car. Raine started up the motor and drove slowly along a curved driveway to pull up in front of the portico. Even after she got out of the car, the other woman didn't move. Her eyes appraising, she waited motionlessly until Raine had almost reached her before she spoke.

"Are you Miss Hunicutt?" Her voice was cool and light with a slight flatness that seemed more eastern than Californian. It also held a tinge of disapproval, making Raine suddenly conscious that the suit she was wearing was inappropriate for the country. Reasoning that since Jonah had only seen her in jeans it might be wise to wear something else, she had chosen the suit. She had also spent a long time on her hair, arranging it in an intricate French knot that made her look older and more mature than her true age. Now this woman's stare made her wish that she'd followed her first instinct, which was to wear something casual.

Realizing she still hadn't answered the woman's question, Raine forced a smile. "Yes, I'm Raine Hunicutt. You must be Miss Arlington. Mr. Partridge told me you would be expecting me."

"Well, as a matter of fact, we were expecting you yesterday. Did you have an accident?"

"No, I was so tired I stopped overnight at the Little River Inn. I didn't realize there was a set time for my arrival or I would have called—"

"It seems we got our signals crossed—and why don't you call me Crystal."

Although the woman's lips curved into a smile,

there was a sting in her words. Raine was glad when she turned and led the way into a large oak-paneled entrance hall. "Luke will put your car away and bring up your luggage. Tilda will show you to your room," she said over her shoulder as she crossed the hall to open wide double doors.

She didn't bother to explain who Luke and Tilda were, and as Raine followed her, she was determined not to ask. She had worked briefly as a tutor for the daughter of a wealthy New York family and had noted that one of the girl's characteristics had been the assumption that since everything and everyone revolved around her own privileged self, explanations simply weren't necessary. Her conversations had dripped with references to places and people and events that had meant nothing to Raine. She wondered if the same thing was true here? Was this woman the product of a privileged upbringing, of exclusive eastern boarding schools? Or was her attitude a subtle way of putting a new employee in her place?

The room Raine found herself standing in was spacious to the point of being barny. She had a brief thought about heating bills as she stared up at the high festooned ceiling, painted in the Victorian manner, a few shades lighter than the walls. Someone with a taste for the authentic had chosen the antique furnishings, the rosewood cabinets, the alabaster lamps and the richly upholstered sofas. Had it been the late Elaine Duncan, or were these the original furnishings of Arlington House, lovingly preserved?

"Maybe I should warn you that we lead a very quiet life here," Crystal said, interrupting Raine's musings. "Also, I've given orders for you to be served your meals in your room since I'm sure your hours will be erratic. Mr. Duncan is a very private person. He seldom welcomes company for dinner. And of course it will save you the bother of stopping your work in order to dress every evening."

Although she nodded, Raine felt a stab of resentment. It suited her that she wouldn't have to face Jonah over a dinner table every evening, but there was a subtle insult in the woman's manner that pricked her pride. What exactly was the relationship between Jonah and Crystal? Was it possible they were lovers? She herself had found out the hard way that Jonah was not a man to let an opportunity pass, and Crystal, for all her cool manner, was a very attractive woman.

She studied Crystal, trying to see her through a man's eyes. She was small, a couple of inches shorter than Raine, and her figure was petite. She wore her brown hair parted in the middle. With her oval-shaped face, her wide-set eyes, she had a demure look, which didn't match the wariness in her glance. Although her clothes were casual, Raine was sure there were designer's labels inside the white silk shirt and impeccably tailored gray-flannel slacks.

As though she knew she was being evaluated, Crystal smiled—a curling of her lips that gave her a catlike look. She went to pull a strip of woven tapestry hanging beside a white marble fireplace, and a few minutes later a woman appeared in the doorway.

The newcomer was large, rawboned rather than fat. Her nod held no hint of servitude as she looked Raine over more thoroughly than was polite, then turned the same unyielding stare upon Crystal, silently waiting for instructions.

"Will you show Miss Hunicutt to her room. You did prepare one of the third-floor guest rooms for her, didn't you, Tilda?"

"I turned it out from top to bottom yesterday morning, just like you told me to do." Raine caught a decided drawl in Tilda's voice as she added, "She'll be comfortable enough there, but one of the second-floor bedrooms would be more convenient, especially since she's having her meals sent up to her room. Luke and me's got more'n enough to keep us busy since you let Marion go."

"I'm sure you can manage until I find a replacement for Marion. And this time I'll make sure it's someone a little more mature who isn't always running off to town evenings to—" Crystal broke off, as if suddenly conscious of the irritation in her voice. When she went on, her voice had resumed its former coolness. "I'm sure you can manage until I get someone suitable."

Tilda muttered something inaudible under her breath. Although Crystal gave her a sharp look, she didn't ask her to repeat it. She turned back to Raine. "When you're ready to start work, Tilda will show you where the book collection is stored.

Mr. Duncan isn't back from New York yet, but I'm sure you know what's to be done.''

"Mr. Partridge gave me instructions.''

"Oh, yes—Mr. Partridge. It's strange he didn't mention that you were so—'' Again she broke off, leaving the sentence dangling, a habit that could get to be irritating, Raine decided.

A few minutes later as Raine followed Tilda's sturdy back up the wide staircase that rose bracket shaped and thickly carpeted from the central hall, she wondered at Crystal's not-so-covert hostility. Mr. Partridge had described her as "a nice little thing,'' and since he was shrewd about people that probably meant the woman could be friendly when it suited her. Well, for some reason Crystal had taken an instant dislike to her.

"Crystal don't cotton to having someone as pretty as you underfoot,'' Tilda said. Since she kept on walking, not looking around, it was a moment before Raine realized the housekeeper had been talking to her.

"I beg your pardon?''

"That's why she fired Marion. She don't like nobody young around here 'cepting herself.''

"I don't understand.''

"She's scared someone'll come along and take Jonah's fancy, make him forget Elaine.'' Tilda gave a contemptuous snort. "As if that could happen. But then Crystal's always been like that, wanting things to stay the same. She's got what you call a jealous nature. What's hers is hers and she don't like changes.''

"She has nothing to fear from me," Raine said. "I'm here to do a job. I'll be working most of the time. I doubt if I'll see much of the family."

"Well, you can be sure of that. Jonah, he keeps to hisself these days. Used to be there was lots of visitors and guests here at Arlington House, but since Elaine was killed and the boy hurt in that car accident—"

"His son was hurt, too? Was it serious?"

"Real bad. Poor little tyke—he's been through a lot. And more misery ahead for him, too."

Before Raine could ask what she meant they had reached the end of a long hall and Tilda was flinging open a paneled door, motioning her inside.

The room, spacious and high-ceilinged, featured a tester bed covered with an ivory comforter, several pieces of mellow cherry-wood furniture and a handmade rug, which covered most of the random-plank floor. Raine smiled, intrigued by the alcove that held the bed. Shaped like a half circle, it was lined with long narrow windows, forming one wall of the room. Tilda caught her smile and returned it, although hers was a little wintry.

"Crystal said to put you in the bedroom at the top of the stairs, but this room is much nicer. If you were a mite higher you could see the ocean from this side of the house."

"I didn't realize we were that close to the beach."

"That's 'cause you came in from the road. There's a path that goes to the top of the cliffs, then a set of wooden stairs that'll take you to the beach. But be careful going down them steps. Sometimes the spray gets them so wet they're right slippery."

"What about swimming? I brought a suit—"

"The cove's too dangerous for swimming. 'Course, Jonah goes out all the time. I keep telling him the current's too strong out there, but he just laughs at me. Says he learned to swim where there's things in the water that's a lot worse than a little undertow. I 'spect he's safe enough 'cause I've seen him out there, fighting the waves, looking like he was born to the water."

Raine had a mental image of Jonah, his brown skin and mahogany hair wet and glistening, his powerful arms rising and falling, and unexpectedly a feeling of loss swept over her, so strong that she closed her eyes, fighting it.

"You okay, Miss Hunicutt?"

Raine made herself smile. "Just a little tired. And please—will you call me Raine?"

Tilda nodded. "That's a right pretty name. How do you spell it?"

"With an *e*," Raine said. "It was a family name—a great-grandmother on my father's side."

"Folks do that a lot where I come from, too. Use family names for first names, I mean."

"Where are you from?"

"Oklahoma. Came here to California with my folks during the depression. My pa got a job working for the Arlingtons as gardener, taking care of the grounds and the greenhouse. When I was old enough I went to work in the kitchen. Never held down another job. After I married Luke, he got on here as the gardener. Mr. Granton—that's Crystal's daddy—was a hard man to work for, particular and all, but the work was steady and paid well, too. When Jonah and Elaine moved back here, right after the old man died, I thought he'd want someone younger, but no, he asked me to stay on so I did. Never regretted it, either.''

"Is he—easy to work for?"

"Well, he don't stand for no foolishness, but if you do your job right you'll get along with him." She went to turn back the comforter on the bed. "Why don't you get comfortable while I have Luke bring up your luggage? It'd be a lot easier if you were on the second floor, but then that's none of your doings, is it? Crystal has her ways. No use trying to figure out what she's up to. If you want anything, I'll be in the kitchen. You can press the button on that contraption at the top of the stairs. It's connected to one of them voice boxes in the kitchen."

She bustled off after pointing out the door to the bathroom. When she was gone, Raine went in and examined the ivory-colored tiles and brass fixtures. She reflected that this was one of the few times in her life that she wouldn't have to share a bathroom with at least two other people. The sparkling tile of the shower tempted her and she stripped off her clothes and took a shower, drying herself on a towel that was downy soft and big enough to wrap around her slender figure at least twice. When she was dressed again she went back into the bedroom to find her suitcase waiting for her on a brass luggage stand.

She felt a moment's regret that she'd missed meeting Tilda's husband. As she crossed the room to start unpacking she caught a flicker of movement out of the corner of her eye and realized the door was slightly ajar. She swung around and for a brief moment was eye to eye with a small dark-haired boy.

From his size she guessed he was probably no older than eight or possibly nine; his face was thin, his eyes dark gray, and his mouth had a vulnerable look that struck some chord deep within Raine's own so recently bereaved heart.

"Hello there," she said pleasantly. "I'm Raine Hunicutt—and you must be Mr. Duncan's son. What's your name?"

The boy stared at her a moment longer, and then he was gone as quickly as he'd appeared, leaving her staring after him, wondering what there was about her that had frightened him so.

CHAPTER SIX

ALTHOUGH SHE SLEPT through the night without awakening, Raine opened her eyes the next morning with the confused memory of a dream in which she had been searching for something she desperately wanted, only to have it snatched away from her time after time just when she was close to grasping it.

Feeling depressed and a little headachy, she lay there for a while wondering if it was still too early to get up. The night before, after she'd gone to bed, she'd given herself a good talking to and had fallen asleep convinced that she wouldn't let personal feelings interfere with her job.

In the clear light of morning that rationalization didn't seem to work. She was too aware of the dangers that lay ahead when she finally met Jonah face to face. Until she'd seen Jonah again in Mr. Partridge's office, she'd been so sure that she'd finally worked her way through the storm of disillusionment that had followed his betrayal. She had even convinced herself that she was a stronger person for it.

Now she wasn't so sure. That one glimpse of him had brought back too many memories of the night of passion she'd spent in his arms, and it shamed her to have to admit that some part of her was still vulnerable to Jonah.

A deep-seated anger stirred within her, an anger she welcomed because at least it was a good clean emotion, one she understood and wasn't ashamed of. What she couldn't tolerate was the part of herself that still dreamed about Jonah and the passion his touch had unleashed. She knew now that everything he'd done that night, his every word, had been calculated to seduce a naive inexperienced girl. He was a despicable womanizer who preyed on the gullible girls who'd flocked around him. So why, *why* this sinking feeling in the pit of her stomach whenever she thought about seeing him again, this tingling along her skin, this dryness in her throat?

Well, there was little she could do about that. At least she wouldn't have to go through the humiliation of having Jonah recognize her as one of his easy conquests. With her hair back to its natural color, she bore little resemblance to the girl he'd known for such a brief time, especially since she must have been one of a long line of adoring fans he'd slept with during his career. So there was little or no likelihood that he would recognize her. After all, he'd stared right at her in Mr. Partridge's office without a flicker of interest in his eyes—

Raine's breath caught sharply as a new idea occurred to her.

Mr. Partridge's office, with its dark paneled walls and its soft lights, had been dimly lit. And

Jonah had just stepped out of a much brighter office. Was it possible that he simply hadn't seen her clearly?

The thought chilled her, but she shook it off and resolutely flung back her bed covers. First things first, like getting dressed and then having breakfast. The evening before when Tilda, looking tired and harried, had brought a superbly cooked roast-beef dinner on a tray to her room, she had made the decision that in the future she would take her meals in the kitchen—at least until Crystal hired some additional household help.

Sliding her feet into her slippers, she went into the bathroom for a quick shower, then made up her face lightly, brushed her hair and coiled it into a knot at the nape of her neck. She hesitated over clothes, finally choosing jeans and a plaid cotton shirt. Sooner or later Jonah would have to see her dressed in the same kind of clothing she'd worn the night of the concert three years ago, but at least she could relax for a couple of days. The evening before, Tilda had told her that Jonah wasn't expected home from his business trip until the end of the week.

After she'd made her bed and tidied up her room, she went downstairs to find Tilda working busily in the kitchen. She looked surprised—and not too pleased—to see Raine.

"So you're an early riser," she observed. "Well, you'll have to wait a bit for your breakfast. I'm in the middle of making cinnamon rolls. Crystal never eats nothing but pastries for breakfast. With that sweet tooth of hers, I don't know how on earth she keeps her figure. You didn't have to come down to let me know you was ready for your breakfast, you know. Just use that intercom contraption Elaine installed. If you go on upstairs again, I'll bring up your breakfast in about half an hour."

"There's no reason why you should," Raine said firmly. "It's ridiculous for you to climb those stairs three times a day when I can eat right here in the kitchen."

Tilda considered her doubtfully, but she finally shrugged. "It's up to you, though I don't know what Crystal is going to say. I have to admit them stairs seem to get steeper every day. Now you sit down over there and I'll fetch you some coffee."

"No problem. I'll get it myself. And toast is all I ever eat in the mornings. Most of the time I'm in such a rush that I skip breakfast altogether."

"Not if I have anything to say about it, you won't," Tilda said tartly. "You'll need a good breakfast before you tackle all them books. After they was delivered from that storage place, I told Jonah he should get Luke to unpack them, but he said the cataloger would probably prefer to do it hisself." She paused to frown at Raine. "Don't know why he said that, seeing as you're a female."

"I was hired by Mr. Duncan's lawyer," Raine said. She poured herself a cup of coffee and then perched on a kitchen stool, sipping it. "I doubt if he knows I'm a—a female."

Tilda grunted, whether from disapproval or not,

Raine couldn't begin to guess. The woman's broad hands slapped the dough expertly before she began pinching off bits of it, putting them in a muffin tin that already held a mixture of brown sugar and butter. Raine sniffed hungrily, recognizing the odor of cinnamon.

Tilda noticed her interest. "You like to cook, Miss Hunicutt?"

"Raine—please call me Raine. And I don't know much about it," Raine confessed. "I did some plain cooking for my father and brother after my mother died, but while I was away at school I mostly lived on junk food. I've always wanted to learn to cook the right way. Maybe I'll get a chance to do it now that I'm out of school and have more time."

"Well, there's no big secret about cooking, although I guess some folks like to think there is. It's mostly plain sense—and of course a good recipe helps." Tilda slid the muffin tins into the oven and set the timer before she added, "Where'd you go to school? At Sonoma State?"

"No, at Juilliard in New York," Raine said without thinking.

"Juilliard? That's where Jonah went—ain't that some kind of music school?"

Raine bit her lip. She had been careless. Would Tilda mention her slip to Crystal or to Jonah? "Yes," she said briefly. "But it's also a regular school."

"Well, if you're interested in music, you'll have to forget it while you're here. When Jonah's home, he don't even allow us to play music on the radio. Been like that ever since Elaine was killed. Just turned his back on music and can't stand to have no reminders of it around him.''

"I understand—and of course I'll honor his wishes,'' Raine said quickly. She hesitated then added, "Maybe it would be best if you didn't mention that Juilliard was my school. It might upset Mr. Duncan. I don't know what his problem is, but—''

"Foolishness, that's what it is,'' Tilda interrupted. "He blames hisself for Elaine's death. He figures if he hadn't been off on one of them concert tours she would still be alive—and the boy wouldn't have gone through so much misery, either. Which is just plain foolish. Elaine always drove too fast. It wouldn't have mattered whether he was here or not. She was always going off in that fancy sports car of hers, speeding along the old coast highway, getting tickets and scaring people to death.''

Raine digested this in silence. "He must have loved her very much,'' she said finally.

Tilda gave her a dark look. "You can call it what you want. I call it sickness, the way he took on after she was killed. Wouldn't talk to nobody, wouldn't see nobody—always brooding and walking the beach. I don't know what would have happened to him if he'd gone on much longer like that. But then there was Michael to worry about and that brought him out of it. Never could understand what went on between Jonah and Elaine.

She was always throwing them tantrums of hers, trying to get him to give up his concerts and stay home with her. Well, they had their troubles, even separated a couple of times, but there's no denying he took her death hard. Far as I know, he ain't looked at another woman since nor touched his piano, either.''

"And now he's a successful vintner, isn't he?" Raine said absently. When Jonah had made love to her, had it been during one of the times when he and his wife were estranged? According to the newspaper article she'd read, Elaine Duncan had been in Mexico on a long holiday. Had she gone away after a quarrel? Was it possible that her own heartache had stemmed from the simple fact that Jonah had been separated from his wife for a while and had needed a woman?

"Oh, the winery's real successful all right," Tilda said, answering her question. "I reckon anything Mr. Jonah does, he does right well. But he can't fool me. His heart ain't really in it. What he *should* be doing is playing his piano and writing them sonatas and things. When the good Lord gives us a talent, he means for it to be used. Maybe it's for growing things, like my Luke, or for making bread, like me, but whatever it is, it's a sin to let it go to waste.''

As if to emphasize where her own talents lay, she began bustling around, putting strips of bacon in a cold skillet, mixing pancake batter, whipping eggs. To Raine, watching her, she seemed to be preparing enough food for a dozen people, and she wondered if Tilda expected the two of them to put it all away. To her relief a middle-aged man, stocky and gray haired, appeared, looking a little sheepish, and she knew she was about to meet the elusive Luke.

"Sit down over there with Miss—with Raine," Tilda said. "Breakfast's about ready. Soon as I take them rolls out of the oven we can eat. From now on Raine's going to take her meals with us. Don't know how Crystal'll like it, but it'll be easier on me, that's for sure."

Raine soon found herself packing away enough food for three people. Although Tilda had shrugged off good cooking as plain common sense, she knew she was in the presence of a culinary genius by the time she finally pushed her plate away with a sigh of pure contentment. "That was absolutely the best breakfast I've ever eaten," she said. "I don't know what you put in those scrambled eggs, but they tasted wonderful."

Tilda looked gratified. "Just a bit of lemon thyme, fresh from Luke's herb garden, and a few grains of curry," she said modestly. "After a bit you get a knack for seasoning things right—but you can ruin a lot of things first, too."

"Tilda was born knowing how to cook," Luke said, grinning. "Reckon the Duncan family's lucky to have her. Not that Crystal is about to admit it. Jonah, he's different. Don't hesitate to say when he likes something for fear you'll ask for a raise or something. And he don't put on no airs, either, or pretend he didn't come up the hard way.

You won't have no trouble working for him, miss, as long as you keep in mind what you're here for. Can't promise the same about Crystal, though. She can be mighty temperamental sometimes.''

As if his burst of garrulousness had exhausted him, he returned to his pancakes. Raine sipped her coffee, feeling relaxed for the first time since she'd come to Arlington House. "What's Mr. Duncan's son like?'' she asked, remembering her brief glimpse of the boy. "I haven't met him yet.''

"Michael? Why, I doubt you'll see much of him,'' Tilda said. "Keeps to himself and don't take to outsiders. But he won't get in your way, either, and make a pest out of hisself like some kids might.''

Luke pushed away his plate and stood up, but he didn't leave immediately. A little diffidently he asked Raine, "If you've got a few minutes before you start work I'd like to show you around the grounds. I'm mighty proud of my roses—don't know when I've had such big ones. This has been a real good year for them.''

Tilda began gathering up the dishes, refusing Raine's offer to help with a shake of her head. "Show her your herb garden, too, Luke. Ain't nothing like the way it smells this time of day when the sun's just come up and the dew's still on the leaves.''

A few minutes later Raine was standing in the middle of what seemed to her dazzled eyes to be a hundred rose bushes, each more lush and beautiful than the next. As far as she could see there wasn't

a dead leaf or a faded rose or a weed in sight, attesting to Luke's industry. As he pointed out the
various varieties, using such names as Charlotte
Armstrong and Peace and Seven Sisters, she knew
that Tilda had been right when she'd said that
Luke had a God-given gift for growing things.
From the proprietary way he talked about the
roses, naming each variety and describing their
faults and virtues as if they were human, she was
sure Luke regarded this garden as his own.

But it isn't, she thought suddenly, *and it's
dangerous assuming that you have a right to a
place—or a person—that belongs to someone else.*
She shivered, feeling chilled suddenly, and was
glad when Luke suggested they take a look at the
vegetables next.

The vegetable garden was at the back of the
house, near the kitchen door. Everything was in
perfect order, laid out as if it were the formal
Italian-style garden they'd skirted as they'd circled
the house. As they walked between rows of lettuce,
green onions, Swiss chard and patches of vari-
colored herbs, she sniffed appreciatively, wondering if the heady odor was rosemary or thyme or
something else equally exotic to her.

Luke bent and pulled up a tiny carrot, wiped it
off carefully with a clean red-print handkerchief
and handed it to Raine. She bit into it, enjoying
the sweetness and the crunch of the crisp vegetable
between her teeth. As a born-and-bred city girl this
was all new to her, and while Luke described the
complications of raising artichokes, she studied
her surroundings with interest.

Beyond the low fence that surrounded the vegetable garden vineyards stretched out of sight, following the rolling contours of the coastal hills. Although the morning fog had already burned off and there was only a slight breeze, Raine caught a whiff of saline-laden air and was reminded that they were very near the ocean.

"Isn't this climate pretty damp for grapes?" she said when Luke had finished his dissertation on artichokes.

"Not in this valley. It gets the sun most of the day—it's in one of the sunbelt pockets. The coastal hills protect it from the worst of the wind and some of the fog." He pointed to the rows of staked vines beyond the garden wall. "Even so, only certain grapes do well here. Most of them out there are Riesling and that German one, what they call Gewürztraminer. They both make mighty fine white wines. Jonah's winery keeps them for his estate wines and won't sell them 'cepting to special customers. They have to put in their orders a year or more in advance, I hear tell."

He jerked his head toward a dark-skinned man who was bending over a vine a few yards away. "That there's José Ortega. He tends this patch for Jonah and lives in a cottage down the road with his wife and kids. Speaks right good English, even if'n he is from Mexico."

Raine hid her amusement, wondering what José Ortega thought of Luke's thick Oklahoma accent. She realized the man had straightened and was staring in their direction. She waved and smiled, and after a moment's hesitation the man waved back before he returned to his work. A small boy trotted between a row of vines, heading toward the man, and for a moment Raine thought it was the boy she'd seen in the hall outside her room. Then, when he was closer, she saw his olive skin and dark eyes and knew he must be one of the Ortega children.

"I see the Duncan boy has someone near his own age to play with," she commented.

Luke shook his head. "Michael don't have much to do with them Ortega kids. Crystal says they're too rough for him."

Before she could question him further, she heard the sound of heels tapping on the stone path behind them. When she turned she saw that Crystal was hurrying toward them. As the dark-haired girl came up, her eyes appraised Raine's jeans and shirt. Although she smiled briefly in acknowledgment of Raine's greeting, her voice held a chill as she told Luke, "I'm sure you have things to do, Luke. I'll show Miss Hunicutt around."

Luke nodded to Raine, then went ambling off toward the house. A little to Raine's surprise, Crystal's voice was cordial as she said, "I see Luke's been showing off his garden. I suppose he told you how many prizes he's won with his roses?"

"No, but I can see why he has," Raine said, equally pleasant. "And the vegetable garden is wonderful, too."

"Yes—well, it's handy, I suppose, although I

sometimes think it would be much more practical to buy what we need at the market. However, Luke is something of a fixture here at Arlington House. I suppose that gives him certain privileges.'' She gave Raine one of her catlike smiles. ''I'll take you to the basement where the crates are stored. I know you must be eager to get started.''

They walked back to the house in silence, but just before they reached the flagstone terrace at the rear of the house Crystal stopped to look at Raine. ''I hope you don't feel that you're in the same— uh, category as the domestic help, Raine. Tilda tells me you insist on eating in the kitchen. With all Tilda's grumbling about how hard she works, I can understand why you don't want to be any trouble, but the Cummingses are here to serve us, you know.''

Raine bit back a retort, knowing it would be unwise. ''I'm not used to eating alone.'' She was careful to keep her tone unargumentative. ''Unless there's some good reason against it, I'd prefer to eat with Tilda and Luke—or maybe I should talk it over with Mr. Duncan when he returns?''

Crystal's eyelids flickered. ''It's up to you, of course, and really of no consequence to me.''

She continued on, and a short time later they were standing in a large low-ceilinged basement room staring at stacks of wooden crates. Raine had expected a large collection of books, but the sheer number of the crates astonished her. She glanced at Crystal and was surprised to find that she was smiling—a genuine smile this time.

"It's horrendous, isn't it? My father was a packrat. He couldn't resist buying books. Whenever they threatened to overflow the house he'd have them crated and hauled off to a warehouse in the city. I'm sure there must be some valuable books in there, but I suspect most of them are junk.''

"Well, we'll soon know," Raine said. "Do you share his interest in collecting books?"

"Heavens, no! I like to read, but when I'm finished with a book, that's it. I'd just as soon toss it out."

Having been raised in a family of bookaholics, the thought of throwing away a book simply because it had been read once was abhorrent to Raine, an opinion she wisely kept to herself.

"Well, I guess the only way to begin is by beginning. Do you know where I could find the tools I'll need to open the crates? And I'll need a ledger, and pens, tags, that sort of thing." She looked down at her hands. "And a pair of work gloves to protect my hands from splinters."

"There are plenty of tools in the potting shed near the greenhouse. And I believe you'll find some stationery supplies in that cabinet over there." Crystal pointed to a steel cabinet near the door. "If you need anything that isn't here, Luke can get it for you."

She hesitated, as if wanting to say something more. If so, she changed her mind, because she gave an abrupt nod and started for the door. A little belatedly Raine called, "Thank you for your help," but Crystal didn't turn around.

Raine stared after her, trying to sort out her impressions of the past few minutes. Jonah's sister-in-law was a strange mixture. Why did she blow so hot and cold? Was it her imagination or was Crystal reluctant to have her associate with the Cummingses? Realizing that she'd get no answers to her questions, she went to get the tools she'd need from the potting shed.

Later, as she was prying the lid off the first crate, she wondered what she would find inside these boxes during the next few weeks. Junk—or something unique and precious? After all, anything could be here. Maybe a collection of incunabula, those rare books printed before 1501. Or something less valuable but just as marvelous like a copy of H.L. Mencken's *Ventures into Verse* or a collectible like a first edition of *The Thin Man*.

Raine smiled to herself. More likely the contents of the crates would be just as Crystal said—pure junk. Collecting books, like anything else, was an art. It was unlikely that an amateur, especially one that had been described to her as a packrat, would have the know-how and good judgment to choose those books that would someday be collectibles.

First editions were issued by the thousands every year. It took luck and a certain rare instinct to choose something like Grabhorn press books or early Faulkner at a time when these items were indistinguishable from other newly published books. It was very unlikely she'd find anything in that category. Still, cataloging a collection for the first time was exciting and an adventure that most people in the antiquarian book industry would love to be in on.

Half an hour later, when she paused to straighten her tired back after unpacking the first few crates, she had little reason to feel optimistic about the value of the collection. So far she had unearthed a dozen children's books, all dating from the twenties, and most of them by authors she'd never heard of. a set of encyclopedias from the turn of the c...tury, at least two dozen cookbooks, all of them printed by obscure regional publishers. Only an assortment of westerns, a couple of them written by Zane Grey before he became famous, had any possibility of being of value.

As she looked at the piles of books, her first optimism dampened. Raine knew she must start a system soon, one that would get rid of the culls of the collection as quickly as possible. She opened the ledger she'd found in the cabinet and began listing the books she'd found, putting a tentative value on them. Later, when she had done some judicious sorting, she would list in more detail anything that might be valuable, or of interest to a collector.

She was trying to decide which general categories she should divide the books into when a sound behind her brought her out of her contemplation. When she swung around, the boy she knew must be Michael Duncan was standing in the open doorway, staring at her. For a moment she thought he would run off again, but this time he stood his ground, his gaze moving down to the books at her feet.

"Hello, again," she said. "Have you come to see what I'm up to?"

When he didn't speak, she tried again. "My name is Raine—are you Michael?"

For a long moment he stared at her, so obviously poised for flight that it startled her when he came into the storage room, closing the door behind him. With a quick movement of his hands that reminded her of Jonah's easy grace, he tapped each of his ears with his index finger, then shook his head back and forth.

Raine's breathing stopped for a moment as a realization came to her. Michael Duncan was deaf.... Why hadn't Crystal or the Cummingses or even Mr. Partridge told her that the boy's hearing was impaired? Had they thought she already knew, or, like music, was it a forbidden subject in this house?

She realized that there was something watchful in the boy's eyes, making her wonder if he had experienced open pity or thoughtlessness or even teasing because of his affliction. Careful not to allow her own pity to show on her face, she nodded, smiling, and after a moment he relaxed and returned her smile with a shy one of his own.

A desire to communicate with him prompted her next movement. She picked up the pen and a pad of paper she'd been using and wrote: "Are you Michael? My name is Raine. I'm here to put your grandfather's books in order."

He read the note, then took the pen from her hand. In large letters, he wrote: "I'm Michael. You are very pretty."

Raine found herself flushing, which seemed to disarm him further, because he was smiling again as he added a note: "Can I help?"

Raine resisted an impulse to hug him, knowing that might scare him away. She nodded and showed him that she'd been doing a crude preliminary sorting, mostly by subject. Afterward they devised a system. After listing the book in her ledger and making the decision where it would go, Raine pointed to a stack and then Michael, trotting busily back and forth, put it on the correct pile.

As they worked in companionable silence, her mind wandered from the books to Michael. All her life she'd been surrounded by music. What would it be like to live in a world of silence, with no music to set the soul soaring, without the sound of a human voice or a puppy's bark or even of the wind, rustling the trees? To Raine, with music so important in her life, it would be even worse than being blind. . . .

And why was Michael mute? Had he been born deaf and mute, or had it been a result of the same accident that had taken his mother from him? If so, no wonder Jonah had shut himself off from the world to devote his life to his son. And why, when Jonah had treated her so abominably, did she find it easy to believe that he would give up his music for love of his small son? Was she falling into the same old trap, believing the best of Jonah on faith? The truth probably was something far different and she was letting her imagination run away with her. After all, she didn't even know for sure that the boy's affliction was connected with the accident.

She was so absorbed in thought that she didn't notice at first that someone else had joined them. When she looked up into Crystal's narrowed eyes she braced herself, but the older woman's voice was pleasant enough as she said, "I'm sorry if Michael's been bothering you, Miss Hunicutt. I'll see that he keeps out of your way in the future."

"Oh, he isn't bothering me! In fact, I enjoy having him here. He's been quite a help."

Crystal didn't seem to hear her. She made a series of rapid finger movements. From Michael's agitated reply he seemed to be protesting, but when Crystal gave him a hard look, his eyes shifted and he dropped the book he was holding as if it burned his hand. His face sullen, he trotted off without looking at Raine.

She stared after him. "I wish I knew how to use—what do you call it? Sign language?"

"It's quite difficult to learn and it wouldn't be worth your while the short time you'll be here." Crystal gave Raine an enigmatic look. "We try very hard to keep Michael from too much outside stimulation. It might be better if you discouraged him in the future."

She turned and was gone before Raine could repeat that she'd enjoyed Michael's company. Feeling disgruntled she returned to her work, stopping only to eat the chicken sandwich and green salad that Tilda brought to her at noon. Although her body ached from the unaccustomed exercise and she knew she'd be stiff the next day, the hope that the next crate might contain some treasure kept her at her task.

A couple of hours later she was rewarded when she came across a first edition of John Gardner's *The Resurrection*. As she thumbed through the slim volume she felt a pang of avarice. If she ever reached the point where she had a little extra money, this was where it would go. To have something that gave pleasure whenever you needed solace or felt lonely was surely the best of all collections.

She recorded the book and then put it into the crate, empty until now, that she'd labeled "Important Books." When she returned to the crate she was delighted to find that the very next item was a bound galley of Salinger's *Catcher in the Rye*.

"Two in a row," she said out loud.

She touched the crude paper binding gently, wishing she were in the position to buy it and give it to Mr. Partridge as a gift. One of his passions was bound galleys, those copies of a book run off on cheap paper by the publishers to be sent to important reviewers and promotional outlets even before the galleys were corrected. Well, this find would go to the museum. Even if it were put up for sale, it would probably be beyond Mr. Partridge's ability to pay.

She listed the book then put it reverently away in

the crate with the John Gardner novel. The rest of the crate she was unpacking held mundane things, mostly first editions of novels written by long forgotten writers from the forties. She had already pried the lid off another crate, the top one of a new stack, when she realized it was too high for her to work out of easily. She used a sturdy ladder to perch on, but when she took out the top book, the shadows in the corner away from the wall fixture were so deep that she couldn't make out the title.

She sighed in exasperation, then uttered a heartfelt "dammit." She would have to move the heavy crate or open up another one until she'd have time to ask Luke to rig up more light for her. She rose, intending to climb down from the ladder, when an amused voice like an echo from the past sent a shock of alarm through her.

"Is that any language for a lady?"

CHAPTER SEVEN

As JONAH SMILED at her from the doorway, it was as if time had suddenly rolled back three years. Knowing she was in the shadows, she stared at him hungrily, and it was at that moment that she finally had to admit how susceptible to him she still was.

The light from a wall fixture near the door fell obliquely across his face, throwing his strong nose in relief and shadowing his eyes. There was an ache deep inside her as she stared at his lips—the upper one so firm and straight, the lower one softer, fuller—and remembered how those lips had felt against hers, against her body. And his hands...those fine strong musician's hands had caressed her, brought her to the peak of passion so many times during their night together. Even now, knowing what he was, she felt a wild desire to run toward him, to throw herself into his arms.

But she *couldn't* give in to this weakness! The wounds his betrayal had left were already too pain ful. She had to keep remembering that he could destroy her again. She must be strong, use that strength to fight against the pull of his physical attraction, an attraction that shamed her and made her so afraid of further disillusionment, further pain. . . .

"I'm Jonah Duncan—I hope I didn't startle you," Jonah said. His voice, too, was just as she remembered—deep and full-bodied, an instrument as compelling as his music had been. She clenched her teeth briefly, fighting for control.

Jonah came into the room, moving with the grace that had always seemed so at odds with his powerful body. He looked around at the stacks of books, the crates she'd unpacked. His gaze lingered on the one she'd labeled "Important Books."

"I was surprised when Arnold Partridge told me he'd engaged a woman to catalog my father-in-law's collection. If you're having any difficulty uncrating the books, I'll see that you get help. You must be finding it physically exhausting, Miss—is it Hunicutt?"

Raine took a long steadying breath, knowing she must speak, must say something. "Raine Hunicutt." To her surprise, her voice sounded almost normal. "And I'd rather do the uncrating myself."

He had been walking toward her. When he stumbled, almost falling, she bit her lip to keep from crying out. "I'm afraid it's like an obstacle course in here," she said thinly. "I'm in the process of sorting out the books by category."

He didn't answer her. He moved closer, skirting a stack of books until he was standing directly in front of the stool where she was perched. Instinctively she started to get up, only to realize that he was too close. Before she could slide her legs sideways, he reached out and lifted her down from the stool easily, his hands on her waist. With the stool pressed tightly against her hips she couldn't pull away, and she felt the warmth of his body as he lowered her slowly to the floor. Still silent, he put his hands on each side of her face, tilting her chin upward, and a slow trembling started up inside her body, immobilizing her.

Gently he kissed her, and as she felt the warmth of his lips against hers a wild yearning swept through her. She was aware of her own ragged breathing, of the strength of his hands, of an overwhelming desire to cling to him, even before his arms tightened around her and his kiss, so gentle at first, became a burning pressure against her mouth.

As the kiss went on she knew she should pull away, show offense, but her own self-serving body betrayed her. For a few pulsating heartbeats of time she let the kiss, the plunder of her mouth, continue, until another emotion came to her rescue, a deep searing anger.

How contemptible the man was, how sure of himself and of his effect upon women! First the concern—undoubtedly phony—about the work being too hard for her, then the helpful gesture of lifting her off the stool, and then, even before they'd exchanged more than a few words, the heavy pass.

Well, this time she didn't intend to be easy prey

for his predatory tricks. This time *she* was calling the shots, and being kissed by a man who had betrayed her was not part of the game.

Violently she jerked her head away, ending the kiss. "Please take your hands off of me, Mr. Duncan," she said coldly. "I don't know how you got the idea that I would welcome your manhandling, but this isn't part of our contract. I came here to do a job—and if you'll let go of me, I'll return to work."

His hands fell from her face. When she moved away from him, out of the shadows, he followed her. In the light from the wall fixture his gaze raked her, lingering on the knot of hair she'd tied back from her face. She braced herself when his eyes suddenly sharpened and his mouth tightened.

"I see," he said finally. "So it's games we're playing, is it?"

"I don't know what that's supposed to mean. For some reason you seem to feel that I'd welcome your heavy-handed pass. Well, let me assure you, I do not! If that's clear, maybe you'll tell me if you have any special instruction so I can get back to work."

There was a long silence. "You weren't so standoffish the first time we met," Jonah said softly.

Shock ran through Raine, setting her nerves on edge. Hoping she hadn't heard him right, she found her voice. "What—what does that mean?"

"It means that you can change your hair color but you can't change other things." Lazily his gaze moved over her face, stopped briefly at her lips, then at her breasts. "So what's this craziness all about, Carmen?"

"Don't call me that," she said sharply. "My name is Raine."

"Raine or Carmen, you're the same girl I made love to in New York."

She knew it was no use then, so she firmly set her chin and gave him back stare for stare. "I'm surprised you remember me."

"You're a little hard to forget."

"Well, *you* were quite forgettable," she retorted, determined not to let him guess how painful her struggle to put him out of her mind had been— how painful it still was. Even now she felt the pull of the old attraction, the old magic, and it angered and shamed her.

"Maybe I owe you an explanation about that note I sent."

She raised one eyebrow. "Note? What note?"

"I sent you a note—and flowers," he said.

"Really? Well, it's been a long time. I do remember a bracelet, though," she went on recklessly, prompted by a desire to get back at him, repay him for some of the agony she'd gone through. "It paid my rent for quite a long time. I guess I should thank you for that since it helped make up for my—my disappointment. When we had our little adventure I was hoping to gain the patronage of a famous concert pianist, which is why I was willing to play along with your—your fantasies. As you yourself pointed out that evening, it's so important when you're just starting out to get the backing of someone who can do you some good.''

"Then it seems I don't owe you an apology, after all," Jonah said, his voice grating. "Sorry I couldn't accommodate you by—no, by god! *It was your first time!* This doesn't make sense—"

"Oh, but it wasn't hard to fool you, especially since you fancy yourself as being irresistible. And it was a pretty good trade-off. You got a night of entertainment, thinking you had seduced a virgin, and I got an expensive bracelet. My roommate got a good laugh out of it when I told him how you'd fallen for my innocent-in-distress act. Oh, I'd had trouble with a man just before you ran me off the road that night, but it was a lovers' quarrel. We made up the next day—but not until I'd made him suffer a little.''

A muscle moved in Jonah's taut jawline. "You're quite an opportunist, aren't you? So why are you here, doing honest work? What do you hope to get out of it? If this is some kind of blackmail scheme your timing is way off. I'm a widower now, and I've retired from public life. These days no one would give a damn about my one-night stand with a cheap little tart. So whatever you're up to, forget it.''

Raine flushed under the lash of his contempt, but she refused to look away. "I came here for one reason only—to do a job that I'm well qualified for.''

"As a book cataloger? That's a likely story.

How did you manage to fool Mr. Partridge, anyway? Don't tell me you tried your sexual tricks on the poor man?''

"I've known Mr. Partridge all my life. He was a good friend of my father, who was an antiquarian book seller. I worked in his shop during vacations and weekends ever since I was a kid. I'm perfectly qualified for this job, which is a relatively simple one."

"But why bother when you have other wares—" his eyes swept over her, lingering on her breasts "—that would bring in far more money for less effort."

It took all her strength not to slap his mocking face, but somehow she managed a scornful smile. "I only use my wares, as you call them, when the price is right. And this job is quite lucrative and something I enjoy doing. I can't say the same about—other things. So if you'll let me get on with it—"

"Oh, no, you don't! I want you out of my house. So pack up your things and get out." His lips twisted into an ugly smile. "I'll even pay for your gas back to the city."

Raine fought to hide her dismay. Several things flashed through her mind. In her eagerness to save her pride she had gone too far. Her personal situation hadn't changed. She still needed this job. If she went back to San Francisco so soon, Martin would turn stubborn again and refuse to take the insurance money. Besides, *she* wasn't the one at fault here. She had taken the job, one she was fully qualified for, in good faith. It wasn't fair that Jonah could so arrogantly dismiss her. . . .

A plan stirred, one that she hoped would extract her from the trap she'd put herself into. "I'm perfectly willing to leave, but of course it will cost you the full fee our contract calls for," she said, careful to keep her voice cool.

"Why the devil should I pay for work you haven't done?" he demanded roughly.

"Because I *am* perfectly willing to stay and finish the job. Why should I be penalized just because you've changed your mind? So if you'll just make out a check for—"

"The hell I will!"

"Then I suggest you let me return to work," she said, hoping he didn't hear the quaver in her voice.

"There's a clause in that contract that says I can fire you if you prove unsatisfactory—"

"But I haven't, have I? I've been working hard for the past eight hours, and you can see that I've already accomplished quite a lot. No, you can't say that I'm unsatisfactory—and you don't really want me to go to Mr. Partridge and complain that you fired me because—because I'm a woman, do you? He's a very fair man who believes in women's equality, and he's also a very good lawyer. That contract he drew up protects both of us. You have the right to fire me if I don't do my work properly—but you'd better be sure of your grounds, Mr. Duncan, because I intend to sue you for breach of contract."

His eyes bit into her, piercing her. "So that's

it," he said finally. "Since blackmail won't work, you think you've found another way to cheat me out of a fat fee. You really are conniving, aren't you? Well, forget it. If you want that fee you're going to earn every cent of it. It might be worth it just to watch you doing some honest work. I intend to check up on your progress every day, and if you slack off, out you go. Under those circumstances, do you think you want to stay?"

The contempt she read in his eyes scorched Raine, and she found it hard to maintain her composure as she said, "I'm staying. I came here prepared to do a good job and that's what I intend to do."

"You can count on that," he said grimly. "There are a few house rules, too. I don't want you contaminating my sister-in-law, who happens to be a particularly innocent and naive person, with your cynical ideas. So stay away from her—and stay away from my son, too. I understand he spent the morning down here helping you. I'll tell him that the basement is off limits from now on, and I expect you to abide by that."

"I have no intention of corrupting your son or your sister-in-law."

"And I'll be keepig an eye on you. Step out of line one time and that invalidates the contract. I understand from what Crystal tells me that you prefer to eat with the Cummingses. Since I don't see why they should be inflicted with your company, I expect you to appear in the dining room on time every evening, appropriately dressed." He surveyed her jeans and shirt. "You do have something other than jeans to wear, don't you?"

Stung by his remark, she started to retaliate in kind, but the feral look in his eyes warned her that he was deliberately baiting her. "I always try to dress appropriately," she said. "But I prefer to eat with Tilda and Luke—"

"You'll do as you're told or you can get out!"

"Very well. But only because it will be easier on Tilda, who is grossly overworked," she said nastily.

He didn't answer, nor did he move away. She discovered that his closeness was becoming increasingly oppressive, and she edged sideways, intending to go around him. But Jonah was quicker. Before she could get away he was upon her, his hands clamping her arms to her side, his mouth covering hers. She tried to struggle, but he was too strong for her. With her back braced against a stack of heavy crates, she was forced to submit to his kiss.

His first kiss had been passionate, but not violent. This one was savage, a bruising assault upon her lips and, she quickly discovered, upon her senses. A familiar warmth started up deep inside her, spread through her body, and she felt a wave of yearning, of need, of wanting.

Oh, God, why can't it be different? Why does it have to be this way—that the one man I've ever wanted is Jonah?

She discovered she was trembling, that her skin was on fire, and with some last bit of sanity she tried to escape. Jonah ignored her struggles and went on with the plunder of her mouth until she finally went limp, her breath gone. His hands moved then, but not to release her. He stroked her hair, her throat, evoking such a surge of response that her senses reeled.

Only when his hand covered her breast did sanity return. Somehow she found the strength to push him away, and this time he let her go, stepping back so quickly that she had to hold onto the crates to keep from falling.

"So some of it wasn't faked," he said, letting her see his satisfaction. "You may be a conniving little opportunist but you have the normal instincts of a woman. Maybe there'll be a few compensations after all for having you around the next few weeks."

Furiously Raine wiped her lips with the back of her hand. "Don't ever touch me again," she said, enunciating her words. "If you try it, I'll—"

"You'll what?"

"I'll take you to court for sexual harassment. This isn't the Middle Ages. There are legal protections from men like you."

"Indeed? And will you stand up in court and testify that you didn't return my kiss, that you honestly tried to get away?"

To her dismay, she felt a wave of heat flood her face. He laughed softly and moved toward the door. "So it's a standoff, isn't it? But don't worry. The truth is, I don't really care much for secondhand property. So I won't bother you again. Just don't provoke me or you can expect more of the same, Carmen.''

"Don't call me that!" she said sharply, using anger to combat the hurt of his disdainful words.

"Why not? I think it's very appropriate—even though you have changed the color of your hair. Originally I called you that because you looked like a young Carmen. It didn't occur to me at the time that Carmen was an amoral and venal woman, but now we both know those words describe you perfectly, don't we? So I think I'll continue to use that name for you.''

He turned away, leaving her fighting the desire to scream, to pick up a book and throw it at him, an impulse so foreign to her nature that she wondered if she was losing her sanity.

At the door he turned to give her one last long look, his eyes hard and remote again. "And one thing more. There'll be no playing of music—or even talking about it—in this house or out you go. And that clause, Carmen, *is* in the contract.''

CHAPTER EIGHT

AS RAINE DRESSED FOR DINNER, her thoughts were turbulent. Even though she had invited Jonah's scornful words by her own behavior, his hostilty had lacerated her self-confidence until she felt raw and hurting. Had she allowed her pride to trick her into making a mistake, pretending to be something she wasn't? Well, it was too late to worry about that. All she could do now was brazen it out. And if Jonah believed that she was the hard calculating person she'd pretended to be, that would only make it easier for her to fight off this weakness she'd discovered within herself.

Ever since she'd gone away to school she'd prided herself on being able to handle any situation that came along. So how was it possible that she'd been thrown completely off-balance by Jonah's kiss? After all, she knew what he was—a man who had seduced a girl years his junior under circumstances that had made her very vulnerable. And to top that off, just a short time ago he'd made a pass at someone who, as far as he'd known at the time, had been a stranger, in his employment only one day. Surely that was the act of a contemptible womanizer. So why, *why*, knowing all this, did something inside her tremble even now when she remembered how Jonah's lips had felt against hers?

Resolutely she put aside her own questions and examined herself in the mirror above her marble-topped dressing table. She had taken pains with her apperance, not only because her feminine pride demanded it but because she wanted to present a picture of self-confidence when she went downstairs.

The long brown-velvet skirt she'd chosen clung to her hips and swirled around her legs, emphasizing her slenderness, and the cream-colored silk blouse was a startling contrast to her dark eyes and skin. It was the same outfit she usually wore for musical recitals and she'd often been told it gave her a patrician look.

Her hair, coiled and looped around her small head, added to the impression of serenity. No one looking at her would suspect the turmoil boiling inside. Or would they? What about the pulse in her throat that fluttered like crazy whenever she was excited or alarmed or even deeply moved? Maybe she'd better wear a neck scarf or her pose of being completely self-possessed might not come off.

Raine made a face at her image, annoyed with her own self-doubt. She was behaving like an inexperienced young girl—and that was something she no longer was, thanks to Jonah. No, she would go downstairs, looking serene and self-possessed, and there was no way he could possibly guess that he had affected her outlook on life for the past three years. At least she could salvage her pride out of this whole mess.

She gave herself a quick spray of cologne, the Windsong her father had sent for her last birthday, and went into the hall. The house seemed very quiet as she ran lightly down the stairs, then paused long enough to take several long breaths in preparation for what she was sure would be an ordeal.

But at first, after she had located the dining room and was seated next to the silent Michael, it wasn't nearly as bad as she'd expected. His voice courteous, Jonah told her that if she were having any trouble opening the crates of books, she should ask for Luke's help.

"That won't be necessary," Raine said. "I'm sure I can manage, Mr. Duncan."

"Since we're going to be living in the same house for the next few weeks—unless you decide the job is too much for you—I think we should go on a first-name basis. So please call me Jonah—and your name is Raine, isn't it? Very unusual. Is it indicative of your nature? Are you as cool and refreshing as a summer shower, Raine?"

Aware that the politeness in Jonah's voice didn't match the mockery in his eyes, Raine decided to ignore his final two questions. "Yes, it *is* a little unusual. It was a family name."

Crystal, dressed in silver gray evening pajamas, her dark hair a soft cloud around her face, gave Raine a bright smile. "I do hope you like southern cooking, Raine. That's Tilda's specialty.

We can't seem to convince her to try anything else.''

To Raine's relief the conversation moved into impersonal areas. Under Jonah's questioning she described her two finds so far—the bound galleys of Salinger's *Catcher in the Rye* and the first edition of John Gardner's *The Resurrection*.

"Mr. Partridge would probably give his eye-teeth for the Salinger galleys," she said, sighing. "He's been collecting bound galleys for years, and I happen to know that he's an avid fan of Salinger.''

She smiled suddenly, forgetting the tension between Jonah and herself. "When I was a youngster he used to play a game with me. He knew how I liked to read, so he'd quote something then attribute it to the wrong author. Naturally I'd be quick to correct him, and then he'd tell me what a smart girl I was. Since I didn't get too many compliments, I hoarded every one of them, and it wasn't until I was in my teens that I finally realized he always quoted from the books currently lying around the living room of our apartment.''

"That sounds like Arnold." Jonah's voice was silky. "He's a compassionate man—and a very good lawyer. Someone told me recently that the contracts he draws up are virtually unbreakable.''

Raine flushed, sorry she'd dropped her guard for a moment. She was relieved when Crystal asked, "Are the Salinger galleys valuable?''

"Very. The Gardner first edition is more in the collectible category. Since it was his first book, written before his *Grendel* became so popular, the printing was small. Someday it could move into the rare category, of course."

"You know a lot about books, don't you?" Crystal commented.

"I agree," Jonah said. "Your appearance is rather deceptive, Raine. I would have guessed your profession as something entirely different."

Raine didn't make the mistake of asking him which profession. Ignoring his comment, she answered Crystal's question instead. "My knowledge can't begin to compare with my father's," she said evenly. "He was quite well-known in the antiquarian book business, not only for his experience but because he never cheated anyone out of a penny."

"And have you tried to live up to his standards, Raine?" Jonah said softly.

Aware of Crystal's speculative stare, Raine gave him a noncommittal smile and changed the subject, telling Crystal about the assortment of children's books she'd laid aside when she'd found Crystal's name written on the frontispiece.

Crystal's gratitude seemed genuine as she thanked her. "My father gave me those books. I guess they were pretty old-fashioned, but I adored them. They disappeared while I was away at school. I've often wondered what happened to them."

Looking as if she were doing them a favor, Tilda brought in their soup, and the conversation shifted to more general things. Beside Raine, Michael ate steadily. His eyes, the same dark gray as his father's, moved from face to face, although his expression gave no hint of what he was thinking.

The food, as Raine had expected, was superbly cooked, and the wine, a chardonnay from Jonah's own winery, was delicate, a perfect complement to the roast chicken and wild-rice dressing. Because she had worked so hard that day, Raine ate heartily, content to let Crystal and Jonah's conversation flow around her. It was later, after they'd finished their chocolate mousse and Michael had kissed his aunt's and father's cheeks, slanted a shy smile in Raine's direction, then trotted out of the room, that the evening began to come apart.

As they lingered over coffee, Crystal's cordiality toward Raine seemed to be fraying at the edges. Had it been summoned up for the occasion, now beginning to drag out too long to please her? Raine decided that she could take a hint, especially since she had no desire to prolong the evening. As she waited for an opening in the conversation so she could excuse herself, Crystal talked about people she didn't know, about the winery business, deliberately shutting Raine out and letting her know that she was the outsider here.

It was no wonder, Raine reflected, that Jonah

spoke of Crystal as being innocent and naive. In his presence she was demure, so soft-spoken that it was hard to realize she was the same woman who'd greeted Raine so coolly the day before. It was only when she looked at Raine that her affability slipped a little.

What was she so afraid of, anyway? That Jonah would be attracted to a woman who would be under his roof for a few weeks, that it might disrupt her own comfortable life? Or was it jealousy of a more personal kind? What exactly was their relationship, anyway? When Crystal looked at Jonah, her face took on animation. Was it affection, friendship, or the glow of love? And Jonah.... Although he treated his wife's younger sister with a sort of amused tolerance, it was impossible to guess how he really felt about her.

Raine winced, ashamed of the pain that stabbed her at the thought of Jonah and Crystal making love. After all, their relationship was their own business and none of hers.

"—from San Francisco, Raine?" Crystal's voice cut into Raine's thoughts.

Raine stared at her. "I beg your pardon? I'm afraid I was woolgathering...."

"I asked if San Francisco is your home."

"Yes, it is. My father had a bookstore on Powell Street. We lived in an apartment above the store."

"So you're a city girl. I do hope you won't be too bored here. Jonah and I are at the winery during the day, so you'll be alone most of the time with only the Cummingses for company.''

''Does Michael go to school in Mendocino?''

''He has a tutor who comes in for a few hours in the morning three times a week.''

''I see. I suppose there isn't a school in this area that—that's suitable. But surely—'' She stopped, realizing she was treading on dangerous ground.

''But surely what, Raine?'' Jonah asked.

''I was going to say that surely there was a school for the deaf in the Bay Area where he could board during the week while he attended classes.''

''Michael's doctors believe he should lead a very quiet life.'' Jonah played with his spoon, his eyes reflective. ''The accident that destroyed his hearing affected his emotional stability, too.''

''I understand,'' she murmured, even though she really didn't. Except for his deafness, Michael had seemed like a very normal boy to her that morning.

Crystal changed the subject back to winery business. Raine sipped her coffee, her mind wandering again, and it was a while before she noticed that even though Jonah seemed to be listening to his sister-in-law's chatter, his mind was obviously elsewhere. She studied him, noting the subtle changes in his appearance. When he wasn't smiling or talking his face looked gaunt, and there was a deep line between his eyes that she was sure hadn't been there three years ago. Was he still mourning his wife's death, or was it worry over his son that made him seem older? And why did she have the crazy impulse to reach forward and smooth out that line with her fingertips?

With a start she realized that Jonah had noticed her interest and was returning her stare. She felt her face flood with heat as his eyes moved over her with deliberate slowness. She had the feeling that he was stripping her naked, and she felt a stirring in her loins that she didn't appreciate. The bastard. Why was he playing with her? Was this more of his harassment, a way of getting rid of her? Well, it wasn't going to work. She intended to stay on until the job was done if it killed her!

She gave Jonah back stare for stare, letting him know that she wasn't intimidated, and she had the satisfaction of seeing his eyelids flicker as if he had received her message.

"I must ask you not to encourage my son's natural interest in someone new, Raine," he said abruptly, as if continuing an earlier conversation. "He's a very impressionable child, and since you'll only be here a short time it wouldn't be wise if he got too attached to you. His doctors tell us it's very important that he lead a very stress-free life. I don't want him confused by—by a stranger."

In other words, don't contaminate my son, Raine thought bitterly.

She forced a smile. "Of course. I wouldn't want to confuse your son." She laid her napkin beside her plate and rose. "If you'll excuse me, I'm rather tired. I want to get an early start in the morning, so I think I'll turn in. Thank you for an excellent dinner. Tilda is a wonderful cook.''

She didn't wait for an answer, and as she climbed the two flights of stairs to her room, she thought over the conversation and her stubbornness stirred. No, she didn't intend to "confuse" Michael. She planned to learn how to communicate with him. It would give her something to do during her free hours, and maybe it would help the time pass faster.

Her mind was alive with random thoughts and images, bits and pieces of the day, but to her surprise she fell asleep almost as soon as she crawled between the snowy sheets of the tester bed.

At first, when she awakened with a start, she thought her alarm must have gone off. But when she reached out for it, still groggy with sleep, the luminous dial showed it was only one o'clock. She lay there staring into the darkness wondering what had awakened her. Then she heard the sound again, this time recognizing it as a child crying.

It must be Michael. Was he having a nightmare? His room, Tilda had told her, was just below hers on the second floor, and Crystal's bedroom was just next door. Surely she would hear him and go to him. Did this mean Michael was physically able to talk, after all? Somehow she had got the impression that his accident had caused injury to his vocal cords, too, leaving him mute and unable to utter a sound of any kind.

The wail came again and it tugged at her heart, all too vulnerable because of her own recent loss. She hesitated, but only briefly, before she made up her mind to go to him. No doubt she would be accused of interfering, but she had to make sure that Michael was all right.

Raine switched on the lamp beside the bed, put her robe on over her nightgown and went into the hall. A safety light burned at the top of the staircase and she moved toward it, then crept quietly down the stairs, stopping once to listen. Although she didn't hear any sounds now, she went on anyway. If Michael had fallen back asleep, no harm done, and if someone else had gone to comfort him, she would make her excuses and leave.

The overhead lights were on in the second-floor hall. She moved toward the door that was the duplicate of her own, her step noiseless on the thick carpet. When she came to the door of Michael's room she hesitated, seeing the door was slightly ajar. Cautiously she peeked through the crack and discovered a lamp was burning next to a small antique sleigh bed, and that Crystal was sitting on the edge of the bed holding Michael's small body in her arms. She was rocking him back and forth, and there was such a look of tenderness on her face that Raine took a step backward, feeling like an intruder.

As though Michael could hear her, Crystal was murmuring soothing words in his ear. "There, there, baby—it was only a nightmare. Go back to sleep. Aunt Crystal won't let anything happen to you. You're safe now.''

As Raine watched the two of them, she discovered a constriction in her throat. So Crystal did love her nephew, and she, Raine Hunicutt, was an overly imaginative fool.

Quietly she turned and retraced her steps down the hall. She had already started up the staircase when she changed her mind. Since she was wide-awake now, a cup of cocoa was in order. Maybe that would relax her enough so she could fall back asleep. Walking on the balls of her feet, she turned and went down the stairs. Her robe swishing softly around her ankles was the only sound until a night bird nearby gave a chuckling cry, making her feel less alone.

Later, she was sitting in the kitchen nursing a hot cup of cocoa between her cold hands, her eyelids drooping, when she heard a sound behind her. She looked around into Jonah's intent stare. He was wearing a maroon silk robe; from his unruffled hair and the book in his hand, she knew he hadn't been to bed yet.

"Were you looking for me, Carmen?" he said. "My room's on the second floor."

As the implication of his words sank in, anger seethed through her. "I came down for a cup of cocoa," she snapped.

"Cocoa? Such an innocuous drink for such a—a sophisticated lady." His gaze locked with hers. "I would advise you not to do too much prowling around in the dark. There are too many things you could stumble over."

"I have no intention of prowling around in the dark. As soon as I finish my cocoa I intend to go back upstairs. In fact, I've changed my mind. I don't believe I'll wait until it cools, after all."

She got up, but before she could escape from the kitchen Jonah had dropped his book on the floor and had intercepted her. She felt his breath against her face as his hands fastened around her upper arms, drawing her up against his hard muscular body. Other than struggling, there seemed nothing she could do to get away. Since she refused to play that kind of cat-and-mouse game, she stood there, her body rigid, staring him straight in the eye.

But Jonah only smiled, obviously unimpressed. With a quick movement he bent his head and his lips touched hers. She felt a curious sinking feeling, as if her bones had suddenly melted, but she remained stiff and unyielding in his arms. Then the pressure of his lips changed and he forced her lips apart, his tongue probing the soft moistness of her mouth, a slow deliberate invasion that was incredibly erotic.

The faint musky odor of his body mingled with the scent of his after-shave lotion was like an aphrodisiac, stirring up memories of when she had come so joyfully into his arms. The pulse in her throat throbbed as his hands slid down her shoulders, taking the robe with them.

The coldness of the air on the exposed skin of her upper arms shocked her, and an awareness of danger stirred beneath the overwhelming desire to yield, to allow the intense pleasure of the kiss to go on. She started to pull away, but Jonah only held her tighter, and the pressure of his body, so obviously virile and masculine, weakened her resolve even further.

Just a few seconds longer, she thought, *and then I'll pull away....*

His lips left her mouth and moved across her cheek in a series of feathery kisses, down her throat to the telltale pulse that throbbed so erratically.

"Soft—so very soft," he murmured, his breath fanning her throat and sending small ripples of sensation through her. His lips found the deep valley between her breasts, and she arched her back, mutely offering the tender mounds to be caressed. Gently he kissed each breast in turn, then bent his head to possess one of them with his mouth. As the warmth, the pressure brought on new waves of sensation, she thought she would drown in the voluptuous stirrings of her own body. Nothing mattered now except the need that had become a raging hunger for Jonah's kisses, his touch, for complete possession.

Easily, so smoothly that she hardly noticed when it happened, he slipped her gown off her shoulders and it fell around her feet in a pool of white silk. There was nothing between them as he gathered her closer, and although she was surrounded by a golden haze now, some part of her realized that he'd slipped off his own robe. They were locked together in an embrace so intimate, bare flesh against bare flesh, that there was no mistaking that Jonah's arousal equaled hers.

His hands, moving in slow circles, caressed her back then fastened over the soft curves of her hips, pressing her even closer. Yielding to a desire to touch him, she leaned away from him far enough so she could trace a path with her fingers through the thick hair of his chest, along the tautness of his stomach, and then, as her touch became more intimate, she gloried in her power to make him gasp with desire. He caught her close again, and as their bodies entwined she moaned deep in her throat, a wordless plea for him to take her then and there....

But still he caressed her, his hands, his lips, exploring and touching and arousing her until she was trembling on the brink of ecstasy. She knew he was as deeply aroused, so when he pulled away abruptly she could only stand there, completely vulnerable and without defenses, staring at his twisted smile.

"It takes very little to bring out the alley cat in you, doesn't it, Carmen? Will any man do? Someone you met in a singles' bar or who you picked up on a bus? Well, it's been a long time since I've had a woman, so I'm very willing to accommodate you—but not here where someone could walk in on us. Let's go upstairs to your room. We won't be disturbed there."

From some source she didn't know she possessed, Raine fought a battle with her senses that even now whispered how easy it would be to give in, to let Jonah satisfy the burning fever his love-making had aroused. But something else, a sense of her own worth, was stronger. It didn't really matter what Jonah thought of her, but she had to live with herself for the rest of her life, and if she gave in to him now, if she allowed herself to be seduced by her own treacherous body, she would writhe with shame every time she thought of this night.

Silently she gathered up her gown and robe and put them on. "You continue to misunderstand me," she said then, and though her voice was thin it held a cutting edge. "I don't do this sort of thing for free, and it's not included in the rate quoted in our contract, either. If you want other privileges, it will cost you extra—a great deal extra."

Jonah's eyes narrowed to dark slits. When his nostrils flared and the muscles of his jaw tensed, she was afraid for a second that he might hit her. Instead he picked up his robe from the floor and put it back on before he turned to look at her. With insulting thoroughness, inch by inch, he examined her. His eyes raked her hair, tumbled in disarray around her shoulders, lingered on her lips, still moist from his kisses, on the mounds of her breasts, the nipples still taut from his ardent caresses. As his gaze moved lower, she felt as if his eyes had some searing power, able to burn through her robe and gown, into her very flesh.

"I'm afraid you overestimate your own value," he said, his voice cruel. "Why should I pay for something that you obviously give away free to other men? So thank you, but no thank you. You simply aren't worth the price.''

He gave her a mocking smile and then he stalked away, leaving her standing there, trembling with frustration and rage. She groped for the back of a chair and sat down heavily, her knees too weak to hold her up. Her arms felt as if they weighed a ton as she folded them on the edge of Tilda's work-table and buried her face in them.

She had won. Oh, yes, she had routed Jonah so thoroughly it was doubtful if he would ever bother her again. So why did she feel as if she wanted to throw herself down on the floor and scream out her rage, her grief?

CHAPTER NINE

DURING THE REST of that long still night, without even the wind for company, Raine tried to come to terms with herself and her emotions. It was time to face up to something she hadn't been willing to admit before. As long as she remained in this house she was in danger of losing her own self-respect, of falling even deeper under Jonah's spell.

Surely it must be a sickness, this effect he had on her. It wasn't love. She was sure of that. Love was tenderness, a commitment, a sharing of one's innermost self with another person. Love was being able to trust. So this wild seductively sweet emotion she felt whenever she was near Jonah must be infatuation, something to be conquered. After all, she knew how cruel and ruthless he could be. The weakness she'd shown tonight couldn't happen again, even if it meant she must go away....

Raine sighed deeply as she thought of the trap she'd fallen into. Yes, she could pack her suitcase and walk out of Jonah's life forever, but only at a high cost to three people she loved very much and to whom she had an obligation. Could she fool Martin into thinking her job here was finished so quickly, that she had enough money to tide her over until the preliminaries for the competition next year? Could she simply stay away from the city for a few weeks, then return later and quietly get a job?

Yes, that might work, but it was so chancy. For one thing, her money was very low. No matter where she went, she had to work to support herself, and jobs were hard to find right now, especially since her work experience was so limited. And what if Martin called Arlington House and found out she was gone? He had said something about bringing Gloria to Mendocino for a couple of days the next time he had one of his rare free weekends. He would certainly call the house, only to find that she had quit. How could she possibly lie her way out of that? And if he caught her in one lie, the whole deception would fall apart. She, who knew her brother's stubbornness so well, since it matched her own, also knew that he would immediately refuse the insurance money, and then they would be right back where they started.

No, she had no choice. She would stick it out. It might even be good for her soul to be forced to stay here and conquer this infuriating flaw in her nature. After what had happened tonight, Jonah would probably ignore her in the future. And if she stayed away from him as much as possible, going to her room as soon as dinner was over, and if she spent every hour possible working, she could get finished in half the time she'd planned for.

In the meantime she would keep her mind occupied. Since her job involved so much stooping and lifting and bending, it would be physically impossible to work more than a ten-or-eleven-hour day—and then not all in one stretch. She would devote her free time to piano practice, provided she could find an available piano. With Jonah and Crystal gone during the day, who was to know if she slipped away in the afternoons for a couple of hours? Even if Jonah found out what she was doing, how could he possibly object? The restriction against music ended at the borders of the estate, and she had to keep her fingers flexible.

That would give her something besides her cataloging to keep her busy. And there was something else, too. As soon as possible she meant to go to the public library in Mendocino and find a book that would teach her sign language so she could start communicating better with Michael, who had already become so dear to her. . . .

Feeling better she fell asleep, and the next morning she was up early, even before her alarm went off. As she went to close her window against the morning chill, she paused to stare out into a world of swirling mist, of gray-shrouded hills and trees.

Her window overlooked the herb garden and she fancied she could smell the pungent odors of mist-drenched rosemary and oregano and thyme. As she was turning away, a movement in the mist caught her eye. She squinted, trying to make out the tall figure who strolled along one of the garden paths toward the rear gate.

Was it Luke, up early to do some job? No, Luke was much shorter than this man. Her breath caught sharply as she realized it must be Jonah. Her mouth dry, she watched as he paused to unfasten the gate. Was he heading toward the beach to do some jogging? Or was it possible that he'd go for a swim on a foggy morning like this? Of course, the water would be much warmer than the air, but still, hadn't Tilda told her there was a dangerous undertow in the cove?

For a moment an image crept into her mind of Jonah's strong arms cutting the rough waters of the cove, of his long brown body moving like a dolphin through the waves. An ache started up deep inside her, and when she realized what was happening she turned away from the window quickly and went to make up her tumbled bed before she dressed for the day.

The kitchen was still dark when she went downstairs, but by the time she had turned on the lights and was measuring coffee into the electric pot, Tilda had appeared to start breakfast. During breakfast Raine explained to Tilda that the change in her dinner arrangements had had nothing to do with her own preference.

Tilda nodded, as if she'd suspected as much. "I figured Jonah would change things around when he got back, but there ain't no use bucking horns with Crystal so I just let it go."

Later, as Raine was busily at work in the basement storage room, she heard a car start up outside and knew that Jonah and Crystal were leaving for the winery. For a moment the notation she'd been making in the ledger blurred, but she blinked hard, shaking off a sudden depression. What did it matter if Jonah was in the house or somewhere else? In spirit they were miles apart even when they were in the same room.

She finished her notation and placed the book, a self-published collection of poems by a poet she didn't recognize, in the pile she'd designated for discard. She felt a pang of pity for the author, who must once have had such high hopes for this slim volume of poetry. As someone else had said, it was as much work to write a bad poem as a good one. And anyway, who was to say that this collection wasn't worthwhile just because the poet was unknown to her or because the book wasn't listed in any of her catalogs?

She started to turn away, then hesitated. With a shrug, she plucked the book off the pile and laid it near the door. She'd take the book to her room that night. At least she could see that the poems got one more reading before they were consigned to the discard pile.

She was smiling at her own foolishness when there was a soft knock on the door. She opened it to find Michael, looking as if he wasn't sure of his welcome, standing there. He returned her smile, his eyes moving past her to the books. She hesitated, remembering Jonah's warning about not encouraging him, but she finally gave a mental shrug and invited him with a gesture. To send him away now without a good reason would surely be more disturbing to the boy than to allow him to stay. Besides, the more help she got, the sooner she would be on her way back to the city.

For the next hour Michael pitched in eagerly, his young legs saving her quite a few steps. Sometimes, when he anticipated what she wanted almost before she had time to point, she wondered if he could read minds. She decided that it must be body language and facial expressions that he could read.

Once, when she caught Michael's interested stare at the gaudy jacket on a book of political cartoons, she sat down beside him on a crate, turning the pages one by one. She pointed to one particularly grotesque caricature, and a laugh tumbled out of his throat and set up echoes in the corners of the room. Raine jumped a little at the unexpected sound and again wondered why he never spoke. If he were truly mute, could he make sounds at all? There was so much she didn't know about deafness—an ignorance she meant to correct as soon as she got to a library.

At noon, when Tilda brought their lunch, she studied Michael's animated face with approval.

"The boy's come out of his shell a mite since you been here," she said. "If you ask me, there's too much fuss about keeping him quiet. It ain't natural for a boy that age—or any age. Them doctors don't know everything, you know."

"Is he mute, Tilda? A while ago he laughed out

loud and he seems to—well, if I didn't know better I'd swear he could hear a little."

The corners of Tilda's mouth twitched; her eyes shifted toward Michael, then back to Raine. "Crystal takes him into the city once a month to see his doctor, but he can't find no sign that the boy's improving. At first they did say his deafness wouldn't be permanent—they've got a fancy name for it, I guess—but they must've been wrong because it's been more'n two years now and he still don't show no signs of improving."

She paused to pour lemonade from a thermos into two cups and to set out forks for their salad before she added, "As for his talking, he ain't said one word since the accident. No reason excepting for the shock. At first they tried real hard to get him to talk, but he just wouldn't. Finally he got so upset the doctors said it was throwing him into one of them depressions, and not to push him. 'Course it would be better if he used his vocal cords. Even if he got his hearing back, he'd have to start learning to talk all over, I reckon."

Raine looked at Michael, who was absorbed in a leather-bound copy of Stevenson's *Child's Book of Verse.* "I wish I knew sign language," she said. "I'd like to be able to communicate without a pencil and paper."

"It ain't all that hard to learn, Raine. Luke and me, we got his tutor to teach us. Makes it easier on all of us, dealing with the boy."

"That was very thoughtful of you."

"Thoughtful?" Tilda bristled as if she'd just

been insulted. "Why, we been with this boy since he was born. It wasn't thoughtful. Just common sense. If'n you're interested I'm sure Reverend Turlock will teach you. You can talk to him when he comes to give the boy his lessons in a little while."

She hesitated, her face troubled. "I reckon I should warn you. Crystal ain't likely to approve. She don't want him getting too close to other people. Says the doctor told her it would only confuse the boy. So if you do learn signing, you'd best keep it to yourself. The boy won't say nothing—he's closemouthed, specially with Crystal. There's a lot of things he don't tell her."

"I don't understand why she'd care if—"

"No reason you should understand. Just mind what I said," Tilda said brusquely.

She bustled out of the room and Raine knew that it would be useless to question her further. In fact, she was surprised the housekeeper had already said so much. Well, she would take Tilda's advice—and her warning. The first chance she got she would make arrangements with Michael's tutor to start taking sign-language lessons, and she wouldn't say anything about it to Crystal or Jonah.

Before she joined Michael at a makeshift table of two upturned crates, she got her pad of paper and wrote him a note.

"I would like to meet your tutor."

"Okay. He is very nice," Michael answered in his large handwriting. He gestured toward the door, as if saying that Reverend Turlock would be arriving soon, and she nodded her understanding. They washed their dusty hands in the laundry sink, then sat down to eat. The silence between them was comfortable as they munched their sandwiches and ate their salad. Afterward they carried the dishes to the kitchen before Michael led the way to a small book-lined room off the downstairs hall.

A man was waiting for them, thumbing through a book. Raine had expected someone old, or at least middle-aged, but she'd forgotten that ministers come in all sizes and ages and was surprised to discover that Reverend Turlock was several years younger than Jonah.

He was tall, sandy haired, with hazel eyes, and his face was pleasant rather than handsome. When he ruffled Michael's hair with obvious affection, smiling at them both, she remembered something her father had once said—to beware of a person whose smile didn't improve his face. Well, when this man smiled, even his eyes seemed to light up.

"So Michael has a new friend," he said in a pleasant tenor voice.

"I'd like to learn sign language," Raine said after she'd introduced herself. "Would you have time to teach me? I'll pay you whatever you think is right, of course."

"I'd be glad to, and there'll be no charge," he said promptly. "I'm only happy that Michael will have someone new to talk to. And it isn't all that difficult to learn the finger positions. It does take time to be able to read sign language, however. That and the nuances come later, with use. Actually it's a good thing for everybody to learn. There are a lot of deaf people out there who are cut off from casual day-to-day contacts simply because few people see the need to learn signing unless they're directly involved with a deaf person. Why don't I give you a chart you can study tonight? I don't come on Wednesdays—that's one of the days I visit housebound parishioners—or I'd start you out tomorrow. The sooner you begin, the sooner you can become proficient.''

"I'll do that, Reverend Turlock,'' she said. "And since you won't let me pay you, perhaps I can contribute to your—well, does your church have a building fund?''

"Please—call me Tim. The Reverend makes me feel a hundred years old.'' The lines around his eyes deepened as he added, "And my church, which is a small one, does have a building fund. Better still, you're welcome to come to church Sunday to see what we're all about.''

He went on to explain about the innovations he'd introduced since he'd taken over the small church, and then asked about her own work. For a few minutes they chatted comfortably about books, and then, armed with the sign-language chart, Raine left him with Michael to return to work. The basement seemed so empty that a warning bell rang inside her. Since her stay here was so temporary, she mustn't let Michael become too important to her or she to him. She would be friendly, yes, but she would keep a certain distance between them, not only for his sake, but for her own.

Dinner that night was an ordeal. She found it difficult to eat in the face of Jonah's stony silence and Crystal's speculative glances. Although she avoided looking directly at Jonah, she was aware of his every movement, of the way the soft light from the overhead chandelier turned his mahogany brown hair to sorrel, of the proud arch of his nose, the coiled energy of his body.

Only Michael seemed unaffected by the general tension. He stopped eating frequently to sign with his father, ignoring Crystal. At one point, he gave Raine one of the smiles that always twisted her heart a little, and when she responded, he winked as if they shared some secret.

Crystal caught their exchange. Her eyes narrowed dangerously, but her voice was honeyed as she said, "I do hope Michael hasn't been pestering you again, Raine."

"Michael was busy with Tim—with Reverend Turlock most of the day," Raine said.

The muscles in Crystal's face tightened. "Then you've met Tim Turlock?"

"Yes—he seems a nice young man."

"Young is right. He's a very immature person, even though he's a minister." She gave Raine a long thoughtful look. "What on earth did you two talk about? I find him such a—an irritating man."

Raine didn't try to hide her surprise. "Why, he was very pleasant. He's interested in the work I'm doing, especially in some nature books I unpacked this morning. He told me he was a book collector himself in a very small way, mainly books on the environment."

"Indeed?" For some reason Crystal's irritation seemed to deepen. "Well, I find him boring. And it's hard to believe he has the money to do any serious collecting. What could he possibly afford on his income?"

"To a true collector, the monetary value of the books isn't all that important except when it limits their own acquisitions," Raine said, thinking of some of her father's clients who had been a drain on his time for very little profit. "I remember one old man who was collecting the complete works of Zane Grey. Most of them, though sometimes hard to find, aren't all that valuable, and I commented to my father that if the old man sold even one of the books in his collection that *was* valuable, he could buy the rest of them easily. Dad told me I didn't understand collectors, which is true. I love books, but I guess it's what's inside the covers that matters to me, not their rarity or the condition of the binding."

"The man couldn't have been a very profitable client for your father," Jonah said, the first direct remark he'd addressed to her that evening.

"I'm sure my father earned only a tiny commission from Mr. Striver, but dad wasn't a mercenary man. He got his payment in helping other people," she retorted.

"And did you point out that he could spend his time in a more profitable way?"

"I did not. My father was—was special. There are few men today who are as kind or as generous with their time as he was." She hesitated, wishing she could see behind his impassive stare. Her motive obscure, even to herself, she added, "Oddly enough, I had the feeling today that Reverend Turlock might be that kind of man, too. I suspect his wife and kids are very lucky."

"He isn't married," Crystal said, her voice flat. Her eyes rested lightly on Jonah, then moved back to Raine. "Don't tell me he invited you to the parish house to see his book collection? Even ministers have their version of the old 'come up and see my etchings' ploy."

Before Raine could think of a polite answer to that, Michael upset his water goblet, ending the conversation—to her relief.

Later, when she was back in her room, Raine discovered that Crystal's attitude had only stiffened her determination to learn how to sign and finger spell. For a long time she studied the charts Tim Turlock had lent her, trying out the various finger positions that designated the letters of the alphabet, then practicing them over and over again until they came with more ease. It was rather like a child learning how to speak, she reflected, but of course she had the advantage of already knowing the language and the alphabet and how to spell.

When her brain seemed unable to take in any more, she put the charts away in a drawer, then took a long hot bath to soak the stiffness out of her body. She went to bed, expecting to fall asleep over the book of poems she'd brought upstairs to read, but the poems touched a chord within her. They were all about unrequited love, and an hour later, when she finally finished the slim volume and put it aside, she felt restless and knew it would be impossible to fall asleep.

After her encounter with Jonah the night before, there was no question of her going downstairs for a glass of warm milk to make her sleepy, so she decided this was a good time to write a letter to her brother and sister-in-law. But when she was seated at the room's graceful little writing table, paper and pen before her, she discovered there was little to say. How could she tell them the truth, that she was miserable here, that she'd made a mess of things—and that her own stiff-necked pride had been the cause of most of it?

So instead she wrote about the eclectic collection she was unearthing. She tried to strike a cheery note as she described the luxury of the Arlington estate, then went on to tell them about Michael. She skimmed around the subject of Jonah, saying only that she seldom saw her employer, who was very busy running his winery.

She was chewing on the end of her pen, trying to think of something to add, when it occurred to her what strangers she and Martin were these days. Their lives were so different—she with her music and he with his medicine, both closed worlds to outsiders. Although she loved Martin, they had been separated so many years that they had little in common.

The thought made her feel lonely, and unexpected tears collected underneath her eyelids. She brushed them away impatiently. Life was a series of compromises, of people drifting apart. It was time to accept the fact that now her father was gone, she was almost totally on her own. Oh, she would keep in touch with Martin and his family, but once she was embarked on a career as a concert pianist she would seldom see him.

And she couldn't even look forward to a family of her own in the foreseeable future. Not if she were realistic. How often had her mother made this clear to her? That a woman who hoped to make a success of the concert stage had no time for outside distractions? The life of a concert pianist was a lonely one, but Raine had made the choice, set her goals years ago. So why was she suddenly having these doubts? Was it because of the judgment she'd read in Jonah's eyes when he'd looked at her last night? Did it lead to self-doubt, being around someone who thought you were. . .cheap?

Well, she wasn't going to let the opinion of one man bother her. She would hold her head up high, feign an arrogance to match his own. After all, *he* was the one who had acted in a despicable manner. She had given him her first passion. He had taken advantage of her and then had discarded her with a casualness that had eaten into her self-esteem like acid, leaving scars that would never go away.

And to compound the damage, he had made another pass at her three years later, arrogantly confident that she would be overwhelmed by his masculine charms or by his fame. That he had recognized her later made no difference. When he'd first approached her, she'd been sitting in dark shadows. He couldn't possibly have known who she was when he'd casually kissed her. And if she hadn't pulled away, would he have tried to seduce her right then and there? Well, she *had* pulled away, but oh, how hard it had been! And how she had wanted him to go on kissing her, to make love to her again....

A wave of heat flooded Raine. Angrily she jumped to her feet and flung the pen down on the half-finished letter. What was wrong with her? Had she completely lost control of herself? Maybe this—this thing was like the passion for collecting they had discussed at the dinner table that night. If so, how had she allowed it to get out of hand, to turn into an obsession?

Well, from now on she would be on guard and doubly determined to stay out of Jonah's way. Maybe she could plead a headache tomorrow and take her dinner in her room. Yes, she would give herself at least one evening's respite. And she would work an hour or two in the evenings not only to get the job done faster but to make sure she was so tired at night that she fell asleep as soon as her head touched the pillow.

And since she couldn't work all the time, she'd keep busy with other things, too. The following day she'd take a trip into Mendocino and locate a piano to practice on, and for a couple of hours every day she would return to music, the one thing that had never failed her.

CHAPTER TEN

THE NEXT AFTERNOON, after checking with Tim to make sure he could spare her a few minutes for her first sign-language lesson, Raine drove into the village of Mendocino.

Although she had passed Mendocino on her way to Arlington House, she had only seen it from a distance. From Highway 1 it had looked to her rather like a combination Maine fishing village and western cow town. Now, as she drove through its narrow streets, she was charmed by its lack of pretensions, by the individuality of its homes, even by its imaginative and unconventional fences, which ranged from elaborate wrought iron to intricately constructed pickets, as if Mendocino's citizens found an outlet for their creative instincts in their fences.

Although she was aware that Mendocino had been described by journalists as a "ramshackle town," Raine decided that it had its own artless charm. The houses varied wildly from staid and proper Victorian mansions to a profusion of cottages, each seemingly from a different decade. Some were in pristine condition, while others seemed to be held together by spit and baling wire, but there was a friendliness here that made her want to get out of her car and walk up to one of the cottages, knock on the door and ask if she could come in and visit for a while.

Smiling at her own fancifulness, she drove slowly along the town's main street, a one-sided thoroughfare that looked across an open pasture to the sea. Since she was still early, she stopped in front of a small weather-beaten building that housed a gift shop and went inside to browse around, finally purchasing a collection of tiny shells for Michael, a stuffed toad for her small niece and, on impulse, a pretty head scarf for Tilda.

When she had paid for her purchases, she asked directions to the town's public library. The clerk, a long-haired young man with a cheerful smile, gave her such elaborate directions that she finally suspected he was trying to prolong their conversation. After thanking him she drove off and soon was examining the rather Spartan supply of books on the shelves of a small public library. Although she couldn't find a book on deafness, she did find one on Mendocino County. Giving Tim Turlock as a reference, she signed up for a card and checked the book out.

Following Tim's directions, she located the spire of his church, which he had described to her as looking like a cracker box with an inverted ice-cream cone on top, and headed toward it, knowing he lived next door. A few minutes later she was pulling up in front of a comfortable-looking bungalow.

Although the house obviously dated from the twenties, its wide wooden porch wore a fresh coat of white paint, and baskets of fuchsia hung from its ceiling, reminding her that this was a moist cool climate despite the unusually sunny afternoons since she'd been there. She was wondering if Tim was the one with the green thumb when he opened the front door and waved at her. "This is the right place. Come on in, Raine."

The living room he ushered her into was as unpretentious as the house, but its sturdy mission-oak tables and desk, a tall bookshelf filled with books, the shabby but comfortable-looking sofa and chairs, well supplied with needlepoint cushions, gave it a homey look.

Here, too, a profusion of growing plants gave evidence of someone's green thumb—not the exotic palms and crotons of a city apartment but old-fashioned, down-to-earth geraniums and creeping charley and wandering jew. As she looked around with bemused eyes, Raine reflected that while Tim looked perfectly at home in such surroundings, he would also fit in anywhere, including a mansion like Arlington House.

"I'd better warn you," Tim said, smiling at her. "My aunt has prepared some of her sinfully rich coconut cookies for you. She'll be insulted if you don't finish off at least three. I have to run a mile extra every day to work off the ones she forces on me."

He patted his lean stomach, looking so rueful that she had to laugh. Maybe because he reminded her so much of her own brother, or because there was none of the speculation she usually saw in men's eyes, she felt as if she'd known him all her life.

"Your aunt lives with you?"

"She's my only living relative, and a great old gal even if she does spend her life trying to marry me off to one of her cronies' granddaughters. So if she has a predatory gleam in her eye when she gets a look at you, you'll know why. I thought about telling her you were married with five kids, but it didn't seem in keeping with my calling."

She laughed again, and as she took the chair he offered her eyes fell on a book, the biography of a famous symphony conductor, lying open on a nearby chair. "Are you interested in biography?" she asked, staring at the title.

"Actually it's the subject of the book that interests me. I dabble in music a bit."

"Piano?"

"No, I blow the coolest oboe this side of San Francisco," he bragged immodestly.

Raine smiled at the smugness in his voice. "I'm a Juilliard graduate myself," she confessed.

"What's your specialty—no, let me guess." He examined her thoughtfully for a while. "Piano," he said finally.

"You should be a detective, or maybe you're a mind reader," she said, impressed.

"Well, I weighed all the evidence, the way you sit—back very straight, knees together. And then there's the slight flattening of your fingertip pads...."

Dismayed, Raine stared down at her hands. When Tim laughed, she realized he'd been teasing her.

"Very funny," she said. "How did you really guess which instrument I play?"

"Because that's the first one that came to your mind when you asked what *I* play," he said.

"So you're something of a psychologist, are you?"

"That's what I started out to be. Then the Lord called me and I changed over to theology." His voice was matter-of-fact, attesting to the sincerity of his commitment. "And if you knew what a hell raiser I was as a kid, you'd understand why my friends still shake their heads in disbelief."

"Well, I have a feeling you're very good at your profession." She hesitated, then added, "Since you must know just about everybody in Mendocino, I wonder if you could help me with a personal problem?"

"Anything I can do, just ask."

"I don't want to stay away from the piano too long as I hope to start training soon for competition. Since music is a forbidden subject at Arlington House—"

"Say no more. I know all about Jonah's musical hang-ups. As it happens, I think I can help you. Follow me." He led her through another door into a sunny dining room. When she saw an upright piano, old but obviously well cared for, sitting between two windows, she gave an involuntary smile.

"Use it whenever you like," Tim said. "It's a veteran of five decades of choir-practice sessions, but it doesn't get much use now. One of our parishioners gave the church a new organ, so we moved the piano over here. My aunt sometimes bangs on it a little, but most of the time it just sits there. Luckily I did have it tuned a few weeks ago. It's available whenever you're in Mendocino."

"Great. I'll rent it from you."

"No charge. At least not money."

"I don't understand."

"The charge will be your continued interest in Michael. The boy worries me. He's become more and more withdrawn during the past few months. But I noticed a big change in him yesterday, which I have to lay at your door. Just continue to be his friend, and learn to sign quickly. He needs to be able to communicate with as many people as possible so that when his father finally decides to let him go to school, it will be much easier for him."

She nodded. "It's a bargain, but I'd do that anyway. I find him a very appealing youngster."

"You're right. He's a wonderful kid who has a way of getting under your skin. But I have to warn you, I'm persona non grata with Crystal since I voiced some of my opinions. I think Michael should be going to school, taking his knocks, learning how to cope with his deafness instead of being wrapped in cotton wool. A group of us here in Mendocino are starting up a school for handicapped children. He wouldn't even have to board away from home. I made the mistake of trying to get Crystal to make Jonah change his mind about sending Michael to school. She threw me out of the house. It seems she doesn't like unsolicited advice from an outsider, especially where Michael is concerned."

"But she loves the boy. Surely she must want what's best for him," Raine protested.

"What she *thinks* is best for him," Tim corrected.

He hesitated, and for a moment she caught a haunted look in his eye. "She's a mixed-up girl, so defensive of what's hers. If you'd known that family of hers, you'd understand. Elaine, Crystal's sister, was one of the most beautiful women I've ever seen. Granton Arlington, their father, doted on her. Crystal was never important to him and yet she was the one who nursed him during his last illness, who was fiercely loyal to him. When he died, Crystal transferred her loyalty to her sister, who treated her like a servant, then to the boy. Now she's scared to death that something—or someone—will upset the status quo at Arlington House and she'll be out in the cold. That's why she's the way she is. Underneath that toughness she's just a scared kid."

"You seem to know a lot about Crystal," Raine said.

"I've lived in Mendocino most of my life. Crystal went to the local schools until her father sent her to an eastern finishing school when she was a teenager. After she came back to Mendocino, we dated briefly. For a while I hoped—'' He broke off, looking rueful. ''You don't want to hear my war tales. This is just a friendly warning from a scarred old veteran. Be careful not to get too emotionally involved with the family. Crystal has a way of seeing things the way she wants them to be instead of how they really are. As for Jonah—he locked his heart away when Elaine died. You could get frostbite if you let your guard down.''

Having given his warning, Tim turned away to run his fingers across the yellowed keys of the piano. ''It isn't in a class with a grand piano, but maybe it will suit your needs,'' he remarked, and she knew he'd said all he intended to on the subject of the Arlingtons.

For half an hour he drilled her in the finger spelling alphabet and set up some words and phrases for her to work on. He gave her a book to study, then excused himself to go on his visiting rounds. Raine opened the piano, sat down at the bench and rested her fingers on the keys, but she didn't start practicing immediately because her mind was too filled with unanswered questions.

Tim must have been very close to Crystal at one time to know so much about how her mind worked. Had that been the pain of unrequited love she'd seen in his eyes when he'd spoken of the dark-haired woman?

Realizing she was wasting time, she tried to put everything else out of her mind. A few notes told her that while the piano was far inferior to what she was used to, at least it was in tune. Not knowing she would be practicing that day, she hadn't brought any music with her. Since the hymns on the music rack didn't appeal to her, she did a few finger exercises, then switched to a Bach Two-Part Invention to relax her fingers, which were stiff from lack of practice and the unaccustomed hard physical work she'd been doing.

Despite her determination to shut out the world while she was practicing, she found it difficult to concentrate. After she'd made a complete hash of a mordent, she finally gave up on the invention and worked on a few difficult phrases from Beethoven's Sonata in F Minor, one of the first sonatas she'd ever committed to memory. The staccato notes of its broken chords seemed to match her own chaotic emotions and she felt herself relaxing as she gave herself to the music.

Later, she couldn't remember changing pieces. Despite her determination to utilize this precious time to full advantage, her thoughts drifted and her mind filled with images of Jonah, of the smoldering passion in his eyes when he'd kissed her in the kitchen, of her own wild and uncontrollable response, and the shock, the shame she'd felt when he'd pulled away, his cynical words reducing her to an object of his lust. . . .

When she came back to reality she realized that she was playing the love theme from *Tristan und Isolde*, a lament to unrequited love. Although she broke off immediately, the melody, so dissonant and full of yearning, so abortive in its unresolved ending, still echoed in her ears, and she felt a wave of grief that a feeling that could have been so beautiful held only pain and disillusionment.

As she sat there fighting tears, the door opened and a tiny gray-haired woman bustled in carrying a tray. She looked Raine over thoroughly, then gave an abrupt little nod as though she'd just passed some test.

"I'm Louise Bodine—but do call me Aunt Louise like everybody else does," she said in a trilling voice that reminded Raine of a sparrow chirping. "You don't know what a treat it is having someone play that piano like it should be done. But now that you've stopped, I thought you'd like some tea and cookies, or would you prefer coffee?"

"Tea will be fine," Raine said, smiling at her. Although it was getting late and she'd stayed away longer than she'd planned, she knew there'd be no getting away until she'd satisfied the curiosity that seemed to radiate from Tim's aunt. During the next few minutes she found out a lot about Tim, including a page-by-page examination of a photograph album that showed him in every stage of development from tiny infant to the present. She also ate several of the sinfully rich coconut cookies, enjoying every bite. In gratitude, she told Aunt Louise a little about herself, describing the job she was doing at Arlington House. At last she rose, saying she must get back to work.

It was almost six o'clock by the time she reached Arlington House. She parked the Mustang next to

Crystal's Trans-Am in the six-car garage and hurried into the house. As she was passing the open library door, heading for the kitchen, Jonah's voice hailed her. Reluctantly she turned into the library to find Jonah and Crystal standing by the French doors that opened out onto a small flagstone terrace, drinking sherry.

"I see you took some time off from work," Jonah said.

Although his voice was polite, she was sure she read censure in his appraising glance and she stiffened, instantly defensive. "I needed a break so I went into Mendocino to look around and do some shopping."

"You went shopping in *Mendocino*?" Crystal exclaimed. "What on earth could you buy there that you couldn't find a better supply of in Fort Bragg?"

Although her question overstepped the bounds of good manners, her tone was so amused that not to have answered her, or to show annoyance, would have seemed an overreaction. *How does she do it?* Raine asked herself. *How does she say the most intrusive things and still manage to sound so reasonable?*

"I wanted to buy a stuffed animal for my niece," Raine said.

"I suppose Tim was giving you advice on kiddies' toys?"

"Reverend Turlock?" Raine said, her heart skipping a beat.

"Oh, I'm sure you're calling him Tim by now," Crystal drawled.

"I'm afraid the point of this whole conversation escapes me," Raine said, fighting anger.

"We stopped at the freight depot in Mendocino on the way home to pick up some equipment for the winery and saw your car parked in front of the parsonage," Crystal said, smiling brightly. "Your private life is none of our business, of course. As a matter of fact, I was just teasing you."

Or testing me to see if I'd lie, Raine thought, very much aware of Jonah's brooding presence.

"I had a personal problem to talk over with Tim," she said. "Since he *is* a minister and used to giving advice, it seemed the natural thing to do."

"Yes, indeed. And was he able to help you?" There were two bright spots of color in Crystal's cheeks that Raine read as anger, which brought up an interesting question. Just what was going on between Tim and Crystal? Or rather, what *had* gone on between them before their quarrel?

"He was very helpful," Raine said. "Will you excuse me, please? I'd like to get ready for dinner."

It wasn't until she'd left the library that she remembered she'd decided to take a tray to her room that evening. Since it was a little late to plead a headache, she decided to reserve it for another evening and hurried to her room.

Quickly she went through her skimpy wardrobe, finally deciding on the same long skirt she'd worn before but with a different blouse, this one a light blue jersey that was loose enough to conceal the fullness of her breasts. With the idea of making herself look as businesslike as possible, she twisted her hair into a tidy knot on the nape of her neck and fastened it with a tortoiseshell clasp before applying light color lip gloss. Satisfied that she looked like the working woman she was, she went downstairs, dreading the meal ahead.

But to her surprise, Crystal had changed her tactics and was friendly, at least outwardly. Raine had taken pains to look as casual as possible, but it was obvious that Crystal had had other ideas. She was wearing a spectacular hostess gown, adroitly draped to show off her petite figure to perfection, and Raine thought she looked rather like a princess with diamonds sparkling in her earlobes and on her graceful fingers.

As Crystal looked her over, Raine fought back an impulse to hide her hands. The work she'd been doing had taken its toll, and after she'd broken several fingernails she'd been forced to file the rest of them down, too. A couple of paper cuts and a bruise on the back of her wrist where she'd banged it against a crate completed the disaster. As she buttered a roll, aware of Jonah's close scrutiny, too, she felt an irrational desire to go upstairs, brush out her severe hairstyle and put on her sexiest dress in an act of defiance.

She must have smiled at the thought of Crystal's reaction if she should give in to her impulse because Jonah's eyes sharpened suddenly and a frown furrowed his forehead. When he returned his attention to his food, she felt absurdly relieved.

During the next half hour, although Crystal included her in the conversation, the patronage in her tone pointed out that Raine was there as an employee, not as a guest. Dispassionately Raine wondered where Crystal had learned her tricks. From her sister? Or was it a natural talent for putting her social inferiors in their place? And which one was the real Crystal Arlington? The concerned and loving woman she'd seen rocking Michael in her arms after his nightmare, or this woman with her thin veneer of politeness, her subtle put-downs?

To Raine's surprise, when he finally joined the conversation, Jonah had put aside his mocking tone, and once again she felt the full force of the charm that had so captivated her at their first meeting. Although he didn't mention music, he did talk about books, revealing a surprisingly wide knowledge of the subject. When she'd enrolled at Juilliard and had been exposed for the first time to large groups of musicians, Raine had discovered that they could be surprisingly single-minded, with little interest in anything that didn't pertain to the world of classical music.

Now she realized that Jonah was different, that his interests were wide-ranging, and she almost forgot the tension between them as she became engrossed in a lively discussion about the latest Nobel prize for literature.

Crystal, looking increasingly restive, finally broke into their two-sided conversation. "Have you found anything more of interest in my father's collection?" she asked.

"I've only unpacked a small portion of the crates, but yes, some of the books I've examined are quite fascinating. Your father collected mostly first editions without much discrimination, so it's quite a mixture. Some of the books are very old but have little value, while some of the newer ones are collectors' items. And there's one full crate of signed books that, well, I'll have to do some further checking, but I think they might turn out to be worth quite a lot of money."

"Something the de Young Museum might be interested in?" Jonah said, setting down his wineglass.

Raine hesitated. "I'm not sure. As I say, I need to check further. It's impossible to be an expert on everything, but it's very possible the books would interest the museum."

Her blue eyes showing interest, Crystal leaned forward to ask, "What are the titles of the books?"

Raine started to answer, then hesitated. Her first thought on finding the books had been that Michael would love to browse through them and she'd been looking forward to showing them to him. Now she was sorry she'd mentioned them. If they turned out to be valuable, would Jonah consent to letting Michael handle them?

"Why don't I check to make sure they're what I think they are?" she said finally.

Crystal's laugh had a cutting edge. "It's good that you come so highly recommended, Raine, or that kind of evasion would make me wonder,'' she said sweetly.

Raine felt a warning warmth in her cheeks, a feeling of congestion behind her eyes. Involuntarily she looked at Jonah, and when she saw the steely look in his eyes, she knew that she couldn't allow herself the luxury of showing anger.

Summoning all her self-control, she produced a smile that she knew must look as insincere as Crystal's. ''Then of course I'll tell you what the books are. I found a crate still bearing a New York postmark dated 1943, and when I opened it I found a collection of Jack London's books, all first editions and all personally signed. I know they're of considerable value, but I'm not sure just how rare they are. I've consulted my catalogs and my father's desiderat list—that's a list of desired books most dealers compile for their own use—but I need to talk to someone with more specialized knowledge.''

Jonah's eyebrows rose. ''Very interesting. Perhaps I'll keep one or two for Michael. He has a weakness for adventure stories.''

Michael, who had been watching them while he stuffed his mouth with Tilda's chocolate cake, must have recognized his own name on his father's lips because he signed a question to Jonah.

Jonah's face softened as he answered his son, his hands moving swiftly. As Raine stared at his hands, so graceful despite the bluntness of his fingers and his square workmanlike palms, an old memory stirred. How surely, how expertly those same hands had taught passion to her inexperienced body, unleashing a hunger that still tormented her....

A hot flush rose to her cheeks. Afraid that Jonah might see and guess what she was thinking, she quickly raised her wineglass to her lips. When she finally lowered it again, Crystal was standing, holding out her hand to Michael.

"I promised I'd play a game of backgammon with Michael before he does his homework," she said. Briefly her eyes rested on Raine. "I'll be back in a little while to have a glass of brandy with you in the library, Jonah."

Raine watched the two of them leave with a feeling of panic, realizing that she would be alone with Jonah. Hurriedly she rose, too, but as she passed Jonah's chair, he reached out and laid his hand on her arm, holding her there.

"What's the problem, Carmen?" he said, his voice mocking. "Don't you trust yourself to be alone with me?"

There was enough truth in his statement to stir her anger again. Somehow she managed to hold it in check and glare at him coldly, but he only looked amused. Although his grasp was light, his fingers felt like hot shackles on her arm, crowding in upon her senses and heightening her awareness of his nearness.

When she tried to pull away, his grasp on her arm tightened and he pulled her down upon his lap. As she felt the muscular strength of his thighs beneath her, as his warmth invaded her own limbs, a protest rose in her throat. But before it could escape, he lowered his head and kissed her parted lips, effectively silencing her.

A sweetness like a tidal wave turned her bones to water. She wanted to escape from his arms, but something reckless and hungry held her there, drowning in his kiss. His hands slid up her arms, under the loose sleeves of her blouse, and she felt an impulse to lean against him, to bury herself in the shelter of his arms.

"Stop playing this silly game with me, Raine. You know you want me as much as I want you," Jonah murmured as he nuzzled her throat. "The pulse in your neck is fluttering like crazy, giving you away. Let me come to your room tonight and I promise it will be the way it was the first time. But first, admit you want me. Because I don't pay for sex."

His words cut through the golden haze that had temporarily blotted out everything else. She felt their cruelty as if it were a physical blow. Drawing upon her pride, she jerked away, extracting herself from his arms. As she hurried toward the hall door, she heard his low laugh behind her, but she didn't turn around. She would not let him guess her humiliation or how much she had been tempted. Not if it killed her.

Her step unsteady but her chin held high and proud, she left the room, and it wasn't until she was well out of Jonah's sight that she stopped to press her hands tightly against her breasts. But even this moment of respite was denied her. When she heard rapid footsteps on the stairs she straightened quickly, and by the time Crystal had reached her, her face was expressionless, her smile fixed and polite.

"Going up to bed already, Raine?" Crystal asked.

"I'm a little tired. I thought I'd read awhile before I go to sleep," Raine said.

"You've had a very busy day, haven't you?" Crystal's eyes narrowed into the appraising look that Raine had already learned to be wary of. "Before you go to your room, there's something I want to show you. It'll just take a few minutes."

Not waiting for a reply, Crystal turned and started back up the stairs. Raine was tempted to call after her and ask if it couldn't wait until another time, but she decided that it wasn't worth the trouble. Crystal had said it would only take a few minutes. Why make a fuss about something so unimportant?

Silently she followed Crystal up the stairs to the second floor and then down a long L-shaped hall. She had assumed they were heading for Crystal's bedroom, but Crystal continued on past her own room, then Michael's room, finally stopping in front of a heavily paneled door.

"This is the master suite. I think you should see it so you'll understand Jonah better." Crystal turned a large brass handle, pulled the door open, and the odor of roses filled the hall. For a brief moment she paused as if bracing herself, before she opened the door the rest of the way, beckoning for Raine to follow her inside.

When she switched on a lamp, a flood of light blinded Raine for a few seconds. As soon as her eyes adjusted to the change, she looked around curiously, not knowing what to expect.

Her first impression was of luxury—a sensuous and lush luxury. A huge four-poster bed with fluted posts sat on a dais, dominating the room. The spread that covered it was made of pink satin, the same material as the window drapes and the upholstery on a low chaise longue. An exquisite hand-painted *poudre* table stood in front of the windows, its top crowded with crystal perfume bottles, an assortment of cosmetics and an ivory comb-and-brush set. Underfoot, a deep pink rug added to the illusion that she was standing in a box of valentine candy.

Raine tried to imagine Jonah here, sitting on the chaise longue, sleeping in the bed, but failed. This must have been his dead wife's room. Why did it look as if its occupant had just stepped out for a minute and would be right back?

Crystal crossed the room to a small alcove. She pressed a light switch, revealing an ornately framed portrait. The woman in the portrait was beautiful; her lips were lush and full, and her face a perfect oval. Her hair, the color of spun gold, molded her small head, emphasizing the provocative slant of her green eyes. She was smiling, but the smile seemed to hold irony, as if she found the idea of having her portrait painted amusing but also rather a bore.

The odor of roses seemed to intensify, and for the first time Raine noticed a large bouquet of freshly cut flowers sitting on a small table beneath the portrait.

She tore her gaze away and turned to Crystal, intending to ask her why she had brought her here, but the question died on her lips. Crystal was staring up at the portrait; her eyes seemed glazed and she looked very young, as if time had been rewound, taking her back to an earlier day.

Even her voice had a childish sound as she pointed to the portrait and said, "This is Elaine. It was painted just before my sister was—before she left us. She always wore pink—it was her signature color. Those albums over there on the desk are filled with photographs of her. Even when she was still a baby she looked like an angel. 'My angel,' daddy called her. He said once that Elaine was his reward for a long hard life. He married so late, you see, and then mother died when I was born. So there was only the three of us. Then when daddy died there was just Elaine and me."

She fell silent, her eyes still fixed on her sister's portrait. The odor of the roses was cloying, oppressive, and Raine wanted to leave, but before she could formulate some excuse, Crystal's voice went on.

"Then Elaine married Jonah, and a year later Michael was born. You might think I'd be jealous, but I wasn't. I knew he belonged to me as much as he did to Elaine. She was—her health was so delicate that I had to take care of him, feed him and bathe him. Elaine didn't want a nurse under-foot. It was just as if Michael were mine. . . . ''

Her voice trailed off, and Raine felt an acute embarrassment, as if she'd blundered into a bath-room while someone was bathing.

"Was your sister much older than you?"

Crystal's eyes returned to her face. "Five years older. Daddy told me once that they hadn't planned to have any more children after Elaine was born. My mother was very delicate and the doctors warned her not to get pregnant again. When it happened anyway, she wouldn't have an abortion. So you see, she gave her life for me and that's why I had to make it up to daddy and Elaine."

Again she fell silent, her gaze wandering back to the portrait.

"You must have been very close to your sister," Raine said.

"She depended upon me for everything. Some-times Jonah was gone so long on his tours and she got very lonely, but she always had me. She met Jonah while she was on a trip to New York, and even after they were married and living most of the time in the East, she asked me to stay on here and take care of things. Daddy had left the house to her, you see, but that's only because he knew I'd always have a home here."

She gestured around the room. "Jonah keeps Elaine's room just the way it was the night she died. He still can't bear to get rid of her things. Oh, he has his women from time to time, but he never brings them here. Even though he's been out of the public's eye for two years, women still pester him. Being a normal man with a man's— well, a man's appetites, he has his affairs, but they never last long, and in the end the women are the ones who get hurt. I sometimes wish I could warn them, but would they listen? What do you think, Raine? Is it *my* responsibility to warn anyone foolish enough to think Jonah could ever forget Elaine and remarry?"

Raine took a deep breath. "I'm sure you don't need my advice," she said. "And if this is some kind of warning to me, I am in no danger of misunderstanding Mr. Duncan's natural courtesy."

Crystal's lips curved into a smile. "Jonah is very attractive. Not that he deliberately sets out to seduce susceptible women. I think he tries hard to fight his, uh, baser impulses. Now that he no longer has his music as an outlet for his energy, he often takes long walks at night when he's unable to sleep. That's why he jogs and swims. Sometimes he goes way out beyond the breakers. But it's only a substitute for music—and for Elaine. And I'm afraid that his women serve the same purpose."

She snapped off the light above her sister's portrait. "Do be careful. You're an attractive girl, and Jonah is between affairs right now."

In spite of herself, Raine found herself recalling how casually Jonah had made a pass at someone he'd thought to be a stranger. Crystal, whatever her motives, was truthful on that point. To Jonah, one attractive woman was like the next, another conquest in a long line of conquests, and to get caught in his tentacles again, now that she was older, wiser, would be sheer insanity.

"Thank you for the warning," she said aloud. "Even though it isn't needed, I know you have my well-being at heart."

Although she'd meant it as irony, her voice must have sounded sincere, because Crystal's face flooded with color. She turned away quickly and went to unlatch a window, throwing it open to the evening breeze. "I'll stay awhile and air out the room," she said, not looking at Raine. "Good night, Raine."

"Good night," Raine echoed.

Feeling as if she'd just escaped from a rose-scented trap, Raine went to her own room, but as she got ready for bed, it wasn't Jonah or Michael or even her own mixed-up emotions she was thinking of, but Crystal, who again had managed to surprise her. She also made a discovery. While she was still wary of Crystal, instinct telling her that the older woman could be dangerous, she was finding it harder and harder to dislike her.

CHAPTER ELEVEN

DURING THE NEXT TWO WEEKS Raine stayed busy, cramming so much activity into her days that when she went to bed at night she fell asleep immediately from sheer exhaustion. Not only was she determined to finish the cataloging job as quickly as possible, but she wanted to make sure there was no time for brooding, for reconstructing in her mind that last humiliating encounter with Jonah, thinking up cutting remarks she could have said. Since it was too late for second thoughts she tried to put it out of her mind and was, in general, successful.

It helped that while she had braced herself for more unpleasantness with Jonah, it didn't come.

At dinner he was cordial, speaking of such unimportant things as books and wine or, when he discovered her interest in old houses, telling her stories about the origin of Arlington House. At other times he avoided her company as if he had finally tired of baiting her. In return she was reserved but civil, and away from the dinner table she was careful to stay out of his way.

Now that Crystal had warned Raine about the danger of getting involved emotionally with Jonah, she dropped the veiled hostility and treated

Raine as she would any other guest. Even so, since Raine didn't care to be the recipient of any more unwanted advice, she avoided Crystal as much as possible, too.

Although she spent her mornings and late afternoons working, she went into Mendocino every day right after lunch for a two-hour session at Tim Turlock's cranky old piano. The practicing she did was unsatisfactory, merely a holding tactic to keep her fingers supple, especially since she often ended up playing to please Aunt Louise, who had a weakness for Chopin and who was such an appreciative audience.

Once, without thinking, she began playing one of Jonah's sonatas. As soon as she realized what she was doing, she stopped and changed back to Chopin. She told herself that it was a natural slip because this particular sonata was one of the pieces she'd committed to memory, but in her heart she knew it was because the image of Jonah seemed to haunt her, hovering constantly in the back of her mind. The realization that he had so much power over her thoughts was sobering. Once again, she wondered if she were making a mistake, remaining in such close proximity to Jonah. Was she playing with fire, opening herself up to more pain than her battered heart could take?

It soon became accepted that after she had finished practicing for the afternoon, she would have tea with Aunt Louise. Sometimes when Tim was free he joined them and helped Raine practice sign language. She found the new skill she was acquiring absorbing, and every day she could see an improvement in her speed and accuracy. Soon she had mastered many common signs, and her excellent memory, trained from years of visualizing and memorizing music scores, served her well.

When Tim praised her she glowed with satisfaction, knowing that his praise was deserved. She still hadn't used sign language with Michael, not only because she wanted to improve her recognition skills first but because she was saving it as a surprise, her gift to Michael on his ninth birthday at the end of the month.

As the days passed and Jonah made no more attempts to see her alone, she allowed herself to relax, to fall into a comfortable daily routine. More and more Michael sought out her company, but only, she noticed, when Crystal and Jonah were gone from the house. In the mornings, soon after she went to the basement to start work, she would hear Jonah's car moving along the driveway in front of the house. Shortly afterward Michael was sure to appear in the doorway with an offer to help.

For an hour or two he helped her stack books or unpack a new crate, then, when she insisted he'd done enough for the day, he curled up on an old blanket with one of the children's books she'd kept out for him. On mornings when he had lessons with Tim Turlock, he returned to eat lunch with her, staying until she left for her own practice sessions in town. On her return he would be waiting to keep her company again. When she insisted that he needed fresh air and sun, he never argued with her. But invariably in an hour or so he would be back, looking so shy and uncertain that she never had the heart to send him away the second time.

Once, when he was helping her unpack a crate, she reached out without thinking to push his tousled hair back from his wide forehead. He turned grave questioning eyes upon her, and then, as naturally as if he'd done it all his life, he returned the favour, tucking a flyaway strand of Raine's hair behind her ear.

She wanted to take him in her arms and give him a big hug, but something stronger than the rush of affection she felt stopped her. She was already becoming too important in Michael's life. It wouldn't be fair if she allowed him to become even more attached to her. As Jonah had pointed out once, Michael had already lost too much in his young life.

So she turned away and went back to work, and after that she was careful not to touch him again.

Three weeks after she'd come to Arlington House Raine returned from Mendocino an hour later than usual because she'd stopped to return the library book she'd borrowed and to browse through the library stacks. As she let herself in the front door she saw Tilda coming out of one of the rooms that opened into the long central hall.

Before she could speak, Tilda, who hadn't seen her, was already heading for the kitchen. Raine started to follow her, then stopped as she came abreast of the room Tilda had just left. Curiously she studied the elaborately carved door. From the rich patina of its dark brown wood she guessed that it was very old, even older than the house, and she remembered Jonah telling her that Granton Arlington's father had collected treasures from all over the world to incorporate into the house. The carvings, of exquisite workmanship, were of musical instruments—violins and cellos and harps—and she wondered what Old World castle or manor house the door had originally graced.

Unable to resist temptation, she gave the door a tentative push. It swung open silently and easily, as if inviting her to come in.

Although the room's four windows, tall and narrow and all on one wall, were fully shuttered, shrouding it in shadows, she realized immediately that this was a music room. The ceiling, like all those in the old house, was very high, festooned with garlands of plaster rosebuds, and the walls were wood paneled, adding to the gloom. Dustcovers, ghostly pale in the dim light, hid a variety of musical instruments, but she recognized a shape that could only have been a harp, another that seemed to hide a small harpsichord.

A ray of late afternoon sun crept through a crack in the shutters and fell across a majestic grand piano sitting in front of the windows. Unlike the other instruments, the piano was uncovered; a folded piece of muslin lay on the floor beside it. Had it been Tilda who had pulled off its dustcover? Surely she wasn't a secret piano player.

And why had she left without closing the door behind her? Did she intend to return?

Raine hesitated, then, yielding to temptation once more, she crossed to the piano, unconsciously moving very quietly as if she might awaken some sleeping guardian of the room. Expecting to find the piano locked, she pushed on the lid, but to her surprise it rose easily. Ivory keys, yellowed with age, gleamed softly as she ran her hand experimentally over them. The tone was full-bodied and mellow, and she saw from the nameplate above the lid that the piano was a Steinway.

As she seated herself on the narrow bench she wondered why Jonah had allowed these reminders of his old life to remain in the house. Why hadn't he stripped the room of its musical instruments and converted it into a den or even a storage room? Was it because even making that kind of decision had been too painful?

On the music stand a yellowed music score caught her eye. She read the penciled-in title and involuntarily winced, recognizing the angular handwriting as Jonah's.

Sonata for My Love....

There was a painful restriction in her throat as she slowly turned the pages of the score, translating the handwritten notes into music in her mind. When she reached the final page she realized the sonata was unfinished, or perhaps the last part had been lost. Did that explain why the sonata was unfamiliar to her, who knew Jonah's work so well?

Without conscious volition her fingers moved

over the piano keys, picking out the notes. The theme was melodious, with the dynamic overtones that were Jonah's trademark, but it also had a lyrical quality that touched something deep inside Raine's heart. Unexpectedly her sight blurred and she was forced to stop because she could no longer see the notes.

How long had this unfinished sonata been lying here forgotten on the music rack? Why had Jonah never finished it? And what a pity that his genius, the pleasure he could still give the world, had been lost. If things were different between them, if her opinion had any influence upon Jonah, she would never stop trying to convince him to go on with his music—

"Oh, you shouldn't be in here, Raine!"

Raine turned to see Tilda standing in the doorway. She was pushing a vacuum cleaner and there was a small wire basket filled with cleaning tools on her arm. "Mr. Jonah don't allow nobody in here."

"But I saw you coming out of this room," Raine said, rising.

"Well, I just can't see letting the finish on that beautiful old piano go to ruin for want of a little lemon oil and a good dusting now and then." Tilda's voice was aggrieved. "The room's real tight, made that way on purpose to keep out the damp, but I slip in and give it a good airing on sunny days, even though Jonah did lock the door and throw away the key."

"When was this?"

"Two years ago, right after Elaine was killed. It's downright criminal, if you ask me, an antique like that piano and that beautiful old harp not being used. Well, I can't do nothing about that, seeing as I don't know one note from another. But I do dust and vacuum in here regular and rub lemon oil into the wood to keep the finish from feathering. A couple of times, when Mr. Jonah and Crystal went into the city for a day, I had a man come in from the village to give it a good tuning."

"Aren't you afraid the piano tuner will talk?"

Tilda snorted. "Lord no! Not that close-mouthed old buzzard. I told him I'd cut off his— uh, ear if'n he told it around town." She gave Raine a long thoughtful look. "I heard you playing when I was coming down the hall with my cleaning tools. It sounded real pretty, and familiar, too."

Raine pointed to the music score. "I was playing one of Mr. Duncan's sonatas, the one on the stand."

"So that's where I heard it before. I've been looking at that piece of sheet music whenever I come in here to dust and vacuum, wondering if it was the one Jonah was working on when he got word about Elaine's accident."

"He was here that day?"

"It was late at night, but, yes, he was home. He'd been in the East on one of his tours, but he got a chance to come back to California for a couple of days to see Elaine and the boy. Then, when he got here, she and Michael was gone. We never did know where she was heading that night, but she had the accident on the old coast highway, going around one of them sharp curves. And why she had the boy with her is a mystery, too. When Jonah got home and found out she'd left the house without saying anything to me or Crystal, he was, well, real upset. He went into the music room, like he always did when things bothered him, and he was still in here playing when I called him to the phone. It was the state police, telling him about the accident.''

She shook her head, looking fretful. ''I never did see a man fall apart like he did. His face, well, it looked like one of them death masks. Run out of here like a crazy man, heading for the hospital in Fort Bragg where they'd taken Elaine and the boy. After the funeral, he stayed in here for a long time by hisself. When he finally came out, that's when he locked the door and threw away the key.''

''How do you get in?'' Raine said, speaking a little loudly because of the thundering in her ears.

''I picked that key out of the trash can.'' Tilda gave Raine a defensive look. ''I told Luke, 'It ain't right, letting Granton's old piano just rot away.' The old man loved that piano. He couldn't play worth a hoot hisself—no natural talent, you see. But he was always having them musical evenings and he sponsored a lot of young people, paid their tuition and expenses so they could study with the best teachers, even sent some of them to Europe— like he did Jonah. Well, when I said that to Luke about it not being right, he told me to mind my own business, but Lord, if everybody did that, what kind of world would this be?''

She stopped to heave a deep sigh, then, with studied casualness, added, ''Mr. Blake, the old man who keeps the piano tuned, did say it was best if someone played it regular. Seems a shame to just let it sit there, nobody getting any use out of it.''

An idea came to Raine then, one she knew had just been planted by Tilda.

''I've been using Reverend Turlock's piano, but why can't I practice here from now on?'' she said. ''With Jonah and Crystal gone during the day, who's to know? It would save me time, and besides, I'm gaining weight eating Aunt Louise's coconut cookies.''

Tilda pursed her lips. She made a show of thinking it over before she said, ''I reckon it would be okay. I won't be a party to going against Jonah's orders, you understand, but if'n you was to come across that key in the kitchen junk drawer, the one next to the range, that wouldn't be my fault, would it? And you don't have to worry. Luke won't say nothing to Jonah or Crystal. He might not approve, but he won't snitch on you.''

''Then it's settled,'' Raine said. ''The old upright at the parsonage is pretty—well, the best that can be said about it is that it has the requisite eighty-eight keys. I'm grateful to Reverend Turlock, of course, for letting me use it.''

''He's a nice fellow. I've knowed him since he was a kid, always getting into devilment. Too bad him and Crystal had that falling out. She was different when they were talking about getting married.''

"Are you saying that Crystal was engaged to Tim Turlock?''

"Well, it hadn't been announced yet, but he'd asked her and she'd accepted. Happy as a lark she was—at least for a while. Then they had that quarrel, and just like that it was all over. The minister, he's got a temper, for all that he's usually so easy-going. And Crystal can be real difficult. From what they was shouting at each other, she took it for granted that after they got married they'd stay here at Arlington House with Jonah and the boy. He told her, well, what he said was, 'No way am I going to live in another man's house.'

"Then they fought some more, mostly about how she'd been coddling the boy, and she finally told him to get out, that she never wanted to see him again. He took her to her word, I guess, although he still tutors the boy. Crystal, she cried for a week, went creeping around here like a ghost, but when he finally called she couldn't talk to him on the phone. I've knowed her all her life and I still can't figure her out.''

Her face gloomy, Tilda bent to plug in the vacuum cleaner and Raine went upstairs to change back into her work clothes. Now that she had time to think it over, she wondered if it was really wise to defy Jonah's edict. She could justify using the piano at the parsonage because it was in Mendocino, miles away from Arlington House. But to go into a locked room to play Jonah's own piano...that was really flirting with danger.

Of course it *would* save her the time she wasted going back and forth to Mendocino—not to mention her pleasant, but time-consuming visits with the garrulous Aunt Louise. Since she was progressing so fast on the signing lessons, she no longer needed Tim's instructions, and she could always enlist Tilda's help since she was proficient in sign language, too. She could spend the extra time working longer hours on her cataloging. As for her chances of being caught, maybe Tilda would agree to warn her if Jonah ever returned home early from the winery, something he had yet to do since she'd been there.

Starting the next day, Raine took a two-hour hiatus after lunch to go to the music room. Although she still felt a little guilty because of the terms of their contract, her conscience didn't bother her all that much. After all, who was she hurting? The piano needed use, and it was the logical solution to her own problems.

Although the piano was vastly better than the one she'd been using, playing it did have one unforeseen result. Now that she could concentrate wholly on her music, a suspicion that had been growing inside her finally crystallized into certainty. Without a music coach, a teacher who was qualified to evaluate her progress and supervise her practice sessions, she was slipping backward, not forward.

Always in the past she had worked under the

close supervision of a teacher. Although she had confidence in her own ability, she was haunted now by a fear that something was lacking in her playing. True, she had won two competitions, and her teachers at Juillard had praised her for her technique and interpretative ability. But it would take far more than that to win the Tchaikovsky competition or even to become a finalist.

Well, there was nothing she could do about it at the moment. She must make do with her own improvised drills, with paying minute attention to details, mastering each phrase of the inventions and the other pieces she played in her practice sessions before she went on to the next, utilizing constant repetition to perfect her technique. When she returned to the city, then she would put herself under the tutelage of the best teacher she could afford. . . .

Several times while she was in the music room she had the feeling she was being watched, but she contributed it to nerves, even to her conscience, which, for all her rationalization, still bothered her a little. Then, shortly after she'd started practicing one day, she glanced up to see the dustcover on the harp swaying slightly. Her first thought was that it was a mouse, until she saw a familiar canvas shoe protruding from one corner of the muslin.

Quietly she rose and went to push the cloth aside. Michael, who was squatting in the space under the tentlike cover, looked so frightened that without thinking she signed a quick "It's all right. I'm not angry."

For a long time he stared up at her, and then a smile spread across his face. He signled four words—"Thank you, Miss Raine"—and she knew that her efforts had been worth every minute of the time she'd spent learning how to sign.

Michael's hands flew, asking questions so quickly that she couldn't follow them. She laughed and put up a protesting hand. "Too fast," she signled.

"Where did you learn to sign?" he asked, slower this time.

"Reverend Turlock has been helping me. Be patient. I'm still slow. I have to spell out half my words."

"I'll help you." He gave her a shy smile. "Are you my friend now?"

Raine fought the sudden thickness in her throat, glad she didn't have to speak out loud. She extended her hand for him to shake, then signed: "Good friends. Forever friends."

"Will you stay here for always?" he asked.

Raine sighed inwardly, wondering how to reply without hurting him and yet still be honest. "I came here to do a job for your father," she told him finally. "When it's done, I must go away. But I'll write you. If your father agrees, I'll come to see you."

When the corners of Michael's mouth drooped, she decided it was time to change the subject. "How long have you been listening to—"

She stopped, not finishing the sentence. Because of course he hadn't been *listening* to her practicing. Which raised an interesting question. How had he known she was in the music room? She was always careful to close the door while she practiced and after all, he couldn't have heard the music. . . .

"How did you know I was here, Michael?" she asked him.

Michael kept his gaze fixed on her face as he answered, "I saw you come in here one day. Next day, I hid behind the harp."

Raine studied him closely. He fidgeted for a moment, and then his gaze shifted down to the scuffed toes of his shoes. He looked so evasive that she was sure he was hiding something. Determined to get to the bottom of the mystery, she touched his arm to get his attention, then asked: "Is it possible that you can hear a little, Michael?"

Michael's eyes widened as if from shock, and then his hands and fingers were moving so quickly that she couldn't follow him. But she caught enough to know that he was denying that he could hear. Because of his obvious agitation she dropped the subject, telling herself that her suspicions were ridiculous. If there had been an improvement in his hearing, why would he keep it secret? From what Tilda had told her, he had the finest doctors in the Bay Area. How could he possibly fool them, much less his father and aunt?

As for why he had been coming here, hiding under the dustcovers while she practiced, that was simple. His father and aunt were gone all day. Tilda was busy with her cooking and household chores and Luke with his garden. Michael had no playmates. He was lonely, and she was someone who had been kind to him, so he liked to be near her. It was also possible that he felt the vibrations from the piano when she played and was intrigued by them. Hadn't she heard somewhere that deaf people could master dancing, using music vibrations as their guide?

Which only proved that once again she had let her imagination run away with her. Her father had warned her so often that she had a way of rushing in, jumping to conclusions and bringing problems down upon herself....

It was getting late, time to lock the door and return the key to its hiding place. But before she did, maybe she'd better explain to Michael why he must keep her use of the music room a secret from his father and aunt. She was searching for the right words when it occurred to her that what she'd really be asking Michael to do was to lie to Jonah. Bleakly she wondered when she had begun taking the evasion of truth—and outright lies—for granted. Well, it was going to end right there. She could only hope the subject would never come up.

Michael touched her arm. "Can it be our secret that you can sign?" he asked, his fingers flying.

Raine smothered a sigh. So Michael had already guessed that it might cause trouble if his aunt found out that she was learning sign language. Did he also realize that his father would be furious with her if he knew that she'd been using the music room?

"A secret is all right," she told Michael, "but it isn't right to lie. If anyone asks we must tell the truth."

Michael stared at her for a long moment before he finally nodded. Sensing his reluctance, she wondered if it was her admonition against lying that bothered him. Or was it simply that he, like most children, wanted to enjoy the delicious thrill of sharing a secret with an adult?

"Will you take me to the beach tomorrow to look for glass balls?" Michael signaled. "A couple of weeks after there's been a storm in Japan, glass fishnet balls sometimes wash up in the cove. Daddy promised he'd take me to look for them, but he's been too busy."

Realizing it would soon be time for Jonah and Crystal's return from the winery, Raine nodded her consent to the outing, then went to close the piano and replace its muslin cover. When she turned around again, Michael was gone.

As she locked the door and went to replace the key in the kitchen-cabinet drawer, she wondered if it was possible that Michael had inherited his father's talent. If so, no wonder Jonah was a bitter man. Was this why he had banished music from his life? Or was it solely because of grief, the wrenching pain of losing the woman he had loved? Maybe part of his reaction was caused by guilt. If he had loved his wife so much, how could he so casually have made love to a stranger?

Raine realized that men sometimes had different standards than women, and a virile man like

Jonah, who was idolized and pursued by adoring fans, must have temptations too great for any normal man to resist. But in her case, none of that had applied. She hadn't been a groupie. She certainly hadn't pursued him. The night he'd rescued her from that lonely country road she had been grateful, trusting, but nothing more. Had he misunderstood her trust and simply taken advantage of what he'd thought was being offered?

How clever he had been! He hadn't made any sudden moves that might have frightened her. No, he had pretended to be carried away, as she had been, overwhelmed by an uncontrollable passion for her. And later, he had kept on with the charade by dropping hints that he wanted to—what were the words he'd used? To court her properly? And she had believed him. What a fool she had been!

Well, she was three years older and a lot wiser now. And she didn't intend to allow her attraction to Jonah to get out of hand again. As long as she recognized the danger, she was armed against him, and just because she had discovered that Jonah was not a complete villain didn't mean she could let down her guard.

In fact, it made him even more dangerous. That he had suffered so from his wife's death and Michael's injury didn't change anything. She was still vulnerable, and that meant she must guard herself against temptation and make very sure that Jonah never got the chance to touch her, much less kiss her, again. . . .

CHAPTER TWELVE

RAINE'S BEDROOM was still dark when a tapping sound, tentative but persistent, awakened her. For a moment, still groggy with sleep, she didn't move. When the tapping resumed she remembered her promise to take Michael to the beach. She groaned, looked at the alarm clock beside the bed, groaned again, then crawled out of bed, slipped on her robe and went to open the door.

Michael, looking eager and disgustingly wide awake, was already dressed in jeans and a denim jacket, but he obviously hadn't bothered with anything as mundane as combing his hair. It stuck up in peaks above his forehead, and Raine had to resist an impulse to smooth it down with her hands as she smiled at him. His fingers moving swiftly, he informed her that it was already getting light outside.

"We have to get there early," he told her, his face earnest. "People climb over the rocks at low tide and come into the cove. If we don't go now, they'll get any balls that wash ashore."

Although she sighed inwardly, Raine nodded and told him to wait outside while she dressed.

In the bathroom she splashed cold water on her

face, brushed her teeth, ran a comb through her hair, then quickly tied it into a ponytail with a bit of ribbon. She hurriedly slipped into jeans and a warm sweater, not bothering with a bra. Remembering the chill of the morning coastal winds, she pulled a favorite old navy watch cap over her hair, then went to join Michael who was waiting impatiently in the hall.

As if he had done it a dozen times before, he took her hand as they hurried downstairs and turned into the long hall that led to the kitchen. With Michael tugging at her hand, Raine decided to sacrifice even a quick stand-up breakfast of buttered toast until they got back, but not without a wistful thought about the cup of coffee that usually started her day and got her wits back together.

It was when they went outside into a morning so fresh and new that the sun hadn't yet cleared the edge of surrounding hills that she was suddenly glad she'd agreed to this excursion. On a day like this anything could happen. *Who knows?* she thought. *We might even find that Japanese glass float Michael wants so badly.*

The sky to the west, toward the beach, was still the color of pewter, but tinges of pink showed at the eastern horizon, attesting to the imminent rise of the sun. The air was crisp and cold. Mingled with the odor of roses was an odd but not unpleasant dankness that evoked images in Raine's mind of sea rocks wet with spray, of surf crashing against the sentinels of stone that guarded the coastline, of sea marshes and tide pools.

A bird called out a sleepy inquiry as if it, too, were reluctant to leave its shelter before the sun was up. It rose from a nearby clump of shrubs in a flurry of black-and-silver wings, and suddenly Raine found herself walking taller, her face into the wind, taking a sensuous pleasure in its moist, satiny feel against her face.

An errant thought came to her. Was this one reason why she'd felt so restless lately? Maybe she had allowed herself to be too confined, stuck in that basement room too many hours every day. Well, all that was going to change. From now on she meant to take time for a daily walk or visit to the beach. What's more, she would take Michael with her whenever possible, making time for him, something his father seemed too busy to do....

After they left the garden they skirted the vineyard behind the house, then, walking single file, climbed a narrow path that meandered up the slope of one of the steep hills that sheltered Arlington House from the full force of the prevailing coastal winds.

Although there were no trees there, the earth teemed with plant life—mosses and lichen and grasses, clumps of fiddleback fern, wind-sheared sage and coyote brush, vegetation that took moisture from the fog and coastal winds. Raine stopped to examine a clump of tiny bell-like flowers, wondering what they were. Almost as if he'd read her mind, Michael tugged at her arm, then signed, "Chinese houses."

"How did you know that?" she asked, smiling.

"Daddy told me. He knows the names of flowers and birds and the things that live in the tide pools."

"Your daddy is quite a surprising man," she said. Then, realizing that she'd spoken aloud, she signed, "When does he tell you all this?"

"We take walks, or we used to. Lately he's been busy at the winery all the time."

There was a droop to his small shoulders that made Raine want to comfort him, but she only nodded before she started on. As they skirted a clump of sour grass that had taken root in the middle of the path, she reflected that the trail had a neglected look, as if it were seldom used. Did Crystal ever go to the beach, or was it too familiar to her, something she had grown bored with? Both Luke and Crystal had mentioned that Jonah often swam in the cove. Was he the only one who used the path these days? There was no sign of him this morning, something she was thankful for.

When she realized she was frowning she gave an impatient shrug. That was the very last time she intended to think of Jonah that morning. She meant to enjoy this hiatus from work and worry. What's more, she intended to make sure that this outing was memorable to Michael, too.

At the top of the hill they paused to catch their breath and stare at the blue green expanse of water sparkling in the early-morning light.

Shaped like a half-moon, the cove was much larger than Raine had expected. Great mounds of gray rock, constantly bombarded with spray from the restless surf, guarded both ends of the cove, cutting it off from the rest of the beach. A narrow strip of sand, like a small oasis, glistened between the outcroppings of rock. It was littered with driftwood, and Raine felt some of Michael's excitement as he gestured urgently for her to follow him down the weather-beaten stairs that angled down the side of the bluff.

She noted that the wooden steps were broad and that the railing, waist-high and sturdy, was obviously in good repair, so she felt no qualms about letting Michael go ahead without offering him her hand, a gesture she knew would not be welcome to an eight-year-old who, as he had told her so earnestly, would be nine in a few weeks.

A few minutes later they reached the bottom of the stairs. No longer obstructed by the hill, the wind blew steadily at their faces, staining their cheeks with color and whipping Michael's brown hair around his face. Raine breathed in deeply, tasting the wildness of the salt-tinged wind on her tongue. A surge of energy that demanded to be unleashed swept through her and she felt an urge to run along the beach, to lose herself in the pure joy of movement.

Something of what she felt must have communicated itself to Michael because he threw back his head and a laugh tumbled out into the air. Raine started to signal a question, then stopped. Nothing must mar these magic moments, certainly not the kind of question that seemed to frighten him.

A few minutes later they were trotting briskly along the edge of the surf. Since Raine was keeping a sharp lookout for the occasional high wave—rogue waves, her father had called them—that were notorious along the California coast, it was Michael who spotted the glass float, bobbing in the surf.

He pulled at her arm urgently, pointing ahead at the glittering object, then began to run. She hurried after him, just as excited, and when they saw that the glass globe, about twelve inches in diameter and still trailing a length of coarse netting, was unbroken, they clutched each other and danced up and down. When reason returned they dragged the ball onto the sand, not caring that the foaming surf had soaked their canvas shoes and their jeans to the knees. After they had examined it to their heart's content, they collapsed on the sand, grinning at each other.

Raine flung herself backward, her arms above her head. How wonderful to be alive, to be here in this world of sand and sea, with no worries or fears for the moment! A line written by a poet who had loved the northern California coast came to her, and she murmured aloud. "I, gazing at the boundaries of granite and spray, the established seamarks, felt behind me mountains and plains, the immense breadth of the continent—"

"'—before me, the mass and doubled stretch of water,'" Jonah's deep voice resounded. "So you're familiar with Robinson Jeffers. Somehow that surprises me.''

Like a dowsing of cold water, his words chilled Raine, destroying her contentment. She sat up and stared into his amused eyes. A shiver ran along her spine and suddenly she was conscious of her wet feet, of her disheveled appearance.

"Why should it?" she asked, not trying to sound pleasant. "I *am* a native Californian, you know."

"Yes, I know. I've been watching you and Michael. Somehow it's hard to reconcile the hard-edged calculating woman I know you to be with a sea sprite running along the beach, pouncing on Japanese fishing floats.''

Raine hid her hurt behind a stiff smile. "And why not? I understand those balls are very valuable," she said flippantly.

Jonah's face hardened. "Is it another of your acts? Something that amuses you. Or are you trying to soften me up with this sudden interest in my son? Well, let me warn you—"

He broke off as Michael descended upon him, gesturing excitedly at the glass ball. For a while he engaged Michael in a serious examination of the ball, finally declaring that since it was the finest specimen he'd ever seen, it deserved a place of honor on the patio.

Michael clung to Jonah's hand, looking into his face with adoring eyes. Raine watched them, her feelings ambiguous. For Michael's sake she was happy that his father was here to share his moment of triumph. Heaven only knew, the boy had too few of them. But she was sorry Jonah had ruined her own morning. Now she must be on guard about the expression on her face when she looked at him.

"I'm going for a swim," Jonah said abruptly. "Stay with Michael until I get back. The surf here is treacherous. Not only is there a strong undertow but the curvature of the cove sometimes forms killer waves that can come up unexpectedly." He pointed to a strewing of debris a few feet from where she sat. "Better stay behind the high-tide line if you don't want to get a surprise soaking."

Shielding her eyes from the morning sun with cupped hands, Raine watched Jonah as he flung off his beach robe, revealing white swimming trunks. His brown muscular body looked almost bronze in the morning light, reminding her of the night they'd made love. How taut and smooth his skin had felt under her touch, how safe and protected she had felt in his arms, and how she had gloried in her belief that the sight, the touch of her own body was having a devastating effect upon this strong virile man, when all the time any woman would have served the same purpose for him. . . .

The hurt of her betrayal was back. To hide it from his too-discerning eyes, she turned her face away, pretending an interest in a high-flying hawk overhead.

"What's the matter, Raine?" His tone was mocking. "Have you never seen a man in swimming trunks before?"

She knew she had to answer him or give herself away. With an effort she let her eyes return to his face, stretching her lips into a scornful smile. "What *are* you talking about, Jonah?"

"Uh-huh. Well, stay here. I'm going to have my swim and then we'll talk."

"I have work to do—"

"Stay here. That's an order. In case you've forgotten, I *am* your employer."

Without waiting for an answer, he turned and plunged into the surf. The wave swelled under him, lifting him. For a moment he disappeared into the trough on the other side and then she saw his arms cutting the water, heading outward.

For a long time she watched him; now that it was safe, she didn't have to guard her expression. When she turned finally to look at Michael, he was watching his father, too, and she caught a look of longing on his face. How he worshipped his father. Couldn't Jonah see that his son was a very lonely boy, that he needed more than just the few minutes of his time in the evenings?

"How often do you and your father do things together?" she signed, knowing Jonah was too far away to see them now.

"Not often lately. He promised to take me to see the giants and the pygmies, but he's been too busy."

"The giants and the pygmies?" she questioned, wondering if she'd misread his words.

"Yes. And the geysers, too. Did you know we have real geysers near here?"

She nodded. "I did know that, but I've never seen them. Have you?"

"No. But daddy is going to take me someday."

He looked so wistful that she decided he needed a distraction. "Show me one of the tide pools," she signed. "I want to learn the names of the things that live there."

Michael gave one last glance toward his father's bobbing head. Together he and Raine walked along the edge of the surf, heading for the rocks at the north end of the beach. The tide pool was in a small concave basin. It was formed by the rocks that surrounded it and fed, Raine surmised, by fresh supplies of water during high tide. Lying on their stomachs on a patch of sand, she and Michael watched a multitude of tiny creatures and plants. Like a small miniature world, Raine decided, enthralled by the variety of life in the quiet pool.

Michael pointed out and named a turban snail, ebony black with a dappled shell, then a starfish, a surprising yellow, which undulated among the fronds of deep green seaweed at the edge of the pool. A purple sea urchin rested in a nest, which, Michael assured her, it had dug into the rock with its own hard spine. As he went on to name a small school of fish as opaleyes, another as rockpool Johnnies, she realized that he could only have learned these things from Jonah, and again she was forced to revise her opinion of him as a father.

They were sitting on the edge of a rock, sunning themselves, absorbed in watching the antics of a homey little rock-colored creature Michael called a sculpin, when Jonah rejoined them. Michael immediately jumped up and held out Jonah's beach robe, which he'd been tending. Jonah's wet body caught the slanting rays of the rising sun and glistened a deep brown as he slipped on the knee-length robe and belted it around his waist.

"I feel almost human again," he commented.

"You couldn't prove it by me," Raine said tartly, and then wondered why she was deliberately provoking him.

A gleam showed in his eyes. "So you don't think I'm human, do you, Carmen? Well, you of all people should know better."

"Don't call me that ridiculous name!" she snapped. "After all, I could call you a few names myself, you know."

"For instance?"

"Names like adulterer, womanizer, seducer of—" She stopped, knowing she'd already said too much.

"I didn't notice any complaints three years ago," he said evenly. "It seems to me that you were all too willing to climb into bed with me."

"I didn't know you were married," she said.

"Oh? Would that have made a difference? I didn't realize you had any scruples at all, Raine."

"I have scruples. And why don't we stop this cat-and-mouse game? You are what you are and I am what I am, and neither of us is perfect. One thing I would draw the line at—if I ever have a son, I won't neglect him."

"What the hell are you talking about?" he demanded.

"I'm talking about Michael. Do you ever take him swimming with you, for instance? How often do you go on a picnic? Couldn't you take a day off now and then just to take him to see the—the giants and the pygmies, whatever the devil they are, like you promised? Of course, you can tell me it's none of my business, but—"

"You're absolutely right about that. It *is* none of your business. I don't owe you any explanations, but as it happens, it is far too dangerous here for swimming. I only go out because I happen to be an unusually strong swimmer. Even with me beside Michael it wouldn't be safe, and I wouldn't advise you to try it, either."

"I'm a very good swimmer. I tried out for the swim team at my high school and would have made it except that my music lessons were at the same time as swim practice."

He brushed her words aside with an impatient gesture of his hand. "No matter how good you are in a pool," he said contemptuously, "it doesn't prepare you for swimming in the cove. As for taking Michael out with me—even at the edge of the water, there's always the danger he could be swept away. Which is why I go to the beach alone when I go swimming. I can't take the risk of leaving him by himself on the beach."

Raine digested his words, but instead of feeling apologetic, her anger only deepened. "But is he confined to this estate? When was the last time he left here? He's a growing boy with an eager questing mind. He needs the stimulation of new things, of meeting new people—"

"And you, Raine Hunicutt, are stepping out of line again!" He towered above her, looking so threatening that she scrambled to her feet. Although she knew he wouldn't do anything to her with his son present, she retreated backward, but only a couple of steps before her pride asserted itself and she stopped, her chin inching upward, her eyes defiant.

Before she could say the tart words trembling on her lips, Michael was between them, his face strained, his eyes anxious. He tugged at his father's arm, so urgently that he caught Jonah off-balance. Jonah tried to recover, but failed. He tumbled over on his back onto the sand beside the tide pool.

For a long moment everything seemed to stop, even the scouring sound of the waves, and then Jonah's shoulders were shaking and he was laughing uproariously. Michael, his body frozen, stared at him. A reluctant smile trembled at the corners of his wide mouth, and then he was laughing, too, doubled over and holding his chest with his arms.

Jonah reached out a long brown arm and grabbed his son around the waist, pulling him down beside him. For a few minutes they wrestled on the sand in a flurry of legs and arms. When they finally stopped, both were panting and, Raine noticed, looking very pleased with themselves. Feeling a little left out, she resisted an impulse to brush the sand off Michael's clothes as he sat up, his face flushed, his eyes bright.

Jonah's fingers moved so swiftly that she couldn't catch more than a few words: *coffee, Tilda, breakfast*. Michael nodded vigorously, then without a glance toward Raine, ran off down the beach toward the cliff stairs.

"What was that all about?" she asked Jonah. "What did you say to him?"

"I told him to ask Tilda to put together a picnic breakfast—including a thermos of hot coffee," he said easily. "You claim I don't spend enough time with Michael, so we're going to have our breakfast here. You're invited, too, although I hope you lighten up a little. You're a very prickly person, you know."

"No more than you," she retorted.

"Oh, I can be very charming." His voice had deepened and his stare was quizzical. "Did you know that when you're angry your eyes shoot sparks?"

"I'm sure they don't. Only electrical wires shoot sparks," she said crossly.

"But they do. And your throat turns bright red, like a turkey."

Involuntarily she put her hand to her throat, then realized she had fallen for his trick. When she glared at him, he gave a satisfied nod. "There! You're doing it again. Sparks—and a turkey-red neck."

"Oh—oh, shut up!" she said, driven to incoherence. "I'd like to—"

"You'd like to what?" he said softly. "Kiss me? Have me kiss you? Make love to me? Have me make love to you? Remember how good it was between us? No matter what your motives, you felt something that night. I couldn't be wrong about that."

"Indeed? I'm afraid you have a more selective memory than I do because I've forgotten all about it. In fact, until I came to work for you, I hadn't thought of you in ages."

"Very interesting. Did you know that when you lie, your lower lip trembles?"

"It does no such thing! And I'd like to change the subject, if you don't mind."

"Oh, but I do mind. What we had was special. Call it chemistry or biology, but making love to you was...memorable. I'm beginning to regret my decision to leave you alone. I may have made a mistake there. In fact, if your price isn't too high, there's no reason why we can't resume our relationship—"

Goaded beyond reason, she flung a handful of wet sand at him. Only his quick movement prevented it from landing in his face. Even so, it showered his shoulder and stained the front of his robe. When she saw the smile slip off his face, she knew she'd just made a mistake.

She turned to run, but he seized her before she could escape. He pulled her down, pinning her arms to her sides so that she was forced to lie full-length on top of him. His warm breath stirred the loosened hairs that had escaped her cap, and his face was so close that she could see the tiny black steaks that radiated outward from the gray of his iris. And because they were locked together, she knew exactly when his anger changed to another emotion.

A flame started up in his eyes and ignited a fire inside her, too. Although she continued to struggle, she was agonizingly aware of the heat, the hardness of his thighs under her own squirming body. A weakness invaded her limbs; a trembling started up deep inside her. Her breasts, pressed tightly against his chest, tingled as if he were caressing them, and she renewed her attempts to get away, afraid that he would guess her growing excitement and take advantage of it.

"Let me go!" she demanded, turning her face away.

"Not until I've exacted a penalty for that handful of sand. When you tease a tiger you can expect to get mauled, and you've been teasing me for the past few minutes, my love."

With a sudden movement he rolled over, taking her with him, and then she was pinioned beneath his body, helpless to move. He forced her arms above her head, holding both her wrists easily in one hand, leaving him free to trace his forefinger, then his tongue across her lips, moistening them, exciting them.

"A man could go crazy looking at that mouth of yours," he said huskily.

He kissed her then, a kiss that was more an invasion than a caress. As his tongue plunged deep into her mouth, penetrating its softness, tasting and exploring, her lips throbbed and began to swell, giving her kindled passion away. Jonah's grip on her hands tightened convulsively, and he probed deeper as if he meant to ravish her innermost soul.

When he raised his head finally, the fever in his eyes told her that he was fully aroused. A ringing in her ears, a slow sweet trembling in her limbs, warned her how close she was to surrendering to the urgency of his passion.

He released her hands, as if he knew it was no longer necessary to hold her there. Roughly, he pushed her cap off and tangled his fingers in her hair, shaking out the ponytail. He spread her loosened hair across the sand, then buried his face in its softness, a shudder rippling through his body.

"I've been wanting to do this for a long time," he breathed against her ear, setting up a tingling along the sensitized skin of her throat.

Raine knew she must escape before her own bottled-up emotions trapped her, but still she lay there, letting him touch her breasts with his hands and caress her throat with his lips. When he pushed up the edge of her sweater, exposing her breasts to the wind, she gasped with shock.

He fondled her breasts gently, lingeringly, as if he were memorizing their contours, their softness, the small dark nipples that hardened under his fingers. His tongue encircled first one then the other, and a sweet agony threatened to overwhelm her. It would be so easy to yield to his caresses. She burned for more, for the consummation of his lovemaking. What did it really matter if she weakened and gave in?

His mouth moved lower, his tongue making tiny circles on the sensitive skin below her breasts, then down to the soft flesh of her stomach. Rising above her, he looked down at her, his eyes glazed, his face flushed, and the responding quickening within her told her that she was fast reaching a point of no return. Gently, he slid the zipper of her jeans down, then pushed the coarse material and her panties over her hips to her knees, exposing her throbbing body to his burning gaze. She tried to protest, but again his kiss ravaged her mouth, silencing her. His hands stroked the softness, the moistness of her most intimate flesh, and suddenly she was aflame, a torrent of desire moving through her veins like molten fire.

He slid his hands under her hips, lifting her until she was crushed against him. As his hardness pressed into her own yielding flesh she felt a wave of panic. What was she doing, allowing this to go on? If she let him possess her again she would never be free of her passion for this man. She knew what he thought of her. Could she live with the knowledge that once again she had given herself to Jonah Duncan, a man who had no respect, no love, nothing but contempt and lust for her?

A word rose to her lips, coming to her rescue. "Michael," she said above the rapid pounding of her heart. "He'll be back any minute. We've got to stop this."

For a moment she thought Jonah hadn't heard her. When he lifted his head, when he let her slip back to the sand, she felt a wave of desolation, even though, once again, she had won out over her own passion.

He rolled away from her. As he sat with his face in his hands, a shudder ran through his body. His eyes were bleak when he finally looked at her. "You're right. I got carried away, which is damnably easy to do with you. You're a natural, you know. All that fire behind that cool look. We have some unfinished business later, you and I, when we won't be interrupted."

Her skin prickled, not from the chill of the morning wind but from the roughness in his voice. Turning her back on him, she pulled her jeans up over her hips, adjusted her sweater and jammed her cap back on her head. When she couldn't find her ribbon, she tucked her hair under the cap any which way, not caring how she looked.

Only when she was sure she could trust herself to speak did she say, "You're wrong. We don't have any unfinished business. I'm afraid you can no longer pay my price."

"What the hell are you talking about?"

"I wangled that cataloging job from Mr. Partridge, hoping I could talk you into taking me on as a pupil," she said, the lie stinging her lips. "Since you have this—this thing about music, you're not much use to me, are you? So why don't we just forget it? I'll finish the job I contracted for, and then I'll use the money to pay for a real coach, someone who can help me win the Moscow competition.''

She knew he believed her when his eyes darkened and his face turned to stone. So why, she asked herself, did she feel an ominous stirring of fear when he told her coldly, ''You've made your point. But just remember this, Carmen. When you play with fire, you can expect to get hurt.''

CHAPTER THIRTEEN

ALTHOUGH RAINE threw herself into her work after she returned from the beach, the croissant and coffee she'd forced down seemed to churn in her stomach, and she had a hard time concentrating. The scene at the beach kept replaying through her mind, getting between her and the books she was sorting and listing. How strange that while her nerves felt raw, as if Jonah's scornful words had some physical power to scourge her, it was his kiss, the firmness and warmth of his lips, that she couldn't stop thinking about.

It was only after she realized that she was standing still in the middle of the room, staring into space, that she finally managed to put Jonah out of her mind and lose herself in work.

When she'd first started cataloging the collection she had quickly discovered that ordinary cataloging procedures were useless, so she'd been forced to devise a simple custom-made system that worked. The first thing she'd done was to have Luke knock together several sturdy bookshelves out of rough lumber. One held the books about which she couldn't come to a firm decision; these would eventually be examined by the New York expert for final evaluation. Others, those that were obviously without any commercial value, she listed carefully, then returned to clearly marked crates, ready for eventual disposal as gifts to local libraries or to a charitable institution.

The ones she knew were valuable or of interest to the de Young Museum she kept in another bookcase segregated from the others. There was another group, too, those books she believed might be of interest to Michael when he was older. Jonah, of course, would have to decide that, but she hoped to persuade him that even though some of the books possessed a respectable monetary value, his son would benefit from having them.

Michael had already picked up her own treatment of books, handling them with respect, often stopping to dip into one, to run his finger along a page, sometimes becoming lost in the magic world of words and ideas, of fantasy and fact. Since it seemed likely he would lead a quiet life, what better companion than books? But oh, she wanted more for him! Friends his own age from whom he could learn the joys of friendship and the give-and-take of life. . . .

Raine gave herself a mental shake. She must remember that Michael was his father's responsibility, not hers. Why did she keep forgetting that?

The basement walls seemed suddenly to be closing in upon her, and she decided that she would go upstairs early and have lunch with the Cummingses. A dose of Tilda's common sense and Luke's good-humor was the best anecdote she could think of for what ailed her.

She was washing her hands when Michael, looking uncommonly cheerful, wandered in. When she asked if he'd like to have lunch with Tilda and Luke, he nodded so vigorously that she laughed out loud, immediately feeling better.

At the big claw-legged oak table in the kitchen where Tilda had set out a lunch of onion soup and bacon-and-tomato sandwiches, Michael was so busy telling Luke about the Japanese glass ball they'd found that morning that he forgot to eat until Tilda nudged him and pointed sternly at his food. By the time lunch was over, Raine was feeling more like her usual self, but, to her discomfiture, when she went to the music room for her daily stint of practice, she found herself thinking of Jonah again.

Why was it that he seemed to permeate her every thought? What was the source of his power over her? Even now when she should be concentrating on her drills, her fingers moved clumsily, thwarting her best efforts and making elementary mistakes that hadn't bothered her in years. In exasperation she finally rested her head on her folded arms. Maybe a rest was in order. Or maybe she should just give it up for the day....

A touch on her shoulder made her start. She turned to smile into Michael's questioning face.

His nimble fingers asked a question. "Are you sick?"

"Just a little tired."

"Don't work so hard to finish the books. I want you to stay here a long time."

She hesitated, then told him, "I have to finish soon or your father will think I'm lazy."

Michael sighed deeply. As he turned away to go to his nest of cushions in the corner, anger flared up inside her. He was so small and so vulnerable. If he were her son, oh, how she would love him and give him the attention he deserved....

As if her anger had cleansed her mind, she discovered when she returned to the Beethoven Three-Part Invention she'd been working on, that her fingers were once more taking orders from her brain. When an hour later a glance at her watch told her it was time to return to her job, Michael accompanied her to the basement and helped her for a couple of hours, then, at her insistence that he had worked long enough, he wandered off in search of Luke, who had promised to help him build a birdhouse.

She was examining the spine of a leather-bound volume of poetry when Crystal's light voice startled her. "Aren't you coming to dinner tonight? It's almost seven."

"Oh, damn. I got so involved I forgot the time. Well, I'll wash up and change and be there in a few minutes."

"Take your time. Tilda's running a little late tonight. Something about a dessert soufflé that fell in the middle." She looked around the dusty room at the stacks of books, the piles of still unopened crates. "Why on earth did you take up this kind of work? It seems like a pretty grubby way of earning a living."

Raine felt a prickle of irritation. "I find it fascinating. For years I helped my father in his bookstore. At first it was just a way to be with him because I hated going home after school to an empty apartment. Later I liked working with books for their own sake."

Crystal's eyelashes flickered, and Raine caught a momentary expression that could have been sadness in her usually guarded China-blue eyes. "Your father raised you alone? Where was your mother? Were they divorced?"

"My mother died when I was twelve. My father did his best to be both father and mother to my brother and me, but it was difficult for him. He had to earn a living and he—well, he was a very private sort of person who found it hard to show his feelings outwardly."

"You said *was*. Is he dead now?"

"He died just a few weeks ago."

"I'm sorry," Crystal said, sighing. "Well, at least you had him that long. I was a teenager back east in boarding school when my father became so ill. I came home to be with him, and then, soon after he died, Elaine married Jonah and they came here to live. Jonah was gone so much on his tours that she needed company, and help with Michael. That's why he's like my own child."

"I can understand that. He's a wonderful boy."

"Yes, he is." Some of the warmth had left Crystal's voice and the wariness was back in her eyes.

As Raine studied her it came to her that this was as good a time as any to approach the subject of Michael's hearing. "About Michael," she said, choosing her words carefully. "Something happened the other day that made me wonder if he's showing some improvement."

"No, that's impossible! As I told you, his doctors are pessimistic about his chances of recovering even partial hearing. And it would be a mistake for you to—to discuss this with him. It could only make things harder for him."

The coldness in her voice warned Raine to drop the subject. Before she could retreat to her room to dress for dinner, Crystal spotted a row of books on a nearby shelf. "My old books, and I thought they had been pitched out long ago during one of Tilda's housecleaning orgies." She hesitated, then added hurriedly, "Thank you for putting them aside for me."

"I had a hunch you'd like to have them," Raine said, smiling.

"I would, I would." Crystal's face held a rare animation now. "I wonder...do you suppose Michael would be interested in reading them? Of course I was about eleven when daddy brought them home for me, but still, Michael's reading skill is very advanced for his age."

"I know. Tim Turlock says he's reading at a fifth grade level."

The animation faded from Crystal's face. "Why

would Tim discuss Michael with you?'' she said sharply.

"He didn't. I commented that Michael seemed to be interested in books intended for much older kids and that's when he told me that he'd tested out at a surprisingly high reading level.''

Obviously not appeased, Crystal demanded, "Has Michael been coming down here again?''

"Occasionally he brings his homework down here to do.''

"The damp is bad for him. I'd appreciate it if you'd chase him upstairs the next time he turns up.''

Raine wanted to point out that the basement was remarkably dry, but since she was unsure of her grounds she merely nodded. Luckily Crystal didn't seem to expect an answer. With a curt, "See you at dinner,'' she turned and left the storage room.

Raine gathered up her notes and ledger and put them away in a cabinet drawer before she followed Crystal upstairs. Later, at the dinner table, she had to force herself to eat. Just sitting there opposite Jonah, the target of his ironic stare, was enough to ruin her usual healthy appetite. She was trying to get down a few sips of chardonnay, one of Jonah's excellent estate wines, when Jonah addressed a remark to Crystal.

"You'll have to go it alone with those IRS reports tomorrow, Crystal,'' he said casually. "I'll be busy for the day.''

His sister-in-law gave him a surprised look. "I

didn't see anything on your calendar for tomorrow."

"I just put it on. Recently someone pointed out to me, more or less correctly, that I've been neglecting my son. According to the weather reports, tomorrow looks to be another sunny day. This seems a good time to take Michael on that outing I've been promising him."

"Why don't I postpone the reports for a day and go with you two?"

"No, this is a father-son outing. No aunts allowed," he said.

In his chair next to Crystal, Michael almost overturned his goblet of milk. Raine caught a flicker of excitement, quickly veiled, in his gray eyes. She'd noticed before that he seemed almost to sense when he was the object of conversation. Had he read his own name on their lips? She made a mental note to ask Tim if it were possible for Michael to learn to lip-read on his own, or had Tim been teaching him that, too?

When Jonah told Michael about the excursion, the joy on his young face was so blinding that Raine found it necessary to blink hard and look away. Automatically her gaze moved to Jonah, only to find that he was watching her, not Michael. Feeling confused, she returned her attention to her food and forced down a few bites of Tilda's superb chocolate soufflé.

Rather than spend the evening with Jonah and Crystal, she made excuses, saying she wanted to finish recording a collection of cookbooks she'd just unpacked while the information was fresh in her mind. Back in her room, she changed into jeans and one of her faded work shirts and went downstairs to the basement. But the job she'd intended to do seemed very boring now. Giving it up finally, she ran her finger along a row of books on the shelf she reserved for "collectibles," looking for something interesting to take upstairs to read in bed.

"You touch those books the way some women might touch a man," Jonah said behind her.

She whirled, her eyes flashing and her cheeks blazing. How was it that he always seemed to catch her off guard? Did he do it on purpose?

Jonah studied her closely for a moment, then asked unexpectedly, "What's your background, Raine? From that tawny skin and those dark eyes I suspect it's Italian—or Spanish. You really shouldn't bleach your hair, you know. It's very striking, but it isn't necessary. You'd get attention no matter what color your hair was."

A thrill of irritation went through Raine, sharpening her voice. "I do *not* bleach my hair!"

His eyebrows soared. "Were you or were you not a brunette when I first met you?"

"That's because I'd dyed my hair brown that year. This is my natural color."

For a long moment he stared at her. "Well, you can understand my confusion. With hair the color of moonbeams, why would you dye it?"

"I don't owe you any explanations, but—very well. I was getting a lot of static during my first year at Juilliard. People tend to put a label on you when you look...unusual. The girls thought I was some kind of man hunter, the boys decided I was fair game for their passes, and my instructors—well, they treated me like a scatterbrain. So at the beginning of my sophomore year I dyed my hair. Later, after I'd grown up a little more, I decided to be what I was and the devil with what other people thought about me. If they misunderstood, that was their problem. So I let it grow back. Sort of a reversal on the usual dark roots thing."

"That must have caused quite a sensation at Juilliard."

She had to smile, albeit a little bitterly. "It did. But it got my point across. After that most of my schoolmates and teachers accepted me for myself."

"I see. And whom do you inherit your unusual coloring from?"

"An Italian mother and an English father. My brother has the same coloring, but on him no one suspects a bleach job. For one thing, his eyelashes and brows are very light."

"Your brother—is he older than you?"

"By four years."

"With just the two of you, you must be pretty close."

Raine hesitated, then answered honestly, "Not as close as I'd like to be. We've both been so busy all our lives that—well, we love each other but we don't really have much in common. And of course we have been separated a lot during the past few years.''

"Is he as ambitious as you, and as ruthless about getting what he wants out of life?"

Jonah inserted the question so deftly that it was a minute before the import of his words really registered. When it did, Raine slammed the book in her hand down on the improvised table she'd been using. "I don't intend to stay here and be insulted!" she stormed.

"Calm down. And why would you take that as an insult? Earlier you seemed proud of your ambition."

"I'm neither proud or not proud. It's—it's just what I am, where I'm coming from."

He winced. "Please. That phrase is on my no-no list."

She started to give him another sharp answer, but to her chagrin she laughed instead. "Mine, too," she confessed. "I hate catch phrases that substitute for real conversation, but I still find myself using them sometimes when I'm—"

She stopped, not wanting to admit that he'd managed to make her lose her temper again.

"When you're having a meaningful conversation?" he said blandly, and she found herself laughing again.

"You should do that more often, Raine. You're still the same sobersides you were three years ago, aren't you?"

"As it happens, I laugh a lot," she retorted. "But only when I'm genuinely amused. I haven't found much here at Arlington House to tickle my funny bone.''

Jonah ignored the barb. "Let's not fight," he said. "I came here with a request. Michael assures me that our excursion tomorrow will be an absolute bust without you. It seems he's anxious to show you all the local wonders. You haven't had a break since you started work here. How about taking a day off and coming with us?''

"But surely you want to be alone with Michael.''

"I have a hunch he'd spend the whole day talking about how wonderful Miss Raine is. Besides, it might be fun showing you the giants and the dwarfs.''

"I don't suppose you'd care to explain what they are?''

"Sorry. If you want to know that, you'll have to come with us tomorrow.''

Raine was silent. A struggle was going on inside her. For the sake of her own peace of mind, she knew it was unwise to be in Jonah's company even for a short while, much less a full day. On the other hand, the thought of taking a holiday from work was tempting. And after all, Michael would be there. Surely there could be no danger with him along. . . .

"Very well. Since Michael really wants me.''

"What if I told you that I also think it's a great idea, that I want your company tomorrow, too?''

"I would think you were playing some kind of game, the very thing you keep accusing me of.''

"You cut me to the quick." There was a wolfish quality to his smile that made her uneasy. "Why don't we put aside our personal animosity for tomorrow—for Michael's sake? We'll just be three people out for a day of sight-seeing. No digs at each other, no recriminations."

Raine nodded agreement, but after Jonah was gone she stood there for a long time, staring at the door, wondering if she was making another mistake, letting herself in for more problems...and more heartache.

CHAPTER FOURTEEN

BEFORE SHE WENT TO BED that night, Raine laid out her clothes for the next day. Jonah had told her to be in the kitchen at six o'clock, dressed for the outing and prepared for one of his famous breakfasts, this time waffles with maple syrup. But when she went downstairs wearing jeans and her prettiest top, a red-and-white jersey with a nautical collar, she wasn't too surprised to find that Tilda, sensing an invasion of her domain, was up early too, and in full possession of her kitchen.

"My, you do look nice this morning with that red scarf threaded through your hair like that," Tilda said. "But then, you always look like an angel, no matter what you wear. Ain't that right, Mr. Jonah?"

Jonah was sitting at the oak table, nursing a cup of coffee between his hands. He looked Raine over thoroughly, his gaze lingering on her lips. When she felt the heat rising to her cheeks, a sardonic glint came into his eyes.

"She does look like an angel," he said, with a subtle emphasis on the word *look*. "And I approve of the sturdy shoes, Raine. Where we're going you'll need them."

"Where exactly are we going?"

"You'll find out, but all in good time."

Raine gave an exasperated sigh. "That's exactly what my father used to say. 'Don't be so impatient, Raine. It'll happen, but all in good time.' It used to drive me up the wall when I was a kid."

The creases beside Jonah's eyes deepened as he smiled at her. "I can just see you as a youngster on a family outing—rushing here and there, trying to cram it all into a few hours."

"There weren't all that many family trips," she said ruefully. "When my dad did manage to get away for a day to take us to the zoo or to Golden Gate Park, I wanted to milk it of every bit of enjoyment."

"And now you see something of yourself in Michael, don't you? That explains why—"

Jonah broke off, and when he spoke again it was to tell Tilda that since they would be getting in after dark, she wasn't to worry about fixing dinner for them.

"Just see that there's some cold meat for sandwiches in the refrigerator in case we come in hungry," he added.

"I'll do that, but don't you go leaving my kitchen in a mess, Mr. Jonah."

Raine bit into a blueberry muffin, watching with interested eyes as Jonah nodded meekly. What an enigma the man was, and wasn't it typical of Jonah's effect on women, old or young, that even while Tilda scolded him there was a softness in her usually uncompromising eyes that gave her away.

It was still dark outside when Jonah stowed the big wicker basket full of food, which Tilda had prepared for their lunch, in the trunk of his Mercedes. Although Raine suggested that she sit in the back, Jonah shook his head. "Michael can curl up more easily on the back seat to take a nap if he gets sleepy."

Rather than argue, she slid into the front seat and buckled her seat belt, prepared for a few hours of strained conversation, provided they talked at all. But Jonah seemed to have forgotten their differences as he headed the car south on Highway 1. He asked her about her progress with the books and she found herself telling him about the first English translation of *The Anatomical Exercizes of Dr. William Harvey, Professor of Physick*, which she'd discovered in a crate of medical books. After she assured him that the de Young Museum would be delighted to have the rare book, she went on to tell him about the collection of juveniles that had once belonged to Crystal and that his sister-in-law hoped Michael would now enjoy.

"We'll have to make sure that anything that might interest the boy, now or in the future, will be saved," he said to her gratification, since it seemed to give her carte blanche in deciding which books to set aside for Michael.

Before she could respond, Jonah took his eyes off the road briefly to give her an amused glance. "Have you figured out what the giants and dwarfs are?"

"No. You're being very mysterious, you know."

"Uh-huh. Well, settle back. The views along this stretch of road are spectacular. We'll park on one of the overlooks. It's pretty late for sighting a school of blue whales heading toward Alaskan waters for the summer, but maybe we'll be lucky enough to see a straggler."

A few minutes later, parked on a high cliff that overlooked a sandy cove, Raine eavesdropped as Jonah's fingers described the migrating habits of the blue whale to Michael, then added, "Right in front of us is the world's largest and deepest ocean. If our eyes were sharp enough and if the earth weren't curved, we could see all the way to Japan—or even to China."

Michael, his face sober, stared fixedly at the blue green waters of the Pacific as if he hoped to see beyond the horizon to those exotic lands. He heaved a deep sigh, then signed that when he grew up he wanted to be a sailor. Raine turned away, pretending to be tucking in the ends of her wildly whipping scarf, suddenly afraid of what her face might reveal to Jonah's observant eyes.

When she looked around again she found Jonah watching her. "You really are lovely, Raine, even without a speck of makeup on your face," he said, his voice reflective. "You'll knock them dead on the concert circuit, provided you make it past the booby traps that lie in wait for aspiring concert pianists. But if you do make it that far, be very careful always to give your best. Never forget that each person sitting in the auditorium has paid his money for that particular performance, not for one you may be doing the next night. For your sake, I hope you have the right stuff. In the end it filters down to that. The hair fades and the skin coarsens, and then all you have going for you is the piano and your God-given talent—provided you have any."

Raine stared back at him, too stunned for the moment to answer. Except when he'd warned her not to bring up the subject in his house, this was the first time he'd voluntarily spoken of music to her.

"I do have the right stuff, and I'm willing to work hard and to take advantage of every opportunity," she said finally. "That's why I'm going to try for the next Tchaikovsky competition."

"You're aiming very high. Maybe too high."

"No higher than you. Just because I'm a woman—"

"That isn't what I meant. I meant that if you intend to try for Moscow, you should be working at it right now, not spending your days in a cellar sorting through old books."

"That's exactly why I'm here," she said tartly. "I need money for a good coach and unlimited time for practice. My contract with you is my ticket to Moscow."

"Especially since your little attempt at blackmail failed? And now you're stuck with the contract you signed. Well, it might be good for your soul and teach you not to play out of your league."

She stared at him angrily, but Michael, always so sensitive to tension, pulled at her hand, his eyes anxious, and she swallowed the sharp words that rose to her lips and even produced a smile.

Jonah, too, must have caught the look on his son's face because he said, "I think we'd better postpone this until later. Michael may not be able to hear, but he's a very sensitive kid, tuned in to what other people are feeling."

"Is that why you won't let him go away to a school for deaf children?"

Jonah frowned at her. "That's one reason. I also owe him something for not being here when he needed me. Another separation from me, and leaving the security of Arlington House, is not the answer."

"Then let the outside world inside," she said urgently. "I saw a boy of Michael's age in the vineyards—one of José Ortega's sons. Tillie tells me he's a very nice boy. I'm sure he wouldn't tease Michael."

Jonah's lips tightened. "You're interfering again, Raine, and you're forgetting our pact."

"I wasn't given much choice about that," she pointed out. "But you're right. For Michael's sake—peace?"

"Peace," he said, extending his hand.

As his larger hand engulfed hers, setting up vibrations along her arm, she was careful to keep her face expressionless. To her amusement, Michael immediately got into the act by shaking hands with each of them in turn, his face reflecting his relief.

In a holiday mood again they drove off, and an hour later they were passing through the rustic entrance of Salt Point State Park. As soon as they had parked, Michael, who was fascinated by the road map he'd been manning, informed them that they were seventeen miles north of Jenner and six miles south of Stewarts Point.

"And a thousand years removed in time from San Francisco," Jonah murmured under his breath.

Raine studied a sign that warned against feeding the bears and building fires without permission. "Is this where we see the giants?" she asked.

"No, this is where we see the dwarfs. But they're very shy. In fact, they're so elusive that you'd better prepare yourself for a long hike, most of it uphill."

Jonah rummaged in the basket for three apples and put them into his son's care. Importantly Michael tucked the fruit away in a small canvas knapsack his father had presented to him at the breakfast table and of which he was inordinately proud. Trying to match his father's long stride, he trotted at Jonah's heels down a tree-shaded path.

As she followed them through a thick stand of Douglas fir and madrona, Raine was conscious of a feeling of excitement and of well-being. Surely it was safe for this one day to let down her guard and just enjoy the outing. Tomorrow she would retreat back into her shell, but for now, why not relax and take advantage of the sun and the fresh air, rich with the odors of growing things and the smell of the ocean?

After a brisk climb past groves of fir and pine and a few redwoods interspersed with brush and grasslands, they reached the top of the ridge, about a thousand feet in elevation, which rose above the beach. In the middle of a large plateau they found the dwarfs, as Jonah called them. By now Raine knew what to expect, having read signs that pointed the way to a grove of pygmy trees, perfect miniatures of the tall redwoods that grew there.

Jonah explained to Michael that the growth of the redwoods had been stunted because the area where they'd taken root was located over hard-pack clay and rock and covered only by a thin coating of soil. "If these same trees were uprooted and replanted in ordinary soil, they would begin to grow, eventually reaching the same height as their full-sized brothers," he signed, his hands moving skillfully.

Fascinated by the doll-like trees, Raine nodded. "Like some people," she said, and thought of Jonah himself, whose growth would have been stunted, his talent lost to the world, if he'd remained on the streets of New York.

Jonah's silence alerted her. She looked up and caught the surprise on his face, and only then realized that she had given herself away.

"So you know how to sign, or at least how to read sign language. Did you learn it before or after you came to Mendocino, Raine?"

Raine straightened her shoulders and gave him a long level stare. "I've been taking lessons from Tim Turlock. I got tired of trying to communicate with Michael on a note pad."

"You decided it was that important to learn to sign for a boy you'll probably never see again after a few weeks?"

"Yes," she said, her tone short because of the skepticism she read in his eyes. Even if she explained further, he wouldn't believe her. So let him think the worst, that she was trying to—what had he called it?—get to the father by being kind to the son?

"Why did you think you had to keep it a secret?"

Raine hesitated. Would he believe her if she told him that Crystal had given her a direct order not to learn sign language? "I thought you might be suspicious of my motives," she said finally. "And I was right, wasn't I?"

He shrugged off her words. "What did Michael think of the secrecy?"

"He thought—he was intrigued at the idea of sharing a secret with an adult," she said.

Michael pulled at his father's sleeve to get his attention. Swiftly his fingers asked, "Why are you mad at Raine again?"

Jonah's face tightened. "I was surprised to learn that she knows how to sign," he replied.

"Don't be mad at Raine. I asked her to keep it a secret."

"Is this the truth?" Jonah asked Raine, and

when she nodded, he added, "Why didn't you say so? Why let me believe that it was one of your—" He broke off.

"Tricks?" she said hotly. "Why do you persist in believing the worst of me in every situation, Jonah? Am I so different from you? Granting that you had enormous talent, how else did you get to the top of the heap? Some people might say that by marrying the daughter of your mentor, *you* were an opportunist!"

For a moment Jonah's face was like granite, and then, unexpectedly, his lips relaxed into a smile. "Some people did—and we're doing it again, aren't we? We seem incapable of being together two minutes without quarreling. But why don't we give it another try? Is it a deal?"

Raine took a deep breath and produced what she hoped was a credible smile. When Michael's small face showed his relief, she made a private vow that in the future she would hold onto her temper—at least for the rest of the day.

They ate their apples, sitting side by side on a slab of rock. As if afraid that they might start quarreling again, Michael sat between them, giving each of them equal attention. On the long walk back to the car, Jonah stopped often to point out a tan oak or a rare brown pelican or a clump of California poppies, a vivid splash of orange yellow in a patch of grass, and Raine had to agree with Michael that his father really did seem to know the names of everything.

Three hours later, after a leisurely ride north to

Willets, they were eating a late lunch in the middle of a grove of sequoia, the grandest of the redwoods, the "giants" Jonah had promised them.

Overhead towered trees as high as three hundred feet, their bases so large that it would have taken twenty men holding hands, to encircle one. As Raine stared up at the trees, forgetting to eat, the quiet, the stillness of the air, the peace of the wooded oasis filled her with awe and she felt a sense of wonder, as if she was seated in a cathedral.

Michael, too, seemed overwhelmed by the sheer size, the majesty of the redwoods. "Are they very old?" he asked his father.

"The oldest living things on earth. Some of these trees, the oldest ones, may have taken root before the birth of Christ. Others were certainly full grown by the time Columbus discovered America."

"Why do they live so long?"

"Because they're virtually immune from killing frosts or insect attack. There is so little pitch in their bark that they can survive forest fires that would kill other species."

Raine touched the buttress, like natural guy ropes, that flared from the bottom of a tree trunk. "How straight and proud they stand," she said.

"They never stand any other way," Jonah said, speaking aloud at the same time he signed for Michael's benefit. "If one is starved for nourishment because of older trees, it simply bides its time. It never bends or grows distorted in order to reach a patch of sun or a bit of open clearing. Then if something happens to its neighbor, it has a spurt of growth, catching up.''

He smiled at the absorbed look on Michael's face. ''These trees do what no nation of man has ever managed to. With man, a few rise and remain erect but the rest are stooped and distorted. We could take a lesson from the redwoods, son.''

And from your own life, Jonah, Raine thought silently, and knew that after this day she would always equate Jonah with the redwoods. She also knew something else. If she got the chance, she would try to return him to his music, to the music that gave so much pleasure to the world.

They finished their lunch, and afterward, while Michael hunted diligently for purplish brown redwood cones, from which Jonah assured him he could plant and grow his own pygmy redwoods, Jonah stretched out on a plot of needles for a nap. Raine dozed, too, curled up against a huge tree stump, awakening only when another party of picnickers arrived to break the silence in the grove.

She opened her eyes and discovered that Jonah was sitting with his back against a tree stump, watching her, his expression so grim that she felt a moment's chill. Michael was gloating over his bonanza of cones. He showed Raine the tiny, almost invisible seeds and told her he was going to start his own forest behind the greenhouse.

When they returned to the car, Jonah headed toward the coast. Lulled by the singing of tires, by the peace of the hilly scenery, Raine fell asleep again, this time awakening as they were passing through a small coastal town at the mouth of a swiftly moving river. She studied the ramshackle houses, a building that was a combination grocery store, filling station and post office and a lone motel. She wondered how the town, one that time and progress had so obviously passed by, could still survive.

When she asked Jonah the same question, he shook his head. "That's what's happening to so many of these small coastal towns. There is so little work in the mills or in the woods, and what there is is seasonal. Of course there's the tourist trade, and some of the people around here work for the government—the postal service, rangers, the like. My winery employs a crew of eighteen, and we buy some of our grapes from vineyards owned by local farmers. A few fishermen still hang on, but it's getting harder and harder to make a living from the sea, especially with the competition from foreign ships, the floating factories that process the fish they catch within minutes of pulling in their nets."

"Well, it seems a shame, and yet if there were too many people living here, wouldn't the coast and the woods suffer?"

"It's a problem, perhaps an insoluble one," he agreed.

Although he said no more, the silence between them was comfortable now. In the back seat Michael had finally given up and was asleep. Raine glanced back at his sleeping face, and she found herself wishing that this scene was what it seemed to be—a man and a woman and their son, returning from a family outing. . . .

But it wasn't, and she mustn't give in to the strangely seductive mood of the day. Jonah had made it very clear that she had been included on sufferance only. And soon, in a week or perhaps a bit longer, her work there would be finished. For a while Michael would miss her, but Jonah wouldn't. He saw her as an opportunist, someone who had come there under false pretenses. It was even possible that some of his hostility stemmed from the fact that she was a reminder of his own unfaithfulness to his wife. Whatever the reason, that's how he would always view her, even though by now she surely had proven herself worthy of the fee she would earn.

And why, when he was the one who had wronged her, was she sitting there stewing over Jonah's erroneous opinion of *her*? Wasn't it about time she came to grips with her own confused emotions where Jonah was concerned?

"Tired, Raine?" Jonah said, his voice sounding strange without its usual ironic edge.

"A little, but it's a nice kind of tired."

"I know what you mean. And you were right. I should do this often, make it a regular thing for Michael and me." He hesitated, his eyes on the road unwinding in front of the car. "But you were wrong about one thing. I wasn't trying to avoid my responsibilities to my son. I'm trying to build something at the winery that I hope Michael will run someday. It was in terrible financial shape when I took it over. That's why I spend so much time there. It isn't enough to leave Michael well provided for financially. He'll need an occupation, an absorbing interest where he'll be accepted for what he is and shielded from the cruelty of the world.''

"I think you're wrong," she said. "Michael is a very strong boy. He can accept the fact that he's different. But the longer you keep him locked away from life, the harder it will be for him to break out.''

In the dusty light of evening Jonah's face stiffened. ''You're doing it again, butting in on something that doesn't concern you. I took your advice about today's outing, but don't let it go to your head. Michael is my concern, not yours. You can't come in here with your dime-store psychology and try to run things.''

A sharp jolt of anger prickled the hairs on Raine's arms, and it was not totally unpleasant, she discovered. She could deal with anger. It was Jonah's disarming friendliness that was the danger....

"I love Michael," she said evenly. "That gives me the right to speak up when I see something that I believe is wrong. You can't keep him wrapped in cotton wool, Jonah. He needs other children, and he has to learn to take his knocks and cope with them. You of all people must know that.''

"What does that mean?"

"You once told me that you were a street kid,

raised in the worst part of the Bronx. Isn't that what gave you the toughness you needed when the going got rough? And I didn't have it so easy, either, although it was nothing like what you went through, of course. Believe me, I know the pain of being locked out. After my mother's death, my father retreated into his own shell. It was years before he emerged, and then it was too late. The wall between us was too high to climb. And during those years I was a very lonely girl. My brother was involved with sports, with his own circle of friends, and didn't seem to be touched by our father's withdrawal. But I have never made friends easily so I didn't have that substitute. This morning you said something about my seeing myself in Michael. Well, that's true. Which is why it breaks my heart to see how eagerly he waits for you to come home at night. Okay, it's none of my business. But think about what I'm saying, no matter how hostile you are toward me.''

Jonah was silent for so long that she was sure he was fighting the temper she knew so well he had. So when he spoke, his voice tired, she was totally unprepared for his words. ''You're right. I must let him go a little. But there's something you don't know. Michael's doctor tells us that his mental health is...delicate. The accident left him unable to tolerate too much stress. That's why he must lead a very quiet life.''

''He seems to have coped very well with our excursion today,'' she pointed out.

He took one hand off the wheel and rubbed his

eyes as if they ached. "You're right again. And I think 1 'll have a private talk with his doctor. It may be that—well, even the best doctors can be wrong."

"What exactly did he say? Could you have misunderstood him?"

"I got it secondhand, from Crystal. After we brought Michael home from the hospital, she volunteered to take him into the city for his appointments. Since it's so blasted painful for me—well, maybe I've abdicated my responsibilities a bit here."

"I doubt that," she said impulsively, and to her chagrin her voice came out warmer than she'd intended.

He turned his head to look at her. As their eyes met, she felt as if he had touched her face with his hands. Then he was watching the road again, leaving her shaken and weak and furious with herself for being so susceptible.

During the rest of the ride, as the sky around them darkened into night, Jonah was silent, much to Raine's relief. She was torn by conflicting emotions. It was becoming increasingly difficult to keep remembering that this man, whose good opinion she found herself hungering for, was the same man who had once sent her world crashing around her head.

Later, when they pulled up in front of Arlington House, only the light on the portico was burning. Jonah stared up at the dark windows of the house for a while before he said, "Why don't you open the door for me and I'll carry Michael inside. Just leave the picnic stuff here. I'll unload it in the morning.''

Carrying Michael's windbreaker, Raine went to open the front door. When she snapped on the front-hall lights she braced herself, half expecting Crystal to appear on the stairs. But the house remained quiet, even when Jonah carried his son upstairs, and as they were passing Crystal's room Raine noticed that no light was showing under the edge of her door.

"Let me get Michael ready for bed tonight," Raine said impulsively.

Jonah nodded. "I'll bring him some milk. And then you'd better get some rest yourself. It's been a long day.''

When she was alone with Michael, Raine shook him gently until he opened one sleepy eye. Helping him get undressed was difficult because he kept falling back asleep, but she finally got him to the bathroom to brush his teeth, then tucked him under his blanket. As she stood beside his bed, studying his flushed face, the crescents of his eyelashes that fanned out across his cheeks, the dark hair that curled over his forehead, she felt a deep pity for his mother, who had died so young and who would never see her son grow up to be a man.

She snapped off the lamp beside Michael's bed, but when she turned to leave the darkened room she saw that Jonah was standing in the doorway. The hall light outlined his wide shoulders and his eyes were hidden in shadows, but she was aware that her own face was spotlighted by the light flooding through the open door. How long had he been there, and how much of herself had she given away as she'd stood beside Michael's bed, staring down at the sleeping boy?

"You look tired," Jonah said. "Why don't you get ready for bed? I'm going downstairs to fix myself a cup of hot chocolate. I'll bring one to your room after I lock up."

She started to tell him not to bother, then changed her mind. Things were on an even keel between them. Why do anything to change that?

She took a quick shower and had just finished brushing the tangles out of her hair when Jonah's knock came. She dropped the brush on a chair, tossed on her robe and hurried to open the door.

"I brought some cookies, too," Jonah said. He had changed into his dark maroon robe and was holding a small tray. "Where should I put this?"

Raine noticed distractedly that there were two cups on the tray, plus a small saucer of cookies. It looked so innocuous—after all, hot chocolate and cookies!—that she nodded toward a small gateleg table by the window.

"Drink it while it's still hot," he ordered. "I hope you don't mind that I brought myself a cup, too. I thought we might have a talk while we had our snack."

Without waiting for an answer he plopped down on an oak rocker, looking impossibly masculine and self-assured. Since she couldn't think of any reasonable objection, she settled herself gingerly on a nearby spool-backed chair, feeling self-conscious in her practical and less-than-glamorous robe.

"What do you want to talk about?"

"Michael," he said. "He's becoming very fond of you, something I think you should discourage. I don't want my son to be hurt when you leave, as you eventually will."

"Love doesn't hurt people," she said steadily. "It strengthens them. And separations are part of life, which is something we all have to learn eventually. Besides, we've talked about it, and Michael already accepts the fact that I won't be here once my job is finished. Also, with your permission, I'd like to write to him after I'm gone."

"What a paradox you are, Raine," Jonah said softly. When he rose and came toward her, reaching out to brush the back of his hand against her cheek, she felt a wave of panic and flinched. "Those were real tears I saw in your eyes when you were standing by Michael's bed. He's managed to get under that very tough skin of yours, hasn't he?"

"He's a wonderful boy," she said, her voice a little unsteady.

"Yes. And even a calculating woman like you has her soft moments."

Raine glared at him, her momentary lapse gone. She jumped to her feet and pointed her finger dramatically at the door. "Get out! *You're* certainly not a paradox, Jonah Duncan! You're just what you seem—an insensitive oaf who never really left the Bronx streets behind."

She started toward the door, intending to fling it open, but her own robe foiled her attempt. Her foot got tangled in the hem and then she was plunging toward the floor—until Jonah caught her deftly and set her back on her feet.

"You're always tripping over your robe and falling into my arms," he said, and now his tone was teasing. "Is it one of your little tricks, or is there something psychological about it?"

She tried to glare into his eyes, but he was standing so close that she was forced to stare at his chest instead. "Let me go," she said through clenched teeth.

"Okay, but first you owe me something for saving you from your own clumsiness." He lowered his head, and when she saw that he meant to kiss her, she tried to jerk away. He laughed softly and cupped one hand behind her head, immobilizing it. Despite her struggles, he held her easily while he leisurely took full possession of her mouth. When the kiss deepened, she made the shameful discovery that she didn't want it to end, even though his arms were holding her so close now that she found it hard to breathe. When he lifted his head she felt so breathless that she was forced to lean against him, her eyes half-closed, her mouth throbbing.

"My God, Raine, you drive me out of my mind." Jonah's voice was hoarse, full of torment. "When I touch you, I forget all my resolutions. I don't really understand this—this hold you have over me."

He captured her face between his hands, forcing
her to look at him. "You're a beautiful woman,
but I've known other beautiful women and none
of them has ever affected me the way you do. So
what is it? Is it your hair?" He filled his hands
with her hair, then let it drift through his fingers.
"Or is it your skin, which looks like ivory, feels
like satin and smells of flowers?" He touched her
cheek with his thumb, ran it over the contours of
her face, following the curve of her cheekbone and
the swell of her throat. "Or is it your mouth,
which tastes so fresh?" He bent to kiss her gently,
his tongue probing the sensitive inward curve of
her lips. "Or is it your body, so obviously made to
give a man pleasure?"

And now he pulled the ends of her belt slowly,
untying it. As if hypnotized by his words, by his
touch, she could only stare into his eyes as the belt
slipped to the floor. The robe fell open, exposing
her still-damp body to his gaze. He drank in her
nudity as if he were tasting her with his eyes, while
she stood there motionless, caught up in the fire
that flamed in his eyes.

He kissed her gently then—oh, so gently! An
ache throbbed through her, a hunger that demanded more intimacy, and she moaned deep in her
throat, pressing herself against him. As if the
moan had triggered off a small explosive inside
Jonah, his kiss became demanding, and his
tongue, a velvet lance, hot and throbbing, pierced
her lips and took total posession of her mouth.

A pulsating started up in her ears, as if giant

wings were fluttering around her, enveloping her, and a barrier that had stood until now, protecting her from her own folly, suddenly tumbled down and she was yielding, compliant in his arms.

The robe fell to the floor, leaving her even more vulnerable, but it didn't matter now. Nothing mattered but the scorch of Jonah's lips, the feel of his hard aroused body against her own hungry flesh. When the kiss ended and he stood back a little, his eyes devouring her again, she gloried in the signs of his aroused passion—the slight swelling of his full lower lip, the pulse that throbbed at his temple, the flush on his cheekbones, the fever in his eyes.

It was that same feeling of recklessness that seemed to guide her hands as she reached out and pulled at the ends of his belt. Like hers, it untied easily, and with a husky laugh he flung his robe aside and stood revealed in all his maleness. Her breath caught as she stared at the brown hardness of his body; it seemed incredibly beautiful to her starved eyes. He touched her, but only to take her hand in his, to lead her toward the bed.

He lifted her high in the air then, as if glorying in the power of his own strength. When he buried his face in the soft flesh of her abdomen, his breath felt hot and scalding against her skin, and as his lips caressed her she gasped aloud from pure pleasure. For a long moment, one she never wanted to end, he held her there, and she rested her hands on his shoulders, buried her face in the crispness of his hair, bending to him, yielding to him.

"I want you, Raine," he murmured, and his words, the throb of his voice were an aphrodisiac, stirring her to wildness. "I want you so much—and you want me, too. Right now your pulse is fluttering like a wild bird and your skin is hot, as if you are blushing all over. Remember how it was the night we made love. Let me love you the same way again...."

Some last remnant of sanity whispered a warning, but it was already too late. In answer her hands tightened on his shoulders and she strained toward him, mutely begging him to end her torment and appease the sweet hunger that had taken her over.

He lifted his head and kissed her breasts before he lowered her slowly to the bed, and the friction of their bodies moving against each other drove her crazy as she felt the hair of his chest rubbing her stomach, her breasts, her face.

She knew the strength of his thighs, pressing against her, his hard unyielding maleness. She knew the delight of having him shudder under the force of his own desire as she pressed herself against him, her thighs holding him, enveloping his maleness with her softness. He rose above her, looking down at her, and she was sure that she would die if he didn't possess her immediately.

But still he held back. He touched her with a fingertip, ran it along the curve of her shoulder to her elbow, then down to her hands. As if he had never seen a woman's hand before, he examined her long slender fingers, kissing them one by one, then tasting the sensitive flesh of her palms with his tongue.

Carefully, so gently that at first it was only a brushing of his lips, he took her breast in his mouth, surrounding the sensitive tip with the warm moistness of his lips and his encircling tongue. A pulsation, infinitely sweet and piercing, started up deep in her loins, as if he was already possessing her wholly.

His hands lifted her full breasts, cupping them, and then drifted lower to stroke the smooth mound of her stomach, the satiny skin of her inner thighs, the soft incredibly sensitive skin that ached to receive him, to be the vessel of his desire. When his lips followed the passage that his hands had already traversed, she felt as if she were floating, as if the bed had melted out from under her, and again the sound of wings seemed to fill her head.

Jonah groaned as if he were in pain, and when he buried his face in the valley between her breasts she stroked his hair, crooning deep in her throat.

"Touch me, Raine," he whispered, and she ran her hands eagerly, willingly over his chest, along his body, his thighs, touching him, stroking him, knowing him as he had known her. And then he was kissing her, this time so passionately that she was sure he would steal her breath away completely.

She strained toward him, offering herself to him, opening herself to him. A heat, an exquisite delight, pierced her as their bodies joined, then moved to a rhythm both ancient and eternally new. She felt a completeness, a meshing, a rush of such joy that it was at this moment that she finally knew the truth. What she felt for Jonah, what she had been fighting so hard against, was love, not desire alone.

And then she was drowning, spiraling upward toward the pinnacle of passion as the world around her dissolved into pure sensation.

A fierce joy, born of her long abstinence, of the love for Jonah she'd just rediscovered, took her will over. She heard her own cry as the room rocked around her, and then there was nothing but the two of them, locked in the most intimate of embraces, nothing but the wonder of this man and this woman melded in perfect union, this blending of life forces, this lifting and falling and lifting again, this climb toward fulfillment, slow at first, then faster and faster, this hardness against softness, flesh against flesh, soul meeting soul on a higher plane. . . .

The world returned in degrees. The feel of crumpled sheets under her body, the warmth of Jonah's thigh beneath hers, the sound of his breathing, of her own breathing. Under her lips, pressed against his throat, she tasted the tangy saltiness of his heated skin and breathed deeply the musky smell, so infinitely dear to her, that was Jonah's alone. Against the bare skin of her back she felt the slow stirring of a cold draft, and although she would have welcomed something warm to shield her, she was too depleted, too content to move.

A shyness crept over her, and then, one by one, came the questions. Why was Jonah so silent? Where were the passionate words he'd whispered earlier? And why were his arms folded above his head instead of holding her, embracing her? Was it possible that he was asleep?

Slowly she raised herself up on one elbow, staring at him. In the soft glow of the bedside lamp, she saw that his eyes were open, that he was watching her. She started to lower her head to kiss the pulse that moved under his chin, but the expression on his face stopped her. What was it she saw there? Was it fear? Why would he look so strange, almost as if he were afraid of her?

"What is it, Jonah?" she whispered.

When he didn't answer, when he looked away and stared up at the ceiling, his face unsmiling, she felt a throb of fear. Had she disgusted him with her abandon?

"I suppose this is when we talk price," he said, his cutting voice dissecting her. "You're very good. Too good for my peace of mind. So what is it you want in return for more of the same? To be let out of your contract? Or is it money?"

Once more Raine's pride came to her rescue. With her world in tatters around her, with a soul-sickness so deep that she felt faint and disoriented, she somehow found the strength to roll away from Jonah, to slip off the bed, to pick up her robe from the floor and put it around her shoulders, instinctively using its spurious protection against his stare as her own thoughts frayed her.

How could she have been so stupid, so weak? He had warned her that he would extract his pound of flesh and yet she had allowed herself to be swept away, had let him make love to her again. No...*not* love. It hadn't been that for Jonah. What had been a soul-searing experience, an exultation to her, had been raw passion, lust, all the ugly words that designated the darker side of love, to him.

She had let it happen again! She had let him seduce her with his kisses, his touch, his words, and now he knew how vulnerable she was, how much she wanted him. No...no, she had to do something, say something to change all that, if only for the sake of her self-respect.

Suddenly she knew what she had to do to erase the past few minutes from Jonah's mind, to turn the tables on him....

She forced herself to look at him then, to meet his narrowed gaze, and when she spoke her voice was so hard that she hardly recognized it as her own.

"But you already know my price, Jonah—your tutelage and patronage in launching my career. Since you're unwilling to pay that because of your—your hang-up about music, then just chalk this episode up to a mutually satisfying experience we both wanted. After all, I'm human. I needed a man and you were available. But this is just a one-time thing. In the future, it's strictly business as usual between us."

Her voice failed her then. Knowing how close she was to tears, she turned blindly and stumbled toward the bathroom. Half expecting him to follow her so he could have his own say, she shut and locked the door behind her, then stood there, her hands crushed against her mouth, choking back the sobs.

She tried to take some solace in having salvaged her pride—her poor pitiful pride. At least Jonah would never know what his lovemaking had meant to her. That much she had to be grateful for. But oh, the pain, the taste of ashes in her throat, this knowledge that while she loved Jonah, he only wanted her body....

She was still standing there, leaning against the sink, her head bowed as if a crushing weight were holding it down, when she heard the bedroom door open, then close softly. Only then did she let go and allow the tears to flow unchecked down her cheeks.

CHAPTER FIFTEEN

IT WAS A SMALL THING that triggered off Raine's tears again just when she was sure she had no more left.

Long after midnight she had finally gone to bed, only to spend a restless night fighting painful emotions that threatened to overwhelm her, trying to make plans for the future—a future that seemed so empty now. She had slept eventually, but even this respite was troubled, filled with nightmares, and at daybreak when she crawled out of bed, she felt as if she had aged a thousand years.

It was when she spotted the tray that Jonah had brought to her room, still sitting on the small gateleg table, that the tears returned, mercifully blotting out the mugs of cold chocolate and Tilda's untouched cookies from her sight. Clutching her upper arms with her hands, Raine rocked back and forth, and when the tears finally stopped she felt drained and empty of all emotion except the last lingering sting of self-contempt, the knowledge that she had contributed to her own unhappiness.

She had been so full of false pride, so intent upon proving to Jonah how unimportant their brief affair had been to her that she'd put on an act, pretending that she'd come here to coerce him into tutoring her for the Tchaikovsky competition. And she'd been so convincing that he hadn't had any trouble believing her. Was it this that had repelled him last night, once the fever of their lovemaking was over?

And why not? It would repel any decent man, and in his own way, Jonah was that. In the past few weeks she had come to realize that he wasn't the despicable man she'd thought him to be. He had his failings—ruthlessness, a self-confidence that bordered on arrogance. But he was also capable of great love—for his wife, even though he'd been unfaithful to her; for his son, for whom he had sacrificed his own career.

Yes, he could be very kind, tolerant and caring, and she had forfeited any chance she might have had to share his life by her own foolish pride. So now she was right back where she'd started three years ago, in love with a man who wanted her but didn't love her. Only this time she didn't have the shield of hate to protect her from pain.

Another question nagged her. Would she have stood a chance to win Jonah's love if she'd been honest at the beginning and had told him how devastated she'd been when his note and gifts had arrived that day in New York, that in her despair she had torn the roses apart, petal by petal, finally tossing them and that hateful bracelet in the trash?

It was so useless asking herself these questions. Because now there was no way of proving that she wasn't the woman he believed her to be, amoral and calculating, willing to do anything to further her career. Oh, yes, he desired her. What she had felt last night he had felt, too. She had seen it in his eyes, heard it in his voice, felt it thundering through his body. But with him it was pure sex, and that wasn't enough for her. She wanted Jonah's love, not just his passion. How could she possibly settle for less when her own feelings ran so deep and strong?

It was better when I believed that I hated him.

There was a prickling behind her eyelids, but she blinked hard, afraid that if the tears started again, this time she wouldn't be able to stop. She went into the bathroom, bathed her hot face with cold water, then took a shower, letting water splash over her body for a long time as if it could wash away the hurt and sense of loss that seemed almost to be a permanent part of her these days.

When she went downstairs to breakfast she used the service staircase, not wanting to take the chance of running into Michael. How could she face his clear eyes this morning, knowing that she'd spent part of the night in bed with his father?

Luckily, Luke and Tilda seemed as disinclined to talk as she did, and it was a silent meal. Several times Raine caught Tilda's sidelong glances, and she wondered if the Cummingses suspected what had happened between Jonah and her. For whatever reason, neither of them commented about her lack of appetite as she pushed her food around her plate, finally managing to force down a few token bites of Tilda's crusty soda biscuits.

The kitchen phone buzzed as she was scraping the remainder of her food into the garbage can.

Tilda answered it, then turned to look at Raine. "It's a man, asking for you, Raine," she said briskly. "Why don't you take it in the hall where you can have privacy?"

Raine's heartbeat quickened. Who could possibly be calling her at this hour unless—was it Jonah? Had he gone off to the winery early, as he sometimes did, then decided to call and find out how she was this morning?

But when she picked up the receiver in the hall, it was her brother's voice that asked, "Raine? Is that you?"

It was so rare for Martin, who detested phones, to call her that her first thought was that something had happened to Gloria or Debra. "Is everything all right?" she asked anxiously.

"Everything's great. Where were you yesterday? I called this number a couple of times but didn't get an answer."

"I guess everybody was out for the day. What is it, Martin?"

"Well, I got a couple of days off, so Gloria and I decided to come up to Mendocino for a little vacation. Gloria's sister is looking after Debra and we wanted to take you out for dinner last night."

"I would have loved that, but I was out all day."

"So how about having lunch with us? There's a pretty decent dining room at our motel. Nothing fancy, but good food. And the price is right for a starving intern's paycheck. We'll be starting back to the city right after lunch, but it would be nice to see you before we leave."

Raine felt a small lift of her spirits. Sharing a lunch with Martin and Gloria struck her as an agreeable way to spend a couple of hours, especially since she needed so badly to be with someone who really cared about her. *And they do,* she thought, smiling for the first time that day.

"I'd love to have lunch with you, Martin," she said. "I set my own hours on my job, so why don't I come to your motel at, say, eleven? That will give us more time together."

"Great. It's the Sequoia, right off the highway. Room 22."

"The Sequoia. Room 22. Okay, I'll be there at eleven."

She was still smiling as she hung up the phone. At least she had a diversion, and she needed one to help her get through the day until she finally saw Jonah again. How would he act toward her? Business as usual, the way she'd suggested, or would his attitude toward her be different? Surely in front of Michael and Crystal he would at least be polite. . . .

"Well, I see you managed to get yourself included in Jonah and Michael's father-and-son outing yesterday," Crystal said. She was standing on the stairs, looking cool and lovely in a sleeveless dress that showed off her tanned arms.

"Michael wanted me to come along," Raine said.

"And of course *that* was his own idea, right? I hope your little excursion didn't give you any false ideas about your role here at Arlington House." Despite the coolness in Crystal's voice, Raine sensed her anger. Or was that fear she saw in those blue eyes? "I wouldn't want to see you get hurt. There are things you don't understand."

"Then explain them so I can," Raine said, suddenly weary of Crystal's innuendos and warnings.

Crystal surveyed her with appraising eyes. She nodded suddenly as if making up her mind. "Come with me. There's something I want to show you. Maybe then you'll see. . . ."

She didn't finish the sentence. She turned and started up the stairs without looking back. Raine was tempted simply to slip away, but her curiosity was too strong. With a mental note to escape as soon as possible, she followed Crystal upstairs, then along the hall, finally stopping at a door near the master-bedroom suite.

"This is Jonah's room. He moved in here after Elaine died because he couldn't bear sleeping in the master suite without her."

"I don't think we should—"

"You've come this far. If you want to understand Jonah, bear with me."

Raine bit her lip, then nodded. She did want to understand Jonah, even if it meant more pain.

A minute later she was standing in Jonah's bedroom; like all rooms at Arlington House it was very spacious with tall windows, gleaming hardwood floors and an ornately decorated fresco that emphasized the height of its ceiling. The dark mahogany furniture, massive and well preserved, was early Victorian, making Raine suspect that it had been part of Arlington House's original furnishings.

As she studied the scroll carvings on the huge

highbacked bed, she decided it suited Jonah. With his scorn for sham and imitations, it was natural that he would choose to live with the original furnishings rather than something more modern. Her eyes lingered on the bed, then moved away quickly when she saw that Crystal was watching her.

"What is it, Crystal? I have work to do."

"Oh, I won't keep you long." Crystal went to switch on a Chinese porcelain lamp. "This is what I want to show you." She pointed to a silver-framed photograph on the nightstand next to the bed. "I think you'll realize then that there's nothing here for you."

Even before she looked at the photograph, Raine braced herself for another assault upon her fragile emotions. It was Elaine's lustrous eyes that stared out at her from the photograph. She was dressed in white, in a bridal gown and veil; her eyes glowed with an inward fire, and her lips, sensuously full, curved into a triumphant smile that held complete knowledge of her own sexual power.

A desire to turn and run seized Raine. That she remained there was only because she refused to show weakness in front of Crystal, who was watching her so closely. "You see, don't you? Any woman who tries to take Elaine's place in Jonah's life can only get hurt. He keeps her portrait by his bed. He won't allow anyone to put it away. And every day he puts fresh flowers beside it."

She nodded toward a bouquet of deep pink roses, glowing softly in a crystal vase beside the photograph. "Elaine's picture is the last thing he sees before he falls asleep and the first thing when he awakens. Oh, Jonah is all man and he has his needs. But his little flings never last long. I scolded him once about his women, but he told me that he only has affairs with women who can't be hurt, that if they show any signs of wanting a deeper relationship, he breaks it off.''

Raine discovered it was hard to breathe. The cloying sweetness of the roses seemed to fill her nostrils. She wanted to leave, to get away from this shrine to a dead woman, but something, a terrible curiosity, held her there, listening as Crystal went on.

"All the men were after her, you know. But it was Jonah she wanted. And of course he wanted her. He's never gotten over her. He never will. Even from the grave she has his love. Did you know that this is the anniversary of the day she was killed? That's where he is right now, visiting her grave with Michael. He doesn't want the boy to forget her, either. That's why he'll never remarry, you see. I pity any woman who takes his attentions seriously.''

Raine knew she had to escape from the room or she would end up disgracing herself by screaming. She murmured an excuse, and it must have made sense because Crystal nodded then turned away to switch off the lamp.

A few minutes later Raine found herself in the storage room sitting on an upturned crate, her face buried in her hands. Although she wouldn't allow herself to cry, her shoulders shook with silent sobs. After a while, because there was nothing else to do, she returned to work. Miraculously she became so absorbed that when she finally remembered her lunch engagement with Martin and Gloria and checked her watch, it was already ten-thirty.

She hurried upstairs to change into a thin summer dress, and it was well past eleven when she knocked on the door of Room 22 at the Sequoia Motel.

Martin, who answered her knock, brushed off her apologies. "Don't worry. Gloria's still in the shower. She says this is pure luxury, not having to wonder if the hot water will run out just when she gets soaped up."

He gave her a solid kiss on the cheek and a warm bear hug before he led her into the room, his arm around her shoulder. Since he was usually undemonstrative, Raine must have shown her surprise, because he grinned cheerfully and told her, "Until recently, I don't think I ever really appreciated how glad I am to have you for a kid sister."

"That's probably my fault," she said, warmed by his words. "I've always been so tied up in my music—"

"And me with my test tubes. Well, we're our parents' children. And since it turned out okay, who's to blame them for pushing us so hard all our lives?"

Raine gave him a puzzled look. "What does that mean?"

"They expected so much from us, you know. Sometimes it was hard to live up to their expectations."

"Well, they were proud of us, of course, but—"

"Sure, but they also expected us to be what they

weren't, and that's a bit hard to take. I was to be the doctor of the family because that's what dad always wanted to be, and you, well, I guess you were compensation for mom's busted career as a concert pianist. Luckily it fell in with our own interests or we might be two very unhappy people right about now. What if the sight of blood sickened me or if you had been tone-deaf?''

It was a new idea to Raine. She had always known that her mother encouraged her in her music because of her own thwarted career, but she hadn't thought of Martin as being pushed in the direction of medicine by their father. And yet the evidence was all there: the chemistry kits he'd given Martin through the years, the math and science tutelage that was so out of line with his income, and later, the expensive prep school that had made Martin a virtual stranger to his family. . . .

"Don't all parents buy thousand-dollar microscopes for their eleven-year-old sons?" she said, trying to make a joke out of it.

Martin laughed and hugged her again. "I'm not complaining. I guess what I'm asking you is if a career in music is really what you want, little sister.''

"Yes," Raine said, thinking of the bleak years ahead when she would have only her music to console her. "I don't know what I'd do without it.''

"Well, I feel the same way about medicine. It's what I want to do for the rest of my life. I think I'd wither up and die if I didn't get to be a full-fledged doctor," he said. "So it's lucky that it's going to happen, thanks to dad's insurance. And your job. Which is my next question. How do like working for the lion of the music world? Lots of deep discussions about Mozart and Bach?''

"Jonah Duncan has retired from music. And anyway, I seldom see him," Raine said evasively.

"Too bad. I had this fantasy that he would take a personal interest in you and become your mentor, or whatever they call it in the music world.''

"Well, forget it," she said shortly. "I'll be finished in a few days, and a month from now I doubt he'll remember my name.''

Gloria, her face flushed and unusually animated, came out of the bathroom looking very pretty in a brown-and-white summer suit. For the next hour, as they ate a leisurely lunch in the motel's comfortable café, the conversation was mostly about Debra, who had been put on a new medicine that seemed to be working. With such good company and her own skimpy breakfast, Raine discovered she was ravenously hungry, and also that it was possible for this short time to put Jonah out of her mind.

But on the way back to Arlington House her mood changed. In a few hours she would be sitting across from Jonah at the dinner table. Would he treat her with open hostility, or had he already put the whole incident out of his mind? Did she come under the heading of "flings," someone he could shrug off? Crystal had told her that his affairs lasted only until the woman showed signs of wanting a deeper relationship. Had she betrayed herself last night in his arms, shown her love for him? That expression she had seen in his eyes after they'd made love had been fear. Was he afraid that she would demand too much from him, get to be a nuisance? If so, her taunting words must have put those fears to rest, once and for all.

She returned to work, but the afternoon seemed endless now. When she found herself listing the same books twice, she finally gave up and went upstairs to get a cup of coffee. She had reached the front hall when she heard a car start up. Glancing through the glass panels of the front door she caught a glimpse of Crystal and Jonah driving away in his Mercedes.

So Jonah had returned from the cemetery and was going off again, probably to the winery to make up for the time he'd lost the day before. That meant the house was clear and she could get in a little practicing. No matter how mixed up her personal life, music was constant, and she would need it even more now that she had shut love out of her life.

A few minutes later as she was limbering up her fingers by doing some simple scales, Michael joined her. She smiled into his eager face and signed a greeting, but she didn't ask him about his visit to the cemetery that morning. If visiting his mother's grave had depressed him, it was obvious that he'd shaken it off. Their excursion the day before seemed to be all that he had on his mind and she finally had to cut him off, promising they would talk later.

Michael settled himself on his floor cushions, his arms wrapped around his knees. As she began her daily routine, she was aware that he was following her every movement with his eyes. An hour later, when she finally stopped to stretch her back and flex her fingers, he rose immediately and approached the piano. He seemed fascinated by the keys, and when he touched one tentatively with a fingertip, she signed, "Do you remember watching your father playing?"

"Yes. The music is still in my mind."

Raine met his clear gaze, and because she felt a fierce desire to protect him from the pain that inevitably lay ahead for him, she had a hard time not gathering him up in her arms. Was *this* what Jonah felt every time he looked at his son, the reason why he was so reluctant to let Michael go to school, to expose him to the sometimes cruel world that lay in wait outside the estate boundaries? He was wrong, of course, but she could understand his decision to keep his son shut away from hurt and disillusionment.

Michael moved restlessly, as if her stare was disconcerting him. She gave his shoulder a reassuring squeeze, then took his hands and positioned them above the ivory keys. When she pressed his fingers down a chord rang out in the room, and Michael cocked his head to one side as if trying to capture the sound. On his own this time, he struck the same keys, looking so pleased that she knew he must feel the vibrations. She showed him how to touch several keys to form the notes of "Chopsticks," and he repeated the sequence carefully, getting it right the first time.

"Why doesn't daddy like music anymore?" he asked then, and she could only shake her head, knowing it would be impossible to explain, especially since she wasn't sure herself what the truth was. Wanting to get his mind off a subject that was potentially painful to both of them, she asked if he'd like to take a walk, and his responding hug was exuberant that he nearly knocked her down.

Afer checking with Tilda, who gave her approval of the expedition, they went down to the beach. The sun was warm against their faces and arms and the sand soft underfoot as they followed the high-tide line, hunting for abalone shells. A voice hailed them, and when Raine turned she saw Rico Ortega smiling at them from the top of a boulder.

Although Michael was reserved at first, Rico, the youngest of the Ortega children, treated Michael's affliction naturally. He would touch Michael's arm and point whenever he wanted him to look at a sea gull or a boat on the horizon, and Michael soon forgot his initial shyness. As they raced along the sand, chasing the waves, it seemed especially poignant to Raine that only one boy should shriek as the water washed over their feet. When they tired, the two boys crouched side by side beside one of the cove's permanent tide pools, watching a school of tiny fish dart back and forth among the undulating seaweed.

Michael signed a question to Raine, asking her the name of a scarlet-tipped crab, and when she replied that she didn't know, Rico sat up, immediately full of his own questions. She explained about sign language, and he was so fascinated that she gave him a lesson there and then. His hands, clumsier than Michael's, found some of the signs especially difficult. Michael thought his efforts so hilarious that he rolled on the ground, laughing and holding his stomach. Rico got his revenge a few minutes later by slyly putting a tiny crab down Michael's back. Michael retaliated by flipping water at Rico, and the two boys were soon embroiled in a splashing battle to see who could get the other one the wettest.

Raine made no attempt to stop them. Let Michael take his thumps, as all youngsters must, but she kept a careful eye on them, too, to make sure that their water fight didn't get out of hand and unduly disturb the inhabitants of the tide pool.

By the time they stopped, each looking very pleased with himself, the sun was low in the sky. Raine got Michael's attention, then gestured toward the stairs. When they had climbed to the top, Rico, after promising that he'd go right home to change into dry clothes, went whistling off, but not before he elicited a promise from Raine to continue the sign-language lessons soon.

Feeling more cheerful than she had all day, Raine wrapped Michael in her sweater and followed him down the path toward the house. The wind, already cooler, cut through her thin shirt and she hurried Michael along, not wanting him to get chilled.

Her heart skipped a beat when she saw Jonah's car parked in the garage courtyard, but she wouldn't let herself think about him, about their next meeting. Tilda was scouring baking potatoes at the sink; she took one look at Michael and threw up her hands. Muttering under her breath, she bustled him off to his room for a hot bath and a change of clothes.

Raine, who was feeling a little guilty, got herself a cup of coffee, then stood by the kitchen window staring out into the deepening shadows of the vegetable garden, reluctant to go upstairs to change. *Maybe this is the night I should develop a headache and eat in my room,* she thought soberly.

She heard someone behind her and turned, expecting to see Luke or Tilda, but it was Jonah who stood there, watching her. "Will you come into the library?" he said. "I have something to discuss with you."

His cold voice and his formal manner chilled her. Silently she followed him down the hall. *All we need is the dirge from* Aida, she thought, unconsciously putting her hand up to hide the tell-tale pulse in her throat. To her surprise, when they turned into the library, Crystal was there, sitting in one of the dark red leather chairs.

When Jonah didn't speak, Raine asked, "Is something wrong?"

A muscle tensed in Jonah's jawline. "When you came here, it was with the tacit understanding that you would conduct yourself in a respectable manner. There's always a lot of local curiosity—and talk—about anything concerning Arlington House and its occupants. Which is why I find it so reprehensible that you would deliberately court gossip."

Raine stared at Jonah in bewilderment. Was he talking about last night? But no one could be that much of a hypocrite. . . .

"I have no idea what you mean," she said.

"Oh, come on, Raine." Crystal twisted the sapphire ring on her finger. "You've been caught out. Don't compound it by lying."

"Since I don't know what you're accusing me of, I can't very well defend myself, can I?"

"I'm talking about that exhibition you gave at the Sequoia Motel this afternoon," Jonah said. "If you find it necessary to meet your lover in broad daylight, at least you could be discreet."

"Jonah is right," Crystal drawled. "It's really too much. Standing in front of a window half-dressed while your friend fondles you is pretty gross."

Raine steadied herself with a deep breath. "And just when was this supposed to have taken place?"

"You know that as well as I do—unless you did it more than once. It really gave the help at the Sequoia something to gossip about. By tomorrow it'll be all over town that one of Arlington House's employees had a hot date in the middle of the afternoon at the Sequoia."

"Well, don't worry about it. No such thing took place," Raine retorted.

"Oh, come on. I overhead you making arrangements with your, uh, friend to come to his room at the Sequoia at eleven. You aren't denying you met a man there, are you?"

"Certainly not—although it's really none of your business. I did meet Martin at the motel. People do that quite regularly when they intend to go out to lunch together."

"Oh, you do like to play the innocent, don't you?" There were two spots of color on Crystal's cheekbones now. "If it was only a lunch date, how come you were standing in your slip in front of the window, the drapes open, at two this afternoon, be-ing—I think the maid who told a friend of mine about it called it 'being fondled by a male guest.' "

Despite her anger, Raine had to smile. So Martin and Gloria had extended their stay long enough for a little last-minute romancing. *Good for them,* she thought.

"I'm sorry that you aren't taking this seriously, Raine." Jonah's voice was like a splash of cold water. "I have no interest in your love life, but what you do in public in an introverted community like Mendocino does reflect upon us, and the winery. In the future, I suggest you be more discreet."

"I see. So you've already passed judgment on me, have you, Jonah?" Raine said, so angry that she forgot they had an audience. "You must think I'm really oversexed. Well, I don't owe you an ex-planation, but I'm going to give it anyway—"

"I'm not interested in—"

"Then why are we holding this conversation? I say you're *very* interested and you're going to hear me out, too. You owe me that for—for listening to the gossip of a malicious woman."

Crystal's gasp cut through her words, but Raine didn't take her eyes off Jonah's stony face. "The man whose room I went to this afternoon, which is probably what started this whole thing, was my brother," she went on. "His name is Martin Huni-cutt. The woman he was kissing was his wife, Gloria. They got a chance to be alone for a couple of days, something very rare in their busy lives, and I feel very honored that they wanted to spend an hour with me. If you don't believe me, you can call the motel and check on the names. And in the future, you might instruct your sister-in-law not to listen in on private phone conversations. In certain circles that's regarded as being very *gross* indeed."

From the corener of her eye she caught the consternation on Crystal's face. She turned her head and gave the dark-haired woman a long level look, not bothering to hide her scorn. A deep flush spread over Crystal's face. Before Raine could move, Crystal stood up and took a step toward her. There was a cry from the doorway and then a whirlwind descended upon them. Michael flung his arms around Raine's waist, his small body trembling. "Don't hit Raine—don't hit Raine, Aunt Crystal," he said clearly.

As if they all had stopped breathing, everyone froze. Raine could only stare down at Michael, too stunned to comfort him. But when he began to cry, she put her arms around his shoulders.

Jonah moved, too. Like a man sleepwalking, he crossed the library, took Michael by the shoulders and turned him around. "Can you hear me, Michael?" he said quietly.

Michael tried to get away, but when Jonah held him firmly, his head drooped and he looked down at the floor, his face reflecting misery.

"You can tell me the truth." Jonah's voice was gentle. His expression was strange, almost as if he were afraid to hope too much. "I won't be angry."

"I—I can hear pretty good now, daddy." Michael's voice was so faint it was hard to make out the words.

"How long have you—when did it happen?"

"It started a few months ago, a little at a time," Michael said. His eyes sought out Crystal's pale face, then moved away.

"Why didn't you tell me?"

"Aunt Crystal told me—she said you would go away if you knew, that the only reason you stayed here was because I couldn't hear."

"And you believed her?"

"She wouldn't lie," Michael said earnestly. "Aunt Crystal loves me best of anyone else in the world. But she wants you to stay with us, too. That's why I had to keep pretending. Only I don't like lying, daddy. It hurts—here." He touched his chest.

Jonah took a deep breath, then let it out slowly before he turned to face his sister-in-law. "Why, Crystal? What was behind this—this craziness? Was it some kind of revenge?"

Hypnotized by the disgust in his voice, Crystal stared into his eyes. When she dropped back into her chair, as if her legs had suddenly failed her, and put her hands up to hide her face, Raine felt a stir of pity under her own anger.

"I—it wasn't intentional, Jonah," Crystal said weakly. "When I realized that Michael's hearing was beginning to return, I just wanted to—to put things on hold for a while, to keep things like they were. Everything was going so well. You had just bought the winery and seemed so content, and Michael was so happy, having you around all the time. I just couldn't stand the thought of you going off and leaving him alone again. So I—I told Michael to pretend that nothing had changed until—until I'd had time to sort things out in my own mind. It wasn't until later that I realized that I was caught in a trap. I was afraid that if I told you the truth you'd make me leave. And where would I go? What would I do?"

"And that's why you robbed Michael of a normal life?"

Crystal made a weary gesture with her hand. "Normal life? With you gone all the time on your concert tours? With his mother dead and only a part-time father? I was only protecting what Michael has a right to."

Jonah ran his hand over his face as if trying to wipe away his own anger. His craggy face seemed etched with new lines, and he looked years older than thirty-seven.

"And what else were you protecting, Crystal? Were you so afraid of being on your own?"

"I admit that I don't want things to change. Can't you see why I want things to stay like they are? Everything else has been taken away from me. I have a right to some happiness, some security."

"You can do anything you like with your life, go anywhere, do anything. You can have a husband, a career, a family. You don't have to cling to the past, which wasn't all that great for you anyway, if you'll be honest with yourself. I think I did you a disservice when I asked you to live with Michael and me. Your values are all mixed-up. Maybe you should get some professional help to straighten you out."

"Are you saying I'm crazy just because I wanted you to make a home for your son?"

"It was the way you went about it. Lying and involving a boy you should have been protecting. Maybe you should leave and find your own way instead of hanging onto the remnants of your sister's life."

Crystal's face was white, her blue eyes filled with desperation. "Please don't send me away! I'll make it up to you and Michael—"

"I think it's time you stopped using Michael and me as your crutch, Crystal. Which is why I want you to pack your things and leave. Go find yourself a new life somewhere else."

Crystal began to cry, and suddenly Raine had had enough. Another minute and she knew she would start crying, too—and she had already shed enough tears in the past few hours to last her a lifetime.

She put her arm around Michael, intending to take him with her, but he pulled away. His face woebegone, he looked at his father and then his aunt. For a moment he wavered, and then he ran to Crystal and tugged urgently at her arm. "Don't cry, Aunt Crystal," he begged.

Raine must have made a sound because Jonah turned bleak eyes in her direction. "This is a private matter, Raine. I think you'd better go."

His words hurt, but she knew he was right. No matter how concerned she was about Michael, about Crystal, about Jonah himself, she was an outsider. Whatever had to be settled between Crystal and Jonah was a private matter that she had no right to witness.

Silently she turned and left the room.

CHAPTER SIXTEEN

DESPITE THE WARMTH of the day earlier, it was cold in the storage room. Or perhaps, Raine thought, it was her own dreary thoughts that chilled her body.

Although she tried hard not to think of the scene in the library, it was impossible to concentrate on her work. The Jonah whose arms had held her so tenderly last night seemed to be a different man from the one who had ordered Crystal out of the house. And yet she had seen his face when he'd realized that his son's hearing was returning. For a moment, until his anger at Crystal had been unleashed, there had been such joy there that it had made her heart turn over.

She shook her head, remembering his cold manner later. For a moment pity welled up inside her for Crystal, who had made a terrible mistake and whose punishment for it was to be banished from Arlington House—and from Michael. Had Jonah always been so hard, or had it been his wife's death that had changed the nature of the man she'd known so briefly in New York?

Or had that man, who had seemed so kind and caring, never existed at all? Maybe Jonah could assume the mantle of a warm loving human being the way an actor assumes a role in a play, using it to quell the resistance of a susceptible girl. That was what she had believed for the past three years, so why was she finding it increasingly hard to accept it as truth?

Of course it didn't really matter which man was the real Jonah or what made him the way he was. He wanted no part of her, and she knew only too well that she still wanted him, still loved him as much as she had that magical night in the Catskills.

The worst of it was knowing that some of her mental anguish was her own fault. Not for allowing Jonah to seduce her at their first meeting. She had been foolish and gullible, an easy mark, but then she'd been so unware of the force of her newly awakened sexuality that she'd had no defense against an experienced seducer. No, she felt no guilt for that, but she did share some of the blame for allowing Jonah to use her a second time as an outlet for his sexual drive.

Raine gave her head a hard shake, repudiating her thoughts, knowing she must stop brooding about what might have been. The thought of returning to the room where she and Jonah had made love such a short time before was unendurable, so she doggedly set to work picking up books, making notes, and then having to make them over again because she'd entered them in the wrong place.

When she had finished recording the contents of a fresh crate, she stood in the middle of the crowded room, looking around. Her work there was almost finished. Only a few crates remained unopened. The contents of the rest had been sorted, cataloged, most of them appraised and given a value. Two bookcase shelves held the books that needed an outside opinion, but that would be remedied when the antiquarian book specialist came from New York at the end of the month.

Wanting to postpone her return to the room that just the night before had held such happiness and pain, she selected another crate at random and pried the lid off. Working feverishly, she tried to bury her personal unhappiness in her work. But inevitably stray thoughts got through, and she finally gave it up when she found that she'd entered half a crate of books under the wrong category in her ledger.

After she'd washed her hands and splashed water on her face, she went upstairs, automatically turning into the kitchen. Tilda was sitting alone, her elbows resting on the scrubbed top of a butcher-block worktable. She was wearing a voluminous chenille robe and her eyelids were swollen and a little pink.

"What is it, Tilda?" Raine asked quickly.

"It's Crystal and Jonah. They had a terrible fight in the library, and then he stormed out of the house. And Crystal, she packed her things and took off, too. She was crying and carrying on so I could hardly make out what she was saying. Wouldn't tell me where she was going. Said she didn't know."

"I'm sorry," Raine said, and discovered she meant it. Crystal had done a terrible thing, but she'd been driven by a fear as strong and compelling as if it were a powerful drug. And Raine, who had her own fears, understood Crystal's desperation, even though she couldn't condone what she'd done to Michael.

"Maybe it's all for the best," Tilda sighed. "Crystal needs to get away from here and live her own life. But I'm going to miss her. Luke and me are right fond of that girl. Her mother died having her, so I took care of her when she was just a baby, you know. She was such a pretty little thing—not that Mr. Granton paid much attention to her. He never treated her right, blamed her for losing his wife, he did. And Elaine ordered her around like she was a hired girl. Always felt so sorry for her, creeping around the edges of her sister's life. Yet it was Crystal who took care of her father before he died and who looked after Elaine when she was in her cups—" Tilda stopped, looking uncomfortable.

"Did Mrs. Duncan drink a lot?"

"There now, my tongue's run away with me again. Well, she was what they call an alcoholic, I guess. No secret about that. And when she was drinking, there wasn't no controlling her. She did wild things. Foolish things."

Raine's heart lurched inside her. "Like driving too fast?"

"You guessed that, did you? Well, she was drinking heavy that night like she always did when she wasn't getting her own way. She must've started in right after she got that phone call from Jonah."

"A phone call? I thought he was here that night."

"He was, but that was later. He called her from the airport to tell her what time he'd be in. But she'd already left the house when he got here. Don't know what happened, but they must've had words on the phone because she was in a terrible temper after she hung up. Slamming things around and carrying on like crazy. She told us to go away, leave her alone, and we went on to bed. But if we'd had any idea she would take the car out when she was in that condition, we would've hid the keys like we'd done before. We was still awake when the garage door went up. A couple of minutes later the car went roaring down the driveway and then it was too late to stop her. We didn't know she had the boy with her until—until we got the news from that state policeman."

"So that's how you found out."

Tilda nodded, her eyes haunted. "We heard Jonah playing in the music room and knew he'd come in from the airport. I got up to fix him some coffee, and so I was the one who answered the phone. It was a terrible thing, having to go in there and tell him about Elaine and the boy. I thought he would go out of his mind. Kept saying he shouldn't've called, that he should've waited until he got home. . . ."

"And now he blames himself for the accident," Raine said dully.

"Never got over it. I don't think he ever will. The boy's a constant reminder of what happened. Giving up his music—that's what you might call Jonah's atonement." She sighed heavily. "And now Crystal is gone, and the boy's going to miss her. He don't have all that many people in his life."

"That might change now," Raine said. "Tilda, have you ever noticed any signs that Michael's hearing is returning?"

Tilda's eyes shifted sideways. "Don't reckon what I think matters much around here," she muttered. "Why you asking me that? Has something happened?"

"Michael spoke to us a while ago. He tells us that some of his hearing has returned."

Tilda's face broke into a wide smile. "Well. . . well, I did notice a couple of things," she admitted. "Like once I hit my elbow on the fool range and I said some words I shouldn't oughta. Michael, he come running in from the back, his face all white and scared until he saw I wasn't hurt. And there was other things. But when I said something about it to Crystal, she told me that if Luke and me wanted to go on working here long enough to get that pension Mr. Jonah promised us, we'd best mind our own business. Since I wasn't sure—well, we're pretty old to go out looking for new jobs."

At Raine's silence, Tilda looked restive, then she gave Raine a sharp look. "You reckon Crystal is gone for good?"

Raine thought of the chill in Jonah's eyes when he'd looked at Crystal; she nodded and Tilda sighed again.

"I was afraid it would come to this someday. And maybe it's the best thing all around. Crystal was too wrapped up in that boy, and in Jonah, too. Well, now she'll have to strike out on her own and it's either sink or swim." Her gloomy face revealed the way she thought it would go. "But it'll be best for Jonah and the boy. Give them both a chance to breathe, and maybe get to know each other better, too."

The teakettle began singing on the range and she got up to make tea. "I went to Michael's room to see why he hadn't come down for dinner, but he was already in bed, sleeping. I put a snack by his bed in case he wakes up hungry in the middle of the night. I'll fix you whatever you want. How about a small rib steak or a sandwich or—"

"I had an enormous lunch," Raine said quickly. "A glass of milk is all I need. Why don't you have your tea and go to your room? I can fend for myself tonight."

"I just might do that. Seems like I'm that upset, what with all the things going on around here."

More to placate Tilda than because she really was hungry, Raine drank a glass of milk and forced down a sliver of cake. Before she left the kitchen she got the music room key, knowing she was too restless for sleep. She unlocked the door of the music room, and when she saw there was a full moon shining in through the tall windows, she didn't bother to turn on the lights.

The graceful curve of the piano lid outlined against the moonlit window tempted her. She sat down on the bench and idly ran her hand across the keys. Almost as an extension of her thoughts, her fingers began playing a piece that had been one of her father's favorites. As the bittersweet melody of Debussy's *Clair de lune* filled the room, she felt herself relaxing, the music that had nurtured her all her life working its usual spell.

Somehow it seemed perfectly natural that a few minutes later, Michael, a dim figure in the shadows, should join her. He slid onto the bench and rested his head against her arm, and although it was difficult playing with him crowding up against her, she didn't stop. Even after Michael had fallen asleep, still leaning against her shoulder, she only stopped long enough to ease him down so his head was resting in her lap, freeing her arms.

The last poignant strains were still echoing through the room when the lights came on. Even before she turned she knew it was Jonah. He had come home. Instinctively she put a protective arm around Michael as Jonah stalked toward her. His face was so gaunt, the lines of weariness so pronounced, that an involuntary sigh escaped her lips. She wanted to put her arms around him, to comfort him as she had comforted his son, but she didn't move. He didn't want her comfort, and she didn't dare offer it. Not with his eyes so remote, his stare so cold. .

"I want to talk to you, Raine," he said.

She felt a stir of anger at the abruptness of his tone. "If you expect an apology because I've been using your piano—okay, I shouldn't be in here without your permission. But if you're angry about what happened this afternoon, I'm not sorry about that. I do think you were too hard on Crystal. She really loves Michael, you know."

He made a chopping movement with his hand, brushing aside her words. "I don't want to talk about her. But it seems I do owe you something for being the catalyst that revealed the truth about Michael."

There was a cynical twist to his lips as he added, "Maybe your motive for learning to sign was to ingratiate yourself with me, but I'm sure he got under your skin a little, too. And that business about you meeting your brother in town—I want to apologize for jumping to conclusions. However, in all fairness, I'll add that since you've made no secret of your sexual habits, it's no wonder the story seemed plausible. Also, since I took advantage of your—generosity last night, I've decided that you deserve your fee."

"What are you talking about?" she demanded.

"You told me that the price for your favors was my patronage. Well, I've been out of touch with the concert world for two years, but I still have some talent as a teacher. You've earned that much.

So I've decided to take on the job of getting you ready for competition.''

At her startled gasp, he held up his hand warningly. "No, not for the Tchaikovsky competition. That involves too much of an investment of my time. But the Gracey Memorial Competition will be held in San Francisco in a month. The prize is a year's tutelage by Joseph Dubois, including living expenses, to be followed by a short tour, provided the winner is ready for it by then. Dubois has the reputation for being able to hone young talent. If you have what it takes, you'll get your shot at Moscow next year.

She started to speak, but again he stopped her. "Before you decide, I want you to know just how things stand between us. After the Gracey Memorial Competition is over, win or lose, we're even. All debts paid. Is that understood? And I'll take this on only after you've auditioned for me. I have no way of knowing if you're even trainable, and I refuse to waste my time if your talent doesn't match your—audacity.''

Stung by the skepticism in his voice, she told him, "I've won competitions before!''

"I'll make up my own mind. If you accept my offer, you'll have to convince me that your talent is worth the inconvenience to me. And I'm warning you. I'm not too impressed by some of the Juilliard graduates who sound like clones out of the same box.'' He gestured to the mother-of-pearl encrusted cabinet where the musical scores were stored. "Look through the material in there and choose something you know. You'll play for me as soon as I put Michael to bed, and you'd better be good.''

Seeming not to notice her stony silence, he bent to pick up Michael; a moment later, he was gone, leaving her sitting there, staring after him.

Until this moment her anger had sustained her, but now she leaned against the piano, resting her hot cheek against the cool wood. Only the fear that she might awaken Michael had kept her from screaming at Jonah, telling him what he could do with his grudging and insulting offer.

The tears dried in her eyes as a tempting thought came to her. That offer...if she turned it down, Jonah would simply shrug and tell her it was her own choice. She would finish her cataloging in another couple of days, and then she would leave, never to see him again. But as long as she was still here, there was always hope, the remote possibility that she could somehow change Jonah's mind about her.

Then there was Michael. Right now he felt lost because Crystal, one of the few people he loved, was going out of his life. If she went too, it would only deepen his loneliness. He needed her, at least for a while, as a buffer against the challenges that would open up to him now that his hearing was returning.

Last of all there was Jonah himself. She had made herself a promise that if she got the chance she would encourage him to return to his music. Wouldn't having him tutor her provide the time, the means? No matter how he felt about her or how much he had hurt her, his music shouldn't be lost to a world that had such need for beauty.

So there were three reasons for accepting his offer. Two unselfish and the other self-serving. The question was, could she possibly endure being with Jonah day after day, knowing what he thought of her?

She never did consciously make the decision. Before she could get her thoughts straightened out, Jonah strolled back into the room. "What are you going to play?" he demanded.

There was such impatience in his voice that her pride stirred again. "Beethoven's Sonata in F Minor."

His eyebrows lifted. "The "Appassionata"? Are you sure you're up to it?"

"I'm up to it," she said shortly.

Her lips set in a determined line, she went to the music cabinet and quickly found the Beethoven score. As she opened it and glanced down at the broken chord of F minor that opened the "Appassionata"s' first movement, she knew Jonah was right. She should have chosen something she'd worked on more recently.

The Beethoven sonata was a complicated piece with its difficult fortissimo chords, with the finger strength demanded in the prestissimo movement. Not only was her memory of it fuzzy, but her practice in general for the past weeks had been little more than finger exercises. She turned to face Jonah, intending to tell him that she would do

Schumann's *Kinderszenen*, a piece she had used for one of the competitions she'd won, but the cynical twist of his lips stopped her. Without a word she went to the piano, snapped on the light, and arranged the Beethoven score on the music stand.

At first, mainly because she was so aware of Jonah's brooding presence behind her, her fingers moved stiffly, without flexibility, and she knew that her playing lacked finesse. But by concentrating on every note, making every phrase, every measure as perfect as possible, she got through the difficult staccato notes of the eleventh measure without making a debacle of it. By the time she had finished the difficult legato at the end of the first movement, where she stopped, she felt rung out and depleted. Her breath quickened by the physical effort of rendering the long movement, she rested her hands in her lap and turned her head to look at Jonah.

He had moved to the window and was staring out at the night; his back told her nothing, nor did his face when he finally turned around. "You play like an automaton," he said. "Where is the fire, the feeling that separates a merely adequate pianist from one with concert quality?"

Again there was that familiar twist to his lips as he added, "If you played the piano the way you make love, you would be ready for competition this minute. As it is, your technique is perfect—and dull as tapioca pudding. What the hell have they been teaching you at Juilliard?"

Raine started up from the piano, her face flushed with anger and disappointment. "I don't have to listen to this—"

"You'll listen to it or you can pack your things and get out right now."

"You're very good at ordering people out of your house, aren't you?" she said bitterly.

For a long moment, he stared at her. She braced herself, expecting more of his cutting words, but instead his eyes lost their hard glitter and he ran his hand over his face as if trying to wipe away a painful memory.

"I didn't enjoy telling Crystal to leave. But I had to make it clear that there was no chance that she could stay on here. Her only hope for pulling her life together is to turn her back on this refuge she's found with Michael and me. And you're right. I shouldn't have ordered you out of the house. It was uncalled for under the circumstances.

"However—" his voice hardened again —"let there be no mistake. If I decide to coach you, you'll have to agree to do exactly what I tell you to do. There'll be no excuses, no laziness. You have a lot of things to unlearn, such as the emphasis on mechanical perfection at the expense of individuality. I'd chalk you up as just one more adequate pianist except that I heard you playing Debussy as I was coming down the hall. You were hitting wrong notes like crazy, and your phrasing was atrocious, but there was something there, the emotion that was lacking when you did the Beethoven sonata. If you can learn to tap that inner well, you just might make a decent pianist. And that's the only reason I've decided to take you on—provided you agree to follow my instructions to the letter. Is it a bargain?"

Raine opened her mouth, fully intending to tell him to take his insults and go to hell. Instead, she heard herself say, "It's a bargain."

"I was sure it would be," he said, his smile thin. "Your conniving has finally paid off and you've got what you've wanted all along, haven't you? Okay, it remains to be seen if it's worth all the bother. One thing you can count on—the next month you'll work harder than you've ever worked before in your life. You'll sit at that piano every day until you're ready to drop, until your fingers are like lumps of ice, until your back is ready to break in two. But by the time I'm finished with you, you'll feel the music in your guts, not just in your head, and you'll be a musician, not a technician. And if you cry foul or try any of your tricks on me, out you go. On the other hand, if you do exactly what I say, I just might make a concert pianist out of you."

CHAPTER SEVENTEEN

THE NEXT MORNING when Raine went down to breakfast she found that Jonah had taken Michael into San Francisco for a complete physical check-up. It was three days before the two of them returned. She spent the time finishing off the book cataloging and psyching herself up for what she knew would be a difficult period ahead, not only physically but emotionally.

One thing that didn't worry her was fear that Jonah would let his feelings for her intrude upon his coaching. No matter what his personal opinion of her might be, he was a professional. He would do his best with her. This she was sure of. But her own emotional reaction...that was something else, something to worry about.

She spent a lot of time trying to come to terms with the painful knowledge that being in Jonah's company for hours every day, yet knowing that he despised her, would be pure torture, and that she was willing to endure it for the simple reason that not to be with him would be even worse. She, who had always been so proud of her independence, who had been so in control of her life, had made the painful discovery that where Jonah was concerned she was helpless against her own emotional needs. Her only consolation was that she could at least salvage her pride by hiding her true feelings behind a wall of professionalism.

When Jonah returned with Michael the news was so good that for a while she forgot her own problems.

"The doctors at the Hardesty Clinic, where Michael was originally treated, ran every test possible, and they're sure that his hearing is nearly back to normal. It seems that when Crystal realized what was happening she withdrew Michael from the clinic, saying that she was transferring him to a doctor in Sacramento because it was closer. After the accident Michael suffered from a small concussion, and when it was discovered that his hearing was gone the conclusion was that the accident had somehow damaged his auditory nerves. Now they're sure that it was shock, a form of hysteria. If Crystal hadn't withdrawn him so quickly they would have discovered the real situation in short order."

"Then Michael will recover completely?"

"His doctors recommend professional therapy for a while in case there should be some latent trauma from the accident—and also from the mental strain he's been under the past few months. Otherwise he's a perfectly normal boy."

Raine's face must have shown her relief because Jonah's lips curved into a brief smile. "He can start school in Mendocino in the fall. I stopped to see Tim Turlock on the way in to tell him the news, and he suggests that I enroll Michael in a local summer program for kids his age. It's pure recreation—swimming and baseball and crafts—but it might make him feel less like an outsider when school opens."

He glanced over at Michael, who was absorbed in putting together a new jigsaw puzzle. "Michael tells me he already has one friend, Rico Ortega. I think I'll ask the Ortegas to enroll Rico in the summer program, too. That way Michael won't feel so alone the first day."

"That's a good idea, although I'm afraid Rico will be disappointed that there's no reason for him to learn sign language now."

He frowned at her. "You seem to know more about my son than I do," he said.

"We met Rico on the beach, and he was so interested in signing that I taught him a few of the letters," she said, wondering why she should feel so defensive.

"Well, maybe he should learn it anyway. Tim tells me that if more people knew how to sign there would be better understanding of the hearing impaired. It's a new idea to me, but it makes a lot of sense."

"Tim is a very compassionate man," Raine said, her voice warm.

Jonah gave her a sharp look. "Yes, I understand you two saw a lot of each other before you decided to ignore my orders and use the Steinway for your practicing. He has quite a good opinion of you. Let's hope you never disillusion him.''

"I don't intend to," she retorted. Her voice was so sharp that Michael glanced up. She gave him a reassuring smile, then waited until he wandered out of the room before she added, "I'm sure Michael will make the adjustment without too much trouble. He has a gift for making friends, maybe because his disability has made him sensitive to other people.''

"Michael has a lot of my father in him," Jonah said. "Dad made friends and kept them because he could always walk in the other fellow's shoes. He died without a cent of savings, but there were so many people at his memorial service that they overflowed the church.''

"Then his life was a success, wasn't it? It was the same with my father. A dozen or more people I didn't know came up to me after his funeral to tell me stories about his kindness," Raine said, her voice colored with sadness.

"Were you and your father close?"

"Not really. We loved each other, of course, and we did share a love of books and music, but it was only after his death that I realized what a truly fine man he was. It's the same with my brother. Ironically, it was our father's death that—that brought us closer.''

"Well, you're lucky to have a brother. I was an only child. My one living blood relative is Michael.''

"I guess we have a lot in common," she said.

"Superficially, perhaps," he replied, the chill back in his voice. "But the way we view life is quite different."

"Meaning that you're so honorable and I'm not?" she said, goaded into retaliation. "Well, at least I wasn't married when I—when we made love that first time."

His eyes bored into hers. "You're under a misapprehension, Raine. The night we met, I thought I was a single man. My wife had gone off with another man, taking Michael with her. She left word that she was getting a Mexican divorce, that it would be final by the time she returned to New York. I had no reason not to believe her. Then the man in question changed his mind, and she returned to New York without the divorce."

Raine fought against a sudden weakness in her knees. So Jonah hadn't knowingly betrayed his wife. She was aware of such a wave of intense relief that for a moment she felt dizzy. Then, as Jonah went on, her relief dissolved into anger again.

"Since you must have believed that I was married, what does that say about your morals, Raine?" he asked harshly.

"How could I know you were married?" she said hotly. "It never entered my mind."

His eyelids flickered. "Okay, I'll give you that. But the fact remains that I did think the divorce was in effect. Otherwise—" He ended the sentence with a shrug. "And I think this conversation is nonproductive. Tomorrow you start your practice sessions. I want you downstairs early—no later than seven. You'll spend an hour exercising before breakfast—jogging or running or bicycling, I suggest. I swim in the cove most mornings, but when it's too cold or windy I'll probably join you for a run."

He hesitated, then added, "In the afternoons I want you to take another hour of exercise. You might take Michael along for company. It would do him good, and he isn't that much of a bother."

"I've never considered Michael a bother," she said tightly. "And I intend to see as much of him as possible while I'm still here. Just because I'll be busy, I don't intend to neglect him."

Her lips set, she got up from the sofa where she'd been sitting. "I'll be on time in the morning. You won't regret that you've decided to coach me."

"I'm sure of that," he said, and to her sensitized ears there was an ominous grimness in his voice.

THE NEXT MORNING Raine was downstairs at six o'clock, wearing jeans and a sweat shirt. Since Jonah hadn't appeared she took off on her own, jogging along the road toward the highway, enjoying the freshness of the morning air against her flushed cheeks. An hour later, ravenously hungry, she was back in the kitchen, putting coffee on to perk and trying to decide what she wanted for breakfast.

Jonah, his hair wet and his skin glowing from an early-morning swim, appeared in the doorway.

She started to ask if she could fix him something to eat, but he was already taking eggs and cheese out of the refrigerator. An old memory stirred, stabbing her with pain, and she put her hand up to cover her mouth, afraid a sigh might escape and betray her.

As if he'd heard her silent sigh, Jonah turned to stare at her, and she knew from the smoky look in his eyes that he too was remembering the first time he'd fixed her an omelet. Defiantly she returned his stare, and it was Jonah who finally looked away and returned to his cooking.

During the next few minutes, while she toasted English muffins and set out butter and honey and Jonah finished the omelet, they spoke of impersonal things. Later, after they'd eaten, they went to the music room, and as she started her first practice session, Raine found out what it meant to be under the control of a tyrant.

She had assumed their relations would at least be cordial, but she soon realized that as far as her feelings or sensitivites were concerned, they didn't exist. Jonah set her to work on scales, but only briefly, then on phrasing exercises, but that, he informed her, was only a warm-up. When he put Beethoven's Sonata in F Minor on the music rack in front of her and told her curtly that she would play the "Appassionata" in the competition and that he would select the encore piece later, she swallowed the protest that rose to her lips, determined to give him no reason to accuse her of being difficult and ending the lessons.

Despite her best efforts, she soon discovered that there was no pleasing Jonah. If she tried to achieve the emotional state he demanded, ignoring technique, he sarcastically asked when she'd made the discovery that she knew more about the score than the composer did. And when she played with precision, using every nuance of the technique she'd been taught, he slammed his open hand down on the piano, declaring that she played like a robot.

"A player piano hits all the right notes," he lectured. "But you aren't a machine. You're the interpreter, the hands of the composer. Through you comes the soul, the essence of the music as it was created in Beethoven's mind. If you have no heart, no passion, it is just unrelated notes strung together. You must feel what Beethoven felt when he wrote this sonata, interpret his emotions as he heard the first stirring of this melody, this counterpoint in his head. What was he saying, what human emotion was he expressing? What do you *feel* when you hear it...play it?"

He bent over her to stab his finger at the score. She caught the faint odor of musk, mingled with the citrus scent of shaving soap, and her heart leapt in her chest like something wild and untamed. The torment increased when he grabbed her hands, massaged her fingers, ordered her to relax, to forget everything she'd been taught because half of it was useless.

It was her inattention that drew his next sally. "No, no, no!" he shouted. "You're sleeping at the

keys! That chord should be played mezzo piano—
and for that you need the proper dynamics. Okay,
your hands are small, but your fingers are strong,
the thumb well placed, the palm sturdy. Your
reach is only adequate, but you've learned to use
one-five fingering when necessary and to roll from
the elbow joint as compensation. So why did you
play that measure as if those bloody keys are made
of eggshells? If you can't hack a simple mezzo
piano, how the hell will you manage the chord in
measure forty-seven that calls for a fortissimo?''

As she stared into his angry eyes, Raine's own
temper flared and she forgot her determination not
to allow him to get under her skin. "I'm not you,"
she retorted. "Just because I don't pound the hell
out of the keys—"

"That's enough! Remember our bargain—no
excuses, no alibis. Either you try harder or I walk
out of this room right now. Start again, and this
time I don't want to hear a schoolgirl practicing a
pretty little tune. I want to hear a woman at those
keys. A woman with fire and passion. And if you
can't feel it, then fake it. Try pretending you're
being made love to by someone you hope to seduce
into furthering your career.''

Stabbed by the contempt in his voice, Raine
swung back to the piano, her eyes so blinded by
tears that she couldn't see the score. She crashed
her hands down upon the keys, and because she
couldn't tell him with words how much he had
hurt her, she let the music say it for her, pouring
out her anger and frustration. Then, as so often

happened when she let emotion take over, she lost herself in the music. As if she were in the eye of a storm, the music soared around her, lifting her onto a plane that was far removed from the hate-love emotion she felt for Jonah.

How strange.... She'd always had to fight against the part of her nature that wanted to treat music as a visceral thing, something more of the emotions than the intellect. How many times had her teachers chastised her for forgetting technique because she'd been carried away by a strong emotional response to music? And yet, this seemed to be the very thing that Jonah wanted from her.

The first movement finished, she stopped, knowing instinctively that she had never played better despite the lack of polish and her inattention to technique. She turned around, suddenly shy, expecting Jonah's praise, but his face was rigid, without expression. If she hadn't known it was impossible, she would have thought she saw pain in the gray depths of his eyes.

"That's a little better," he said. "Now try the first movement again, and this time follow the score. Your fingering is as sloppy as hell. As for your pedaling, you stomp on those pedals like a football player."

Her hands shaking with anger, Raine turned back to the piano and this time she concentrated on phrasing, letting her head guide her fingers, trying for technical perfection. If Jonah recognized this subtle slap at him, he said nothing, only nodded when she was finished, and set her to work on a

Bach invention, declaring that her fingers seemed stiff.

The next days were a torment. One part of Raine was content just to be with Jonah, living for the rare moments when he snatched up her hand to demonstrate a position or to caution again about the too-high rise of her wrists, waiting for the times when he leaned over her, so close she could feel his body heat, to point out a particularly troublesome phrase.

But the rest of the time she had to endure his in-difference, which became increasingly hard to take. Now that she knew that Jonah had believed himself to be divorced when he'd made love to her that first time, she was without even that defense. It hurt that he had discarded her as soon as his wife had returned to him, but it also proved that once again she'd misjudged him, that he hadn't been the dishonorable man she'd believed for so long. And if Elaine hadn't changed her mind about a di-vorce? Would he have "courted" her the way he'd promised their night together. And if he had, would his love for his wife have intruded, even-tually destroying their relationship?

In an effort to stay so busy she didn't have time for more of these inner dialogues, Raine threw her-self into the rigorous routine Jonah had set up for her. Her sessions at the piano took up most of her mornings and afternoons, broken only by lunch, by an hour of exercise in the morning and another late in the afternoon before she went upstairs to dress for dinner.

Jonah even supervised her meals, insisting on a well-balanced diet rich in vegetables, fruit and salads—and no desserts. Since she had a well-developed sweet tooth, Raine couldn't resist when Tilda, clucking like a mother hen, sometimes slipped her a few cookies on the sly. But she still watched wistfully at the dinner table when Jonah, his smile mocking, leisurely demolished a piece of Tilda's delicious pecan pie.

Evenings she practiced another hour and then spent the remainder of the evening memorizing the Beethoven score and the encore, which Jonah had decided should be Rachmaninoff's *Rhapsody on a Theme of Paganini*. Although she would have preferred something less traditional, Jonah had been adamant.

"I know Johan Graussmeyer, who will be one of the three judges at the Gracey competition, and he's a hard-bitten conservative. He considers any composer later than Rachmaninoff an upstart. Even Stravinsky is beyond the pale as far as he's concerned. Of course, the other two might outvote him, but he's a domineering bastard who usually gets his way. So the Paganini theme seems the best bet—provided you can master it by then. Of course, you can always go the crowd-pleaser route and choose one of Chopin's nocturnes. You might not get the judge's votes, but you'll get an ovation from the audience."

Although Raine didn't respond to the gibe, she was determined to master the Rachmaninoff rhapsody in record time, if only to prove to him that she was a serious musician, not the lightweight he obviously thought her to be. In one way, his constant criticism and his lack of praise made it easier for her. She was discovering that anger was a good defense against the sometimes raging physical needs of her own body. Every time Jonah looked at her, every time he came near, the aching need returned, keeping her in a constant state of frustration. He had obviously lost all interest in her as a woman, which, while in some ways a blessing, was also an added torment.

Only when she was with Michael was she able to retain some balance. Although the boy missed Crystal and talked about her wistfully, he was happy with the new horizons that had opened up for him. When he prattled on about the friends he was making at summer school, it was impossible not to catch some of his enthusiasm, and Raine felt both sad and gratified by the knowledge that when she finally left for good it wouldn't have the same effect on Michael that it would have had earlier.

Sometimes, when Jonah was late getting home from the winery, she took time away from her studies to read to Michael from his favorite Jack London adventure stories. Other times she stole away to the beach with him for an hour. If the day was clear they would lie in the sun, studying the tide pools, or if it was foggy, walk along the beach, sometimes talking, sometimes silent.

But this was her only recreation, and often Jonah's words came back to haunt Raine. He had warned her that there would be times when she would hate the piano, and sometimes, after hours of repetition, while she tried to master the difficult intensity that ends in the dramatic Dies Irae of the Rachmaninoff rhapsody, she would gladly have seen the music score—and even the piano—go up in smoke.

But she kept on, enduring the whip of Jonah's voice, the endless repetition, the hours of visualization that were involved in memorizing the long scores. Part of it was pride, and part of it was her determination that if she couldn't win Jonah's love, at least she would gain his respect.

When her fingers became numb and lost all feeling, when her eyes burned from staring at the score, then she often wished she was the automaton Jonah had accused her of being. With her feelings so close to the surface that she sometimes felt as if her skin were raw, she had to clamp down and force strict discipline not only upon her body, but on her own errant thoughts. That Jonah praised her so rarely, and even then with a hint of acid in his voice, only strengthened her stubbornness. Sometimes when he bullied her into repeating a trill for the tenth time, demanding perfection, she wanted to throw his own haphazard training in his face and remind him that it was well-known that he seldom practiced for a concert and certainly had never in his life spent hour after hour repeating one stupid phrase. But she restrained herself, remembering how precarious the truce between them was.

Then, gradually, as the days passed something

changed. Like a long-distance runner who must reach and then conquer a state of exhaustion before he can finish the race, Raine reached a stage during which she was sure she could no longer go on, only to pass it, almost without knowing it. Always before when she was playing, she was conscious of the music in front of her, of tempo and legato and phrasing, of the touch of the keys, the feel of the pedals under her foot. Now when she sat down to play, the mechanics were so automatic that the music was produced almost as if by magic, her fingers and hands and feet attending to business without her attention, as if the keys were an extension of her brain, freeing her to concentrate solely on the results she wanted.

It seemed ironic to her that the very thing she'd been striving for all her life had come to her at this time, and that it was like ashes in her mouth. Jonah never commented on the leap of improvement in her playing. If anything he drove her harder, almost savagely sometimes, his words like lashes from a whip, telling her that she still wasn't ready for competition, that she must work harder if she hoped to be chosen as a finalist for the Gracey competition.

It was because of Jonah's trigger temper these days that Raine never mentioned Crystal to him, so it was Tilda who told her that Crystal was still in Mendocino and that when she'd tried to contact Jonah, he had refused to talk to her.

"That man—he can be so hard," Tilda sighed. "Sure, Crystal was wrong. But she's sorry now, and she only done those things 'cause she was afraid Mr. Jonah would send Michael off to one of them private boarding schools and she wanted him to have a father who was around all the time. She's had time to do a lot of thinking and she's changed—maybe 'cause she understands herself a little better now.''

"Where is she staying, Tilda?" Raine asked.

"At the Mendocino Inn. I reckon she's awful lonely, although Luke and me go by to see her as often as we can. I don't think she's eating much at all. She must've dropped ten pounds since she left here. I don't know how much longer she can go on like this, and that's the truth.''

"Do you think she'd talk to me if I called?" Raine asked hesitantly.

"Why, she don't hold no grudge against you. She told me that if things had been different, maybe you two could've been friends.''

"I think I'll call her. The Mendocino Inn, you say?"

"That's right good of you." Tilda shook her head, looking doleful. "I asked if she'd seen Reverend Tim, but she said she's sure he don't have time for her these days.''

"Well, I'll see what I can do," Raine promised.

That afternoon, when Jonah went to the winery, she phoned the Mendocino Inn and asked for Crystal's room. When she heard Crystal's voice, she identified herself, half expecting to be hung up on, but Crystal seemed very pleased, if surprised, that she'd called.

"I thought you might like to hear how Michael is getting along," Raine said. "Is it possible for us to meet somewhere—maybe have dinner together tomorrow evening?"

"Oh, I'd love that. I've been wanting to apologize for the terrible way I treated you. It—it wasn't personal. It was just that—well, I was so mixed up, Raine. I was afraid that Jonah would become seriously interested in you and then you would change things and—and I wouldn't be needed anymore." Her brittle laugh made Raine wince. "I didn't need any help along those lines, did I? I did a great job of messing up everybody's lives all by myself."

"Don't keep blaming yourself, Crystal. There's no way you can change the past. And we'll talk some more about this tomorrow. Should I met you at the inn, say, at seven? Do we need a reservation?"

After they'd made arrangements to meet, Raine hung up, feeling very troubled. There had been a feverish quality about Crystal's voice that worried her. She knew so well what it meant to be thrust out of a comfortable cocoon into a totally new environment. Her freshman year at Juilliard had been very lonely until she'd made her first friend. But even at her loneliest, she'd been very busy with the demanding academic work of the school, with her music. Crystal, brooding alone in a hotel room, had no outside interests, nothing to keep her mind off her troubles.

An idea came to her then. Impulsively she

picked up the phone and dialed Tim Turlock's number. When his pleasant voice came on the line she identified herself and asked if he had time to talk.

"I always have time for you, Raine. I don't see anything at all of you or Michael these days, but it's a good trade-off. Finding out about the kid's hearing has got to be the best news I've heard in a long time."

"Yes, we're all very happy about Michael." She hesitated, then decided to come right out with it. "Tim, have you seen Crystal since she left Arlington House?"

"No." His voice sobered immediately. "I've been stewing around about that, trying to get up the nerve to call her, but—well, I don't think she'll talk to me. There was a lot of bad feeling when we broke up. We both said things that were pretty hurtful."

"But you do want to see her?"

"I do. I'm very concerned about her. She's— well, she's really a wonderful person with a lot of warmth to give. She should have kids of her own to worry about, you know, and if things hadn't gone so wrong between us, maybe that's where she'd be today. If you knew how that family of hers treated her, you'd understand how she could go off on the wrong track. All her life she had her father and sister as behavior models. They ran roughshod over everybody who got in their way. It's no wonder Crystal got her values mixed up. I just wish there was some way I could help her. My mom used to say the Turlock men are like a dog with one bone. We're one-woman men. And Crystal is the woman I've wanted ever since we were kids.''

His rueful words made Raine smile, albeit painfully. "Then I think I can help you. I'm meeting Crystal tomorrow for dinner at the Mendocino Inn at seven. Why don't you meet me there an hour earlier so we can talk. Maybe we can figure out a way for you to join us for dinner and then—well, see what happens.''

"Great! I'll be there at six.''

He sounded so eager that Raine was smiling again as she hung up. She went to tell Tilda that she'd be eating out the next evening, but prudently she decided not to mention it to Jonah. The less he knew about her plans, the fewer explanations she'd have to make. She wouldn't put it past him to forbid her to have dinner out. And if he got angry because she went without asking his permission? Well, she'd face that when the time came. After all, she could always plead ignorance of the law.

Jonah's law, that was.

She dressed carefully the next evening, taking pains with her hair and makeup. After a debate with herself, she finally decided to wear a rather brief cocktail gown, one that she hadn't worn before because it had seemed out of place for family dinners, even at Arlington House. She was aware that the blue silk accentuated the contrast of her skin tone and her hair, and that her three-inch heels showed off her slender legs. She smiled at her own reflection in the dressing-table mirror. Briefly, until she banished the thought, she wished Jonah could see her in something sexy for a change instead of her usual jeans.

She gathered up her purse and a light wrap and hurried down the hall toward the rear service stairs. She didn't want to take the chance of running into Jonah. But when she turned into the kitchen, intending to use the back door, Jonah was sitting at the oak table drinking a cup of coffee. It was too late for retreat so she raised her chin a fraction of an inch higher, trying for insouciance as she strolled into the kitchen.

Jonah looked her over, his eyes lingering on the small gold chain that lay in the hollow between her breasts. His lips twisted into a smile that said he suspected the worst. "Going out? Or is that outfit for my benefit?"

"I'm having dinner at the Mendocino Inn with a friend," she said shortly.

"I see. Well, your curfew is ten o'clock. Don't be late."

"Curfew? What are you talking about? It's been a long time since I needed someone to oversee my social life."

"I couldn't care less about your social life. What I am interested in is your physical stamina. I don't want you fighting a hangover, alcoholic or otherwise, tomorrow morning. So get your socializing over early and be back here by ten."

He drained his cup and rose. He was almost to

the door before he added, "Have a good evening."

The café doors were swinging on empty air before she could stop sputtering and say the hot words that rose to her lips. She was tempted to follow him, but prudence stopped her. She could only be the loser if they had an open quarrel now, but how she'd love to tell him what she thought of his ugly suspicions!

All the way to Mendocino she fumed, thinking up things she wished she had said to Jonah, simmering down only when she saw Tim. He was waiting for her in the lounge when she arrived at the inn, looking very attractive, and unusually grave, in a tweed jacket and sport shirt.

"We just have a few minutes so I'll talk fast," she said after Tim had ordered white wine for her and mineral water for himself. "You told me once about a school for handicapped children you and a church group were starting. Is it still in the works?"

"Indeed it is. Unfortunately, the financing delayed us for a while. The children's parents were willing to contribute enough to keep it going once we got it on the road, although some will have to donate services instead of money. But the initial expense, such as bringing the building the church donated up to local building codes and installing additional plumbing and ramps and modernizing the kitchen, took a lot of potluck suppers and bazaars. So we're having to start small with only fifteen children. Later we hope to be able to expand. Right now our most pressing problem is teachers. We can afford the salary for one full-time teacher, and I can donate a couple of hours an afternoon, but I have my own obligations. I can't short my parishioners. Even a couple of part-time teachers would ease the burden."

"You have one potential teacher you're over-looking. Crystal knows how to deal with the handicapped, has real rapport with children. With all that love she's got bottled up inside her—"

"I agree she would be a godsend, but there's one big problem. I'm not her favorite person at present. If I suggest she help out, she's going to think—well, that I'm trying to interfere in her life again. And besides, I couldn't pay her much, if anything. I was thinking about volunteers."

"Crystal doesn't need money. She has a good income from her father's estate. What she needs is to be useful."

"You're right again." He shook his head in mock wonder, then reached across the table to kiss her on the cheek. "You're a surprising woman, Raine. You look so ethereal and yet you're so practical and down-to-earth."

A few minutes later he left, after telling her that he would be back for that "accidental" meeting later. As she finished her wine, Raine reflected that she might have advice for other people but she was doing a lousy job helping herself. Why was it always so much easier to tell other people what to do than to figure out the answers to your own problems?

"You look troubled, Raine. Is something wrong?" It was Crystal, standing beside the table. From the uncertain look on her face, she still wasn't sure Raine had forgiven her.

Raine smiled up at her, noting the dark shadows under her eyes. "Everything's great. I'm tired, that's all."

Crystal slid into a chair opposite her. "I appreciate this, Raine. I know I don't deserve your— your friendship, but even when I was so rotten to you, I liked you and wished we could be friends. It was only because I was so afraid of...." Her voice faltered.

Raine reached out and touched her hand. "I know—and I understand. If I started telling you some of the mistakes I've made, we'd be here all night."

Crystal still looked teary, so Raine quickly changed the subject. She was relating Michael's latest adventure at his summer program when Tim's tenor voice said, "Talk about the luck of the Irish! Two of my favorite ladies together, and hopefully in need of an escort for the evening."

Raine smothered a smile. Tim's rather hangdog look didn't quite match the flippancy of his words. "Why, hello, Tim," she said sweetly. "Why don't you join us? We were just getting ready to order."

Although Crystal made no objections, a wave of color stained her throat, and she was silent as Raine and Tim talked about Michael, then about the Gracey competition. With what she hoped was adroitness, Raine steered the subject to the school

314 SONATA FOR MY LOVE

for handicapped children, and she noticed that Crystal listened intently as Tim told them the trouble he'd been having getting the school started.

"One problem is teachers. The mothers are willing to take turns supervising the playgrounds and helping to prepare and serve lunch, but we need volunteers to act as classroom helpers. One requirement is a knowledge of sign language, or a willingness to learn it, since four of the children are hearing impaired. It's a big job and requires understanding, incredible patience—and love."

"But surely there must be plenty of volunteers for the job," Crystal said, speaking for the first time.

"It's a matter of dedication. Even the most well-meaning people have a bad habit of treating volunteer work as a hobby, something they can turn off when it suits them. And most of these kids have already had too many disappointments in their lives. We don't want someone who will drop out after a month or two, just when the kids are beginning to feel secure. That sort of thing can be detrimental to children who are already so vulnerable."

Crystal stared at him, her eyes very bright. "Would you consider someone like me?" she asked in a small voice.

"You?" Tim sounded so surprised that Raine was afraid he was overdoing it. "It's quite a commitment, Crystal, and you do understand there isn't any money to pay the helper."

"I don't want pay. And if you remember, I took

some classes at Sonoma State on dealing with handicapped children.''

During the next few minutes Tim allowed himself to be persuaded, and by the time they had finished dinner it was all settled. Crystal was radiant, the haunted look gone from her eyes.

Using Jonah's curfew as an excuse, Raine left the two of them sitting there over coffee, feeling as if she had just won some kind of victory.

CHAPTER EIGHTEEN

RAINE WAS STILL THINKING about Crystal and Tim the next morning as she sat at the piano, waiting for Jonah to appear for their morning session. The two of them were so right for each other. Would they make it this time? Or would the past rise up to haunt them and ruin things between them again?

Preoccupied with her thoughts, she touched the keys lightly, then began playing idly, letting her fingers pick out a melody, only to realize that she had chosen Jonah's unfinished sonata, the one he called *Sonata for My Love*. Charmed by its haunting quality, the poignancy of its principal theme, she had played it so often during her earlier practice sessions that she knew it by heart. Had the song been a present to Jonah's wife, something he meant to dedicate to her? If so, no wonder he'd never finished it.

When she heard the door open behind her, she stopped playing immediately, only to find it was too late. Jonah's hands seized her by the shoulders and gave her a hard shake, almost making her lose her balance.

"Don't ever play that sonata again," he said, his voice dangerously quiet. "That piece has a personal meaning to me that you couldn't possibly understand.''

In her hurt she wanted to strike out at him, but she was silent as he slapped his hand on the Beethoven score. ''*This* is what you should be playing. Your time is getting short and you still play as if you're wearing handcuffs. So get to work. And if your social life is interfering with your practice, then give up one or the other. At this point, I don't care which.''

Raine straightened the music score, but her hands shook so badly that she almost dropped the sheets on the floor. When she played a discordant phrase, Jonah snatched up the sheaf of music and thrust it in her face.

''Where the hell do you see a B-flat chord?'' he demanded. ''Point it out to me. Or are you improving on Beethoven now? Play it the way the master wrote it. A broken chord of F minor, from middle C to A-flat above the treble staff. You *can* read music, can't you?''

His irritation seemed out of proportion to her mistake, and she forgot that her eyes were still wet with tears as she turned to stare at him. His face changed and he frowned. ''What's wrong with you today? Too much sleep? Or too little? Did Tim Turlock keep you up too late?''

''How did you know that I had dinner with Tim?''

''I had business in town and I went into the inn to—to have a drink at the bar. I saw you two with your heads together. That chaste little kiss on the cheek was very touching. I wonder if he has any idea what kind of woman he's playing footsie with?''

In stony silence Raine turned back to the piano and began the Beethoven piece again. Her hands felt numb and clumsy, and despite her attempts to concentrate she hit one wrong note after another. Jonah finally stopped her.

"If you can't do any better than that, you'd better take up the accordion instead," he said contemptuously. "A child could outplay you today."

She swung around to face him. "What do you expect? You've been on my back ever since you came in. First you insult me with your innuendos about Tim, and then you expect me to play as if nothing's happened."

"If you can't separate your personal from your professional life, you're in the wrong profession," Jonah told her. "There'll be times when your emotions will be tied up in knots, when a love affair has gone sour on you or a promoter has cheated you out of a fee. But when you're up there in front of that audience, they don't give a damn about that. All they know is that they've paid their money and they expect to hear your very best. So no matter what's happening in your personal life, you hang in there until the last note of the last bar is played."

Raine stared into his eyes. "Then why did you give up music when *your* personal life went sour?"

She was sorry as soon as the words escaped her lips. Jonah's face, already so glacial, turned white.

He swung around, turning his back on her. "I've had enough of your incompetence for one day," he said over his shoulder. "Take the rest of the day off to pull yourself together. And when you come in here tomorrow morning, I expect to hear that sonata played the way Beethoven wrote it."

He stalked out of the room, slamming the door behind him. Raine put away the music and then, because she felt a little shaky, she went upstairs to lie down. But when she had stretched out on the bed and was staring up at the ceiling, she knew that what she really needed was a long walk along the beach, not rest.

Snatching up a scarf, she ran down the service stairs, stopping only long enough in the kitchen to get an orange from the refrigerator. Although the morning had been gray and misty, the sun had already burned off most of the ground fog, and as she walked briskly toward the beach stairs her nerves began to unwind and she threw back her head, taking long drafts of air into her lungs.

She walked along the beach until she reached the rocks that formed such a formidable barrier at one end, protecting the cove from intruders except at low tide. There was something exciting about having a small part of the Pacific all to one's self. What a pity she couldn't utilize it for a swim. Jonah had warned her about an undertow, but surely if she stayed just beyond the surf she would be safe. After all, she was a strong swimmer.

She made up her mind quickly, solving the problem of a swimsuit by stripping off her jeans and sweat shirt and tying her head scarf over her breasts. During the time she'd been coming here, she'd never seen anyone except Rico on the beach, but in the unlikely event that someone was lurking about at the edge of the cliff, it would look as if she were wearing a two-piece bathing suit. Besides, she would only be in the water for a few minutes.

After the initial shock of the surprisingly cold water, Raine felt energized to the bone. She played at being a dolphin for a while, cavorting and splashing and diving under the slow rolling waves to spy on a small school of black-and-white fish. But she was careful to stay close to shore, venturing out only far enough to avoid the breaking surf, mindful of the old saying that he who swims alone is swimming with a fool.

When she began to tire she floated on her back, feeling lazy and relaxed. The waves, at low tide now, lapped her body, rocking her gently, and it seemed impossible that the same waves could lash and tear at the rocks during high tide or when the wind was up.

Perhaps she dozed. The first warning she had that she wasn't alone came when a strong hand reached out to grab her arm. In her shock, she went under. Greenness closed in around her head, and she came up furious and spluttering. Jonah, looking grim, was waiting for her. He grabbed her arm again, and when she tried to push his hand away he only held on tighter, forcing her to tread water to stay afloat.

"What the hell do you think you're doing? I

told you how dangerous the undertow is in the cove," he said through clenched teeth.

"I was careful not to go out too far. And besides, I was only floating."

"Way out here? You must be crazy."

For the first time Raine looked toward shore. She gasped with dismay. She was at least a hundred yards away from the beach, and from the tug at her feet, an undertow was pulling her out to sea.

But she wasn't about to admit her shock to Jonah. "I was just getting ready to go back," she said airily.

A wave washed over her, and Jonah grinned sourly as she spit out a mouthful of water. She gave him an angry look and kicked upward. Using the Australian crawl, she headed for shore. It was more difficult than she'd expected and she realized that Jonah had been right in his warning. Within a few feet she was already tiring, but she forced herself to keep moving. Although she was a good swimmer, Jonah's stroke, unorthodox as it was, was much stronger, and he kept up with her with infuriating ease.

When they were close enough to shore for her to touch bottom, Raine remembered that she was wearing bikini panties and a very thin scarf. As a wave washed against her shoulders, she tried to decide what to do. Brazen it out? Or hope that Jonah would be gentleman enough to guess her predicament and turn his back while she put on her clothes?

"Where did you learn how to swim?" she asked

when it was obvious that he was going to wait her out.

The sardonic look in his eyes told her that he knew what her problem was, and that he had no intention of making it easier for her. "In a city swimming pool, and in the East River when there wasn't too much garbage floating around," he said bluntly.

"I've never seen a stroke like that before. What is it called?"

"You can call it the Bronx crawl. Not to be confused with a Bronx cheer, of course," he said.

His quip took her by surprise and she flung her head back, laughing. After a moment Jonah laughed, too, and then, as if their laughter had started a chain reaction, both of them stopped and stared at each other.

Unbidden, a warmth invaded Raine's cold body and suddenly she was on fire, wanting to feel Jonah's mouth on hers, his hands on her breasts, his hard body against hers. Jonah's eyes darkened, and then he reached out for her and was crushing her tightly in his arms.

Through her panties and the flimy scarf that bound her breasts, she felt the heat of his body and she knew that he wanted her as much as she wanted him. His mouth came down upon hers, further igniting the desire that had been simmering there for the past two weeks.

A wave broke over them, and Jonah lifted her to keep the water from splashing her face. The wave receded; as he let her slide downward again, the feel of his skin, moving against hers, drove her wild. With a gasp she clutched his shoulders and pressed herself frantically against him, wanting a closer intimacy. His hand slipped down to cup her soft hips, holding her hard against him, and the swell of the waves, rocking them back and forth, was like the movements of love.

With a groan, he picked her up and carried her back to the beach. Her arms locked around his neck, she buried her face in the hollow at the base of his throat, breathing in the iodine odor of seawater, tasting the saltiness of the ocean on his skin.

On a sheltered spot beneath the cliff, he lowered her to a small circle of sand. For a long time he stared into her eyes, as if searching for the answer to a question, before he began a slow exploration of her scantily clad body with his hands, his eyes burning with a fire that echoed her own rising passion. When he bent his head and pressed his lips against the hollow in her throat, she felt as if her heart would stop from wanting him. Gently he pushed aside the scarf, baring her breasts to his ardent gaze.

"Your breasts are the color of wild honey," he said, his voice husky. When he lowered his mouth to possess the dark aureole, so tight and firm now, she clutched his shoulders with both hands, arching her breasts up to meet his burning lips. Like the touch of butterfly wings, he showered her with kisses, then slid off the wisp of silk around her hips, exposing her nude body to the wind and the surf's spray—and his burning eyes. Swiftly, he stripped off his own swimming trunks, then stretched out beside her.

As his eyes moved over her, Raine lay motionless, smiling up at him, proud that her skin was unblemished, that her breasts were firm and taut, that her hips were softly curved, her thighs silky smooth. Not from personal vanity, but because it gave Jonah pleasure to look at her, just as his own body, so strong and virile, sent small ripples of desire moving through her flesh.

He touched her then, his hand moving skillfully, arousing her to a fever pitch. And because she wanted him to share the same pleasure, she touched him, too, taking joy in the pulsating response of his body, in the knowledge that it was the sight of her, the feel of her, that made him tremble, that softened the lips that could be so tight and hard, that made his eyes burn as though he had a fever.

Then he was pulling her close, capturing one of her thighs between his legs, locking their bodies together in an embrace so intimate that she felt as if they were one. She waited breathlessly for the ultimate intimacy, her chest heaving from the force of her need.

"Sweet, sweet Raine," he whispered against her ear. "These past two weeks have been hell, wanting you, burning for you. I have to have you, no matter what it costs me this time...."

His words seemed to possess a sharp edge, cutting into her, maiming her, as she realized that even in the throes of passion, a passion she knew to be as strong and driving as her own, he still thought of her as a saleable item, someone whose price was open for negotiation.

A shudder shook her from head to foot. With a twisting motion she pulled away from Jonah and scrambled to her feet. He raised up on one elbow, and if she hadn't been so crushed the surprise on his face might have made her laugh.

"What the devil's wrong, Raine? Are you cold?"

"Yes, I feel cold all right. But not from the wind," she said bitterly. Feeling soiled and tainted, she turned her back on him and struggled back into her clothes, making a hash of it because her body was still damp from her swim. Although she hadn't looked at him since she'd answered his question, she was aware that the expression on his face had changed.

"If you don't want to be seduced," he said, his voice grating, "then I suggest you keep your clothes on in the future."

She whirled to face him. "I didn't know you were within miles of the beach. And my pants and scarf cover me as much as a swimsuit would. So don't lay that on me."

"The water made them transparent, as you couldn't help knowing. And you also know I come down here to swim every chance I get," he said. "I don't know what game you're playing now, but if it's money you want—"

In her fury, she turned to flee from him, but before she could get away he was upon her, pulling her down on the sand. He kissed her, but there was no tenderness in his kiss. As he ravished her mouth the sand grated against her hair and she struggled frantically to get away, sure that he meant to take her by force. But his arms were too strong, and then, to her shame, she didn't want to get away. Because the passion that he'd aroused earlier was still unsatisfied and she was lost in the vortex of her own desire, wanting him so much that his scorn, even her own pride didn't matter. All that existed was the hunger inside her, the seductive hardness of his body against hers. Without shame she stopped struggling, mutely begging him to take her, possess her.

He gave a short laugh, a scornful sound, and then he was unlocking her arms from around his neck, pushing her away.

"I've changed my mind." The cruelty of his words was reflected in his eyes. "From now on, don't try your little tricks on me. I'm probably the only man on earth who can see through them."

He picked up his swimsuit, pulled it over his taut hard hips, not bothering to turn away. She lay there, too stunned to move, and because her shame was so deep, her eyes were hot and dry as he gave her a mocking salute, turned on his heel and stalked away.

THE NEXT MORNING it took every ounce of courage Raine possessed to face Jonah again. She had gone to her room when she returned home, refusing supper even when a worried Tilda brought soup and a sandwich to her room. Desperate for oblivion, she had finally taken two of the sleeping pills her doctor had given her the day before her father's funeral. Although she finally slept, in the morning she awoke with aching eyes and a nagging headache.

She skipped breakfast and substituted an extra half hour of jogging, returning to the house only when it was time for her morning practice session. Not knowing what to expect from Jonah, she waited quietly, sitting at the piano, her hands in her lap.

When Jonah came in he was unsmiling, expressionless. If he hadn't looked her over so thoroughly, she would have thought the incident on the beach had been a figment of her imagination—or a nightmare. Aware that her face, despite the makeup she'd applied so carefully, was pale and her eyes hollow from lack of sleep, she turned away and opened the piano.

The Beethoven sonata was lying on the music stand, just as she'd left it the day before. Without waiting for Jonah's instructions, she plunged into the first movement, playing automatically, not caring if she struck a wrong note, wanting only to get it over with. But perversely her fingers moved with the ease that had come to them so recently, and as the music swelled, something within Raine responded to the sonata for the first time, and suddenly she understood the emotions behind the music and was deeply moved by the regret and loneliness, the awareness of the folly of pride, all the human faults she had in such abundance.

When the sonata was finished, the last arpeggio and crescendo and triplet played out, she leaned against the piano, too debilitated to move. It was Jonah's silence that finally made her turn her head to look at him. He was watching her; his smile held irony—and something else she couldn't read.

"Okay, you're ready for competition," he said so matter-of-factly that she could only stare at him. "Tomorrow we tape the Beethoven, and if it wins you a place as a finalist, then we start thinking about other aspects of being in big-time competition—including what you should wear."

He started out of the room, then turned at the door. "Back to your practice, and watch your left hand in the ninth measure. Your timing is off. You're passing your thumb under your fingers too quickly again. This time get it right."

CHAPTER NINETEEN

IT WAS THE DAY of the competition. At the Fair-
mont, in the suite Jonah had arranged for, Raine
had discovered that she was too restless to take a
nap, as ordered by Jonah, so she'd dressed early.
Now she had nothing to do but stand by the window, staring out at the afternoon fog just beginning to roll in from Marin County across the bay.

Three days earlier they had come into San Francisco to get ready for the competition. Not the
least important of their preparations had been to
choose the gown Raine was now wearing. "Part of
that edge I told you about," Jonah had said when
she expressed surprise at how patient he'd been
during an arduous shopping trip, how adamant
he'd been that the waist of the gown they'd finally
chosen was altered slightly to give her a perfect fit.

In contrast there'd been the rehearsal session
with the Gracey Auditorium Symphony Orchestra,
during which Jonah had remained totally aloof,
sitting in the rear of the darkened auditorium while
Raine coped alone with the orchestra's rather temperamental conductor, her professionalism finally
winning the man's approving nod.

And with all that, Jonah made sure she spent

several hours during each of those three days in the practice rooms made available to the six finalists. Although she was curious about her fellow competitors, he discouraged her from anything more than a polite exchange of nods and smiles. "Think of them as the enemy," he said grimly. "And you don't fraternize with the enemy."

"More of that winner's edge?" she murmured.

"Exactly. Remember—this is a competition. Keep that word in mind and don't forget it, even for a moment." His eyes glittered as he added, "Once it's over, you can follow your instincts and get cozy with that Swedish competitor who's been coming on to you for the past couple of days."

She hadn't answered, afraid that if she said aloud the words that trembled on her lips it would break the unspoken truce between them.

But now, as she waited until it was time to go downstairs, she wished she had told him off, good and proper. It rankled that even at this late date he treated her like a spoiled child, or like an athlete he was training for some sports event.

The previous night when they had dined at Ernie's, one of San Francisco's fine restaurants, he had ordered a Spartan meal of one broiled lamb chop and a small salad for her, and then had sat there demolishing a steak with obvious relish. Resentfully she had picked at her food, barely touching it, something he had ignored. Later they had gone to their individual suites, separated not only by two floors of the hotel, but by Jonah's elaborate politeness.

Since their disastrous encounter at the beach, his attitude had become even more remote, and although she wanted desperately to believe it was a defense against his own feelings for her, she couldn't forget the scorn in his eyes when he'd repulsed her and walked away. Sometimes, when her own longing to feel his arms around her kept her from sleeping, it was all she could do not to go to him and beg him to make love to her again. Then her natural good sense would reassert itself, reminding her that Jonah's passion without his love and trust would be pure hell. It didn't help to know that she had forfeited any chance with him she might once have had by her actions.

I should have gone in for acting, I'm so damned good at it, she thought in despair.

Bleakly, she stared down at the glittering street below. Then, because this *was* her hometown, which she had missed sorely while she'd been away to school, her mood changed.

Maybe she could salvage at least one thing from the past weeks by proving to Jonah that his efforts hadn't been wasted. Tonight, whether she won or lost the competition, Jonah's part in her training was over. That was the bargain they had made. But if she won, then surely he would remain interested in her career and keep in touch. Perhaps in time. . . .

Raine groaned aloud as she realized the trap she'd almost fallen into. No, it was over—*over*! And she must become reconciled to never seeing Jonah again after tonight. But she would still have her music, and although it was a poor substitute for the love she felt for Jonah, it was an anchor to cling to, something to give her life purpose and meaning.

So for herself, *not* for Jonah, she would do her damndest to win tonight.

As she turned away from the window, her own reflection in a brass-framed wall mirror seemed to mock her. In the gown that Jonah had chosen for her, she had never looked lovelier. The dress was silk crepe, the color of champagne and simply cut, its only decoration the tiny bead pearls that were set at random in the bodice. It clung to the soft curves of her body in a seductive way that still managed to seem artless and uncontrived.

"You need every advantage you can get, Raine," Jonah had said when she'd protested at the high price of the gown, which he had insisted on buying for her, calling it a "bon voyage" gift. "These competitions are cutthroat affairs—even your appearance is crucial. You don't want to look too virginal, so we won't make it white. Champagne is a good compromise. It has more sophistication than pastels and yet is not as obvious as jewel colors would be. It will also be a nice contrast to the black suits of the orchestra, and the male contestants."

He had smiled then, although his eyes had remained cold. "A touch of the vixen and yet very chaste. Yes, that's the look. And of course you're a master of that combination, aren't you? But don't forget. When the chips are down, it's your talent that counts. Anything else is just frosting on the cake.''

Well, at least the frosting looks okay, Raine told her own image in the hotel mirror.

She had arranged her pale hair in the classic simplicity of a French twist, exposing the nape of her neck, but with softening waves around her face that accentuated her patrician look. And her makeup was carefully discreet. Although she'd spent half an hour applying it, she was aware that only an expert would guess that it wasn't nature that gave her skin a luminous glow, the faint blush to her cheeks and the rosy tint to her full lips. Since she owned no jewelry except a couple of gold chains and a wristwatch, and an inexpensive ring, which would have been an encumbrance to her playing, she had decided to forego it entirely, and her bare fingers seemed to mock her, reminding her that no matter if she won or lost tonight, she would never wear Jonah's ring.

A knock at the door startled her. She whirled away from the mirror, her heart beating very fast. Had she been daydreaming and forgotten the time? No, her small travel clock told her it was still too early to meet Jonah in the lobby.

But when she answered the door, Jonah stood there, looking handsome and self-assured in impeccably tailored evening attire. He had an odd smile on his face, as though he were laughing at a private joke. When she stepped aside, wordlessly inviting him to come in, he complied, then produced a small velvet box.

"This is for you. You've earned it by your hard work. It should set off that gown very nicely."

Raine's fingers trembled as she opened the box. Inside, like a small echo from the past, was a necklace. Although plain, the gold chain was very heavy while the large pearl that was suspended from the chain in a filigreed teardrop setting had a creamy glow that proclaimed its perfection—and value. Inevitably, a memory of Jonah's first gift of jewlerly stirred, but she pushed it away. Not for anything would she let him know how strongly his gift had resurrected that old pain. Still silent, she took the necklace from the box, intending to slip it around her neck. But her fingers seemed clumsy and she fumbled with the chain, almost dropping it.

"Here—let me do it." Jonah took the necklace from her and turned her around. With the delicacy that always seemed so at odds with the bluntness of his fingers, he fastened the clasp, and her awareness of his nearness, of his warm breath on the nape of her neck, was so strong that it was almost painful.

She started to move away from him, unwilling to prolong the agony of his closeness, only to stop, arrested by his reflection in the brass-trimmed mirror. His eyes were half-closed and his expression, unguarded and without the mask he usually wore, was full of torment, as if he too were in pain. Her heartbeat accelerated as a realization came to her. No matter what Jonah thought of her as a person, his feelings for her as a woman were still strong. Was it lust or love, or both?

But even as she watched, his lips took on the cynical twist that she had come to hate. As quickly as it had come, the hope that had surged through her vanished. What did it matter if he did feel some form of love for her. He would never trust her. And love without trust was unendurable. Yes, she could make him desire her again. Just by turning now and putting her arms around his neck, she could break down at least one barrier. But then what? After he'd made love to her, would he ask how much he owed her? No, it was best to pretend she hadn't seen behind that aloofness he wore like armor. Best to hide her own vulnerability.

"Thank you, Jonah," she said, her voice a little husky. "It's lovely."

"A reward for your application to work. You rather surprised me, you know."

"Surprised you? How?"

"I didn't realize that your ambition was based on genuine talent and a willingness to work hard. I thought you wanted to buy success without paying your dues. For that, I apologize."

"Thank you." This time her words had a hollow ring.

He moved away and he was all business again. "After we reach Gracey Auditorium, I want you to speak only when absolutely necesary. Don't expend your energy on conversation. You'll be waiting in the green room with the other contestants. Be polite, but don't indulge in confidences, gossip, small talk. Just stay as loose as you can, let the excitement build, don't peak out too soon—"

"You sound as if you're psyching up a prize fighter," she said dryly.

"A competition is a competition. If you don't retain that edge, you don't win. Talent counts the most, yes. But there's something—call it winner's fever—that affects some fighters when the bell rings. Some competitors never experience it, but the ones who do are the ones who win, whether it's a long-distance race, a boxing match or a music competition like the Gracey. It gives those people the edge, and sometimes they aren't the ones with the most talent."

"And no doubt you had winner's fever in abundance?"

He looked grim. "Oh, yes. I was hungrier than the rest. That made all the difference. But I never won anything I didn't work hard for or that I didn't deserve. And I developed strength from every setback I got, too. Of course I also had the natural talent," he added, and she knew it was a statement of fact, not braggadocio.

"Had?" she said softly.

His face stiffened. "I'm no longer interested in performing."

Liar, she wanted to say, but she held back the word. She had seen the pain in his eyes those times when he'd refused to touch the piano, not even to show her the correct fingering for a difficult phrase.

So the hunger was still there, as strong as when

he was clawing his way up from a Bronx ghetto. But another passion was stronger—his love for his dead wife. He still blamed his dedication to his career for her death, which was why he hadn't touched the piano since Elaine's funeral, and why he hadn't finished the sonata that he'd started for her. Oh, yes, that song—so enchanting and poignant that it tore out the heart to hear it—gave away his secret. And to hope that by some miracle he might someday love again was stupid and futile and oh, so painful....

Her lips fixed in a smile, Raine went to get the silk shawl and evening purse that complemented her gown. When she looked at Jonah again, he had moved to the door and was holding it open for her.

"So this is it," she said, her throat suddenly dry.

"This is it. The thing that separates the winners from the also-rans. The competitions you've been in before are nothing next to this one. Every one of your competitors has won or placed very high in other competitions. Their talent and training is top drawer. The judges are completely professional, disinterested, nonpartisan, which can work to your advantage. But remember—whatever happens in that auditorium tonight will be on your record. So do your very best."

Raine nodded soberly, knowing that his advice was good, that he spoke the truth.

THE ROOM where the contestants waited, traditionally called the green room, though it was actually a rather dirty gray, was near the dressing room, easily accessible to the wings. Although there were several shabby couches and chairs, Raine was too restless to sit. Avoiding the eyes of the other contestants, she walked slowly up and down, listening to the music that for the third time that evening was echoing through the room. The two contestants who had already finished, both young men a little older than Raine, had a relaxed look as they sat side by side on a couch, chatting together like members of some exclusive men's club.

Consciously Raine shut out their voices and listened to the music, a Beethoven concerto, that the third contestant, the young Swedish man, was playing. Lars Bjorborg had been a child prodigy and was now the student of one of the finest teachers in the country. His music was crystallike in its perfection. Part of her thrilled to the lyrical passages of the concerto, even while she felt depressed, knowing that the competition was every bit as good as Jonah had warned her it would be.

She wished that she hadn't drawn the final slot. As Jonah had pointed out, it was not a favored one since the piano they were using, although one of the best to be had, was apt to lose its fine tuning by then, and the judges would have become a bit jaded from an overdose of music. Still, there were advantages, not the least of which was that once her stint was finished, she would be spared the agony of having to wait a long time before she found out if she had won or lost.

And if she won she would study with Dubois,

one of the country's top teachers. All her living expenses would be paid, and after her training was completed, if she proved worthy, she would go on tour. She wouldn't appear with the nation's important orchestras as a soloist but would serve a long apprenticeship, sharing the bill with other young hopefuls, appearing with semiprofessional symphony orchestras in smaller towns. With luck she would collect a few favorable clippings for her scrapbook, while her talent—and certainly her repertoire—grew. And after that, if she were lucky, she would get her chance to compete in Moscow.

"What do you think of Bjorborg?" The voice was young, feminine and self-assured. Raine turned to look at the girl standing beside her. Her name was Maile Wong; she was nineteen years old, of Hawaiian-Chinese ancestry, with a pale oval face and large lustrous eyes. Her dress was demure, a white organdy confection that made her look as if she'd come from a high-school prom.

"He's very good," Raine said.

"Too much emphasis on technique. He makes it seem too easy." Maile dismissed Bjorborg and his talent with a flip of her slender hand. "My teacher is Louis Constantine. Who's yours?"

Raine hesitated. Jonah had deserted her at the auditorium door and he hadn't offered to accompany her backstage. Was it supposed to be a secret that she was his pupil? "Jonah Duncan," she said with a mental shrug.

The girl's eyes widened, then narrowed. "Are you kidding me, Hunicutt?" she demanded.

Raine shook her head, reflecting that this was one competitor who was obviously not worried about anything as nebulous as losing her winner's edge by indulging in conversation before the competition.

A latecomer, the sixth competitor, ambled into the room. He was the youngest of the group, a loose-limbed boy of fourteen with a shock of unruly brown hair. Ignoring the others, he dropped into an empty chair and began playing with a yo-yo.

"That's Luxor Levine. He won the Oakland Symphony Young Artists' Award last year," the Oriental girl said, not bothering to lower her voice. "He's fourteen but he looks about twelve. Imagine trying for the Gracey at that age."

"Well, he *is* a finalist, so he must have turned in a good recording," Raine pointed out.

The girl flipped the ends of her long glossy hair. "Anyone can make those tapes. Who's to know? Sometimes the teachers do it themselves."

"I heard him practicing yesterday. He's good. Besides, what would be the point of having someone else make the entrance tape for you? You still have to play in the competition."

"Well, judges are human. Sometimes they make mistakes. At the Bach International in Washington a few years back, the winner only had two pieces in his repertoire." She giggled suddenly, looking very young. "Imagine the flap when they tried to get him ready for a concert tour. The whole thing was a riot.''

Raine started to reply, then, realizing that she was doing just what Jonah had warned her against, she murmured something about needing a drink of water. But when she was outside in the corridor, she didn't seek out a water fountain. Instead she leaned against the wall, her eyes closed, breathing very deeply.

As she listened to the final movement of Beethoven's Concerto in C Minor, it came to her that Maile Wong was right. Bjorborg did put too much emphasis on technique, the flaw that Jonah had seen in her own playing. Looking back, she knew now that she'd been so caught up with perfection, with winning the praise of her teachers, that she had forgotten that music was essentially emotion, magically converted into sound.

Well, she no longer was the same girl who had played so earnestly at Juillard. Jonah had done that much for her, turned her into a woman who was in touch with her own passions and talents and shortcomings. She knew what love was, the kind that can lift one to heaven if returned or destroy with equal ease when it was unrequited. Would any of this show in her music today?

A wave of sound jolted Raine out of her thoughts. Bjorborg had finished, and from the applause he had scored heavily. Would the judges be influenced by the approval of the audience? Jonah had told her that no matter how experienced or impartial the judges might be, they couldn't help but be swayed a little by the enthusiasm—or lack of it—from the audience. Would this weigh strongly in the Swede's favor?

Raine gave into temptation and moved to the wings. On the stage, the young Swedish man was bowing, his long hair damp with perspiration. Beyond him, in the front row of the auditorium, she could see the impassive faces of the judges— two men and one woman. She looked at them searchingly as they bent over their pads, writing busily, wishing she could see behind their professionalism to the real people within. They held so much power over the lives of six strangers. Did it bother them that they would be labeling five of them losers?

She was still standing there a few minutes later when Lars Bjorborg finished his encore number, again to enthusiastic applause. She couldn't help smiling when the Levine boy, looking for all the world like a modern-day Tom Sawyer, sauntered out onto the stage. If he was impressed with the seriousness of the occasion, it didn't show. She wouldn't have been surprised if he had taken out his yo-yo to play with instead of plopping himself down on the piano bench, his freckled hands hovering above the keys. Turning away, she began walking up and down, listening with her newly heightened judgment as the boy played Bach. Within a few minutes she knew that while he had a natural talent that might someday mature into something truly formidable, he was no real competition to her now.

Later Maile Wong passed Raine on her way to the stage. Looking composed and serene, she gave Raine a sidelong glance, acknowledging her automatic "Good luck" with a complacent smile. A few minutes later when the sentimental strains of a Chopin nocturne filled the wings, Raine resumed her pacing and worrying. Chopin was always an audience pleaser, and from the way Maile played with the keys, emphasizing the romantic aspects of the nocturne, Raine knew that she had gone the opposite route of Bjorborg. Had Jonah made a mistake, choosing the purity of Beethoven for her? Well, it was a little late to worry about that. She would do her best, and the rest was in the lap of the gods.

Raine discovered that she was breathing too fast, that the palms of her hands were wet and clammy even while her face felt as if it were on fire. Suddenly she had to fight off an irrational compulsion to dash out onto the stage, push Maile off the bench, ending that maudlin rendition that cheapened Chopin's genius, and take over the piano herself. Was this the winner's fever Jonah had been talking about, or was it just plain nerves?

Knowing she must get control of herself, she leaned against the wall again, her eyes closed. A hand cupped her elbow. She opened her eyes to stare at Jonah's unsmiling face.

"Are you okay, kid?" he said softly.

Unexpectedly Raine's eyes misted with tears and she was fighting a different battle, this time to keep from throwing herself into Jonah's arms. "Okay, coach," she said, trying to smile.

"You've got the right stuff. Go out there and prove it," he said. He bent his head and kissed her forehead, and then he was gone so quickly that she stood there in shock for a moment, wondering if she had imagined it. No, Jonah had been real enough. He had come, after all, and just at the moment when she needed him the most. Did that mean he had sensed her need because he loved her, or was she being foolish again, trying to read something more into what was probably the normal concern of a teacher for a pupil?

Putting the question aside, she returned to the green room, and this time she found it easy to wait quietly, letting the tension build, but in a constructive way. Then Maile Wong had finished the nocturne and had done her shorter encore piece to a respectable wave of applause. The monitor, a tall elderly man, beckoned to Raine from the doorway and she rose to follow him, with only the slightest quivering of her lower lip.

As she waited in the wings while the monitor introduced her she heard the rustling of programs, the subdued murmuring of voices, a few coughs, and sensed the audience's restlessness. Had they become jaded by the length of the competition? This was, after all, a very partisan audience since most of the people there had come at the invitation of one or another of the contestants.

Well, she had her own claque, small though it might be. Martin and Gloria were there, as well as two of her former teachers, a few family friends and a sprinkling of old schoolmates, and to her delight she had seen Crystal and Tim sitting together near the center of the auditorium, too. And with the knowledge that Jonah was rooting for her, how could she possibly feel alone out there on the stage?

The monitor had finished the introduction to a splattering of polite applause. He turned, looking toward the wings. Raine took a deep breath, held it for the count of five, then expelled it before she resolutely stepped forward. The glare of the lighting was a small shock to her eyes as she walked to the center of the stage to give the requisite three bows—one to the judges, one to the audience, one to the conductor, although the orchestra wouldn't be accompanying her first piece since it was a sonata.

Instinctively her eyes sought out the seat on the aisle where she knew Jonah would be sitting. Although still half-blinded, she saw his head towering above those nearby, and as if he had wrapped her in a warm security blanket, her nervousness vanished. She seated herself on the piano bench, her back ramrod straight, and then her fingers, supple and strong, were dancing over the keys, playing the opening chord of the "Appassionata."

Although it was permitted in this competition, she had eschewed the use of a score, not wanting the distraction of a page turner. After all, the Beethoven sonata had been etched into her brain by long hours of repetition. At night before she went to sleep she had visualized it a hundred times, playing it out in her head, seeing each note, each mark in her mind's eye.

This was the culmination of a lifetime of grueling practice, the end result of years of mental and sometimes physical pain. She knew instinctively that she had never played better, that Jonah had goaded and bullied and shamed her into doing the thing her teachers hadn't been able to do—make the breakthrough into that rarefied state beyond technique where music comes from the heart as well as the intellect. The dozens of separate techniques that went into making up the whole were so automatic that they no longer required conscious thought, and she became one with the sonata, losing so much of herself to the music that when she finished the last rolling movement she felt disoriented for a brief moment, as if she had been lost in another world.

There was a pulsating moment of silence, and then the applause started. It swelled, rose higher, became tumultuous, and as she turned dazed eyes toward the audience, still breathing very hard from her physical exertion as well as her mental exultation, she saw that they were standing, that she had just been given the rarest of accolades, a standing ovation from that most partisan of audiences.

Her eyes sought out the seat on the aisle where Jonah was sitting, only to find that he was standing, too. As she met his eyes it was as if nobody existed but the two of them. What she saw there turned her knees to water and gave her a new surge of hope. Suddenly nothing mattered but the necessity of proving to Jonah that she was not the woman he believed her to be, that she loved him not only with her flesh, but with her heart and soul.

An idea came to her, one so clear and beautifully logical that she inhaled sharply. Of course. There *was* a way to prove to Jonah that she loved him more than anything else in the world, including her music and her future career as a concert pianist. He knew the depth of her ambition, how hard she'd worked to win this competition. If she deliberately threw away her chance of winning by a foolish gesture, then he *must* believe in her love....

She didn't allow herself to think about consequences or lost opportunities or burnt bridges. If she did, she might not have the courage to carry out the plan. So even while the applause still roared, she rose and went to speak quietly to the conductor. When the edges of his mouth drew downward into a frown, when he turned away from her, obviously irritated, to signal to the orchestra to put down their instruments and close their Rachmaninoff scores, the applause died, and she sensed the puzzlement of the audience.

She turned, and although her eyes remained on the judges, she was speaking to the one person in the audience who mattered now. "I won't be playing the Rachmaninoff variation," she said, her voice very steady. "Instead I will play a sonata, still unfinished and unpublished, that was written by a friend. It's called *Sonata for My Love*."

There was a buzz of voices, and she caught the disapproving stare of the judges—"those very conventional fellows," Jonah had once called them. She returned to the piano and without any fanfare began the first haunting measures of Jonah's sonata.

Time stood still. She lost all consciousness of the audience, of the judges, even of Jonah. There was just the piano, the music and herself, a perfect meld of instrument, melody, performer, each complementing the others, three parts of a whole. The sonata had been written by a man in love with a woman he feared he had lost, and this was how she, who knew the same kind of fear and loss, played it—with her heart, from the soul. Her technique, imperfect because she hadn't practiced the piece adequately, didn't matter. She cared only that she was revealing her love to Jonah with the music he had written for another woman.

When she reached the abrupt end of the unfinished sonata, she stopped. With the last poignant notes still throbbing through the auditorium, she sat there, her head bowed, feeling weak and drained because she had poured all her emotion and energy into the music.

At first the sound was like a muted groan, or like the surf breaking upon the rocks behind Arlington House. Then she realized it was applause, but unlike any she'd ever heard before. She rose and looked at the audience, her eyes widening in disbelief when she saw that this time even the judges were standing and there were tears on the face of the woman judge.

But it was Jonah whose approval she hungered for. She turned her eyes toward the left aisle, and her world crumbled around her yet another time.

Jonah's seat was empty. Jonah was gone.

To Raine, the decision of the judges was an anticlimax. It shouldn't even have happened. She had done the unconventional, the unforgivable, changing her program in the middle of the competition, choosing an unfinished sonata by an unnamed composer. But judges, as Jonah had once pointed out, were human too, and because they had been deeply touched by her rendition of Jonah's sonata, they gave her the prize.

A few minutes later she stood in the middle of the stage, acknowledging the applause, the congratulations of the other competitors, but it was all automatic. Nothing mattered but one thing. Jonah wasn't there to congratulate her. He had left the auditorium without even saying goodbye.

CHAPTER TWENTY

IT WAS CRYSTAL who suggested that Raine go to Jonah and have it out. She and Tim were among the ones who came to the party given in honor of the contestants after the competition. Although Raine was sure she had carried it off well, not wanting to ruin the pleasure of her brother and friends, it was Crystal who guessed that something was wrong and took her aside for a private chat.

"What is it, Raine?" she asked quietly. "Can I help you? I owe you so much—"

"You owe me nothing," Raine interrupted. "You've put your own life in order. I had nothing to do with it."

"But you were the one who made me see that I had to turn my thinking around. And Tim told me you suggested that he get me interested in the school—and after I was so horrid to you. So let me repay you. Tell me what's the matter. Is it Jonah?"

Raine looked into Crystal's troubled eyes, and something inside her, a wall of reserve, gave way. "He was in his seat and then he left before I finished the encore. He didn't even care enough to find out if I had won."

"I'm sure there's some explanation. I talked to him earlier and he seemed so proud of you. Did you know that I'm welcome to visit Michael?" Crystal's smile was painful to see. "But I don't intend to—to fall into the old trap. I'm going to take an apartment in Mendocino so I can be near the school, and Tim. We're talking about marriage. I think I'm going to like being a minister's wife."

"I'm so glad," Raine said warmly.

"And it's all because of you, Raine." Her smile wavered suddenly. "You really love Jonah, don't you?"

"Yes," Raine said, hopelessness flattening the word.

"Does he love you?"

"I think he does, but not enough. He doesn't trust me, and that's my own fault. Like a fool I gave him every reason to believe that I'm a scheming calculating woman. Now there's no way I can change things."

"Is that why you played his sonata tonight?"

"You knew it was Jonah's?"

"Oh, yes. It's been on the music rack of the Steinway ever since Elaine died." For a moment the old Crystal showed in her smile. "There wasn't much that went on at Arlington House that I didn't know about. I had nothing else to occupy my mind."

"Then you know Jonah wrote it for your sister. And when I played it tonight, I hoped he'd understand that I did it as proof that my love for him is more important to me than winning the competition. But he must have misunderstood and thought I was using him again. Or maybe—maybe it was just too painful, being reminded of Elaine.''

Crystal's eyes were full of pity. "Elaine went through life strewing pain in her path. I think I've always known what she was and yet my whole life revolved around her. It's only now that I can see how she used me. Even after she was dead, I did everything in my power to make sure Jonah never forgot her. Her room, kept like a shrine, and her photograph beside his bed. I convinced Jonah that if he changed her room or put her photograph away it would be detrimental to Michael. And I was the one who put fresh flowers by her pictures every day. Perhaps if I hadn't, Jonah would have forgotten her by now—or at least be willing to open his heart to another woman.''

"But why did you lie to me? I thought—"

"I was afraid of what I saw in Jonah's eyes when he looked at you. And later—well, later I was too ashamed to tell you the truth. Besides, I thought things were all right between you and Jonah. I didn't know that Elaine's old poison was still ruining things.''

Crystal's voice was unsteady as she added, "I'm taking therapy now from a psychiatrist in Mendocino and I'm beginning to understand myself, and maybe even Elaine. She was a very unhappy woman, insatiable for attention. Perhaps it was my father's fault, or maybe it was just because she was so incredibly beautiful that everything came too easy to her. After she married Jonah she wanted him to give up the concert stage and stay with her all the time, but music was his life. It was an even stronger mistress than Elaine.'' She laughed harshly. ''Well, Elaine won after all. After her death, Jonah did give up his music and stay home. I made sure of that, me and my scheming.''

''Don't blame yourself too much. You were a victim, too,'' Raine said, her voice weary.

''I'm so ashamed, Raine. And I still feel empty sometimes. Elaine—and then keeping her memory alive—was my crutch, the thing that held me together and gave my life purpose. It hasn't been easy, getting along without a crutch.''

''But you're making it, aren't you?'' Raine said, and it wasn't really a question.

''I am, with Tim's help. He—he really cares for me, you know.''

''I'm glad.''

''I know you are, Raine. You told me once that when you had to fight hard for something the prize was all the sweeter. Well, take your own advice now. Don't give up—not until you've talked to Jonah. I'm sure he's returned to Mendocino. Go to him, talk to him, tell him the things you've just told me. Maybe you can get through that hard shell he carries around with him. I think he really loves you. He just has to learn to trust you.''

Someone came up then and during a new round of congratulations Raine thought about Crystal's words. *Go to him.* A small thrill of excitement stirred until she remembered that she'd come to the city in Jonah's Mercedes. Her own car was still parked at Arlington House. Well, that was no obstacle. There was always Martin's car.

As soon as she got the chance she took her brother aside and asked to borrow his car.

"You intend to drive all the way to Mendocino tonight?" he said, frowning. "Why don't you wait until morning? Showers are forecast. Those roads can be treacherous as hell when they're wet, you know."

"I'll be careful," she said impatiently. "But I have to go. Why don't I drive you and Gloria home first? I promise to have your car back to you by tomorrow afternoon."

An hour later, shortly after she had dropped Martin and Gloria off and driven away in their seven-year-old Toyota, she discovered that her brother had been right about the weather. She was crossing Golden Gate Bridge when the clouds opened and a fine misty rain began to fall. She stared up at the gaunt structure of the bridge, its upper reaches shrouded in low-lying clouds, and wondered what her life would be like when she next drove over this bridge. Would Jonah reject her, once and for all, or by some miracle would they work things out?

There was very little traffic once she'd left Santa Rosa. She had chosen Highway 101, the most traveled route north, but only an occasional truck and a few cars passed her now. When she reached the first grove of redwood trees, memory assaulted her and she found herself reliving the day she'd spent with Jonah and Michael among the sequoias.

It was the hope that somehow she could make the happiness she'd felt that day permanent that strengthened her resolve even when the drizzle changed to a downpour. She turned on the heater to unfog the windows and when she caught herself yawning she rolled down the window at her elbow to let in the cold moist air. The only sound now was the whine of tires on wet cement, the swish, swish of the windshield wiper and the rapid beating of her heart, sounding out a litany of hope and despair.

When she saw a truckers' stop near Albion that was still open she pulled up and went inside, knowing she needed a break and a cup of coffee. Several truckers were sitting around a formica-topped counter. They eyed her curiously, and she realized she must look out of place in her long gown, rain-splattered now, and her silver shoes. A bleary-eyed waitress brought her a steaming mug of black coffee. She seemed to welcome Raine's company because she lingered, staring through the steamed-up windows at the misty rain outside.

"Really weird weather for this time of year," she commented. Not waiting for an answer she added, "You're out pretty late. You still got far to go?"

"Just the other side of Mendocino," Raine said. She took a sip of the scalding coffee.

"Well, be careful. It's always slick when the

first rains come. Oil on the road or something, they say.''

A few minutes later when Raine got back into the car the coffee had dispelled her drowsiness, although her eyes still smarted and her head had developed an ache. Despite her eagerness to have her confrontation with Jonah, she drove carefully, even pulling over once when the wind began to gust, waiting until it slackened off before she went on.

It was almost morning when she finally pulled up in front of Arlington House. The old house with its witches' hat tower, its turrets and slanted roofs, loomed against the gray light of early dawn. No lights showed in its tall arched windows, which meant that it was too early even for Tilda and Luke. For a few minutes Raine sat in the car, wondering what to do next. Jonah must be asleep too. Should she go to his room and awaken him? And if she did, what could she say? That she had come to explain why she had chosen his sonata for her encore after he'd told her so vehemently not to play it? Would he believe that it was unplanned, an impulse? More important, would he believe her motives?

She felt a wave of despair. It seemed so hopeless. And yet it was the only chance she might ever have to salvage some happiness out of the fiasco she'd made of her life. Even if Jonah only wanted her on one level, she would be willing to settle for that. The thing was, he hadn't tried to touch her since that day on the beach. And that look she'd thought she'd seen in his eyes before the competition—had that been her imagination? If so, could she endure another rejection from Jonah?

With a long sigh she got out of the car and went up the front steps. She let herself into the house with the key Tilda had given her, then stood for a moment, listening. It was cold in the entrance hall, and the only sound was the sigh of the wind, the creaking of old boards.

Should she wait until Jonah got up, or go to his room to tell him she was willing to take him on any terms? And if he no longer wanted her? Then she would go away and somehow she would learn to live without him. Crystal was turning her life around—painfully, step by step, day by day. She would do the same, go through the motions of living until she gained some kind of peace. One thing she knew for sure. She had made a mistake, using Jonah's sonata, but the price she was paying for that mistake was too cruel!

At the bottom of the staircase she slipped off her shoes. As she climbed through the shadows her stockinged feet whispered softly on the carpet, her pulse keeping time with her footsteps. What would Jonah say when she came to his room? Would he ask her to leave him alone with his grief? Or would he, having been deprived of sex for several weeks, make love to her, and then despise her for giving in to the same weakness?

She had almost reached the first landing when she stopped. From her vantage point halfway up the stairs she was looking directly down at the music-room door, and she saw that a dim light filled the doorway. Invariably the music-room door was kept shut to prevent dust from harming the delicate instruments stored there. Was it possible that Jonah had been playing the Steinway since he'd come home? If so, it would be the first time he'd touched the piano in the weeks she'd been there.

She had started on when a familiar sound stopped her again—the creaking of the piano bench. Hardly daring to breathe, she retraced her steps to the bottom of the stairs, then moved quietly along the hall until she was standing in the open doorway of the music room. Jonah, his body silhouetted against the window, was sitting on the piano bench, and at first she thought he was asleep because he sat so motionlessly, his head slumped against his chest.

Then, as she watched, he raised his hands and brought them down upon the keys, sending a crash of sound through the room. Afraid the noise would awaken Michael, she quietly closed the door before she moved toward him. As she drew closer, she could see him plainly in the light from the window, and the tormented look on his face told her the truth.

She had always assumed, as did everybody else, that Jonah had given up the piano out of grief or guilt. Now she knew that it was music that had turned its back on Jonah. He could no longer play the piano. Was it some physical affliction, like the arthritis that had ruined her own mother's budding career?

As soon as the question arose, she rejected it. There was nothing wrong with Jonah's hands. She had felt their sensitivity, the delicacy of their touch, and when he was angered, their strength. So it had to be something else, some kind of mental block.

Pity welled up inside her. She of all people could understand the depth of his despair. Was it possible that she was the one person who could help him, give him back his music? She moved forward quietly, not thinking, not planning what to do, wanting only to comfort him. She was close enough to touch him when he groaned aloud, a piteous sound that set up echoes in the corners of the room. An involuntary sigh escaped her lips; he heard it and turned his head to stare at her.

"I have to finish the sonata," he said, as though he were continuing a conversation they had started earlier. "Don't you see how important it is that I finish the sonata?"

Raine knew she had lost him then, that there was no hope. But because he was in pain and because she loved him, she forced back her own despair and, standing behind him, encircled his body with her arms, fitting her hands over his. One by one she pressed down his fingers, just as she had once done with Michael, his son. The notes, the first chord of his sonata, sounded harsh and discordant, and his fingers were rigid and unyielding, taking all her strength to push them against the keys. Doggedly, refusing to give up, she persisted, and slowly, painfully, his fingers began to move of their own accord.

And then he was playing on his own, his eyes closed, his head thrust back, and she knew that he had forgotten her, that he was lost in his own private world—a world that she would never be invited to enter.

At first the notes were poorly executed, but as he warmed up his touch changed, and she caught hints of the talent that had galvanized the world of classical music. For a moment she felt a personal envy, knowing that what was a painfully achieved level of skill for her was pure genius in Jonah because it was natural, something he had been born knowing by instinct.

But the moment passed, replaced by a far deeper and more hurtful emotion—grief. In the act of giving Jonah back his music, she had just deepened the gulf between them, destroying the one chance she'd had to be with him. Now he would return to the world of music and he would have no need for her. There would be plenty of other women, eager and willing, and there would be no doubts, no suspicions to sour those relationships.

Jonah reached the end of the sonata, but he didn't stop. He played on with such surety that she knew the sounds must have been in his mind all along, although only now was he able to play them.

Raine turned. By concentrating all her energy on putting one foot down in front of the other, she left the room, left Jonah still playing, oblivious to her, to everything but his music. As she ran down the dark hall and out into the grayness of false dawn, the golden notes of his sonata followed her and she knew that they would haunt her for the rest of her life.

CHAPTER TWENTY-ONE

As Raine left her apartment building and stepped out onto the sidewalk, she shivered and pulled the collar of her sweater up around her neck. The dreariness of the afternoon, the swirling wisps of fog, reflected her own depressive mood. Would the clear days of fall never come. And when they did, would she feel any better? It had been so long, almost two weeks, since she'd felt any joy. How long did it take for a broken heart to heal? A year? Ten years? A lifetime?

It wasn't as if she had given in to her depression. No, she'd done all the proper things. She'd gone on with her life, keeping so busy that she was often too tired at night to think about anything except crawling into bed. Although the money she'd earned cataloging Jonah's books would have been more than enough to support her without working until her lessons with Joseph Dubois started in the fall, she had taken a part-time job a week ago with a ballet school in return for the use of their piano for practicing. In the evenings, following a three-hour practice session, she went home to her tiny furnished flat, fixed herself a real meal and sat down at a table to eat it—no snacking on junk foods while standing at the sink for her! Afterward she worked on her visualizations, memorizing scores, or she read or watched TV if there was something on that she wanted to see.

And she hadn't been neglecting her social life. Whenever Martin and Gloria invited her for dinner, she accepted and had an enjoyable evening playing with her niece, talking, laughing and acting so normal that sometimes she felt like an actress in a soap opera. She had even accepted a couple of dates. Once she'd gone out to dinner with the son of the woman who owned the ballet school, and another time she'd attended a concert with the nephew of one of her old piano teachers, himself an aspiring baritone.

All very normal, and all so futile. Well, no more self-pity. She was working hard, and eventually she would make it to the Tchaikovsky competition. And if she won? A whole world of possibilities would open up for her. From then on it would be up to her, which had been true all along, hadn't it?

Meanwhile she had each day to get through. Her job, playing for the ballet class every weekday morning, was fun. For a while every day as she played the old standards she could forget her own problems, and wasn't that all she dared ask for just now?

So why didn't the heaviness of her spirits go away? Why did the least little thing—a piece of sentimental music on the radio, the flower stands on Market Street, the sight of a tall dark-haired man—still hurt so and stir up memories of what had been, what could never be again?

Maybe she should go to a psychiatrist, only what could she say that would make sense? "Please give me a pill to mend a slightly bent heart, doctor?" No, a doctor couldn't help her. She would have to fight it out on her own and somehow, day by day, get through the rest of her life.

A few minutes later she parked her father's old Mustang in the parking lot next to the neat white building in the Avenues that housed the ballet school. As she ran lightly up the stairs to the second floor, the familiar sound of the intermediate dance class, all talking at once, greeted her. The rehearsal room took up all of the second floor; it smelled of rubber and dust and overheated young bodies. One wall was mirrored, equipped with practice bars; an upright piano, in surprisingly good condition, stood at the far end, flanked by a stack of canvas-covered floor mats.

Raine looked around for the ballet teacher, but only the students, eleven girls in the eight-to-ten-year-old range, were there, most of them still dressed in their school clothes. "Where's Mrs. Norton?" she asked, raising her voice above the hubbub.

Esther Jamison, who was the class's self-appointed spokeswoman, answered her. "She's out today, Miss Hunicutt," she said importantly, pointing to a handwritten note that had been taped on the piano. "She stayed home with a cold."

"So why are you girls still here?"

"We took a vote and decided to stay and listen to you practice."

Raine hid her amusement. "Oh? You enjoy listening to scales?" she said blandly.

"Not that! We thought you'd play some good stuff—you know, like you did when we had the birthday party for Mrs. Norton last week."

"Uh-huh. And I suppose I don't have anything to say about this?"

"Oh, we knew you'd do it. You're so nice. You will, won't you, Miss Hunicutt?"

Again, Raine had to hide her amusement. How could anyone resist that kind of stroking? "Okay, it's a bargain. I'll play whatever you want. Any requests? Or do you prefer Bach?"

She laughed at the hasty chorus of voices, all calling out the names of popular songs. The girls arranged several of the mats on the floor and settled down to listen. Raine played one song after another, enjoying their pleasure, but eventually her mind wandered, and it was a while before she realized that she'd finished a popular ballad and was now playing Jonah's sonata. When she realized what she was doing, she broke off, her hands dropping to her lap.

There was a chorus of disappointed protests. "That's so pretty, Miss Hunicutt," one of the girls said. "Why don't you finish it?"

Raine shook her head. "The song has no ending," she said.

"Miss Hunicutt's wrong about that, young ladies." The voice, deep and masculine and achingly familiar, spoke from behind her. "The song has a very happy ending, if she wants it that way."

In her shock, Raine whirled too quickly, and only Jonah's strong hand kept her from taking an ignoble tumble to the floor.

"Why is it that I always seem to be picking you up off the floor, Miss Hunicutt?" he murmured in her ear. His words were humorous, but when she looked up at Jonah she saw that his expression didn't match. His face was gaunt, and his eyes were sunken deep in his head while his mouth—Raine started violently. His smile—it held such tenderness, without that ugly twist she hated so! Or was it her imagination, her deep yearning to see him looking at her with love in his eyes?

Jonah slid onto the bench beside her. He kept his left arm around her, as if to make sure she wouldn't run away, while he continued on with the sonata, using his right hand. Hesitantly at first, then with more confidence, Raine played the counterpoint with her left hand, all the time acutely aware of the warmth of Jonah's thigh pressed against hers, of the rapid rise and fall of his chest, of the strength of his arm around her shoulders.

When the first movement of the sonata was finished, Jonah stopped to look around at the girls. As if the presence of a man in this essentially feminine world had some mesmerizing power, they stared back at him with fascinated eyes.

"Okay, young ladies, the concert's over. I have

some private business to discuss with your teacher," he said.

"Is it all right, Miss Hunicutt?" Esther said doubtfully.

"Yes. Mr. Duncan is an old friend."

The girls, looking over their shoulders, gathered up their rehearsal clothes and left. For a few moments their giggles and high sweet voices funneled up from the staircase and then there was silence. His step purposeful, Jonah went to the door and turned the key in the lock.

"What—what are you doing?" Raine asked.

"I don't want to be interrupted for the next few minutes," Jonah said, returning to the bench. He was unsmiling now and there was a thin coating of perspiration on his face. "I should have done this the night you followed me back to Mendocino," he said, pulling her into his arms.

Before she could speak again she was being kissed. At first, she was too stunned to respond, but as the kiss continued, as his mouth throbbed against hers a great surge of joy swept through her. She strained against him, wanting more, hating the clothes that separated them and kept her away from the stirring of his body, so evident against her thigh.

With a muffled groan Jonah moved away, but only long enough to pull Raine's sweater over her head and unfasten her bra, and then he buried his face between the soft swell of her breasts.

"You don't know how many times I've dreamed

of doing this, Raine," he said, his voice muffled against her moist flesh.

"And I've dreamed of doing this," she said, her voice catching. With trembling hands she removed his sports jacket, then unbuttoned his open-necked shirt, slipping it down his arms until it fell to the floor. For a moment she allowed herself the pleasure of burying her face in the thick mat of hair on his chest, inhaling the odor that haunted her dreams, before she pulled away again.

Her eyes lowered to the task, she unfastened his belt buckle, then slid her hands inside the waistband of his slacks, wanting to feel his hard maleness beneath her fingers.

"Oh, God, Raine—you're killing me!" he groaned as his body pulsated under her touch.

His eyes steady on hers, he stood motionlessly while she finished undressing him—lovingly, tenderly. As if taking in nourishment, she drank in the strength of his brown body before she reached out to touch him, exploring him with her hands. The hair of his chest felt crisp and alive as it curled around her fingertips, and when her hands moved lower, making seductive circles against his skin, the muscles above his stomach rippled and his body leapt, as if eager to possess her.

He reached for her then and began to undress her, taking his time, kissing the flesh he uncovered as he removed her jeans, her pants, her socks and shoes. Her eyes closed, she swayed as he touched his lips to the pulse places of her body, stoking the flames of passion, driving her mad with the force of her wanting, her need.

And when she could wait no longer, she threw away all restraint and flung herself into his arms, pressing her breasts to his chest, crushing her hips against his brown body. He gave a triumphant laugh and caught her up in his arms, then lowered her gently to one of the floor mats.

The world receded, became misty and unreal, and all that existed was her own throbbing hunger to be possessed, totally, completely, by this man she loved with all her heart. His hands, which she knew to be so strong, were gentle as he touched her, stroked her, raising the fever to an even higher pitch. She was aware of a pulsating sound and she realized it was their hearts, beating in tandem in the same frenzied rhythm. She moaned softly, wanting his lips to possess her mouth again, wanted to taste the freshness of his lips and tongue, even while, paradoxically, she wanted the erotic things he was doing to her body with his mouth never to stop.

When the torment bordered on pain, Jonah rose above her, and for a long time he stared into her eyes. His lips, usually so firm and straight, had a swollen vulnerable look. His eyes were the color of smoke just before it bursts into flame. He lowered himself into the cradle of her thighs. As his hardness became one with her yielding softness she was sure that her soul would leave her body under the force of a pleasure so exquisite that it seemed to move the earth under her.

The pleasure of their joining flowed, ebbed, flowed again, intensifying finally into the sweet peak of pleasure. And in that moment of ecstasy the wonder of being in the arms that she loved above all others, of being possessed by this man she thought she had lost, added another dimension to the act of love, and she felt a soaring of her spirit, a wholeness that she knew would sustain her through whatever else life had in store for her.

Afterward she lay in a daze, her body still shuddering in the after-vibrations of passion, and she felt alive and strong and incredibly happy. Jonah touched her cheek gently with the back of his hand; his eyes were filled with wonder, and she knew that he had shared the depth of the experience.

"You felt it, too, didn't you, Raine?" he said softly. "As if the world stopped for a few seconds?"

"Or as if we left the world altogether," she murmured, burying her face in the hollow of his throat.

"My God, but I love you, Raine," he said, his hand stroking her hair. "The night of the competition—I should have waited long enough to tell you that while you were playing my sonata, I suddenly knew how it should end. My only thought was to go home to Mendocino and get it down on paper before it got away from me. It was as if I was possessed."

"I thought you didn't love me," she said, and

the remembrance of that pain throbbed in her voice.

"I was a fool—all along I was a blind, insensitive fool," he said. "Those first weeks I tried to make myself believe that what I felt for you was only sexual attraction. I fought against the truth for so long that I almost lost you. But you should have stayed that night. When I finished playing in the the music room you were gone. We're two of a kind—too quick to jump to conclusions, too proud to ask questions or explain ourselves for fear of showing how vulnerable we are. We're going to have one hell of a stormy marriage, but a wonderful one, too. Because, against all odds, we found our way back together, and that gives us an edge."

Dreamily she touched his lips with her fingertip, then laughed as he kissed it, then kissed the others in turn. "I fell in love with you that night in the Catskills," she said. "I didn't care about your fame. If you had been a salesman or a truck driver, I still would have let you make love to me. It was like a thunderbolt, and nothing that's happened since has changed the way I felt."

"It was the same with me. Do you know what that night meant to me? It was as if I'd been given a second chance at happiness. I was a lonely disillusioned man and you gave me love, something to live for. We had that one perfect night, and then, after I left you and went back to my apartment, Elaine was there, waiting to tell me the divorce was off. I told her that it was too late, that I wanted my freedom. But she had a whip to hold over me, the same weapon she always used—Michael. She threatened to take him away from me, to stir up a scandal that would not only damage my career but shame my son. Even then I would have held out, but she guessed that there was someone else. Like a fool, when she accused me of it I admitted it, told her I wanted to marry another woman. She flew into a fury and screamed that she would hire detectives, find out who the woman was, and then she'd shout her name from the housetops. I couldn't allow you to be dragged through the mud. You were too vulnerable, so damned young, and unfortunately, because my name was news I knew her threats were valid. So I wrote that note, one calculated to turn you off me for good.''

"It almost destroyed me, Jonah.''

"I know—God, I'm sorry about that now. But at the time it seemed the only way to save you from Elaine's jealousy. I was afraid that if I saw you, talked to you and tried to explain, that I would have weakened. And you didn't deserve a shabby backstreet affair. You were so young. I felt guilty as hell about that, too. What did I, a burned-out shell of a man, have to offer you? So I sent the bracelet and the flowers.''

"I tore the roses to pieces and then I tossed them and the bracelet in the trash.''

He groaned and pulled her closer. "We've wasted so much time, Raine, so much time. We could have been together these past two weeks. Do you know that I almost went out of my mind trying to find you? Mr. Partridge was out of town but someone at his office told me you had moved to New York, and that's where I've been, trying to find you. Yesterday, when I returned here to make arrangements to sell the winery, it suddenly came to me that your brother was an intern at a local hospital, that his name was Martin. I ran him down this morning, and he told me where I could find you. Then when I came over here I found you playing my sonata, and I knew what I had to do to prove to you that we belonged together.''

Raine touched his cheek, sighing. "I've made so many mistakes. I should have stayed with you in Mendocino, had it out, but when I heard you playing the sonata you'd written for your wife, when you said you had to finish it as if—as if your life depended upon it, I was sure it was no use, that you could never forget Elaine.''

Jonah's arms tightened around her. "I wrote the sonata for you, Raine. *You* are my love, my only love. I never loved Elaine. Oh, she was beautiful—like a cold, perfect statue. You have to remember that several years ago, for all my sudden fame, I was still a street boy at heart who couldn't believe his own luck in attracting a woman like that—and some of it may have been gratitude toward Elaine's father, too, who helped finance my career. Well, my illusions about Elaine didn't outlast the honeymoon. She was a passionless woman, totally self-centered, already drinking heavily, but by the time I realized my mistake she was pregnant with Michael. So I stayed with her, poured all my energy into my career. Then, just when I thought I was free of her, I met you—and lost you the very next day. I went back to Mendocino the night of Elaine's accident to try one more time to talk her into going through with the divorce. I was going to offer her everything I had for my freedom and custody of Michael. Then I made the mistake of calling first, of telling her to think it over before I got home. But she didn't wait for me. She went storming off in her car and killed herself and almost killed Michael."

"And so you punished yourself by giving up music?"

"It was never my own choice. When I sat down at the piano again, I discovered that I could no longer play."

"Is that why you didn't come to me once you were free?"

"That and the knowledge that I had failed Michael so miserably. When I realized I could no longer play I almost went out of my mind. And when I got back on an even keel, I knew I had nothing to offer you, Raine. A man who has messed up his own life has no right to ask a young woman like you to share his prison. No, I couldn't do that. And I believed our night together meant nothing special to you."

"Why would you think that? I didn't try to hide the way I felt about you."

"It was the bracelet, Raine."

"The bracelet?"

"It was one of a kind, from a very well-known jewelry designer. Someone pawned it the same day

I sent it to you. Later the pawnbroker tried to authenticate the designer in order to get top price for it. He contacted my jeweler, who immediately called me to ask if it had been stolen." He looked at her steadily. "Do you understand now why I was so ready to believe that our night together wasn't important to you?"

"Yes. Someone must have found it in that trash can."

"The pawnbroker described her as a dark-haired girl—she fit your description perfectly."

"That must have been Marsha Wright, one of my roommates at the time. Little things like stockings and makeup were always disappearing until she finally went off with her lover."

"I knew it must be something like that, but only recently, when I was finally forced to be honest with myself and admit that I was in love with you. I fought it so long, trying to convince myself that what I felt for you was just sexual attraction, not love."

"Well, you don't have to fight it now," she said softly.

"It was a battle I couldn't win. The day I heard your voice in the dark corner of my storage room and realized that you'd come back into my life, I forgot all my convictions. I thought it was fate, that life had given me a third chance at happiness. But then you seemed like a different woman than the one I remembered, and suddenly all the doubts were back, and I kept remembering that you'd pawned that bracelet the same day I'd sent it."

"And I thought, when you kissed me, that you were making a pass at a total stranger," she said, shaking her head. "That's why I put on that act, not wanting you to know how devastating your note had been to me."

He rubbed his chin against her cheek. "So much time wasted, or maybe it isn't a waste. Maybe we're both stronger because we came so close to losing each other."

"Well, I could have done without the lesson," Raine said ruefully, remembering the pain of the past few months.

"I feel the same way, but now we have each other."

"And we have other things, too, including a few decisions to make." She gave him a searching look. "Do you want me to go on with my music, Jonah?"

"What do you think?"

"That you know my career is as important to me as yours is to you. Am I right?"

"You're right. And as far as the logistics of having two careers are concerned, we'll work it all out. You'll always have my support, Raine."

She gave a sigh of pure happiness. A loud banging at the door made her start.

"Miss Hunicutt, are you in there? Why is the door locked?"

Raine started to giggle, and then couldn't stop. Like two guilty children they dressed hurriedly, throwing on their clothes and helping each other with zippers and buttons.

"Not exactly the most romantic place to make love," Jonah said wryly, looking around the barren room as if he had just noticed his surroundings.

"It's the most wonderful place in the world. I'll never forget how we made love on that mat."

Jonah pulled her into his arms and kissed her lingeringly, ignoring the insistent pounding on the door. Raine returned the kiss, then looked up at him, letting him see the love in her eyes. "You'll finish the sonata now?"

"It's done. I'm introducing it at my first concert in New York in the fall. And I've changed the name. It's *Sonata for Raine*. I want everybody to know how much I love my wife."

"Your wife. It sounds wonderful."

"The best word in the dictionary when things are right—and the worst when things are wrong." For a moment the old bitterness twisted his mouth, until Raine stood on her tiptoes and kissed it away.

"The past doesn't matter now. All that matters is the three of us—you and Michael and me. Do you realize that I'll be a stepmother soon?"

"He loves you, you know, and it was the postmark on that letter you sent him three days ago that told me you were still in San Francisco."

"I couldn't just disappear from Michael's life without a word," she said.

The banging on the door started up again. "Is everything all right in there, Miss Hunicutt? If you don't answer, I'm going to call the police...."

Raine went to unlock and open the door. She

smiled into her employer's worried face. "Everything's just fine. I've never been better in my whole life," she said, and because of the happiness soaring inside her, her voice had the confident, clear ring of truth.

ABOUT THE AUTHOR

Writing her first Superromance was a "labor of love," says Irma Walker. To inspire her as she worked on *Sonata for My Love*, Irma treated herself to some new Beethoven tapes, which she played as she wrote. To help her with the musical aspects of the book she drew on the experience of a close friend who had studied to be a concert pianist, and the setting, close to her own home in the rugged coastal country of northern California, allowed her to make all sorts of lovely excursions to "soak up atmosphere."

As an air-force wife, Irma has lived with her husband, George, now retired, in numerous states—including seven years in Hawaii—and the Philippines. A love of travel is second only to her love of people, and topping her list of favorites is her four-year-old grandson Mickey—"the world's greatest kid."

A true believer in happy endings, Irma is the perfect romance writer, but she also has other novels, mysteries, science fiction and one historical, to her credit. With Irma's vast storehouse of people and experiences we can look forward to many more Superromances.

Enter a uniquely exciting new world with

Harlequin American Romance T.M.

Harlequin American Romances are the first romances to explore today's love relationships. These compelling novels reach into the hearts and minds of women across America... probing the most intimate moments of romance, love and desire.

You'll follow romantic heroines and irresistible men as they boldly face confusing choices. Career first, love later? Love without marriage? Long-distance relationships? All the experiences that make love real are captured in the tender, loving pages of **Harlequin American Romances.**

What makes American women so different when it comes to love? Find out with **Harlequin American Romance!**

Send for your introductory FREE book now!

Get this book FREE!

Harlequin American Romance

Twice in a Lifetime
REBECCA FLANDERS

BOOK MATE PLUS®

The perfect companion for all larger books! Use it to hold open cookbooks . . . or while reading in bed or tub. Books stay open flat, or prop upright on an easellike base . . . pages turn without removing see-through strap. And pockets for notes and pads let it double as a handy portfolio!

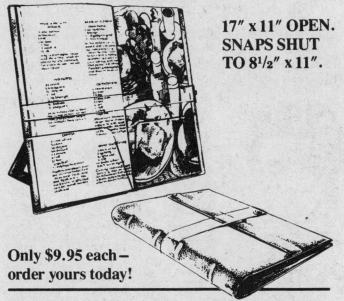

**17″ x 11″ OPEN.
SNAPS SHUT
TO 8¹/₂″ x 11″.**

**Only $9.95 each —
order yours today!**